THE WOLVES OF NIFELHEIM

Paul Adam

Endeavour Publishing

First published in Great Britain in June 2024
by Endeavour Publishing

Copyright © Paul Adam 2024

The moral right of the author has been asserted.

All characters in this publication other than those clearly in the public domain are fictitious and any resemblance to real persons, living or dead, is purely coincidental.

All rights reserved.
No part of this publication may be reproduced, stored in a retrieval system, or transmitted, in any form or by any means, without the prior permission in writing of the publisher, nor be otherwise circulated in any form of binding or cover other than that in which it is published and without a similar condition including this condition being imposed on the subsequent purchaser.

A CIP catalogue record for this book is available
from the British Library.

ISBN 978-0-9571913-8-9

Printed and bound by CPI Group (UK) Ltd, Croydon, CR0 4YY

Endeavour Publishing
19 Bents Drive
Sheffield
S11 9RN

Praise for Paul Adam

'Tension that resonates like flawlessly tuned strings'
Guardian

'Brilliantly imagined, fiercely authentic and wholly gripping'
Literary Review

'An intelligent, civilised mystery...beautifully written...
a real pleasure to read'
Sunday Telegraph

'Paul Adam has the great gift of narrative drive'
Tribune

'A distinctly atmospheric thriller'
Mail on Sunday

'Adam always handles his massive canvases with real panache.
The requisite pulse-racing action is wedded superbly
to the serious theme'
Good Book Guide

'Beguiling mystery'
New York Times

'Brilliantly researched and informative... a turbo-charged,
white-knuckled thriller by a brilliant storyteller'
Daily Record

'Mystery fans and music lovers alike will be captivated by Adam's
excellent contemporary thriller'
Publishers Weekly, starred review

'An enthralling mix of Italian ambience, history
and – most of all – music'
Booklist

Paul Adam is the author of thirteen previous novels for adults, and the Max Cassidy series of thrillers for younger readers. He has also written television and film scripts. He lives in Sheffield and is married with two sons. For more information visit www.pauladam.com

Also by Paul Adam

An Exceptional Corpse
A Nasty Dose of Death
Toxin
Unholy Trinity
Shadow Chasers
Genesis II
Flash Point (U.S. title Oracle Lake)
Enemy Within
Knife Edge
Dixieland

The Cremona Mysteries Series
Sleeper (U.S. title The Rainaldi Quartet)
Paganini's Ghost
The Hardanger Riddle

The Max Cassidy Series for Younger Readers
Escape from Shadow Island
Jaws of Death
Attack at Dead Man's Bay

For Susannah

PROLOGUE

Bavaria, March, 1886

The palace was in darkness. The king, still fully dressed though it was long past midnight, came out from his bedroom and made his way through the dimly-lit chambers, his bejewelled slippers padding softly on the parquet floors. A liveried footman, jolting awake from his doze just in time, stood up to follow him, but Ludwig waved him away. He wanted to be alone.

He crossed the vaulted entrance hall outside his private apartments and went into the Throne Room. No lanterns burned on the walls, no candles flickered in the high candelabra that stood like sentinels in the corners of the chamber. But in the moonlight that flooded in through the windows, Ludwig could see clearly the inlaid marble floor, the extravagant gilt decoration and the paintings that adorned almost every surface: sanctified kings, Archangel Michael defeating Lucifer, Saint George slaying the dragon and, on the ceiling at one end, the figure of Christ seated on a rainbow flanked by Mary and angels in prayer.

The plinth in the apse, where in a Byzantine church the altar would have stood, was strangely empty. The elaborate, canopied throne that Ludwig planned for the space had not yet been constructed – one of the many missing pieces in this new palace he was building high on a crag on the southern fringes of his kingdom.

Pulling open a glass door, he stepped out onto the balcony. After the warmth of the interior, the cold took his breath away. The night air seared his lungs. He braced himself and huddled in a corner out of the wind, looking west over the countryside. Was there ever a more beautiful land? he thought. Was there ever a more impressive view from a balcony? Below him, a kilometre away, was the village of Hohenschwangau, the houses dark, their occupants asleep. On a low ridge above the village, lights glimmered in the courtyard of the old palace. The lakes on either side – Alpsee and Schwansee – were frozen, their surfaces shimmering like burnished pewter in the light of the moon, and the whole landscape was cloaked in a thick layer of snow, the jagged line of the Allgäu Alps on the horizon glazed with ice. It had been the longest, harshest winter anyone could remember. Sub-zero temperatures for weeks at a time, new falls of snow virtually every day. And it showed no signs of ending.

Somewhere in the distance a wolf howled, sending a prickle up his spine. Ludwig turned his head. Had he imagined it? He listened hard, but the sound didn't come again. He gazed across to the forests that blanketed the lower slopes of the mountains and his mind strayed onto the forbidden myths he'd read secretly as a child. The tales of Odin and Thor and the other gods. Their eventual destruction, Ragnarök, had been preceded by a winter just like this one: Fimbulvetir, when the snows never melted, the seas and rivers froze and the Earth was cast into perpetual twilight.

Ludwig thought back to those private moments in his bedroom at Nymphenburg, eight years old, reading by candlelight long into the night. He could still recall his feeling of horror at the Armageddon of the gods. How the ash tree of life, Yggdrasill, began to wither, its leaves to fall; how the apples of youth that gave the gods their immortality shrivelled and started to rot and the Well of Life turned to ice. And then the wolves came. Always the wolves in Norse mythology, the creatures that more than any other encapsulated the primeval fears of the ancient peoples. They came prowling out of the forests, jaws slavering, hungry and looking for prey.

In Muspellheim, the land of fire, the ground was shaken by volcanic eruptions and violent earthquakes that convulsed the whole universe. The bonds around Fenrir the wolf, an animal so terrible the gods had kept him chained up for all eternity, split and fell apart. Jörmungandr, the great serpent encircling Middle Earth, rose up angrily from his undersea home and the oceans boiled and foamed with his venom. The gods and the Einheriar warriors in Valhalla buckled on their armour and swords and crossed over Bifrost, the rainbow bridge separating Asgard, the home of the gods, from Midgard, the land of men. They were ready to fight, ready for the Last Battle. But their enemies were more numerous and more powerful.

The great wolves, Skioll and Hati, who had been pursuing the sun and the moon for aeons suddenly seized their chance. They sank their teeth into the horses pulling the chariots of Day and Night, ripping out their throats, then catching the sun and moon as they fell, swallowing them whole. Heaven and Earth were plunged into darkness, the only light the glow of fire from Muspellheim which grew slowly brighter as the guardian of the land, the dark fire giant Surtr, came north into Midgard, his flaming sword shining brighter than the devoured sun. Beside him was Loki, the scheming trickster wanting revenge on his fellow gods.

Odin and Fenrir fought one-on-one. Odin drove his magic spear, Gungnir, into the wolf's mouth but the wolf snapped it in two and seized hold of the god, crushing his body in his jaws and gulping him down. The king of Asgard was gone. Thor tackled the hissing Jörmungandr with his thunderous hammer, staving in his skull. In his death throes the snake spat out his poison. Thor staggered away only nine paces before collapsing lifeless to the ground. Loki and Heimdall, the watchman of the gods, engaged in combat and killed each other, then one by one the other gods fell until only Odin's wife, Frigg, was left and she was enveloped in fire from Surtr's sword as the nine worlds of the universe burned in an ineluctable inferno.

Ludwig saw all this vividly in his imagination. Is this never-ending winter my Fimbulvetir? he thought. The pagan Germanic tribes had believed in pre-destination. That the fates of men were determined by the Norns, three gnarled old women spinning beneath the roots of Yggdrasill, and your destiny could not be changed. Has my future already been decided for me? the king wondered. Can I do nothing to influence it?

A wolf howled again, far off in the forests, and Ludwig shivered – not the wind or the cold, but a premonition of his own end.

ONE

Bavaria, March, 1886

A woodcutter named Josef Vogel found the body.

It was approaching mid-day and he'd been out in the forest since early morning. There'd been a fresh, heavy fall of snow overnight and it was bitingly cold. The ground in the thicker parts of the forest was relatively clear, protected from the snow by the canopy of branches, but in the glades and clearings the drifts were sometimes thigh-deep.

Vogel's breath was a fine white mist when he exhaled, his grizzled moustache and beard gilded with tiny shards of ice. His fingers, even cocooned in his woollen mittens, were numb and he'd lost all sensation in his toes, moisture seeping in through his boots despite the strips of sackcloth he'd tied around them to block up the holes. The last thing he'd wanted to do was venture out into the wilds on such a bitter day, but his wife, Helga, had insisted. The weather was to his advantage, she'd said, hostile enough to deter most people from collecting wood for themselves. Whatever he brought back would command a premium from customers desperate to feed their fires.

All right for her, Vogel grumbled to himself as he pulled his cumbersome sled along the track. She's warm by the hearth. I'm the bugger freezing his knackers off in the middle of nowhere. I'm the one with the frost-chewed toes and the aching back and sore arms. At least it was over now. He was on his way back to the village, the sled stacked so high with logs it was almost too heavy to haul. He comforted himself with the thought of the price they'd fetch in Schwangau, and the prospect of a hot bowl of soup when he finally reached home.

He paused to rest on the edge of a clearing. The forest was still, quiet enough for him to hear the sound of his own breathing, the slight wheeze of the chest infection he'd had for weeks and couldn't seem to shake off. A light breeze gusted suddenly through the trees, stirring the branches as if some giant, invisible hand were stroking them. The cloud cover split apart momentarily and sunlight scintillated on the diamond crust of the snow.

Vogel rubbed his chest where the rope from the sled had cut into the skin. He was tired and hungry, anxious to get home before the light began to fade and the temperature dropped even lower. His eyes roved around the clearing, taking in the undulating carpet of snow, the trees on the periphery, sprawling ash and maple mingling with the more compact forms of pine and spruce.

That's when he saw it.

It was in the middle of the clearing, a single length of timber protruding vertically from the snow like the mast of a small sailing boat. It was out of place in the forest. No tree, no shrub grew like that, with a perfectly smooth, rounded surface. It had to be man-made. Curious, Vogel left his sled and waded across through the drifts to take a closer look. He touched the piece of wood. He knew his trees and could see at once that it was ash. About a metre and a half long and five centimetres in diameter, it had had its bark removed and the underlying wood planed to a sleek finish.

Strange. What was it doing there? Vogel passed through this clearing regularly and he hadn't noticed it earlier in the week. It looked like a staff – of the kind hikers sometimes used in the mountains, but no one would have been out walking these past few days. Not in the blizzards and sub-zero conditions. Only wretched woodcutters were stupid enough to do that. A stake, then? A stake rammed into the ground for some reason, perhaps to mark a particular place. But why?

Vogel bent down and brushed away some of the snow. And saw something even more peculiar. Wound around the lower part of the stake was the pale green stem of a plant, with small, oval leaves and clusters of white, waxy berries. Mistletoe. Vogel stared at it. Mistletoe? That couldn't be right. Mistletoe was a parasite that attached itself to a living host, like a tree, and fed off it. Yet this smooth pole of ash wasn't alive.

He scooped away more snow, expecting to find the forest floor beneath, but a few centimetres down he encountered what looked like cloth. A dark blue material with brass buttons attached to it, like a jacket or a coat. Somewhere inside him, he felt a stirring of unease. He hesitated, then uncovered more of the material.

Dear God! He straightened up so violently he almost fell over backwards. He crossed himself instinctively and took a deep breath to calm his throbbing heart. He'd seen a face gazing up at him, the eyes wide open but unseeing. The mysterious piece of ash wasn't a staff, or a stake. It was a spear. A spear buried deep in a dead man's chest.

Vogel glanced around nervously, suddenly on edge, wondering whether he was being observed, whether there were more eyes watching him from the cover of the forest. But that made no sense. The body must have been here since at least the previous day for it to have been covered by so much snow. The woodcutter didn't want to look at it again, but he felt he should. Perhaps he would recognise him, perhaps it was someone he knew.

Crouching down again, he cleared away more snow, careful not to touch the man's skin. The face was chalk white and unlined, a young man in his twenties, the flesh frozen solid, ice in his light blond hair. Vogel had never seen him before, but he felt a shiver pulse up his spine, a pang of something in his core – sympathy, loss, pity, fear, horror, that universal human connection with the end of a life.

He leaned back on his haunches, the snow cold on his thighs, and considered what to do next. Just walk away and leave the body? That was his first inclination, the natural response of a powerless man who didn't trust the authorities, who didn't want to bring unnecessary trouble his way. But what if someone else discovered it? What if they saw his footprints, the tell-tale marks of his sled and the police came hammering on his door, demanding to know why he hadn't reported the body? Maybe even pointing the finger at him, accusing him of killing the man. The thought frightened him. That was the kind of thing the police did to little people like him.

But right now, he had no choice but to walk away. Moving the body felt wrong and, besides, what would he do with it? His sled was fully laden and he had no intention of abandoning his logs to transport a corpse to the village. He'd do what he always did when a difficult decision had to be made: leave it to Helga.

The least he could do, however, was give the poor devil, whoever he was, some protection from the scavengers in the forest – the rats and foxes and wolves which would quickly devour the body. Shovelling snow with his mittens, he re-covered the man's torso and head, burying them even deeper than before. Then he returned to his sled, looped the rope under his shoulders and continued on his way.

"A body? What do you mean, you found a body?"

Helga Vogel looked at her husband, who was seated in front of the hearth, wolfing down a bowl of broth. His feet were bare, his pale, frozen toes as close to the fire as he could safely put them, the flesh thawing, starting to tingle. His sodden socks were draped over the cast-iron range, filling the room with an odour of damp wool and sweat. His boots – what was left of them – were drying out close by. They'd shrunk in the snow, bonding themselves to his legs so tightly it had taken Helga a good ten minutes of tugging and twisting to get them off.

He was a sorry sight: thinning hair still slicked down across his head, his bony frame shivering beneath the blanket wrapped around his shoulders. Helga felt a tiny twinge of pity, worried that he might lose some toes – and then where would they be? But she suppressed it ruthlessly. What else could he do but chop wood? He had no trade, no skills, and they had five children to feed.

"Josef? Talk to me."

Vogel had his mouth full of soup. He was chewing on a chunk of turnip which, despite its two-hour boil in a pot, still had the consistency – and some of the taste – of antique leather. He swallowed.

"What I said. A dead body. Spear stickin' out his chest, his eyes lookin' up at me somethin' terrible. Never saw him afore. Young feller."

Another slurp of soup.

"Funny thing is, the spear was wrapped in misseltoe. Why would someone be doin' a thing like that?"

"Never mind the misseltoe," Helga said. "What we needs to be thinkin' 'bout is what we do."

Vogel spooned more broth into his mouth. It was thin and watery, but it was hot. He could feel himself warming up. He had pins and needles in his toes, which was painful, but a reassuring sign that the nerves were still intact.

"What you reckon?" he said.

Helga pondered for a moment.

"You must tell the consable."

"You think?"

"That's the right thing. Let him decide what to do."

"When?"

"Now, course. You must go there now. And while you're goin', you can drop some wood off at the Kreisels'. Bertha, she was around earlier, said they're runnin' badly short."

Vogel sighed. Going back out into the cold was not something he wanted to do – not when he was still trying to recover from his last expedition. He wondered if he could eke out the bowl of broth to delay the inevitable for a while longer, but Helga was already taking his socks down from the range and getting them ready for him to put on. Best get it over with, he thought. Rather now than later when it'll be even colder.

Finishing the last few morsels of potato, he raised the bowl to his lips and drained the final mouthful of liquid. Then he swung each leg up in turn and massaged the toes until the tingling subsided. His socks weren't fully dry, but they were the only pair he had, so they had to go on. Then Helga slid the boots over his legs, tugging hard, before binding the sackcloth around the soles. Vogel slipped into his wet coat and soggy mittens, jammed his hat over his ears and braced himself.

"Remember to get the money from Bertha now," Helga instructed him. "We don't want no payin' later. You understand?"

Vogel nodded, pulled open the door and went out into the yard where he'd left his sled. Transferring some logs to a sack, he swung the load over his shoulder and headed out into the village. The Kreisels' house was a short distance away, another small wooden hut like the Vogels' – one living room, one bedroom where the whole family slept – with a privy outside at the back which they shared with three other households. He delivered the wood and took payment, asserting himself with uncharacteristic vigour when Bertha tried to avoid it, Helga's wrath always at the back of his mind if he came home empty-handed. Then he walked a further hundred metres to what passed for the village's police station – in reality, the home of the constable, Wolfgang Huber.

Huber was at his kitchen table – the house blessed with four rooms, luxury by Schwangau standards. In front of him was a plate of sausage and fried potatoes and a large mug of ale. He wasn't pleased to see the woodcutter.

"What do you want, Vogel?" he asked irritably. "Can't you see I'm having my dinner?"

Vogel eyed the plate with unconcealed envy, almost tasting the food on it. Even something as basic as a sausage was a treat he ate very rarely and as for ale, well, that was a drink he only managed to indulge when Helga wasn't paying close attention to the family finances – which wasn't often. Huber saw the look and pulled the plate protectively close to his belly. And it was a large belly, its swelling bulge a testament to the volume of sausage and beer to which it was regularly exposed.

"What is it?" he snapped.

Vogel described his discovery in the forest, the very act of recounting it bringing back unpleasant sensations: that stiff, icy face buried in the snow, those sightless eyes staring up at him – dead, but still somehow threatening – that bizarre spear plunged into the man's heart. All of it sent a renewed chill through his body.

There was a moment's silence when he'd finished. Huber gazed at him sceptically. The tale was so extraordinary it was difficult to believe. But Vogel wasn't a man with a reputation for making things up.

"You're sure it was a body?" the constable asked.

"Course I'm sure," Vogel replied indignantly. "A dead body. I seen it with my own eyes."

"All of it?"

"Uh?"

"You saw the whole body?"

"Well, jus' the head and chest."

"Not the rest of it? Not the legs?"

"No, but what diff'rence does it make? It's still a dead body, legs or no legs."

"We need to get the facts right," Huber said.

He had some more sausage and a swig of ale. This was trouble, and he didn't like trouble. He was clearly going to have to do something about it and he wanted to make sure he finished his dinner first. It was never a good idea to contemplate any kind of work on an empty stomach.

"Where was this?"

"East. Over towar' the von Wildenstein place."

"And there was a spear in his chest, you say?"

Vogel nodded. "Spooked me bad, I can tell you. So bad a feller could do with a drink."

He looked pointedly at the constable's beer, hoping Huber might offer him a mug, although past experience, and the constable's reputation for stinginess, told him that was unlikely. Huber ignored the hint. He concentrated on his fried potatoes for a while, trying to give the impression of a man deep in thought, a man mulling over the best course of action to take when, in fact, he'd already decided exactly what he was going to do: pass the buck to someone higher up the food chain. A violent death like this was outside his experience. He'd seen the occasional hunting fatality or a fall in the mountains, but those were always accidents. This body in the forest didn't sound like an accident, it sounded like murder. He cleared his plate, finished his ale, then belched and pushed back his chair.

"I need to consult with my colleagues in Füssen," he announced pompously. "You will come with me."

Vogel didn't waste his breath protesting. It was unavoidable that he was going to have to show the police where he'd found the body. He watched the constable preparing to go out: summoning his wife to help him pull on his shiny black, knee-high boots – no sackcloth bandaging for him – donning his thick winter coat and peaked cap, then strapping his billy-club to his belt.

It was getting colder now. The effects of the hot broth had worn off and Vogel shivered as they stepped out into the street and began the three-kilometre trudge to Füssen. The wind had picked up, a raw easterly that plucked at their backs as they plodded along the road, walking in the tracks left by sleds to avoid the deeper snow along the edges. The sun was already dipping behind the mountains, casting a broad shadow over the plain. Lights gleamed in the windows of Hohenschwangau and Vogel wished he was back at home in front of the hearth. It was going to be night before this was over.

They crossed the bridge over the Lech, the river raging through the arches beneath them, and walked up Lechhalde past the monastery of Saint Magnus into the centre of Füssen. The cobbled streets were treacherous, their icy sheen glistening in the glow from the gas lamps on the walls. Shops were beginning to close for the day, traders bringing in their wares and shuttering their windows. The police station was on Hinteregasse, a small, two-storey building housing the town's complement of two constables, a sergeant and a captain. One of the constables, a hefty, ruddy-faced man named Lehmann, was manning the front desk, a fire burning in the grate behind him.

"I need to speak to Captain Beck," Huber said, his chest swelling with self-importance.

"Oh, yes," Lehmann replied, yawning. "What about?"

"A serious matter."

"Serious, eh? How?" Lehmann didn't sound impressed. To him, and the other officers in Füssen, Huber was nothing but a country bumpkin – a constable in name, but not the real thing like them.

"I'll explain to the captain," Huber said. "It's important."

"Yeah?" Lehmann gave him an amused look and twisted round on his stool to call out into the back room. "Sarge!"

A middle-aged man carrying just about as much weight as Huber, but differently distributed, most of it in his capacious backside, appeared in the doorway.

"What?"

Lehmann smirked. "Huber has something important to tell the captain."

"Does he now? Well, he can tell me first. We can't have you wasting the captain's time. What is it?"

"A body," Huber replied. "A dead body. Out in the forest." He paused and his voice took on a lower, more confidential tone. "Murdered. By party, or parties, as yet unknown."

"Murdered? What're you talking about? Murdered how?"

"A spear to the heart."

This was such a melodramatic statement that even the sergeant – determined to maintain his cool – flinched visibly.

"A *spear*? You've seen this?"

"Not me. But this fellow here has."

The sergeant looked Vogel up and down and didn't much like what he saw.

"And you are?"

"His name's Vogel," Huber butted in. "A woodcutter. He found the body."

Sergeant Krause pursed his fleshy lips, considering the situation. The captain didn't generally concern himself with day-to-day matters. He was far too grand, far too absorbed with strategy and policy and dinner to bother himself with the petty crime that was the staple diet of the Füssen police force. But this was different. Murder – if that was really what this was, and Krause had his doubts – was something Beck couldn't leave to his subordinates, even one as competent and efficient as me, the sergeant thought modestly.

"Wait here," he instructed, then heaved himself up the stairs, the treads creaking ominously beneath his feet. A few minutes later, he reappeared on the first-floor landing and beckoned them up.

The captain's office was spacious and plainly furnished, one end occupied by a large desk and the other by another blazing fire. Vogel took off his hat respectfully and looked around, struck by how warm the police station was, and how well-upholstered its occupants, for Lothar Beck was another ample man: solid chest giving way to flabby stomach, round face with fair hair cropped short above a pair of pink, prominent ears that gave him a porcine appearance.

"Now, what's all this about a body?" he said.

"Well, sir – " Huber began, but was cut short by the captain.

"Not you. Him." He jabbed his finger at Vogel.

The woodcutter repeated his tale, Beck listening, interjecting occasionally with a question. Then the captain stood up, went to the window and gazed out. It was getting late. The light was fading fast. Ideally, he would have liked to wait until morning before going to look at this body, but time wasn't on his side. The woodcutter claimed to have covered it up again, but the fellow looked like a half-wit so it would be rash to assume he'd done it properly. If the wildlife picked up the scent, there might be nothing left by the next day and that wouldn't be good. Beck, already assessing how best to cover his arse, didn't want to have to explain to the regional commissioner in Kempten that a homicide victim had rather unfortunately been eaten by wolves.

"Sergeant!" he said decisively.

"Sir?"

"Have my horse saddled. And get out the sled. We'll need ropes, shovels, a tarpaulin and lanterns."

"Yes, indeed, sir."

The preparations took a little over ten minutes, Lehmann and the other constable, Böhm, drafted in to help, then the search party headed off. Captain Beck was on horseback towing the sled. Krause, Huber and Vogel followed behind on foot. The woodcutter was obviously essential for leading them to the correct location. Huber, on the other hand, was not really needed now, but Krause suggested he come along because someone was going to have to do the digging and it wasn't going to be him.

It was a long hike. Through Füssen, then past Schwangau, then a further four kilometres east into the forest. Vogel's feet, courtesy of his leaking boots, were wet and freezing within half an hour. He glanced grudgingly at the lightly-laden sled. Why couldn't he ride on that? After all, unlike the others, he'd been out for most of the day already, had probably walked a good ten kilometres. He needed a rest, but he knew he wasn't going to get one. If he were allowed on the sled, then the two police officers would certainly demand equal treatment and their combined weight would probably give the horse a seizure.

Leaving the main track through the forest, the trees became denser and Beck was forced to dismount and lead his horse. It was only twilight, but beneath the foliage it felt like night. Lanterns were lit and Vogel led the way, the flame gleaming on the snow, exacerbating the darkness beyond so it felt as if they were walking through a claustrophobic tunnel.

By the time they reached the clearing, it really was night. Vogel paused and held his lantern up high. To his relief, he saw that the spear was still there, sticking up through the snow. The shovels were unloaded – conveniently only two – so Vogel and Huber, reluctant but resigned, undertook the excavation.

"Careful now," Beck ordered them. "We don't want any damage to the body."

The outer layers of snow were removed cautiously, then Huber stepped back and let Vogel use his hands to clear away the remainder. Gradually, the body emerged into the light. Vogel averted his gaze from the face – he didn't want to see those staring eyes again – and brushed the snow off the torso and legs. The body was complete, no apparent damage from scavengers.

"Let me see."

Beck came forward with a lantern and made a closer inspection of the corpse. The jacket and trousers looked good quality, the boots, too – not the knee-high pair you'd expect in deep, snowy conditions, but ankle-length: town boots. The spear was disturbing, the mistletoe wrapped around it puzzling. Beck touched it. The shaft was icy cold. He gave it a tentative shake, but it didn't move – it was frozen solid into the chest. Should he try to pull it out? It would make transporting the body back to Füssen easier. Probably not. The captain's knowledge of forensic medicine was slight, but there'd have to be a post-mortem examination and the pathologist might want to see the murder weapon *in situ*.

Beck moved the lantern up to the head and gave a start. Even frozen and deathly white, it was a handsome face: striking blue eyes, full lips, flawless skin, all framed by golden hair. Far too young to have departed the world, particularly in so violent a manner. He felt a sudden frigid tremor at the top of his back, like snow slipping down his spine. Then he took another look at the corpse and the sensation was replaced by an equally icy sense of foreboding. He knew who the young man was.

TWO

Reinhardt Neumann stepped down from the stagecoach and was struck immediately by the intense cold. After the relative comfort of the carriage – the warm atmosphere sustained by the hot bricks slotted in beneath the seats at each stop, not to mention the body heat of the other occupants – the air in Füssen was a shock, an icy blast swirling across the square, tainted with the acrid stench of smoke from the chimneys of the town.

He coughed, clearing his throat, and pulled the collar of his greatcoat up around his neck. He was thirty-six years old, deputy head of the Criminal Investigation Division of the Berlin police. Tall, muscular, black hair cut short, lean face softened by warm hazel eyes, ramrod posture giving away his former life as an army officer. He'd been on the force for five years, brought in when the Ministry of Justice had finally grown weary of the endless allegations of brutality and corruption made against the police and decided to recruit some new brooms to sweep out the dirty stables – their first preference military men like Neumann who were reliable, accustomed to command and, above all, honest.

Behind him, the other passengers were disembarking. There'd been four of them on the taxing six-hour journey from Munich: Neumann, a timber merchant and his wife, and the sales director of a ropemaking factory in Füssen. Discovering his ignorance of their home town, they'd spent a lot of the trip enlightening him about the history of the settlement – from its key position on the ancient Roman road across the Alps, the Via Claudia Augusta, through its five-century-long rule by the prince-bishops of Augsburg to its current status as a major trading centre of southern Bavaria. Among its more successful industries were violin and lute making and timber, the felled trees being rafted out from the mountains on the turbulent waters of the Lech.

Neumann hadn't been so forthcoming about his own reasons for making the journey, despite his companions' evident curiosity. Not because he was anti-social or wanted to be mysterious, but because he didn't really know why he'd been sent to Füssen. The Berlin police chief, Bernhard von Richthofen, hadn't been sure, either. A telegram had come in from Bavaria for Neumann's immediate superior, Colonel Olaf Wolff, but Wolff, much to the force's embarrassment, had just been suspended from duty, having been caught taking bribes from an organised crime gang.

"You'd better handle this, then," von Richthofen had said. "There's an urgent job for you down south."

The telegram hadn't explained exactly what kind of job, just that it was a homicide investigation and someone from the German legation would meet him on his arrival in Füssen. Neumann looked around now to check if anyone was waiting.

Across the square was a short line of three horse-drawn cabs, all dirty and splashed with mud and slush. Beyond them, keeping itself distinctly apart, as if it didn't want to be contaminated, was a much smarter carriage – highly-polished black bodywork, the doors embossed with the coat-of-arms of some noble family, a coachman in a beaver hat perched on top and two elegant stallions standing patiently in harness, their backs draped with thick blankets to keep them warm.

Huddled next to the carriage, trying in vain to find some shelter from the wind, was a thin young man of about seventeen or eighteen. He wore dark green livery, a jacket and breeches, but no coat, and he was shivering visibly. Neumann glanced at him sympathetically, proof, if any were needed, that the aristocracy treated their horses better than their servants.

The young man was scrutinising the passengers from the stagecoach. He took in Neumann's greatcoat with the officer's insignia on the shoulders, the traces of dark blue uniform beneath it, and his cap with the Berlin police badge above the peak and he came forward.

"Sir?" he said hesitantly. "Colonel Wolff?"

"You're waiting for a Colonel Wolff?" Neumann asked.

"Yes, sir."

"Colonel Olaf Wolff?"

"I don't know his first name, sir."

"A police officer from Berlin?"

"Yes, sir."

"That's me. My name is Neumann. Major Reinhardt Neumann. I believe I'm expected."

The young man looked confused.

"I beg your pardon, sir. I was told to pick up a Colonel Wolff."

"You're from the legation?"

"Yes, sir. From His Excellency, Prince von Auerswald."

"Then I'm your man. Come on, let's get out of the cold."

Neumann swung his battered old army kit-bag over his shoulder and strode across to the carriage. The young man removed the blankets from the horses, folded them away under the coachman's bench and was about to climb up to the rear seat when Neumann touched his arm.

"Travel inside with me."

"Sir... I'm not allowed to –"

"You'll freeze up there."

Neumann pushed the young man into the carriage and clambered in behind him. He hammered on the roof with his fist and, outside, the coachman flicked his whip and the vehicle pulled away.

"Sir," the young man said. "It's strictly forbidden for me to –"

"Yes, yes," Neumann interrupted. "But we don't need to worry about that now. What's your name?"

"Keller, sir. Jürgen Keller."

"Well, Jürgen, I've seen what the elements can do to a man and I didn't want to pull your stiff, lifeless body down from that seat when we get to wherever we're going. Where *are* we going, by the way?"

"To the legation, sir. Schloss Lichtenberg."

"Is that far?"

"No, sir."

Neumann looked out of the window and saw that they were already in what looked like the outskirts of Füssen, the red-roofed houses petering out into what had to be countryside, although the land itself was featureless, hidden beneath a thick blanket of snow.

"Is it always this cold down here in March?" he asked.

"It's been a long winter, sir."

"And yet you have no coat."

Keller shifted uncomfortably. "I have my uniform, sir. His Excellency gives me a uniform."

"Let's hope he doesn't also give you hypothermia," Neumann said dryly.

The carriage was slowing now, turning off the road up a steep drive that had been cleared of snow. At the top of the drive, set back into the hillside, was a large, stately mansion constructed of white stone, the entrance porticoed, octagonal towers at either end of the frontage. Even before the carriage had come to a stop, Keller was leaping out on the side away from the house and scuttling round so he was on hand to open the door for Neumann. He reached in and lifted out the major's kit-bag, then accompanied him up the steps to the front door which swung open with perfect timing to reveal a frock-coated butler waiting in the hall.

"If you'd come this way, sir," the butler said, leading him to an internal door and in one slick, well-practised movement knocking, opening, then stepping back to allow Neumann to enter the room alone.

A man behind a desk looked up from a sheaf of papers, then rose and offered his hand.

"How do you do, colonel. I'm Anton Maisel, His Excellency's secretary."

He was in his early-thirties, a slim, neat man in black jacket and trousers, the high collar of his white shirt almost touching his chin, restricting the movement of his head so he appeared rather stiff and formal. A former military man, Neumann surmised. Probably one of the select units, the Guards or maybe the cavalry, for him to have his current position.

"It's a pleasure to meet you – Herr? – Maisel."

"Captain," Maisel corrected him, confirming Neuman's guess. "You are a little later than expected."

"The stagecoach was delayed, I'm afraid."

"No matter. These things happen. His Excellency is waiting for you."

He made a move towards a door at the side of the room.

"Captain…" Neumann said and the secretary turned. "I think there may have been a misunderstanding. A mix-up of names. You were expecting my colleague, Colonel Wolff, I understand."

Maisel frowned. "That is correct. You are not Wolff?"

"I regret that Colonel Wolff is..." How could he put this? "...temporarily indisposed. I am Major Reinhardt Neumann, Colonel Wolff's deputy."

"I see." Maisel seemed perturbed for a moment, unsure what to do. Then he gave a thin smile. "If you'll excuse me, I will apprise His Excellency of the situation."

He disappeared through the door. Neumann wandered over to the window. It was warm in the room, but there was no fire. He could feel hot air blowing in through vents in the floor, hear the low hum of a pump somewhere beneath the house. Impressively advanced, he thought, then reminded himself that the Romans had had a similar heating system. Rediscovering something that was two thousand years old: that was progress for you.

"Major..." Maisel had returned. "His Excellency will see you now."

Neumann went through into the adjoining room, a much larger office with a leather-topped desk at the back and a more informal seating area near the window – a sofa, two armchairs and a low table. The floor was polished wood, the furniture elegant and expensive: not the sort of fixtures generally found in public buildings, but then this – the standard portrait of the emperor on the wall notwithstanding – wasn't really a public building. It was the private residence of the man who came forward to greet him: Prince Ernst Heinrich von Auerswald, German legate to the Bavarian government.

"Major, how do you do. May I offer you a glass of Tokay?"

"Thank you, sir."

Von Auerswald went to the mahogany sideboard and poured two glasses of the sweet Hungarian wine. He was a tall, courtly man, pushing fifty but still trim, his dark suit immaculate, his shirt studs and cufflinks silver, his greying hair cut short around a handsome, slightly aquiline face. On each of his cheeks was a thin duelling scar that had not been acquired in an actual sword fight, but put there deliberately – cut cleanly into the skin so they healed without much disfigurement – as a mark of his class.

"Please." Von Auerswald gestured at the armchairs and they sat down.

"You had a good journey?" he asked, the patrician putting his guest at ease.

"Yes, thank you, sir."

"Good." The legate took a sip of wine and looked at him quizzically, sizing him up. "We were expecting Wolff, but I suppose you will do just as well. You are a career policeman?"

"No, sir. I was in the army before."

"Which regiment?"

"The XI Corps."

"You fought in the French war? Or were you too young?"

"No, I was there, sir. With the Third Army. At Wörth and Sedan."

"I went to the Front with King Wilhelm – as he then was." Von Auerswald shook his head. "A terrible business. Terrible. How is your wine?"

"Very good, sir."

"I imagine you could do with a hot bath and a meal. Maisel has arranged accommodation for you at an inn in Füssen. Plain, but perfectly adequate, he tells me. That will be your base for the duration of your stay, but I will expect regular reports from you."

"Of course, sir."

"How much do you know about the case?"

"Almost nothing, sir. A murder, I understand."

"A particularly nasty, perplexing one. A young man named Christoph Geissler. One of ours, a diplomat here at the legation. That's why I insisted that the investigation be handled by someone from Berlin. This doesn't go beyond these walls, major, but I don't trust the Bavarians to do it properly. You are in charge, remember. I've agreed that with the Minister of Justice here. But tread carefully, be tactful. They're touchy down here."

"Yes, sir. I understand."

Neumann made a mental note of the legate's comments, but he didn't find them reassuring. He could foresee problems ahead. Germany had been unified for the past fifteen years. In theory, it was one country – one empire – now. But to allay the fears of the regions that the new Germany was really just a synonym for Prussia, the lesser states, like Bavaria, had been given a certain amount of autonomy to conduct some of their own affairs. Within limits, of course. Bismarck was not a chancellor who believed in too much independence, too much freedom for anyone except himself. Von Auerswald was in an anomalous position. He was like an envoy to a foreign kingdom that wasn't strictly foreign, an ambassador who reported not to the foreign ministry in Berlin, but to the chancellery.

"Well, thank you for your time, major," the legate said, draining his glass. "I'm glad I've met you. I will leave everything in your capable hands, but keep me posted."

"I will, sir."

On the drive back to the town, Neumann felt a knot of unease in his stomach. The prince had made it all sound very straightforward, but the locals weren't going to take kindly to an outsider, particularly a Prussian, coming in and running a criminal investigation, telling them what to do. He had enough experience of leadership to know that it depended on trust and respect and those were not going to be afforded him easily. He would do his best, of course, but already he was beginning to taste a hint of poison in the chalice.

"So you're the policeman from Berlin," Johanna Hoffmann said and Neumann was aware of the saloon bar behind him falling suddenly silent. He didn't turn his head, but he could sense a dozen or more pairs of eyes examining him, assessing him, this stranger from the north, from Berlin, a city that was probably as alien to them as Timbuctoo.

Johanna checked the register on the counter.

"Colonel Olaf Wolff."

"There's been a change. My name is Neumann. Major Reinhardt Neumann."

Johanna corrected the booking and shrugged phlegmatically.

"Makes no difference to me so long as you pay your bills." She peered more closely at the register. "Invoice to be sent to a Captain Maisel at Schloss Lichtenberg, Prince von Auerswald's place?"

"Yes."

Her lip curled into a cynical smile. "Toffs, they're always the worst payers. I'll want something on account before the end of the week."

"I'm sure that can be arranged."

Johanna looked at the kit-bag by his feet.

"That your only luggage?"

"Yes."

"You want someone to take it up for you?"

"I can manage."

"This way."

Neumann followed her up the stairs. She was a big, broad woman with a blunt, no-nonsense manner that was no doubt essential in her line of work. He could see her handling her staff, her customers, the drunks that would be an inevitable consequence of running an inn. Forthright, formidable, a landlady with a sharp tongue and probably a useful pair of fists when she needed them.

"Best room in the house," she said, opening a door at the end of the landing and showing him in. "How long are you staying? No one told me."

"I don't know. It depends how quickly I finish my work."

"The big murder? Young Prussian fellow from the legation." She saw the surprised look on his face and chuckled. "Everyone knows about it. There are no secrets down here. The privy's next door, the bathroom's down the corridor. We don't have running water, hot or cold. You want a bath, it'll be a long wait. The maids are all busy in the kitchen at the moment."

Neumann glanced at the large enamel basin on the washstand at the side of the room.

"A jug of hot water would be welcome."

"We can stretch to that. You want supper?"

"If it's available."

"Nothing fancy, just a bit of roast pork and potatoes."

"That will be fine."

"Come down when you're ready."

Neumann looked around the room when the landlady had gone. Plain, but perfectly adequate, the prince had said, and that was a fair description. Maybe three metres square, it was clean and warm, a fire smouldering gently in the grate. The floor was varnished wood, the furniture dark and old-fashioned: the washstand, a wardrobe, a chest of drawers, an armchair, a small desk by the window and a bed topped with a horsehair mattress that was slightly lumpy, but comfortable enough – as Neumann discovered when he tried it out.

He was used to simple living, both in his army service and now as a city police officer. His two-bedroom apartment in Berlin was far from luxurious. Kristina had added a few softer, feminine touches, made it homely and welcoming, but since her death, he'd reverted to the more Spartan life of his bachelor days.

The window overlooked Brotmarkt at the front of the inn. There were shops opposite: a bakery, a grocer's, a hardware store, all now closed up for the night. Above the rooftops, he could see the towers of what he knew from his fellow stagecoach passengers were the Saint Magnus monastery and the High Castle which dominated the town. In the distance behind them were the Allgäu Alps, their peaks shrouded in thick mist.

He gazed out for a time, thinking back over his conversation with von Auerswald, grim memories of the war reawakened in him the way they were in the nightmares that still afflicted him sixteen years on. I went to the Front with the king, the prince had said. That would have been the entourage of aides and hangers-on and noblemen who'd turned up in their opulent rail carriages like sightseers on a grand tour, to enjoy their champagne dinners and gawp at the troops before they were sent out unprotected into the French guns. Were you too young? the legate had asked. Too young? Neumann thought. Was there ever a good age to be senselessly butchered?

There was a knock on the door. A skinny maid, about twelve or thirteen, entered with a jug of hot water.

"Thank you," Neumann said. "Can I get my laundry done here?" The girl gaped at him blankly. "Laundry?" Neumann repeated. "My shirt, can someone wash it?"

For a second, he wondered whether perhaps she was deaf, then she said something in a strange, unintelligible tongue that he realised was dialect. She didn't understand his High German, his Prussian German.

"Never mind," he said, waving a hand to dismiss her. "I'll ask Frau Hoffmann."

Stripping to the waist, he washed at the basin, soaping away the sweat of the journey. He'd been on the road, or rails, for two days. Six hours on the train south from Berlin with an overnight stopover in Munich, followed by the stagecoach to Füssen. He was feeling suddenly weary, and very hungry. He put on a fresh shirt and went downstairs. A table was ready for him in a corner of the bar. The landlady herself brought him his plate of pork and potatoes. Neumann asked her about laundry and she nodded.

"Twenty pfennigs for small items like socks and underwear, thirty for shirts or trousers, fifty if you want them ironed."

That was expensive. In Berlin, he could get a whole week's wash for three marks, but he knew that down here he would be regarded as a rich northerner from the capital, a legitimate target to be milked for whatever the locals could get away with. He wasn't going to argue. Captain Maisel had told him to keep a record of all his expenses for reimbursement at the end of his stay and he didn't seem like a man who would quibble over a laundry bill.

"You want some beer?" Johanna asked.

"That would be good, thank you."

The food was tasty and there was plenty of it. Neumann wasn't one for elaborate cooking or rich sauces. Unpretentious country fare like this suited him perfectly. The maid who'd brought him his hot water earlier came over with a tankard of ale and placed it gingerly on the table with her arm at full stretch – in case I bite, Neumann thought – before scurrying back to the bar. The Bavarians were renowned for their passion for brewing – and for their equally enthusiastic consumption of the end product – and the beer was good: a light, refreshing ale without too much bitterness.

Neumann ate and drank, trying not to feel too self-conscious, although he could see that he was the main object of attention in the room. The other customers were staring at him with hostile eyes, as if he were a dangerous species they had never encountered before, whispering to each other in their incomprehensible dialect. Here was double cause for suspicion: an outsider *and* a policeman. It didn't get worse than that.

Back upstairs in his room, he unpacked his kit-bag and put his clothes away in the chest of drawers and wardrobe. The fire was just embers now, but still giving off enough heat to keep the chill of night at bay. He undressed, hung his uniform up carefully, and slipped into the bed, the sheets unpleasantly cold against his skin. He was exhausted, but sleep didn't come easily. He felt disorientated. His mind was restless, adapting to the unfamiliar surroundings, jumping around from thought to thought but always coming back to the same preoccupation: the murder of Christoph Geissler, the reason why he was here.

He'd handled enough investigations to have acquired a sixth sense about each new one he undertook, to have somehow gained a foreknowledge of what was to come. Lying there in the darkness, the anxiety that had struck him in the carriage from the legation flooded back with a renewed intensity. He had a bad feeling about this case.

THREE

He awoke next morning with a thick head and the sensation that during the night someone had sneaked into the room and pummelled his body, for he felt stiff all over – no doubt the result of the previous day's long incarceration in a cramped stagecoach. Rolling out of bed, he did a few exercises to stretch his muscles and warm himself up. The fire had died overnight and the room was freezing. Outside, when he opened the curtains, he saw a new covering of snow on the street and rooftops. A dense mass of low cloud obscured the mountains.

The skinny little maid arrived shortly afterwards with a jug of hot water. While Neumann shaved, she busied herself lighting the fire. Hoping that she might perhaps understand a few basic phrases of High German – despite his experience of the evening before – he asked her name but was met by another blank look of incomprehension.

Downstairs, he found a small dining room at the rear of the building where breakfast was being served. Two other lone men were seated at separate tables. They nodded at him and exchanged a polite "good morning", but didn't appear inclined to engage further so he sat by himself until Johanna came out from the kitchen.

"Breakfast?" she said.

"Please."

"Liesl!"

The maid appeared in the doorway. So that was her name. The landlady gave her instructions in dialect, then turned back to Neumann.

"You are happy with your room, major?"

"It's very comfortable, thank you."

"Will you be wanting dinner?"

He hesitated. "I'm not sure at the moment. I'll say no, to be on the safe side."

"If you change your mind, we can always find you something. We keep a pot of soup simmering on the stove."

"Thank you, Frau Hoffmann."

"Until later, major."

Johanna moved away to allow Liesl access to the table, her tray bearing a plate of cheese and hard-boiled eggs, two bread rolls and a pot of coffee.

"Thank you, Liesl," Neumann said and was rewarded with a shy smile.

As he ate, he reviewed the situation and didn't find much to his liking. His knowledge of the case was scant. A diplomat murdered – his name, Christoph Geissler – but that was all he'd been told. He knew nothing about the victim, nothing about the circumstances of his death. All that he would have to find out from the local police, and they were an unknown quantity. They might be cooperative, but they might equally be obstructive. He was in charge – von Auerswald had made that clear. In theory, he could control the course of the investigation, but in practise, he was going to be reliant on local help and that was not necessarily going to be willingly given. Human nature being what it was, they would more than likely be wanting him to fail.

Breakfast finished, he returned to his room and put on

his greatcoat and cap, then went back downstairs to the dining room where Johanna was coming in and out of the kitchen, supervising breakfast whilst also overseeing the cook who was preparing the day's food.

"The police station," Neumann said. "Can you tell me where it is?"

Johanna's eyes glinted with amusement. "A policeman who can't find the police station. Not much of a detective, are you?"

Neumann took it in good part, sensing it wasn't intended maliciously.

"That's what detectives do," he replied. "Ask people who know more than they do."

"Hinteregasse."

"And where exactly is that?"

"Go out the front door and turn right, then… Wait a minute, there's a better way." She opened a door at the side of the room and yelled through it. "Tobias!"

A young man emerged. Eighteen or nineteen years old, dark haired, dressed for going out in thick coat, hat and scarf.

"My son," Johanna said. "He can show you the police station on his way to work."

The cold outside was penetrating. Neumann felt it seeping deep into his bones even through the heavy layers of his greatcoat.

"Where do you work?" he asked Tobias as they headed away from the inn.

"I'm a clerk at the telegraph office."

"You don't help run the inn?"

Tobias smiled. "Oh, yes. Mother makes sure of that. Those soft rolls you had for breakfast? Who do you think went to the bakery at six to collect them? Who do you think will be working behind the bar this evening, serving beer and schnapps, bringing the kegs up from the cellar, clearing tables, washing glasses? Muti takes the term 'family business' very literally."

"Is your father around? I haven't seen him."

"He died ten years ago."

"Oh, I'm sorry to hear that. You're an only child?"

"I have an older brother, Axel. He works at the palace."

"The palace?"

"Footman to the king."

"A plum position."

"Until you see the wages. There you are, that's it."

Tobias nodded at a building across the street. Neumann thanked him, then dodged a passing horse and wagon and went up the steps into the police station. The front desk was unmanned, but in the office behind it a constable and a sergeant were having what looked like their breakfast: coffee and a mound of sticky pastries. The officers' lips were smeared with sugar. Neumann could smell the sweet aroma of cinnamon. The sergeant looked up and saw him. His mouth tightened with irritation and he was about to tell this stranger to come back in half an hour when he noticed the man's peaked cap and badge and had a sudden inkling who he was. Wiping his lips, he stood up and walked over to the desk.

"Yes?"

Neumann noted the surly tone. "Major Reinhardt Neumann. From Berlin. You're expecting me."

"Are we?"

"Who's in charge?"

"Captain Beck."

"Is he here?"

"Upstairs."

Neumann started for the stairs. Behind him, Krause was exclaiming, "Hey, you can't just – " But the major was already halfway up and he knew the sergeant wasn't built for any kind of speedy pursuit. He knocked on the door at the top and walked in without waiting for a response. Lothar Beck was sprawled back in his chair, a cigarette in one hand, a cup of coffee in the other. He stared at Neumann, mouthing silent questions – Who? What? – then his brain clicked, supplying the answers. He swung his feet off the desk, belatedly remembering the cigarette and stubbing it out in an ashtray as he stood up. Before he could speak, Krause puffed into the room.

"I'm sorry, sir. He just came up without –"

"Thank you, sergeant."

"Gave me no time to –"

"That will be all, sergeant."

"Shall I –"

"You may go back downstairs, sergeant!"

Krause delayed for a second, still breathless from the stairs, then he waddled out of the room and closed the door behind him. Neumann contained his emotions. He was appalled by the sloppiness on show. Smoking on duty, eating, the place so insufferably hot he wondered how any work got done. It probably didn't, he reflected. But he didn't want to start off with confrontation so he offered his hand instead.

"Captain. Reinhardt Neumann. Pleased to meet you."

"Likewise," Beck said, though his face expressed the opposite emotion.

The two men gazed at each other for a moment, then Beck remembered the basic courtesies and offered him a chair.

"Please."

Neumann did a quick, preliminary appraisal of the captain. Mid-forties, overweight, small, rather mean eyes. A posture that was slightly defensive, but which, Neumann sensed, could swiftly turn aggressive if he felt himself under threat. A small-town police officer, probably promoted beyond his capabilities. Lazy, slack on discipline – if first impressions were anything to go by – but likely cunning and calculating. Honest? Maybe up to a point, but you couldn't rely on it. He'd no doubt use his position to do favours for chosen people, take a few "gifts" on the side in return. His loyalties would be suspect, but he would have influential friends in the local community ready to protect him. Not a man to underestimate.

Neumann was aware that Beck was doing the same to him, trying to work out what kind of adversary he was – for that was almost certainly the way he'd view him. Trying to decide how best to handle him. Neumann knew he had to establish his authority right away.

"You are the commanding officer of the Füssen police force, I understand."

"That's right."

No "Sir" at the end of the reply, Neumann noticed. And it wasn't accidental.

"I hope we're going to work well together on this investigation," he went on. Make it sound collaborative, that he wasn't some martinet here to throw his weight around.

"I hope so, too."

"Perhaps you would be good enough to outline the facts for me."

Beck shrugged. "There's not much to outline. The victim, Geissler, was twenty-six years old. Came from Berlin. Worked at the legation for Prince von Auerswald. He was found dead in the forest on Tuesday."

"Cause of death?"

"He'd been stabbed through the chest with a spear."

"A *spear*? What kind of spear?"

"Wooden. Metre and a half long. Not much else to say."

"Has an autopsy been carried out?"

"The pathologist's coming down from Munich this morning."

"Let me see the file on Geissler."

"The file?"

"You have a file, I presume?"

"We opened one, naturally. But there's nothing much in it yet."

"The body was found on Tuesday. It's now Saturday," Neumann said icily. "What've you been doing all this time?"

"Well," Beck began and Neumann saw a hint of smugness in the curl of his mouth. "It was found Tuesday, but late in the evening, so we didn't really get started until Wednesday. And that's when we were told it was being handed over to the Prussians. Since then, we've been waiting for you."

So that was how he was going to play it, Neumann thought. Blame me.

"Who found the body?"

"A woodcutter named Vogel."

"He's made a statement?"

"Not exactly. Fellow's an idiot, can't write, not even his own name."

"But one of your officers could write it for him, couldn't they?"

"There's not much for him to say, to be honest. He just found the body in a snowdrift."

"I'll need to speak to him."

Beck waved a hand airily. "Whatever you wish."

"What about the murder scene? You examined it, of course?"

Beck shook his head. "There was no point. It was covered in snow. Probably a lot more now, the weather we've had this week."

Neumann took a deep breath. This was beyond sloppy; it was downright negligent. He was beginning to see why von Auerswald didn't trust the locals to lead this investigation.

"I want to see the scene today," he said.

Beck pulled a face and glanced out of the window.

"The weather's still bad. Is that really necessary?"

"I will decide what's necessary," Neumann said sharply. "And captain, I'm not a stickler for formalities, but we are both police officers and know the protocol. You will address me as 'Sir', or 'Major'. Do I make myself clear?"

Beck took a few seconds to answer, the resentment obvious in his face.

"Yes, sir."

"How far away is the murder site?"

"Six, seven kilometres."

"I'll need a horse."

There were five of them in the party: Neumann, Beck, Krause, Vogel and Huber, the last two joining them as they passed close to Schwangau, and all of them, bar the major, oozing discomfort at the weather and resentment at being forced to go out in it. If anything, it was colder now than it had been earlier. The wind had picked up and it sliced through their clothes and the exposed skin of their faces like a frozen knife. To the south, the cloud cover had lifted a little, giving a hint of the size of the mountains, though not even a glimpse of their summits. But at least it wasn't snowing.

Neumann and Beck rode at the front, the major on a docile bay mare from the police stables. The others were on foot, Vogel carrying his axe, which Neumann had expressly instructed him to bring. They headed east in a line and the major tried to engage Beck in conversation. He knew his arrival had ruffled feathers, wounded local pride, and he wanted their relationship to be as amicable as possible.

"Do you have much crime in Füssen?" he asked.

It was intended as a straightforward question, a simple search for information, but Beck interpreted it differently: as something inherently patronising, the big city policeman sneering at his rural counterpart.

"We have our share," he replied defensively. "Not as much, I'm sure, as you do in Berlin, but we have enough to keep us busy."

"I wasn't making a comparison. I'm just interested, that's all. How much is serious crime?"

"Not a lot," Beck conceded, slightly placated by Neumann's conciliatory tone. "Minor theft, drunkenness, assault, that kind of thing. Most of it attributable to the workers at the rope-making factory. Immigrants, you see, from Austria and Bohemia."

"Any murders?"

"Very few. And none unsolved."

That was better than Berlin, Beck was pretty certain, where homicides would be more common, but probably harder to clear up. In Füssen, by contrast, the occasional killing nearly always had witnesses, a very obvious perpetrator.

"That's impressive," Neumann said. "What's your view of the Geissler case?"

"My view?" Beck repeated warily. Was the major trying to catch him out?

"You know the area, you know the people. Why do you think he might have been killed?"

"I don't know." That's for you to work out, Beck thought. Isn't that why you're here?

"A young man like him, a diplomat working at the legation. Who would want to kill him? Is there anti-Prussian feeling in Füssen?"

"None," Beck said, perhaps a little too quickly, too firmly. "I mean, we're one country now, aren't we? We're all Germans."

It was a disingenuous reply, Neumann reflected. Legally correct, but spiritually questionable. Unification had not been an accident, or even a particularly concordant act. It had been engineered by a scheming Bismarck, forced on the smaller states by a chancellor determined to create an empire in which the first among so-called equals would always be Prussia. There were plenty of people in Bavaria who would feel affronted by that, maybe angry enough to take violent action.

Neumann looked around, trying to get his bearings in this unfamiliar land. To his left, the plain stretched away north into the distance, a snow-clad landscape of fields interspersed with patches of woodland and isolated farmhouses. The wind had sculpted the snow into an undulating vista of hollows and lumps and teasing shapes that gave only a suggestion of what might lie beneath: walls, ponds, perhaps even buildings where the drifts were at their deepest. In the other direction, the mountains were still veiled with mist and cloud that eddied across the peaks, occasionally ripping apart to reveal stark rock faces and ridges frosted with ice. An echelon of swans swooped past overhead, low enough to hear the flap of their wings, then dropped down out of sight beyond the trees.

"Is there a lake over there?" Neumann asked.

"Two," Beck replied. "Alpsee and Schwansee."

"And that sandy-coloured building I can see, with the castellated towers?"

"That's Schloss Hohenschwangau, the king's palace. Well, one of them. He's building a new one up there on the clifftop. You see it?"

Neumann nodded, studying the edifice that was half hidden by the mist. All turrets, Romanesque arches and sheer white stone walls soaring up into the sky, most of it covered with scaffolding.

"Impressive," he said. "When's it going to be finished?"

Beck chortled. "Probably never, if you ask me. It's taken them seventeen years to get this far and it still looks like a building site."

The captain, like most locals, looked on the new palace with a mixture of bemusement and resignation. No one could understand why Ludwig was constructing such an extravagant confection when he already had Hohenschwangau just a kilometre away. But kings were kings and they could do whatever they liked, spend their money as they pleased, even though Ludwig's subjects, respectful and obedient for the most part, had a suspicion that the vast sums being expended on this opulent vanity project were actually *their* money.

Neumann had heard all about the king's passion for palaces, not just these two but others in Bavaria, at Linderhof and Herrenchiemsee where he was reportedly building a mini-Versailles on an island in a lake. The Berlin press gave regular reports on the projects, generally in a tone of fascinated disapproval at such profligacy, their jingoistic cheering for the glories of the empire always tempered by suspicion of its constituent parts, particularly the more independent ones like Bavaria, which was regarded as unreliable and a potentially subversive thorn in Bismarck's side.

Beck turned in his saddle and shouted something at Vogel, the woodcutter replying, but Neumann understanding nothing for it was all in dialect.

"This way," Beck said, reverting to High German and steering his horse off the main track onto a smaller path through the trees. Neumann fell into line behind him, the path too narrow to ride abreast. Schwangau and Füssen were well behind them now. There were no houses out here, just the dense, semi-impenetrable forest. Neumann listened to the sound of the wind in the branches, the muted clop of the horses' hooves in the snow. His bay mare whinnied, unsettled by the trees closing in around them. Her breath puffed out like flurries of steam, condensing momentarily before vanishing into the air.

As they progressed deeper into the wood, Neumann and Beck dismounted and continued on foot. Vogel came to the front to lead the way, his experienced eye picking out paths that the others would have missed until, finally, they broke out into a wide clearing.

Vogel pointed and said something.

"Would anyone care to translate that for me?" Neumann asked.

"This is where he found the body."

Neumann surveyed the area. It was roughly circular, about ten metres in diameter, the trees surrounding it underpinned by shrubs. Since Geissler's body had been removed, there'd been more snow. The clearing was blanketed forty or fifty centimetres deep, the surface untouched by any marks. No footprints, no paw prints.

"Show me exactly where it was."

Beck translated the instruction and the group moved out towards the centre of the open space. Vogel stopped and gestured at the ground. Neumann interrogated him, the captain acting as intermediary.

"When you found the body, tell me what you saw."

"The spear," Vogel replied. "Just here. Course I didn't know it was a spear. It just looked like a branch sticking up out of the snow. But a funny branch, you know. All smooth and very straight. That's why I took a closer look at it."

"Did you see any footprints, any sign that someone had been there before you?"

"No."

"Any blood?"

"Blood?"

"In the snow."

"No."

"Had you encountered anyone earlier?"

"No one. I had the forest to myself."

"So what did you do?"

"When?"

"After you'd inspected the spear."

Vogel shrugged. He made a guttural noise that Neumann took for some obscure word of dialect, but which turned out to be the woodcutter clearing his throat preparatory to a satisfying spit.

"Scooped away the snow," he said. "That's when I saw the body underneath. Gave me a fright, I can tell you."

"Did you touch the body?"

"No way. Those dead eyes staring up at me."

"You didn't remove anything?"

"From the body? Didn't touch it, like I said. Just covered it back up and went to find the constable."

He nodded at Huber who was standing next to Krause, both men feeling the cold despite their well-padded frames, both tired after the long walk. Beck was also cold and getting impatient.

"Have you seen enough... sir?" he asked.

"We need to search the area," Neumann said.

Beck gazed at him incredulously. "It's covered in snow."

"I'm aware of that, captain. But I need to see the ground and we can't wait for nature to do the job for us. We must remove the snow."

"Remove it? What, dig it away with our bare hands?"

"I want fires lit to melt it. A circle of them... round here." he indicated the spots.

"Fires? You want us to light fires? With what?"

"Vogel's a woodcutter, isn't he? Get him to cut some wood."

Neumann walked away to terminate the discussion. He circled round the edge of the clearing, peering into the undergrowth – not sure what he was looking for, but wanting to familiarise himself with the location: get a feel for the place. It was very remote, a long way from the legation. Had Geissler come out here for some reason, or had his body just been dumped here? Clearing away the snow, he hoped, might shed some light on those questions.

Behind him, Beck was issuing orders to the others, sending them out into the surrounding woods to collect fallen branches and logs and twigs for kindling, exorcising his anger in the time-honoured fashion of taking it out on his subordinates.

Neumann found a break in the trees that was obviously a path and headed out along it. A hundred metres in, he heard the unmistakeable sound of someone chopping wood. He thought at first that it must be Vogel, then realised that the noise was coming from the forest ahead of him. Pushing on along the path, he emerged into another clearing and saw a sturdy pony harnessed to a cart piled high with wood. A few metres away, a young man was wielding an axe, chopping a large log up into more manageable sections. Neumann could see him only from behind. He was medium height and slim, wearing scuffed knee-high leather boots, rough wool trousers and a cap on his head. The young man sensed, or heard, the major's presence. He lowered his axe and turned. His face was dirty, gleaming with sweat.

Neumann gaped at him, suddenly aware of his figure, the swell of breasts under the shirt that was unbuttoned at the top, revealing a glimpse of cleavage. For a second, he was lost for words. Then he found his voice.

"Good day, fräulein."

The young woman looked at him with clear blue eyes flecked with orange. Her face, beneath the grime, was more mature than he'd thought. He put her in her mid-thirties.

"Well..." he began, feeling unusually discomposed. There was something about her gaze that unsettled him. "You live near here?" he went on, realising as he spoke that this peasant woman would probably only understand dialect. But, to his surprise, she replied confidently in High German.

"At Waldblick."

She inclined her head to her right. In the distance, through a gap in the trees, Neumann caught sight of a large stone and wood house with tall chimneys.

"Who is your master?" he asked.

"There is no master."

"Your mistress, then? Who owns the house?"

"The Freiherrin Sophie Hals von Wildenstein."

"This land here, it belongs to the freiin?"

"All of it. The forest, the farmland out on the plain."

The young woman turned away from him and resumed her work.

"Are there no male servants who could do this kind of heavy labour?" Neumann said.

She made a point of chopping through a section of log before she replied.

"I can do it as well as a man."

She swung the axe again. Neumann watched her. He didn't often see women wearing trousers – although it wasn't uncommon in the more Bohemian quarters of Berlin – but maybe it was different down here in this rural backwater. The terrain, the weather, the nature of the work, dresses were probably impractical.

"You come out here frequently, I suppose?" he said. The woman ignored him. "To collect wood, I mean."

She chopped off another section and let the axe drop to her side. She was breathing heavily, her chest rising and falling.

"Why do you ask?"

"A body was found a few days ago in a clearing just over there. On your mistress's land. Were you out here on Monday or Tuesday?"

"A body? Whose body?"

"Were you out here? Did you see anyone?"

She wiped her brow with the sleeve of her jacket.

"You're a stranger here, aren't you? Who are you?"

Neumann found her manner pert, bordering on insolent. There was none of the deference he would have expected from a servant.

"I'm a police officer," he said curtly. "Answer my questions."

She seemed more amused than intimidated.

"Ah, your questions. Let me think. No, I wasn't out here on Monday or Tuesday. And, thus, I didn't see anyone."

She picked up the wood she'd chopped and stacked it neatly on the cart.

"You've finished?" Neumann said. He glanced back towards the clearing. There was no sign of any smoke. He had plenty of time. "Take me to your mistress."

Gisela Winter wrapped a shawl around her thin, stooped shoulders and went out of the cottage, a two-room wooden hut hidden away in the forest, trees growing almost to the door, a steep rock escarpment behind. She moved slowly and with some difficulty. The arthritis in her joints was always worse in cold weather.

At the base of the escarpment was a spring that trickled out into a stone trough. The spring never froze, even in sub-zero temperatures, but the water in the trough did. Gisela picked up the fist-sized rock she kept nearby on a ledge for just this purpose and smashed the film of ice on the surface. Then she dipped her kettle in and filled it.

She was old. She didn't know exactly how old – her date of birth had never been recorded, although it was at least seventy years ago. But there was nothing wrong with her ears or eyes. She heard the noise first and cocked her head, listening. The faint rhythmic squeak of a rusty axle, wheels turning. Then she saw them: a man and a woman walking along the track to the big house, the woman leading a pony and cart. They were less than a hundred metres away but neither of them looked in her direction. Gisela watched them. The woman she knew well, but the man she'd never seen before. Tall, powerfully built, wearing a long, dark grey greatcoat that covered the tops of his polished black boots. Gisela studied him pensively for a time then, when the couple disappeared from sight behind a thick stand of trees, she shuffled back inside the cottage.

It was warmer than outside, but she kept the shawl on as she hung the kettle from the hook over the fire and settled down in her armchair. Above her, hanging from the ceiling beams, were bunches of herbs and flowers – sage, thyme, lavender, rosemary, echinacea, marigold – the ingredients of the potions and ointments she made and sold to support herself. Their scents, sweet and fragrant, suffused the room.

Gisela picked up the drop-spindle from beside her chair and spun some wool. Her fingers were stiff and swollen at the knuckles, but still dextrous enough to twist the strands together as the spindle rotated. The flames of the fire flickered into life, revived by a sudden draught from under the door. Gisela watched the fluttering red and orange tongues, the tendrils of smoke curling up into the chimney, seeing shapes in them, seeing signs, a gift she'd had since childhood. A gift that the local people still trusted, still called upon regularly to predict the future.

Gisela gazed into the fire, her hands busy with her spindle, trying to understand the signs, to interpret them. Nothing was clear. In her mind, she could see only a mist obscuring the truth. She attempted to draw the veil aside, but it remained stubbornly fixed, occasionally fragmenting to give her a tantalising glimpse of what lay beyond, but never enough for her to see it distinctly. Yet she sensed it wasn't good. A sudden chill shivered through her and she pulled the shawl tighter around her shoulders and leaned instinctively closer to the fire.

Neumann and the servant woman walked in silence along the track, the only sound the muffled pad of their boots in the snow and the creak of the cart beside them, the pony pulling hard, keen to get home. As the trees thinned out, the major got a better view of the estate house. It was an impressive, well-proportioned building, three storeys high, the ground floor stone, the upper floors clad with wood that had silvered over time, softening the edges of the house and giving it a feeling of age, as if it had somehow grown out of the surrounding forest, a natural feature that had always been there.

Emerging onto the tree-lined drive at the front, the servant said, "If you go to the main door, one of the maids will see to you," then she veered off diagonally, heading for the stable block at the eastern end of the building. Neumann walked up the short flight of steps and rang the bell by the front door. The maid who answered was in her late teens, a white apron over her black dress, her hair concealed beneath a white cap.

"Is your mistress in?" Neumann asked.

"I'll see, sir. May I have your name?"

"Major Reinhardt Neumann."

"If you'd care to come inside, sir."

The maid stepped back, pulling the door wider to allow him to enter, then closing it behind him.

"One moment, sir."

She scurried away into the back of the house. Neumann removed his cap and looked around the entrance hall. It was homely rather than grand, the walls panelled with dark wood, the floor overlaid with a rug that was worn so thin in places the pattern had been obliterated. It smelt of polish and old timber and dust.

"This way, sir."

The maid had reappeared. Neumann followed her along the corridor and into a drawing room.

"The freiin will be with you directly, sir," the maid said, then left him alone.

The room was spacious, furnished with armchairs and sofas that looked as if they'd been chosen for comfort rather than style. Like the hall rug, they were a little threadbare, the upholstery shiny and torn in places. A fire burned in the stone hearth that occupied most of one wall. Neumann wandered over to the windows, tall glazed doors that gave onto a paved terrace outside. With the covering of snow, it was difficult to make out what the grounds were like, but he could see what he guessed was a formal garden: flower beds, a broad lawn leading to a shrubbery, an ornamental pool in the centre with a tier of stone bowls above it that had to be a fountain when the water supply thawed. Beyond the gardens was the frosty surface of a frozen lake.

The door clicked open. He turned and saw the servant woman from the forest coming into the room. She'd changed into smarter trousers and jacket, exchanged the dirty knee-high boots for a cleaner pair of black shoes. The cap was gone, revealing a mass of dark hair tied up and fastened with a silver clasp, and she'd washed away the grime and sweat from her face.

"You wanted to see me, major."

"No, I'm waiting for..." Neumann stuttered to a halt, the realisation suddenly hitting him. "*You*? You are the Freiherrin von Wildenstein?"

"I'm pleased to make your acquaintance."

Her gaze was direct, unapologetic, almost mocking. Neumann felt the anger rising inside him, knew he should control it, but he was too outraged to hold it in.

"I suppose you found it amusing, pretending to be a servant? Making a fool of me."

He could hear he sounded like a prig and was annoyed with himself. But her behaviour was unseemly for a baroness.

"I pretended no such thing," Sophie replied tersely. "You assumed I was a servant because your own prejudices told you I had to be. Collecting wood, that's what menials do. Not in this house. Tasks are divided up according to ability, and chopping wood happens to be something I'm good at." She paused. "As for making a fool of you, well, you seem more than capable of doing that without my help."

Neumann was astonished by her rudeness. He sensed she was seeing how far she could provoke him and that he would be wise not to take the bait.

"Now, what is it you want?" she went on. She'd taken an instant dislike to him in the forest. Like all Prussians, he was arrogant, like all policemen, officious.

"A young man has been murdered," Neumann said, trying to reassert some of the authority that had slipped away from him. "A diplomat from the German legation named Christoph Geissler."

"And you think I know something about it?"

"His body was found on your land."

"That's meaningless. I allow open access to my estate. To collect wood, to hunt small game, to fish in the river. Anyone can come into the forest."

"You said you weren't out there yourself on Monday or Tuesday. What about your staff, your servants? I'll need to question them."

"That's not something I will permit."

He stared at her, wondering if he'd heard her correctly.

"I beg your pardon?"

"Some of them are very vulnerable. I won't have a policeman bullying them."

"I've never bullied anyone in my life."

"Haven't you? Are you sure about that?"

She looked him in the eye and he was struck by that same uncomfortable sensation he'd felt when he'd first met her: uneasy, a little flustered, fearing – absurdly – that she could see into his mind, could identify his flaws and weaknesses. She was a striking woman. Not conventionally beautiful; at least, not in a pretty, feminine way. Her jaw was too strong, her eyes too fierce and searching. But she had a powerful aura, a sort of defiant sexuality that he found strangely attractive despite her obvious hostility towards him.

"You know I can compel them to answer my questions," he said.

"Can you? And how will you do that?"

"I can get a court order."

"That will take you time. Then you'll need a warrant to come back here and enter my house. That will take more time. Much quicker to let me question them."

"You presume to know what I wish to ask."

"It's hardly difficult. You want to know whether any of them were out in the forest where this diplomat's body was found. Whether they saw or heard anything that might be relevant to your investigation. Am I correct?"

"Yes," he had to concede.

"I will make the necessary enquiries and send word to you. Where can I find you?"

"At the police station, or the Gasthaus Hoffmann, in Füssen."

"Is there anything else?"

"No."

Those intense blue eyes came to rest on his face again. "You're from Berlin?"

"Yes."

"Sent here specially? You don't trust the local police to investigate this properly?"

That was not something he could acknowledge.

"It's a joint investigation between Prussia and Bavaria," he said and she smiled cynically, not deceived for a moment.

"They will not welcome you here," she said.

"Who won't?"

"The men who matter." She moved away towards the door. "If that's all, major, allow me to show you out."

FOUR

The encounter preoccupied him on the walk back to the clearing in the forest. He hated to admit it to himself, but the freiin had got under his skin more than any woman he could recall. Her manner, her self-assurance, that unquestionable sense of entitlement of the landed aristocracy. All of it had infuriated him. The deception, too. Perhaps she was right that she hadn't actually pretended to be a servant, but the difference was purely academic to Neumann. As far as he was concerned, she'd misled him. She'd played a game with him, humiliated him. Then she'd taken the initiative in the meeting, taken away the control that rightly should have been his. She seemed to pamper her servants, but she'd treated him almost with contempt – a *public* servant who deserved no respect. She'd denied him his legal right to question potential witnesses, then dismissed him like an under-butler. What made it worse was the feeling that he could have handled the situation better. *Should* have handled it better. He'd allowed her to outmanoeuvre him and that was a blow to his professional pride.

He smelt the smoke, saw the sooty clouds drifting up above the trees as he approached the clearing. Four fires had been lit in a rough square about three metres from the spot where Geissler's body had been found; far enough away to ensure that any evidence uncovered wouldn't be compromised by the blazes. *If* any evidence were there, Neumann thought. He wasn't optimistic about discovering anything of importance, but this was a procedure that had to be carried out. You couldn't investigate a murder without examining the scene of the crime.

The snow was already melting fast. Vogel and Huber had been allocated the laborious task of providing the fuel, going to and fro into the woods to bring out timber, while Beck and Krause stood by, ostensibly supervising but, in reality, doing little more than keeping themselves warm by the fires. Neumann joined Beck by one of them.

"You've done an excellent job, captain. The snow's almost gone," he said.

Beck nodded, but wasn't going to be charmed by the obvious flattery.

"You've been away a while," he replied bluntly. "Must've been a long walk."

"I met the landowner, the Freiherrin von Wildenstein."

"Did you now." Beck's voice was non-committal.

"Do you know her?"

"Know *of* her."

"What's her reputation locally?"

Beck shrugged, gauging his reply, his natural deference towards the gentry tempered by an equally innate misogyny.

"She's regarded as, well, eccentric."

"She seems to run a rather unorthodox establishment."

"The House of Women, that's what it's known as," Beck said. "Not a man in the place. The freiin won't allow it."

"No male servants?"

"Not a butler, a coachman, a stable boy. It's all women."

"She isn't married?"

Beck snorted. "Who'd marry a woman like that? Dresses in men's clothes, they say. Not in the town, though. She puts on a gown when she comes to Füssen. Looks the proper lady." He surveyed the ground on which the snow had pretty much all melted. "What're you going to do now?"

Neumann moved away from the heat of the fire and studied the area. It was waterlogged and slushy, littered with twigs and dead branches and soggy leaves. He could see nothing to indicate that a body had once lain here. No indentation in the soil, no traces of clothing, no obvious signs of any blood. Hitching up the hem of his greatcoat, he got down on his knees and began a search, his fingers sifting carefully through the debris. The others watched him, Beck rolling his eyes at Krause, both of them regarding this operation as a waste of time.

Neumann didn't hurry. He could feel the cold, the moisture seeping into his trousers from the damp earth. His fingertips, too, were rapidly cooling as he scooped up leaves and examined them. The area was far from pristine. There were marks that had probably been caused by feet, but they were worthless as evidence. More than likely they had been made by Vogel, or by the police when they recovered the body. None of them, in any case, was clear enough to identify a particular shape or pattern on the sole of a boot.

Bending lower, he saw a small strand of dark blue cloth caught on the sharp side-stem of a twig. He detached it, took an envelope from his coat pocket and put the strand inside, then continued his meticulous search. Behind him, the others fidgeted impatiently, wanting only to be finished and away from this inhospitable place.

Neumann worked slowly across the ground, noting, in particular, what wasn't there. It was difficult to be certain because the soil was so wet, but he was fairly sure there was no blood. A spear wound to the chest would have produced a lot of blood, an arterial spurt that would have left deposits on the area around the body. But he could see no sign of any on the leaves or twigs. Conclusion: Geissler had probably been killed elsewhere and his body dumped here. But dumped by whom?

Something glinted in the mud by his fingers. Digging down a little, Neumann discovered a ring. He wiped the dirt off it. It was gold, embossed with a white enamel letter W set in a navy-blue enamel surround. From the size, it had to be a man's ring. He showed it to Beck.

"Does this mean anything to you?"

The captain peered at the ring. "No."

"A letter W. What would that signify?"

Beck shrugged. "I've never seen anything like it before."

"Sergeant?"

"Means nothing to me either."

Was it Geissler's? Neumann wondered as he stowed the ring away in another envelope. Or did it belong to someone else? Wildenstein, he thought suddenly. This was the freiin's land. Was this ring somehow connected to her or her family? Had somebody dropped or lost it here? He had to keep an open mind, not jump to conclusions. It was entirely possible the ring had nothing to do with Geissler's murder.

Ten minutes later, he completed his search, having found nothing more of any interest. He brushed the muck off his trousers and dusted down his greatcoat and turned to the others, seeing the relief in their faces

"I'm done here. Thank you for your assistance."

They made good time on the return journey. All of them were eager to be home before nightfall. Already the sun had sunk behind the mountains and the shadows of dusk were creeping through the forest. As they neared

Schwangau, Neumann heard the howl of a wolf. He reined in his horse and turned his head towards the sound. It seemed uncomfortably close.

Huber, walking just behind him, confirmed that suspicion.

"They're getting bolder, sir," he said. "It's been a long, hard winter. They're hungry. They've even been seen on the outskirts of the village, scavenging for food. It's not good."

Neumann looked back towards the forest, trying to see any shapes, any movement in the fading light.

"There's a whole pack of them," Huber went on. His hand reached protectively for the billy club on his belt. "They start threatening people, they'll have to be dealt with."

Neumann listened a moment longer, but the sound didn't come again. He dug his heels into the flanks of his mare and they walked on, the howl lingering inside his head like a distant, mournful echo.

Neumann had seen bodies before – too many bodies. Corpses on the battlefield, both friend and foe. Young men ripped apart by shells and bullets, by the bloody reality of war. Many he'd watched die, soldiers alongside him, brothers in the infantry, picked out in a random lottery that chose some for slaughter and left others standing, wondering how and why they'd been spared. The numbers, in the end, became too large to count. Nameless carcasses scattered across the killing grounds, sometimes three, four deep, limbs severed, guts spilling, faces shattered beyond recognition. Neumann a subaltern supervising the burial parties, his men slipping in the pools of blood, retching and vomiting as they tossed the dead into their makeshift, unmarked graves.

He'd seen bodies since as a police officer, but, thankfully, not many. A few accidental deaths, a handful of suicides, a greater number of homicides, Berlin a city where poverty and deprivation were commonplace, where violence was rife in the criminal underclass and murder its all too frequent outcome. Professional detachment notwithstanding, they all touched him in some way. How could they not? Those lives lost, those families grieving, that sense that with every one, a little part of him also died.

But few had affected him the way Christoph Geissler did. The young man's body was laid out on a table in the outhouse behind the police station that had been turned into a temporary morgue. He was naked, covered by a white linen sheet. The room was unheated, but not cold enough to preserve the corpse. Over the days since its discovery, it had thawed and was now beginning to decompose, filling the space with the sickly odour of putrefaction.

Neumann gazed down at the face. The skin was growing slack, the flesh beneath it losing some of its structure, but it was still arrestingly handsome. No, not handsome, beautiful. Not an adjective that was generally ascribed to the male of the species, but then there was something distinctly feminine about Geissler. He had none of the coarseness of the stereotypical man. His jowls were smooth and almost hairless, only a close inspection revealing a sheen of fine, blond stubble. His features, particularly his nose, were delicate, his eyes a vibrant blue, his lips soft and full, all framed by luxuriant golden hair, worn quite long, which, even in death, had lost none of its lustre.

It was a shock to see him cold on the slab. So young, so fair, his face serene, untouched by any mark of violence, and yet the life had gone from him. Neumann pulled down the sheet to expose the torso. To expose the crude line where the pathologist had cut open and then stitched shut the chest, and the gaping hole in the left breast. Neumann bent over the table to examine the wound. It was wide and circular, about five or six centimetres across, but relatively shallow, certainly not deep enough to reach the heart.

Doctor Arnold Jaeger watched him. He was a short, stout man in his forties, his chin garnished with a neat goatee. He'd already put on his overcoat and packed up his black medical bag, impatient to get away now he'd completed his work. Neumann picked up the spear that had caused the wound in Geissler's chest. It was light and smooth, one end tapered to a stubby point. The wood around the tip was stained with something dark, presumably blood.

"This is surely too blunt to have killed him," he said.

"It didn't," the pathologist replied. He stepped over to the body. "You see there, deep inside the wound? There's a darker line, a thin incision."

"I see it."

"A stab wound. He was killed with a knife or similar blade, about twenty centimetres long and three centimetres at its widest point. It went right through the chest and pierced the heart."

"So the spear was inserted after death?"

"Exactly. Someone thrust it into the knife wound and applied pressure – quite a lot of pressure – to force it through the chest muscles."

"Why would anyone do that?"

"That's your job, major, not mine," Jaeger said tartly.

"And this?" Neumann indicated the stems of mistletoe wrapped around the shaft.

"It appears to be mere decoration. It had no part in the death."

"The berries are poisonous, aren't they?"

Jaeger glanced at him sideways. "Not to a man who's just been stabbed through the heart."

"What about pagan tradition? Could it be something

to do with that?"

"I'm a doctor. I don't deal with superstitious nonsense. There was no sign of any poisoning, no sign of any disease. The deceased's organs were healthy. I can say with absolute certainty that the stab wound was the cause of death. Now, can I go?"

"One more thing. Time of death?"

Jaeger clicked his tongue and held out his arms, hands spread in a gesture of helplessness.

"Impossible to say with any accuracy. The body had been frozen, invalidating the usual signs – the body temperature, the onset of rigor mortis and so forth – that we use to try to estimate time of death."

Neumann nodded, his gaze wandering back to the pale shape on the table.

"Do you have any further need of the body?"

"No, I've completed my examination."

"So it can be released for burial?"

"Yes."

"Thank you, doctor. I look forward to receiving your full report."

Jaeger picked up his bags and hurried out before the major could think of any more questions. Neumann didn't want to linger, either. It was unpleasantly cold in the outhouse and the smell of decomposition was beginning to turn his stomach. He pulled the sheet back over the corpse and they returned to the warmth of Beck's office.

"Who identified Geissler?" Neumann asked.

"Captain Maisel, from the legation."

"Next of kin have been notified, I assume?"

"The legation was taking care of that."

"Let them know that the family can now have the body."

"Yes, sir."

"Take me through the chronology."

Beck squinted at him. "The *what*?"

"The timeline. Geissler's body was discovered on Tuesday, you said. What time exactly?"

"The middle of the day. I can't be more precise than that. That's what the woodcutter, Vogel, told us, but he didn't report it to the police until later. It was nightfall by the time we brought the corpse in."

"And Geissler's movements before that? Had he been reported missing?"

"Tuesday morning, we had notification from the legation that he hadn't turned up for work either that day or the day before."

"When was he last seen?"

"Sunday evening. He has lodgings here in Füssen. His landlady gave him supper."

"She didn't see him on Monday?"

"No."

"And she didn't think that odd?"

"Not odd enough to tell us."

"So his whereabouts between Sunday evening and Tuesday mid-day – say, forty hours – are unaccounted for?"

"Yes, sir."

Neumann didn't ask whether any attempt had been made to explain those missing hours. He knew what the answer would be. He couldn't work out whether this laxity was the norm here or whether there was a degree of bloodymindedness involved – we're not regarded as good enough for a case like this so let the big noise from Berlin, whoever he is, figure it out for himself. See how far he gets without our help. The answer was ultimately immaterial. Neumann would have to start from the beginning, take responsibility for everything the local police had failed to do.

"Where are his clothes and possessions?"

Beck got up from his chair and opened the door of a cupboard against the wall. He took out two cloth bags, one large, one small, and handed them to Neumann. The larger bag contained Geissler's clothes – his trousers, boots, socks, underwear, jacket, shirt and cravat. The outer garments were caked with mud, the left breast of the jacket torn apart where the knife and then the spear had been inserted. The material around the tear was stained with what looked like dry blood.

In the smaller bag were the dead man's possessions: a handkerchief; a leather wallet with his business cards and eighty marks inside and a pocket watch on a golden chain with a small gold swan attached to one of the links – good quality, expensive, perhaps surprisingly expensive for a junior diplomat, but maybe he had had rich parents. The money and the watch, that probably ruled out robbery as the motive for the murder.

Finally, there was a piece of folded paper with some writing on it. But not writing in any language Neumann could recognise. It just seemed to be a collection of random ink marks, some identifiable letters like F and R and B, others strange symbols he'd never seen before, all of them slightly smudged, presumably from the damp when the note had thawed out with the body.

"What's this?"

Beck shrugged. "It was in one of his pockets. We don't know what it is."

"Some kind of code?"

"Maybe."

Beck's manner was indifferent. Neumann got the message loud and clear: your problem, not mine.

Neumann replaced the items in the bags and returned them to Beck.

"We'll continue in the morning, captain."

He walked back through the quiet streets to the Gasthaus Hoffmann, washed and changed his clothes, then went downstairs with his dirty garments to ask Johanna if they could be laundered. She looked at his soiled trousers, the knees plastered with mud, and raised an eyebrow.

"Have you been digging a grave, major?"

Neumann laughed. "I've been out in the forest."

He paused. Operational matters were confidential, but he was acutely aware of his outsider status here, of how little local knowledge he had. Gathering information, however slight or apparently inconsequential, could only help him in his investigation.

"On the von Wildenstein estate, actually," he added. "The freiin seems an interesting woman."

"You met her?" Johanna replied. "And you're still in one piece?"

"One piece?"

"Most men who go there she sends packing with their tails between their legs." She gave a bawdy chuckle. "And not just their tails."

"She doesn't like men?"

"Not ones who try to court her. Who want her money. And there are plenty of those. She's a very rich woman."

"There are no men in her house, I understand. No male servants."

"Male servants are always trouble, particularly when there are female servants around. They take liberties, their hands have a tendency to wander, they bully and take advantage of the young girls. That's why I get Tobias to do most of the heavy work around here. I know he won't misbehave with the housemaids. And if he does, he'll feel the back of my hand."

"It seems an unusual set-up for a big estate like hers."

Johanna shrugged. "She's wealthy enough to do as she pleases. There are men on her farms and managing her forest. It's just in her home she won't tolerate them. I don't blame her, personally. The girls she employs, most of them are, well, fragile."

"Fragile?"

"Waifs and strays. Girls who've been abused or knocked about. Girls who've got in the family way and been thrown out into the street. The freiin takes them in, looks after them or finds them a suitable position somewhere outside the area. Some people say she's a soft touch, a fool, but who are we to judge? No offence, major, but it's a man's world. We women need to stick together."

Johanna folded up his trousers and tucked them under her arm. "I'll put them in the wash tomorrow morning. Now, I suppose you'll be wanting your supper."

Later, back in his room, Neumann reflected on the day, running over exactly what he knew about the murder of Christoph Geissler. The diplomat had been stabbed to death with a knife. That in itself wasn't uncommon. What made this case exceptional, however, was the spear that had then been thrust into the chest wound afterwards. It was a bizarre, apparently pointless act, but it must surely have had some reason behind it. The mistletoe wrapped around the shaft seemed equally senseless, but that, too, had to have some meaning. Why had the killer done it? Why, in fact, had he murdered Geissler in the first place? The diplomat was young, very junior and powerless. Why had anyone wanted him dead?

He took out the two envelopes from his coat pocket – the evidence he'd gathered in the clearing. The strand of cloth wasn't of any great interest to him, but the ring was. He washed the dirt off it in the bowl on the washstand, then examined it more closely under the oil lamp on the bedside table. It was gold, but there was no hallmark on it, nor any other inscription except that letter W on the top. Why W? He was going to have to visit the freiin again, to ask her about the ring, a prospect that held little appeal for him. He was still smarting internally from their last meeting. He still felt he'd come out the loser, that she'd demeaned him deliberately. He thought back over their conversation and her parting remark, in particular, came to the forefront of his mind. They won't welcome you here, she'd said. The men who matter. What did she mean? Who were these men who mattered?

FIVE

Christoph Geissler had had lodgings in the south-east corner of Füssen where the old town wall was still intact, running in a straight line behind the Franciscan monastery before coming to an abrupt stop on the bluff above the Lech. The house was perched on the hillside next to the wall, accessed from a flight of steps that led down to a footpath running along the north bank of the river. His landlady, Monika Seidel, was a widow in her mid-fifties, a tall, stringy woman with sharp, inquisitive eyes set deep into her gaunt face. Courteous from the moment Neumann knocked on her door, she became positively fawning when he identified himself.

"A major? From Berlin? This is indeed an honour, sir. Please, take a seat in the parlour."

She showed him through into the front room, a small space crammed with ugly furniture, vases, ornaments and other bric-à-brac, like an antiques shop full of objects no one wanted to buy. It was unheated and almost as cold as outside.

"May I offer you some refreshment, major? Perhaps a glass of French brandy? I don't drink myself, you understand – except for medicinal purposes – but I always keep a bottle of cognac in the house for visitors. It's very fine."

"Thank you, Frau Seidel, but no. I don't wish to inconvenience you any more than I have to. I'm here about Herr Geissler. I'd be grateful if you could answer a few questions."

"Of course." Frau Seidel spread her skirts and settled herself down on a lyre-backed chair. "I don't have much contact with the police as a general rule. I keep a respectable house here, you know. But I'm always happy to oblige an officer of the law. Particularly one from Berlin. Is that the uniform of the Berlin police? It's rather smart, isn't it? My late husband, Gerd – God rest his soul – was butler to the Diefenbach family for many years. He looked so elegant in his livery. I do like a man in uniform, you know."

"Herr Geissler," Neumann said. "He'd lodged here for how long?"

"Oh, since he first arrived in Füssen. The accommodation I provide is first class and the legation always wants the best for its staff. The prince is most insistent on that. I met him once, you know. Such a dignified man, but very easy with his manners. A true nobleman."

Neumann could see that he was going to have difficulty keeping Frau Seidel on the subject. "And when did Herr Geissler arrive?" he asked.

"Last summer. He'd been here nine months. Not all the time, of course. The legation moves between Füssen and Munich according to where the king is staying, but the court has been here for most of the winter."

"What sort of man was he?"

"Most personable. Polite, considerate, quiet. His rooms were always immaculately kept. I wish I could say the same for all my lodgers." She gave Neumann a knowing look. "Young gentlemen, they're not always as fastidious as they might be, are they? That's why this whole terrible business has been so shocking. A sweet, pleasant young man like him. Murdered! When Captain Beck told me, I almost fainted, and I'm a woman with a generally robust constitution."

"You last saw him on Sunday evening, I understand?"

"That's right. I gave him supper, a rather nice piece of roast lamb and some pickled cabbage, if I remember correctly. Herr Geissler was always very complimentary about my cooking."

"And you didn't see him again after that?"

"No."

"He wasn't here for breakfast on Monday morning?"

"No."

"And you didn't find that strange?"

Frau Seidel pursed her thin lips, her posture becoming more defensive.

"Well, you see, major, it wasn't unusual for Herr Geissler to stay out overnight. A handsome young man like him, you know how it is."

"You think he slept somewhere else?"

Frau Seidel leaned towards Neuman and lowered her voice, as if she feared she might be overheard.

"Far be it for me to spread gossip, but I think he might have had a... lady friend. I do his laundry and I've sometimes noticed traces of scent, of cologne, on his clothes."

"Have you seen any other evidence of this lady? Letters, or notes from her, perhaps?"

"Oh, no. I don't go snooping around my lodgers' rooms, unlike some landladies I can think of." Her tone became even more confidential. "Of course, he might have gone to one of those houses men go to in the evenings. You know, for company. I'm a woman of the world, major. I was married for twenty-six years. I know that men have...needs."

"Is there such a house in Füssen?"

The woman of the world suddenly appeared

scandalised by the question.

"I wouldn't know anything about that! But I'm sure Captain Beck will be able to help you."

"What about Herr Geissler's other activities? Did he have a social circle, interests outside his work?"

"Not many. He was a man of moderate habits. I don't believe he frequented any of the inns in the town. The only social events he attended regularly were the monthly meetings of the Wagner Society."

"The Wagner Society?"

"A group devoted to the composer's music. The king's kapellmeister, Herr Steimitz, runs it and the king himself is a frequent guest at the meetings."

"You go yourself?"

The idea appalled her. "Certainly not! I would not wish to be associated with such a disreputable figure. Please don't think me disloyal to the king, but his friendship with – that man – has brought no honour whatsoever to the royal family."

"How about friends? Visitors?"

"The only visitors I ever saw were a young boy from the legation – one of the prince's servants – who would sometimes bring despatches or messages."

That would probably be Jürgen Keller, Neumann thought.

"And Johanna Hoffman's boy," Frau Seidel went on.

"Tobias?"

"No, the older son, Axel. Works at the palace."

"Did he come often?"

"Not particularly. And he never stayed long."

"Do you know why he came?"

"Oh, no. I never pry into the private lives of my lodgers."

Neumann showed Frau Seidel the ring he'd found in the forest.

"Have you ever seen this before?"

"Never."

"Herr Geissler never wore it?"

"Not that I saw."

"You mentioned the Wagner Society. Could this be something to do with that? A sign of membership of the group, perhaps?"

"You'd have to ask them that."

"Thank you, Frau Seidel. You've been most helpful. Now, I wonder if I could see his rooms?"

They were upstairs on the first floor: a bedroom and an adjoining sitting room, both with windows overlooking the river. A bathroom, just along the landing, had been reserved for Geissler's exclusive use, Frau Seidel explained. She herself had her own bathroom next to her bedroom on the ground floor. Neumann looked around the sitting room. The landlady lingered intrusively by his shoulder.

"I will call you if I need anything," he said diplomatically.

"Oh, yes. As you wish."

Neumann waited for her to leave before he began his inspection. The sitting room was small, but adequate for one person. An armchair, a table with a lamp on it, a bookcase and a desk against the wall. All of it spotlessly clean. If Frau Seidel had any faults as a landlady, skimping on the dusting wasn't one of them.

He began with the bookcase. Seeing what a person read told you a lot about them. There were quite a few books on the shelves. Classics by Goethe and Schiller. Zola and Dickens in their original languages – an educated man who understood French and English. A man with an enquiring mind, too, evidenced by books on science and philosophy; maybe with a Romantic streak if works by von Arnim, Brentano and von Eichendorff were an accurate indication of his tastes.

What was he looking for? Neumann asked himself. A

clearer picture of Geissler, a man he'd never met, never seen except white and lifeless on a mortuary table. To gain some idea, some insight, into what kind of person he'd been. Neumann needed that connection, partly for personal reasons: to *know* the victim of a murder he was charged with investigating, a process that was going to use a lot of his time and almost certainly cause him some pain – no homicide he'd dealt with had ever left him unscathed. But for practical reasons, too, he wanted a deeper knowledge of the young diplomat, for it was only by understanding him that he was going to discover who had killed him.

He tried to picture what Geissler's life had been like. A young, single man from Berlin, working in Bavaria, a part of the empire that had good historical reasons for mistrusting Prussia. It couldn't have been easy for him to fit in, to make friends here. He had his work, of course. What would his routine have been? Breakfast in his lodgings, then the walk to the legation. Neumann couldn't see him having his own horse in Füssen – the cost of stabling, of maintenance, it wouldn't have made sense for a fit 26-year-old like him, particularly given that much of his time would have been spent in Munich. And a cab every morning, that would have been extravagant on a junior diplomat's salary. So a bracing half-hour walk out of town to Schloss Lichtenberg before he began his day's duties. And what would those have been? What did an official of his rank do with his time? The prince and Anton Maisel would almost certainly have handled all the high-level work, the interesting stuff, so Geissler would no doubt have been stuck with the boring, menial, clerical tasks. Not very stimulating.

And in the long evenings, what did he do? Return home to his lodgings and a landlady thirty years his senior with whom he had little in common, little to share. He must have been lonely. After supper, he would probably have come upstairs to these two modest rooms and sat in the armchair reading, the routine broken only by his monthly outings to the Wagner Society gatherings. Was that where he'd met this lady friend Frau Seidel had mentioned? Or was his female companionship confined to the more sordid surroundings of the local brothel? Male desire being what it was, the latter was quite likely, but Neumann decided to give Geissler the benefit of the doubt and assume he had a friendship, probably of a sexual nature if he stayed out regularly overnight, with a rather less transactional young woman. How would they have communicated with each other? By letter? If so, had Geissler kept any of those messages? If he had, they wouldn't have been left lying carelessly around the place. Whatever Frau Seidel's protestations, she struck Neumann as a landlady who would certainly snoop around her lodgers' rooms. So where would they have been hidden?

Neumann took the books out of the bookcase one by one and riffled through the pages. Not there. Then he crossed to the desk and tried the drawers, none of which was locked. They contained only stationery, writing paper, pens and ink. He pulled out each of the drawers in turn and looked underneath them. Nothing there either. That didn't leave many other potential hiding places in the sitting room. Neumann lifted the rug and checked the floorboards. None of them was loose or had been visibly tampered with in any way.

Moving into the bedroom, he searched the wardrobe, chest of drawers and bedside table, looked under the mattress, then examined the floorboards, too. Still nothing. Had he missed something? He went back into the sitting room and looked around. Where else could letters have been concealed? He'd ruled out the bookcase, the desk, the floor, but that didn't leave anywhere else obvious. Maybe Geissler had simply destroyed them.

Frustrated, he went to the window, rested his hands on the sill and looked out. The Lech was below him, a broad strip of fast-flowing, vivid turquoise water choked with chunks of floating ice. It was the coldest looking river he'd ever seen. Beyond it, the south bank was so narrow there was room for just a single row of houses and the road before the land rose steeply up the craggy base of the mountains.

The windowsill rocked suddenly beneath his fingers. He glanced down, shifting his weight. The sill wobbled again. It was loose. Very loose. Neumann gripped the edge and pulled the varnished wooden plank away from the window, revealing a shallow cavity in the wall underneath. Inside the cavity was a brown manilla envelope. Neumann lifted it out and removed the contents: ten separate pieces of paper, all with writing on them – the same peculiar ink marks as on the note that had been found on Geissler's body. Neumann studied them. They didn't look like love letters from a woman. They looked like something much more sinister. But whom were they from? And why would a diplomat like Geissler be receiving messages in what appeared to be code?

SIX

Neumann saw the shiny black carriage drawn up outside the police station as he came round the corner onto Hinteregasse. The horses were standing quietly by the kerb, the coachman hunched on his seat above them, his whip dangling limply by his side. Going into the building, Neumann found Jürgen Keller sitting in the reception area in his thin, dark green livery. At least he'd had the sense to come inside into the warmth. The youth stood up when he saw him.

"Sir... His Excellency would like to see you."

Neumann followed Keller back out onto the street and, once again, as the youth prepared to clamber up onto the rear seat of the carriage, he made him come inside with him.

"Sir – " Keller started to protest, but Neumann cut him off abruptly.

"I want to talk to you."

Keller eyed him nervously as the carriage pulled away from the police station.

"You know why I'm here?" Neumann asked.

"Yes, sir."

"How well did you know Christoph Geissler?"

"Me, sir? I'm just a servant, a messenger boy."

"But you had contact with him. What kind of man was he?"

Keller was flustered, confused. "Sir, I couldn't possibly comment on that."

"Forget your position. This is just an informal chat between the two of us. It will go no further. Did you like him?"

Keller gave his reply some thought, his face betraying his anxiety.

"Yes, sir. He always treated me very well."

"Do you know anything about his private life?"

"Oh, no, sir," Keller replied quickly. "Nothing at all."

"You went to his lodgings, I understand."

The youth looked at him sharply. His eyes were wide open, alarmed.

"Just to deliver messages – from His Excellency or Captain Maisel. I never stayed long."

"So you don't know whether he had friends in Füssen?"

"No, sir, I'm just a servant," he repeated. "I know my place."

"I'm trying to identify your accent. Where are you from?"

"Saxony-Anhalt, sir. A small village outside Stendal. His Excellency has an estate near there."

"Doesn't the chancellor also own land in that area?"

"Yes, sir. Prince Bismarck and His Excellency are almost neighbours."

"You've met the chancellor?"

"He has visited His Excellency, yes. And I have had the honour of serving him."

"And His Excellency brings you with him to Füssen when he comes."

"Yes, sir. He brings all the staff."

"There are no locals employed at the legation?"

"No, sir."

More Bavarians von Auerswald doesn't trust, Neumann thought. Probably a wise assumption to make here in the heart of Ludwig II's kingdom.

The prince was waiting for him in his office. There was no offer of Tokay this time, no social niceties. Von Auerswald got straight down to business.

"Where are you with your investigation?"

Neumann outlined what he'd been doing, his discussion with the pathologist, his visit to the site where Geissler's body had been found. Then he showed the prince the ring.

"Have you seen this before?"

Von Auerswald shook his head. "You think it's important?"

"It was right where Geissler's body was dumped. In a clearing in a remote part of the forest. I don't believe that's a coincidence. It has to be connected to the murder. Either it was Geissler's, or it was his killer's."

"I never saw Geissler wearing it."

"He was a regular supporter of the Wagner Society, I gather. I'm going to make enquiries, see if the ring has anything to do with them."

The prince regarded him sceptically. "With the Wagner Society?"

"You don't think that's likely?"

"You must do whatever you think fit, major. But I've been to a few meetings of the society. The king is their patron, you know, so I've occasionally been obliged to go." He grimaced. "Not my idea of an evening's entertainment, I can tell you. The operas – *music dramas*, as Wagner so pretentiously styled them – are ludicrous. Dwarves, giants, gods, knights arriving in boats pulled by swans. I can't imagine anything more ridiculous. And as for the music, well, it just witters on and on. The fellow was an incontinent bore, taking half an hour to say something that Mozart could do more effectively in thirty seconds. The members of the society, in my limited experience, are tedious cranks. I really cannot see any of them killing Geissler."

"That's my fundamental problem with this case, sir," Neumann said. "Why would *anyone* want to kill him? As far as I've discovered, he seemed to be a likeable young man."

"He was."

Neumann hesitated, wondering how to broach his next question.

"Sir… could I ask what work Geissler did here at the legation?"

"His work? Well, mostly fairly routine stuff. He handled correspondence, drafted letters and reports, looked after our files and archives, did whatever Maisel allocated him, I suppose."

"Was any of it classified?"

Von Auerswald frowned. His forehead wrinkling, combined with the duelling scars on his cheeks, transformed his face, giving it a harder, more menacing edge.

"What are you getting at, major?"

"Was he engaged in any kind of work that might have put him in danger?"

"What do you mean, danger?"

"Jeopardy. Anything that might have made him enemies, or put him in a situation where his life might be at risk."

"Absolutely not," the prince said firmly. "All classified material is handled by either Maisel or myself. Geissler took encrypted messages to the telegraph office in Füssen for transmission to Berlin, but he never had any part in writing them. Only Maisel and I have access to the codebook."

"Let me show you something, sir."

Neumann took out the pieces of paper he'd found

under the windowsill in Geissler's sitting room and slid them across the desk.

"These were in his lodgings, in a secret hiding place. Do they mean anything to you?"

Von Auerswald studied the marks on the papers.

"You think this is some kind of code?"

"It looks like it to me."

"I think they're runes."

"Runes, sir?"

"The ancient Germanic alphabet. Doesn't mean they might not also be code, of course."

"A similar message – if that's what these are – was also found on Geissler's body."

The prince pushed the notes back across the desk, his expression pensive now.

"What are you suggesting? That Geissler was involved in something underhand? Espionage?"

"I don't know, sir. But it looks suspicious. Messages in a strange language secreted away in his lodgings. Why would he do that?"

"Why indeed? You need to find out what these messages mean, major."

Von Auerswald got up from his chair and paced across the room to the window. He was agitated.

"There's a fellow in Füssen. I forget his name, but Maisel will give it to you. He writes books about this kind of stuff – runes, myths, local folklore. He gives talks, lectures on it. He might be able to help you."

He turned, the light from the window behind him. He was frowning again. With his face in shadow, his duelling scars were more pronounced, like gashes underlining his eyes.

"This is all starting to look very peculiar, very... *pagan*. Spears, mistletoe, runes. What's going on?" He walked back to his desk and gave a brief gesture of dismissal with his fingers. "We'll talk again in a few days, major."

"Yes, sir."

Neumann left the room. In the outer office, Captain Maisel was curled over his desk, writing what looked like a letter. He looked up. Neumann asked him about the local folklore expert and Maisel pondered for a moment.

"Yes, I know the man. Went to one of his talks, in fact. Not long after I first came to Füssen. I wanted to improve my knowledge of Bavaria's history and customs. Let me think. Ziegler. I think that's right. Norbert Ziegler. I don't have an address for him, but the local police will know where to find him."

"Thank you, captain. One other thing. Do you have a photograph of Christoph Geissler I could borrow?"

"Of course."

Maisel stood up and went to a filing cabinet. He pulled out a thin cardboard folder with a small photograph attached to the front.

"His personal file. It's not a very good picture, I'm afraid, but it's all we've got. The chancellery isn't exactly renowned for its photographic skills."

"It will do, thank you," Neumann said.

The carriage took him back to the Gasthaus Hoffmann where Johanna served him a light dinner of soup, bread and cheese. He'd barely started eating before a man plonked himself down uninvited on the seat opposite. He must have been in his forties, almost bald, with chubby red cheeks which gave him the appearance of an overgrown baby.

"Gunther Krämer, *Füssener Blatt*," he said. "Welcome to our humble little town, major."

He took out a notepad and pencil and placed them on the table in front of him. Neumann sighed inwardly. It had to happen some time, the local press taking an interest in his arrival. Who had tipped the journalist off? he wondered. One of the local police officers, Beck perhaps? He wouldn't have put it past him. It certainly wasn't Johanna because she came thundering across the dining room and laid into the journalist fiercely.

"Out! I won't have you bothering my guests, Krämer, Now! Shift yourself."

She rolled up the sleeves of her dress to show she meant business, exposing a pair of brawny forearms. Neumann watched with disinterested fascination. Krämer was pretty bulky, but if it came to a brawl, his money was on Johanna.

"It's all right, Frau Hoffmann," he said equably. "I'll deal with it."

"You're sure?" Johanna seemed disappointed. "Well, don't let him spoil your dinner."

She glared at the journalist and headed back to the kitchen. Krämer smiled, his fleshy mouth moist with saliva.

"I see you're a reasonable man, major."

"What can I do for you, Herr Krämer?" Neumann asked. It was never sensible to be hostile towards newspaper reporters. You had to placate them, treat them like hungry dogs – toss them a bone, even if it had no meat on it.

Krämer was blunt and to the point. "You solved the Geissler case yet?"

"It's early days, I've only just arrived, but our enquiries are ongoing."

"That's it?" Krämer said. "That's the best you can do?"

"I can't comment on the details. I'm sure you understand that."

"You got any suspects?"

"I refer you to my previous answer."

"Is that what you call it? Do you know why he was killed?"

"I've nothing else to give you, I'm afraid. If anything changes, I'll let you know."

Krämer's lip curled. "That's very good of you, major. But it doesn't fill many column centimetres. It doesn't give our readers confidence that this heinous crime is going to be dealt with swiftly, or properly."

"It will be, I can assure them of that."

"Let me check my facts," the journalist said, consulting his notebook. "You're deputy head of the Criminal Investigation Division in Berlin, aren't you?"

"That's correct."

"Used to be in the Prussian army. Decorated twice for bravery during the war with France."

"You're well informed."

"I do my homework. And now you're down here, leading an investigation that some would say could, and should, be handled by the Bavarian police. Don't you trust them?"

"I have full confidence in the local police," Neumann said smoothly. "This is a joint operation. We are working together to solve the crime."

Krämer laughed sardonically. "Forgive me, but that sounds like something you've been told to say. A line from the chancellery, perhaps?"

"It's the truth. Now, if you'll excuse me, my soup is getting cold."

The journalist put away his notebook and pencil and stood up.

"I'll leave it there for the time being, but this is just the beginning, major. You can rest assured I'll be back."

"I'll look forward to it," Neumann replied.

Journalists could be trouble, he thought as he ate his dinner. He knew that from Berlin where the newspapers had long been railing against the inefficiency and corruption of the police. They might be less strident down here, but he doubted it. Controversy and polemic were good for circulation wherever you published. He'd have to take care with Gunther Krämer. He was already isolated enough in Füssen; he didn't need an enemy in the local press, too.

Dinner over, he went upstairs to his room and was just settling down in the armchair to mull over the morning's work when there was a knock on the door.

"Yes?"

A man entered. In his early thirties, tall and well-built, he was wearing a uniform that even by the flamboyant standards of the military was a touch over the top. Neumann had seen a few dandies during his time in the army, but this man was a veritable peacock. Black jackboots polished to a high sheen, silver spurs attached to the heels; royal blue breeches with gold stripes down the seams; a matching blue tunic adorned with gold braid – on the sleeves, on the front, on the epaulettes – and hanging from his side, a sword with a jewelled hilt and a golden scabbard engraved with what looked like glorious battle scenes. Tucked beneath his left arm was a golden helmet topped with ostrich feathers that, if they'd been on his head, would have brushed the ceiling.

"Major Neumann?" the man said, clicking his heels and inclining his head in a respectful nod. "I am Captain Wilhelm Schirmer, adjutant to His Majesty King Ludwig the Second of Bavaria."

Neumann stood up, straightening his back and shoulders, his military training ingrained for life.

"Captain. This is an unexpected pleasure. How may I help you?"

"The king commands your presence at the new palace of Hohenschwangau," Schirmer declared imperiously. His helmet caught the light from the window, sending coruscating flashes of gold across the room. "Have you met royalty before?"

Neumann shook his head. "I haven't had that honour."

"There are strict rules of etiquette that you should

observe. Permit me to explain them to you. When you enter His Majesty's presence, you must bow to him."

"I understand."

"If you would be so kind as to demonstrate for me."

Neumann stared at him. He appeared to be serious.

"You want me to bow?"

"If you please."

Neumann bowed.

"A little lower," Schirmer instructed. "That's better. No flourishes, please. His Majesty cannot bear any kind of ornamentation in a bow. And you must not look him directly in the eye, yet at all times you must give him your full attention. His Majesty is most particular about that. If you would be so good as to look at me as if I were the king. No, your gaze should be slightly more to the left of His Majesty's face. Not that far left. That's just right. Perhaps a brighter hint in your eyes, major. So His Majesty knows you are fully focused on him."

For two or three minutes the adjutant drilled him on the finer points of gazing into space while trying to look attentive. Neumann went along with it, acquiescent, but amused. He'd seen numerous staff officers during the war with France. Captains and majors and colonels loitering around the generals at the Front. Or, rather, *near* the Front. None of them had actually been anywhere close to the sharp end of the action, to the bloody chaos that passed for military strategy in that campaign. Schirmer had the appearance of a fop, but if you looked beyond the rococo uniform, there was a toughness in his lean face and pale blue eyes that Neumann sensed was a more accurate reflection of his character.

"Excellent, major," the adjutant said. "We'll make a courtier of you yet."

His mouth twisted into a semblance of a smile. Neumann got the impression that he knew how absurd this charade was, but was enjoying putting him through it.

"Now, manners," Schirmer went on. "It is forbidden to clear your throat, cough or sneeze in His Majesty's presence. Also, to spit, belch or break wind."

The attention to detail was impressive, but Neumann was a little offended that he had to be warned off farting in front of a king.

"I think that covers everything." The adjutant puffed out his chest and clicked his heels again. "We will send a carriage for you at three. Please ensure you are ready."

The sun was breaking through the clouds, sending glittering rays across the snow-covered garden, as Sophie left the house and headed for the forest. She walked across the rear terrace, past the silent fountain, past the hidden lawns and borders where, beneath the white mantle, bulbs were lying dormant, awaiting the change in temperature, of season, that would trigger a vibrant burst of new spring colour.

Despite the brightness, it was still cold. The snow showed no sign of melting, the lake was still frozen, its surface grey and ridged with ice. She was wearing a cloak over her jacket and trousers which she pulled tight across her chest to keep out the chill wind. As she left the formal grounds, the forest closed around her protectively, sheltering her from the elements. Some people feared the woods, found them dark and threatening, but Sophie loved it out here. She loved the wildness, the dense thickets, the open glades, the quietness, the sense of nature untamed which chimed with her own feeling that she was a spirit untamed.

She'd grown up here, had roved these secluded corners of her estate since she was a child. It had been her way of rebelling against the strictures of her upbringing, of escaping the suffocating routines and rules that dictated what children, particularly girls, could and couldn't do. The house to her had been a straitjacket, but out here in the woods was liberation. Her parents both dead, she was her own mistress now. This was her territory. She could do as she pleased in the house, but she still found a special freedom in the forest, a connection to the trees and the wildlife that brought a warmth to her heart.

The track she was taking was familiar and well-worn. She came this way several times a week. It led up the slope behind the garden, then turned to the west for a couple of hundred metres before emerging into the small clearing in front of Gisela Winter's hut. Sophie pushed open the door and stepped inside. The old woman was sitting at her table, crushing herbs with a pestle and mortar. Sophie put down the bag she was carrying and decanted a loaf of bread, a hunk of cheese, a small earthenware pot of pork stew and a few apples from her store, almost the last of the autumn harvest which had been eked out over the winter months. The fruits were wrinkling, starting to dry out and get tough, but they still had flavour. Gisela would cook them with a few preserved blackberries, soften the flesh to make it easier for what was left of her teeth.

"I've brought you a few things," Sophie said.

"Bless you, child."

"The stew's fresh, made today. I'll put it in the oven to keep warm. You can eat it later."

Sophie went to the hearth, opened the oven door and slid the earthenware pot inside. The fire was getting low and she noticed that the stack of wood to one side was almost gone. Going back outside, she scooped up an armful of logs from the wood store and brought them into the hut.

"What're you making?" she asked, sitting down on the bench at the table. She could smell the strong aroma of crushed rosemary.

"Gretchen Brandt asked me for a poultice. Her

husband cut his hand skinning a rabbit and the wound's gone septic. She needs something to draw out the pus, bring down the swelling.

Sophie watched Gisela mix the rosemary with warm milk, softened onion and fine oatmeal. She'd been coming here for more than twenty-five years, since as a nine-year-old she'd first plucked up the courage to venture near the hut, to break her parents' strict instruction to stay away from the strange woman in the woods, a warning that, of course, had only made the forbidden more attractive to her.

Gisela frightened people, even supposedly modern, enlightened couples like Sophie's parents who sneered at old customs and superstitions but still saw danger in a woman who dared to be independent, who dared to be different. For Gisela lived outside society, alone in a rundown wooden shack, foraging for mushrooms and berries in the forest, growing vegetables and selling her creams and elixirs to pay for her other necessities. In earlier times – not that long ago – she would have been branded a witch, been dunked in the lake or even burnt for her magical powers. But as she told everyone who came to see her: "I don't dispense magic, I dispense medicine." And that, in fact, was the establishment's real problem with her. Healing, for generations, had always been a female skill. Not any longer. It had become male territory and the doctors, for all their diplomas and expensive consulting rooms, were terrified that Gisela, this elderly, uneducated woman, knew more about medicine than they did.

The local people certainly thought she did. The women came to her for help – for themselves and also for the men in their lives. They were mostly poor families who couldn't afford the doctors' fees, but, in any case, they trusted Gisela far more than any arrogant, patronising physician. She spoke their language, understood the hardships of their lives. She knew their histories, their intimacies, and she had the time and inclination to listen to them, to comfort them. Ointments to soothe rashes and cuts and grazes, she made those. Draughts to ease insomnia or muscle ache or girls' monthly pains. Tonics for depression and anxiety and more hazardous concoctions to take away unwanted babies. Even occasionally love potions which everybody, including the purchasers, suspected wouldn't work, but didn't really care, for in love hope is more important than reality.

Sophie had watched her make all these medicines, always sitting opposite her on the bench at the table – as a young girl, her legs swinging in the air, too short to reach the floor, and now as a mature woman. Asking questions and learning as Gisela measured out ingredients, ground willow bark and liquorice, crushed rosemary and thyme and juniper to make oils with which to blend her unguents. Sometimes she helped in the process, did some of the work, particularly in recent years as Gisela's arthritic hands had become more incapacitated. She enjoyed these times together. Like mother and daughter, one passing knowledge and insight to the other, the two of them shut away in their own secret world.

"Who was the man I saw you with yesterday?" Gisela asked.

Sophie looked at her blankly. "Man? Oh, the policeman, you mean."

"Policeman?"

"From Berlin. An aggressive, insufferable individual. Sent here to investigate a murder. Typical Prussians, think we can't do it for ourselves."

Gisela paused in her mixing, her fingers coated with oil and oatmeal.

"What murder?"

"Some young diplomat from the German legation in Füssen. His body was found in the forest not far from here."

"What did this policeman want with you?"

"He asked me if I'd been out on Monday or Tuesday. He wanted to interview all the staff as well, but I refused. Those girls have suffered enough without some heavy-handed brute browbeating them."

"Where exactly in the forest?"

"He didn't say. A clearing, I think, over that way. Why? Did you see or hear something?

Gisela shook her head. "No, but as you know, I don't go far from the house these days, especially in weather like this."

She finished the poultice and scooped the ingredients into a cloth bag for her customer to come and collect later.

"I must go," Sophie said. "Is there anything you need?"

"You keep me well provisioned, freiin. Thank you."

"I'll come again in a couple of days."

Gisela sat for a while at the table after Sophie had left. She was troubled. A *murder*. Close by, too. That was unsettling. Yet she'd seen nothing. Sensed nothing, either, and that worried her because the forest was her domain. She usually knew everything that went on in it or, at least, felt the undercurrents that would have been disturbed by something so violent as the killing of a human being.

Pushing herself up from her seat, she went to a shelf on the wall and took down a yellowing linen bag. She spread a white cloth out on the table, then opened the linen bag. Inside were small pieces of wood inscribed with different marks – her runesticks. She dipped her fingers in to jumble the sticks up, then closed her eyes and focused hard on the murder of the diplomat. Taking a handful of the runesticks, she cast them out across the tablecloth. When she opened her eyes, the sticks were scattered in a pattern that looked entirely random, but which to someone with the right powers to interpret them had much more meaning.

Gisela had those powers. Her mother had been a seer and the daughter had inherited the same gift. As a child, Gisela had had vivid dreams in her sleep. Then the dreams had started coming during the day when she was awake. They'd frightened her. There she was in the family home, or in the classroom at school. With her eyes she could see her surroundings, but with her mind she was seeing something completely different – strange scenes and signs that puzzled and disturbed her. It was like a foreign language that was confined to her head and only she could understand it. Except she didn't understand it. Not at first.

Troubled and genuinely scared that she had some form of insanity, she finally confided in her mother and found that she had had the same experiences in her childhood. That she still had the dreams in adulthood, only they weren't dreams, they were premonitions. With her mother's reassurance and help, Gisela learnt how to cope with the visions, to try to work out what they meant. Sometimes, on the most basic level, that was straightforward. She saw things that were either good or bad, signs that made her happy or fearful. Other times, the dreams seemed more specific, as if they were predicting a particular event or outcome. Those were harder to understand so to help her, her mother introduced her to the runesticks. She taught her the symbols, the letters and how to use them to see into the future. Even now, sixty years on, Gisela still felt she was a beginner in the art. So many times she read the runes and found nothing clear in them, nothing certain. But then the future wasn't certain unless you believed in the inexorable power of fate, that everything was predestined and could never be changed.

Today the runesticks weren't helping her – like recalcitrant children who knew exactly what they should be doing but refused to carry it out. Gisela cast them again, the fragments of wood skittering across the tablecloth and coming to a stop in a different pattern. She leaned over and examined them. The dominant sign was the *berkana*, which meant a birch twig, the traditional symbol of fertility, of the birth of new life. How could that be? She was asking for guidance on a murder, on a *death*, so why were the runes predicting life instead? It didn't make sense.

Putting the sticks back into their bag, she shook them up again, then took a new handful and threw them across the table. That was better. She could see clearly now the pattern of symbols: the *purisaz*, which meant a demon, and the *raido*, meaning journey, the two together combining evil and the passage of the soul after death. But what was this? The symbols were repeated. There were two identical patterns. Gisela stared at them, her skin going suddenly cold and clammy. She saw only one possible interpretation. The diplomat in the forest was only the first death. There were more to come.

SEVEN

The carriage wound its way up the steep road from the valley, thick forest on both sides. Through the trees, Neumann caught glimpses of the scenery below: the tiny village of Hohenschwangau and its old palace overlooking the frozen waters of the Alpsee which sparkled like a huge crystal mirror in the late afternoon sun. Above the road were more trees that blocked out the view until the carriage rattled round the final bend and he saw the new palace towering over them.

From the valley, the building had looked quite small, perched high on its crag, but now he was close to it he could see what an enormous structure it was – or would be, for it was still very much a work in progress. One side appeared to be finished, a vast six-storey wing of dazzling white stone, topped with black conical turrets in imitation of a medieval fortress. The rest of the palace, however – as Captain Beck had described – was a building site, a complex web of scaffolding and walkways from which more walls and window openings were gradually emerging.

The carriage passed a collection of wooden huts that provided toilets, medical services and a canteen for the two hundred masons, carpenters and labourers who were still working despite the inclement weather, then drove through the arched entrance of the gatehouse. Neumann disembarked, the guards noting down his name in a logbook. The courtyard was teeming with men, boys, wheelbarrows and carts. Stacks of bricks and piles of sand and cement occupied most of the available space, a giant steam-powered crane hovering overhead to swing the materials into place. At the back of the site, the land fell away into the deep Pöllat Gorge in which Neumann could hear the roar of cascading water. On the other side of the gorge rose a sheer cliff, the exposed rock frosted with ice and snow, small conifers sprouting from ledges and crevasses where surely it should have been impossible for anything to grow. Waiting nearby, looking incongruous amid the dirt and slush, was Captain Schirmer in his blue and gold finery. His helmet was on his head now, the ostrich feathers fluttering in the breeze.

"Major, if you would follow me, please."

They went through a door into the finished wing, along a corridor of servants' rooms and up a winding staircase to the king's quarters on the fourth floor. Neumann was struck immediately by the ostentation of the surroundings. The entrance hall had a graceful ribbed-vault ceiling richly painted in blue, gold and maroon. Figures of animals sculpted from marble decorated the bases of the arches and the walls were adorned with murals depicting scenes from the great German Sigurd saga that Wagner had used as a key source for his *Ring* Cycle. From the ceiling hung three large chandeliers set with candles and wrought iron swans.

Schirmer led them through a door on the right into what he called the Throne Room. This was quite breathtaking in its opulence. Elaborate paintings on the walls and ceiling, an inlaid marble floor, everything embellished with gleaming gold leaf. The room thronged with people, most of them middle-aged men in dark suits who seemed to have nothing much to do. They broke apart as Schirmer approached to allow him a clear passage, Neumann trailing along obediently in his wake. At one end of the hall, on a raised platform in the apse, sat a man – not on the splendid throne one might have expected, but on a plain wooden chair. There was a space around him, like a forbidden zone that no one was allowed to enter. Neumann realised with a spasm of shock that this was Ludwig.

All the adjectives that were commonly applied to royalty – regal, imperial, majestic, noble – none of them seemed apposite here. The king looked ordinary and non-descript, a fat, jowly man whose cheeks and body were sagging under his excess weight. What had been a handsome face in youth was now bloated in middle-age. His eyes were bloodshot and watery, his hair thinning and his moustache and beard wispy and insubstantial. Even his clothes were a disappointment: a dark-grey suit, white shirt and blue cravat which were smart enough by most standards but looked drab and ill-fitting on a monarch, particularly one ensconced in a room as gaudy as this.

"Sire," Schirmer said, making the announcement to the whole assembly which promptly fell silent. "Allow me to present Major Reinhardt Neumann, of the Berlin police."

Ludwig looked at Neumann with dead eyes. He clearly had no idea why he was there. Neumann was equally in the dark. Why *had* he been summoned to the palace? Schirmer stepped forward and lowered his voice, leaning down towards the king, obviously explaining the situation for Ludwig's mouth opened in an "Aah" of understanding and he nodded. He beckoned to Neumann. The major advanced a couple of paces and bowed, hoping it met the adjutant's exacting standards. He kept his gaze, as instructed, on a point just to the left of the king's face.

"Major," Ludwig said. "You are most welcome." He squinted around the room, aware that everyone was listening, then stood up. "Walk a little way with me."

Schirmer made a move to join them, but the king waved him away.

"Just Hoffmann."

A footman in the blue and yellow livery of the Wittelsbach dynasty fell in behind them. Neumann glanced at him. This had to be Axel. He could see the facial resemblance to Johanna and Tobias

"You like this room, major?" Ludwig asked.

"It's most impressive, sire."

The king gestured at the ceiling, at the huge dome painted blue and decorated with stars and a great golden sun in the centre.

"It's modelled on the famous Hagia Sofia, in Constantinople. The framework above the dome is iron to support the weight of the stone. And you see the floor, the mosaic depicting trees and animals? The dome represents heaven and the floor earth, and in between the two you have me. Ruling over my kingdom with a power bestowed on me by God. Do not think of this as vanity. I take my duties very seriously. Look over there, in the alcove. The image of Jesus and below him the six holy kings who watch over me, who ensure I lead my subjects along a true Christian path. Stephen of Hungary; Henry the Second, the Holy Roman Emperor; Kasimir of Poland; Louis the Ninth of France; Edward of England and Ferdinand of Spain. All of them canonised. I feel their eyes on me, guiding me to be a better monarch. Would you care for a biscuit?"

The non-sequitur took Neumann by surprise.

"A... biscuit, sire?" he stammered.

"I'm most partial to a biscuit at this time of day."

Ludwig lifted a finger and Axel Hoffmann hurried forward with a silver dish containing an assortment of biscuits: gingerbread, almond, chocolate. The king took two and bit off a chunk of one. His teeth were decaying and there were noticeable gaps in his mouth.

"Help yourself, major. I have an excellent Viennese pastry chef. You should taste his cream meringues. *Mmm*."

Neumann took a biscuit and they resumed their walk, going out into the entrance hall and across to the king's private apartments. Ludwig had a strange gait, throwing his legs out in long strides then bringing his feet down heavily onto the floor as if he were crushing a cockroach.

"It's a tad chilly at the moment, don't you think?" he said. "I'm having a central heating system installed which will keep the place nice and toasty in even the coldest weather. But it's not ready yet. We're having a few teething troubles." He chuckled, a throaty noise that sounded as if he was gargling. "You could say the same about me. Do you have good teeth, major? I'm a martyr to my molars."

Neumann mumbled a reply. This really wasn't the kind of conversation he'd been expecting. The king rambled on, talking about the weather and his health and the building work on the castle and how difficult it was to get the right stonemasons and carpenters and plasterers. Neumann listened to the monologue, wondering if he was supposed to respond, but Ludwig seemed almost oblivious to his presence.

They went through into the king's study, an oak-panelled room containing a leather-topped desk, heavy green curtains and, on the wall, a rather distracting painting of the knight, Tannhäuser, being seduced by a naked Venus and her similarly unclothed nymphs.

Ludwig said abruptly, "So what's going on?"

This did seem to require an answer.

"Sire?"

"This dreadful murder. Young Christoph Geissler.

You're here to investigate it, I understand."

"Yes, sire."

"So tell me what progress you've made. *They* won't tell me, you can be sure of that." The king inclined his head in the direction of the Throne Room, clearly meaning the men in dark suits. "They keep everything from me. Miserable, scheming creatures. They tell me nothing, you know. Just treat me like a child, conspire against me to thwart my wishes."

"Well, sire," Neumann began. "We're at a very early stage, but we're working hard to solve the case."

Ludwig glared at him angrily. "That's exactly the kind of weaselly reply *they'd* give me. I want better than that, major. That's why I've summoned you here. Why was he killed? Who did it? Those are the questions to which I want answers."

Neumann reconsidered. Ludwig was sharper than he first appeared. In normal circumstances, the major would have declined to be too specific about a case in progress, but this was the king of Bavaria. Neumann felt an obligation to be open and honest with him. He outlined what he'd discovered so far and Ludwig listened intently, flinching visibly when Neumann mentioned the spear.

"A *spear*? Lord have mercy on us. Who would do such a thing?" He looked away and murmured, "My Baldur. My beautiful Baldur."

"I beg your pardon, sire. I didn't catch that."

Ludwig turned back to him. His eyes were glistening. His voice took on a different tone, soft and intense.

"You must be my champion, major. My knight. Find the man who did this. You will have my full support. You will keep me informed of your progress. Do not tell *them*." He spat out the word. "Communicate with me only through Captain Schirmer. I trust him implicitly. You understand?"

"Yes, sire."

"You may go."

Ludwig marched away from him, his feet hammering down onto the wooden floor. He called Hoffmann over. The footman presented him with the silver dish again and the king grabbed a few biscuits and consumed them greedily. Neumann made his way back to the entrance hall where the men in dark suits were spilling out from the Throne Room. Who were they? he wondered. Courtiers, advisers, maybe ministers? He thought suddenly of Sophie Hals von Wildenstein. Were these the men who mattered?

One of them followed Neumann out onto the landing at the top of the stairs.

"Major, one moment if you please," he said, his tone indicating that this was an order rather than a request. "Allow me to introduce myself. I am Baron Friedrich von Breckendorf, Minister of Justice."

He was a slim, elegant man in his early forties, about half a head shorter than Neumann. His hair was receding at the front, exposing a smooth, shiny expanse of skin above his forehead. Below that were dark, shrewd eyes with hooded lids, and a neat black moustache and beard trimmed short and flecked with traces of grey.

"You will know already from Prince von Auerswald, I imagine, that you will have the full cooperation of the Bavarian government in your investigation. But I wanted to confirm that now to your face. Whatever resources you need will be forthcoming."

"Thank you, sir," Neumann replied. "I'm grateful for that."

"The king, as I'm sure you know by now, has taken an interest in the case. But he can be a little...well." Von Breckendorf cast around for the right word, careful not to sound disloyal whilst being exactly that. "Emotional. He has a sensitive temperament that is easily upset. We who advise him, who *protect* him, would not want him to be exposed to anything overly distressing. I hope we understand each other, major." The baron fixed Neumann with a steely gaze. "I would be obliged if any communications you wish to make to His Majesty came through me."

Neumann took a moment to reply. He was a policeman. This was the first time he'd ever encountered royalty. The last thing he wanted was to become embroiled in the politics of the court.

"Of course, sir," he said diplomatically. "You can rest assured that I will follow the correct channels at all times."

"Make sure you do."

Von Breckendorf smiled, but there was no missing the hint of menace in his words. He gave a curt nod and went back into the Throne Room. Captain Schirmer escorted Neumann down the stairs to the courtyard where the carriage was waiting for him.

"If you need to get in touch with me," the adjutant said. "Send word to Hohenschwangau. The message will get to me."

"*Neumann?*" A shout rang out from across the courtyard and the major turned.

"By God, it is you."

A soldier in a blue and yellow uniform was walking towards them, his boyish face breaking into a grin.

"Hafner!" Neumann exclaimed. "What are you doing here?"

He held out his hand, but Lukas Hafner embraced him in a bear hug instead.

"I might ask the same of you, Reinhardt. I work here, but what the hell are you doing so far from Berlin?"

"You know each other?" Schirmer asked.

"Fought together at Wörth," Hafner replied.

The adjutant looked at Neumann, a new respect in his face. "You were in the army?"

"The Prussian XI Corps. Alongside this rogue's Bavarian II Corps," Neumann said. He took in the gold crown on Hafner's epaulettes. "You got your majority?"

"I command the royal garrison. Here, and in Munich when the king's there."

"Congratulations."

"My God, I can't believe it." Hafner shook his head. "How long has it been? Ten years?"

"A long time."

"But what brings you to Bavaria?"

"A murder case."

Hafner's eyes opened wide with understanding. "Ah, that one. You're here for long?"

"I don't know at the moment."

"Where are you staying?"

"The Gasthaus Hoffmann, in Füssen."

"The barracks are just outside the town. We must get together. Come to the mess one evening."

"I'd like that."

"Until then."

The two men shook hands, then Hafner strode away across the courtyard and Neumann climbed into the carriage. On the descent of the hill, the coachman taking it very slowly on the icy road, he reflected on his meeting with the king. The summons to the palace had been a surprise, and not a particularly pleasant one. Neumann knew from grim experience that powerful outsiders taking an interest in a criminal investigation was rarely good news. It inevitably led to interference, to the undermining of police independence – although that, he also knew from experience, was largely a myth. The police did as they were told, looked hard at offences and individuals deemed deserving of close scrutiny, but ignored others where vested interests were more important than justice. In Berlin, there were men who mattered, too.

But the interference had never come so directly from

an influential figure, let alone one so exalted as a king. And it had never been so overt. From Schirmer's thorough briefing on the importance of etiquette at the court, Neumann had expected a brief, punctilious audience with the monarch, a bit of bowing and scraping followed by a summary dismissal. That it had turned out instead to be a lengthy, informal private conversation had astonished him. Just the two of them, no advisers or ministers in attendance, Ludwig chatting to him as if he were an old friend, his opinions frank and not a little indiscreet. Neumann wasn't sure whether to be flattered, or terrified, by the king's attentions. It certainly added another worrying layer of pressure to his investigation. And it puzzled him, too. Geissler's murder was a horrific event, but it wasn't something that Neumann would have expected to attract Ludwig's interest – an interest that felt very personal. Had he imagined it, or had he really seen tears in the king's eyes? The questions went round and round in his head as the carriage took him back to Füssen. One, in particular, preoccupied him: Who was Baldur?

EIGHT

The Singers' Hall, at the top of the main building, was the most magnificent room in the palace of New Hohenschwangau. A vast, opulent chamber with golden chandeliers hanging from a panelled golden ceiling and carved angels and dragons on the beams, the walls – in keeping with the king's obsession with German myths – had been decorated with scenes from Wolfram von Eschenbach's Parzival – the story that inspired Wagner's last opera: Parsifal being crowned king of the Holy Grail by the enchantress, Kundry, Parsifal's wedding to Condwiramour and his battle with the Red Knight. Everything about the room had been designed to inspire awe, to celebrate the mysteries of the Grail and reinforce Ludwig's perception of himself as both a latter-day knight inheriting Parsifal's legacy and a divinely-chosen king whose legitimacy came directly from God.

The grandeur of the surroundings, and the Christian philosophy underpinning them, however, were lost on the cabinet ministers who were meeting there that afternoon. All they could think about was the temperature – the unheated room was freezing and draughty – and the noise coming from the construction work going on elsewhere on the site: the incessant hammering and banging and shouting that intruded on their thoughts and discussions. None of them liked coming here. The old palace down the hill was far more convenient and commodious, not to mention warmer. But the king insisted on dragging them all up here to this inhospitable wasteland. It was his main residence now and this was where government business would be conducted.

Not that much business was actually getting done. The meeting wasn't going well. The cabinet wanted to talk about the budget and public spending, chiefly how to reduce it. The king, though, had other priorities.

"Herrenchiemsee," he said, referring to one of the other palaces he was building – this one a hundred and sixty kilometres away to the east and even more extravagant than New Hohenschwangau. "I want to know when work is going to resume there."

The honest answer – if honesty had been an attribute of the cabinet – would have been "over our dead bodies". But that wasn't a reply that any of them wanted, or dared, to give to Ludwig. The king was notoriously unpredictable. He had a ferocious temper that none of them was eager to provoke.

"Well, Your Majesty," the cabinet secretary, Konrad Baumgartner, began, "That's a tricky question to answer."

"Why's it tricky?" Ludwig retorted. "It looks very simple to me. Work could restart tomorrow if you let it."

"Yes... yes, that is correct in theory. But if Your Majesty will permit me, it's a little more complicated in practise."

"How is it more complicated?"

"Well, sire..."

Baumgartner was floundering. An inoffensive, mild-mannered man, he was a staunch monarchist whose faith in royalty was sorely tried by the present incumbent. He looked appealingly around the table and the finance minister, Count Walther Ehrenbeck zu Freudenberg, came to his rescue. The count was a much tougher character, a bruiser who liked speaking the truth to power – although he was less keen on having it spoken to him. But even he had to be diplomatic with the king.

"It's a question of timing, Your Majesty," he said smoothly.

"What do you mean, a question of timing?"

"I wouldn't want to bore Your Majesty with too much detail, but essentially it all comes down to cash flow. The state revenues come in at a certain time and are allocated to various spending departments and at the moment there is nothing to spare for this particular building project, close to your heart as we know it is for Your Majesty."

This last remark was something of an understatement. Herrenchiemsee was Ludwig's passion, the latest, most expensive addition to his already fairly extensive portfolio of palaces. He had Nymphenburg in Munich and Hohenschwangau, but those had been his father's before him so they didn't really count. Ludwig had not created them. The Residenz, also in Munich, he held in higher regard because he had added a Winter Garden to its roof – a vast iron and glass greenhouse containing a lake with an artificially illuminated moon above it, a Moorish pavilion, trees, flowers, peacocks and a parrot on a golden hoop which could speak German – well, it could say "Good evening".

That the lake was leaking so badly the unfortunate servants occupying the bedrooms immediately beneath it had to sleep under umbrellas was of no concern to him. What mattered was the imagination – his – that had gone into the garden. Imagination was also the key to his other palaces at Linderhof and New Hohenschwangau, and also at Herrenchiemsee where he had acquired a disused monastery on an island in the middle of Bavaria's largest lake and was turning it into a version of Versailles, complete with a Hall of Mirrors which, at ninety-eight metres, was twenty-five metres longer than the Sun King's – not that he was trying to compete with a French monarch who'd been dead for a hundred and seventy years.

"Why can't these revenues be allocated to Herrenchiemsee?" Ludwig asked petulantly.

He'd been posing this question at every cabinet meeting for the past six months and was getting increasingly fed up with his ministers' evasive answers. Didn't they see that this was important, that this was his dream they were frustrating?

"That is not straightforward, Your Majesty," zu Freudenberg replied. Then he took a risk. "The palace has already cost the public purse more than sixteen million marks, only six million of which has been approved by the cabinet."

If he was hoping the figures might give the king pause for thought, he was grievously misguided. Numbers meant nothing to the king and, as far as he was concerned, the public purse was *his* purse.

"*So?*" he said. "Whether you've approved the spending or not is immaterial. That money was absolutely necessary to undertake the building work and more will be required to complete it. Don't you see that? What use is a half-finished palace?"

What use is a finished one? zu Freudenberg thought, but wasn't reckless enough to say it out loud. Instead, he said, "We fully understand Your Majesty's desires. However, at the moment, the money is just not there in the budget."

"Where is it then?" Ludwig demanded, hammering the table with his palm.

Baumgartner, sensing the beginnings of a royal meltdown, stepped in to try and smooth the waters.

"Rest assured, Your Majesty, that Herrenchiemsee has not been forgotten by any of your loyal ministers." How could it be, given that the subject came up every week?

"Then give me the money" Ludwig replied. "Where's it all gone?"

"We have commitments, sire. Essential expenditure on education and roads and other important projects. And we have to make payments to Berlin for defence and foreign affairs."

"Damn payments to Berlin. Damn the Prussians," the king said, banging the table again, his face flushed. "Why should we give our money to them?"

"We are part of the empire now, Your Majesty. We have treaty obligations."

"Then break them."

Even by his standards this was a rash statement, close to sedition. The cabinet ministers exchanged glances, trying to pretend they hadn't heard it. But Ludwig was not to be deterred.

"Do you hear me? Break these obligations, I say. What are the Prussians to us? They have done nothing but exploit and oppress us. Even if you pathetic little creatures have forgotten what they did to us in sixty-six, I haven't. I haven't forgotten their aggression, I haven't forgotten the humiliation of defeat."

He was shouting now and thumping the table with his fists like an angry toddler. Fortunately, there was nothing he could throw. No one could look him in the eye.

"How feeble are you, how spineless? I will have what I want. Do you understand? You find me the money to finish Herrenchiemsee or I will dismiss the lot of you."

And with that, he was off. Thrusting back his gilt chair so violently it toppled over onto the floor with a crash, then stomping out of the chamber, his footman and adjutant scurrying after him.

Baumgartner waited a while for the dust to settle, the

tirade and the king's threat to sack them running easily off their backs. They had heard it all before. And would probably hear it again soon.

Then the cabinet secretary said, "Gentlemen, shall we move on to the next item on the agenda?"

Ludwig was something of a nocturnal creature. He liked to stay up all night, rarely going to bed until dawn, his household's timetable arranged around him accordingly. This wasn't insomnia – he had no trouble sleeping – it was a choice he'd made. Consciously, or sub-consciously – he had never troubled to work out which – he had rejected the day in favour of embracing the night. Day was when all the tedious, demanding stuff happened. When he had to engage with his dullard ministers and – very occasionally – his subjects. He had to listen to them, take in information, make decisions. Do his *duty*. The word was anathema to him.

It hadn't always been that way. When he first came to the throne, twenty-two years earlier, he had taken on his new responsibilities with an earnest seriousness. Only eighteen years old, he had committed himself fully to serving his country. He had carried out his duties conscientiously, earning the respect of both his ministers and his people. But in the years since, something had changed. He had got tired of responsibility, tired of dealing with government, with politicians whom he despised. He saw himself as the people's king. His power came from God, but he could only exercise it with the trust and consent of his subjects. There was a mystical bond between them that politicians interfered with. They placed themselves between the parties, attempting to control both, and in the process undermined Ludwig's almost priestly function as leader of Bavaria.

He was an innately shy man, but he had always been comfortable with the ordinary populace, particularly when he could mix with them without the intervention of courtiers or ministers. Hence his penchant for riding around the country, making surprise visits to villages and handing out gifts. There was probably an unconscious element of *noblesse oblige* about these occasions, but, nevertheless, Ludwig found real pleasure in them, in marked contrast to his advisers who regarded them with unconcealed horror. But those informal, unplanned trips had become less frequent in recent years. Ludwig had stopped going out much in public, even to the theatre which he had always loved. He couldn't bear being stared at by the audience. His shyness was metamorphosing into misanthropy and he had taken to retreating into the nocturnal world when he could avoid contact with people other than just a few trusted attendants.

His palaces, too, were a way of creating another world for himself, a private, secure enclave that was infinitely preferable to the real world outside. They had been his comfort since childhood. Nymphenburg, where he could escape into the huge expanse of the park and be alone with his thoughts, where he could hide in the Chinese Pagodenburg, or in the grotto of the Magdalenenklause, or in the Mirror Room of the Amalienburg – to him, enchanted places that would later inspire the exotic designs for his own palatial creations.

Hohenschwangau he'd loved, too, the Alpine palace named after the swans that lived on the nearby Schwansee and which his mother had taken him regularly to feed. Queen Marie had loved swans, telling her young son the Greek myth of their origins: how Venus had been born from a wave of the sea and the other waves, jealous that they'd been overlooked, complained to Zeus who, in compensation, scooped up some foam from their crests and created a swan. Hohenschwangau abounded with images of the birds.

They were painted on the walls, there were vases in their shape and a silver candelabrum with a swan base. And if Ludwig went to the windows, he could see the real things paddling on the lake and longed to be free like them.

The palace also had murals of German myths: of Tannhäuser and the Grail Knight, Lohengrin, who travelled in a boat pulled by a swan. Ludwig had spent hours studying the paintings and reading the stories they illustrated. They fascinated him, appealed to something deep in his core. The strength, the nobility, the essential Germanness of those medieval heroes. He could identify with that, aspire to be like them.

He had taken those myths with him when he embarked on the construction of New Hohenschwangau. Their images were everywhere, not just in the Singers' Hall but also in his private apartments. In his salon, from the Swan Alcove where he liked to sit and read, he could see a mural depicting the miracle of the Grail and Lohengrin's selection as its knight.

He was sitting there now, gazing at the painting, every detail of it familiar to him, from the steadfast figure of Lohengrin with his hand on his sword to the golden glow emanating from the Grail high up on the holy altar. It was gone midnight and Ludwig was feeling wide awake and restless. He got up from his chair and paced around the room. He needed something to distract him, to calm his agitated mind.

"Hoffmann!" he called.

Outside in the dressing room, Axel stirred, half asleep on the divan that served as his bed. He was fully clothed, always on standby in case the king needed him.

"*Hoffmann!*"

Axel slid off the divan, yawning, and went through the door into the salon.

"Sire?"

"Send for Doctor Steimitz. Tell him to bring the score for *Lohengrin*."

"As Your Majesty wishes."

"And we'll need coffee and something to eat."

Axel hurried downstairs to the coach-house by the main gates and roused the coachman and one of the grooms from their quarters next to the stables. Neither was happy to be dragged from their beds in the middle of the night, but it was hardly an unusual occurrence. The king frequently called on them at strange hours. The horses were harnessed and a carriage despatched to collect the royal kapellmeister from his home. Then the footman went to the kitchens where the staff were always on hand to provide food for the king during the night. The chef was snoozing on the couch provided in his pantry, the kitchen boys and scullery maids curled up on the floor in front of the massive coal-fired range. Axel woke them and ordered coffee and pastries, then went back upstairs to the private quarters and lay down on his divan to snatch a few more minutes sleep before his services were required again.

An hour later, Hubert Steimitz arrived, his cloak flapping around his ankles, his hands clutching the music for Wagner's opera. He was a short man in his mid-fifties with a round, genial face and wire-rimmed spectacles that changed according to the task he was undertaking: one pair for distance, one for reading and a third for playing music or conducting from a score. He came into the salon, panting audibly from the climb up the stairs, and went straight to the piano, a small white instrument embossed with elaborate decorations of flowers and leaves, a portrait of Apollo, the Greek god of music, on the underside of the lid. Removing his cloak, he sat down on the stool, placed the score on the music rest, then turned to the king.

"What is Your Majesty's pleasure tonight?"

"You know my favourite passages. Let me hear them again."

Steimitz began to play, starting with the Prelude, then moving on through the opera: the heroine, Elsa, recounting the dream in which she has seen a vision of the man who will come to champion her; the arrival of the mysterious silver-armoured knight in the boat pulled by a swan who tells Elsa he will fight for her and wed her, but only on condition that she never asks his name or whence he has come; the prayer before the combat between the knight and the evil Frederick, then the rejoicing at the knight's victory; the moving love duet between Elsa and the knight after their wedding and then the fateful moment when she can bear the mystery no longer and she asks his name, forcing him to abandon her and return to Montsalvat and the temple of the Holy Grail.

The kapellmeister was a superb pianist, his score-reading abilities exceptional. There were no singers present, but he managed to bring out both the vocal line and the accompaniment to vivid effect. Ludwig listened in rapture, the coffee and cakes beside him forgotten, as the exquisite music enveloped him and soothed his troubled soul. He loved *Lohengrin* perhaps more than any other Wagner music-drama. It had been in his life since he was twelve years old and his governess had described to him a performance she had been to in Munich, arousing in the young crown prince a fierce desire to see the opera for himself. He was fifteen before that ambition was realised, but it was a seminal moment in his development, and a beginning of a passion for Wagner that would never wane.

He became obsessed with the composer, began a long, intimate relationship in which Wagner was The Friend and Ludwig his Parzival. He paid off Wagner's debts, showered him with money to support his musical enterprises and in return Ludwig – and the world – got the sublime delights of *The Ring*. To Ludwig, it was about far more than just music. He saw it as akin to a religion in which Wagner was a deity. His music was pure and holy (even though the man was far from it), the antithesis of the real world which Ludwig was coming increasingly to see as ugly and corrupt and evil. As he listened to Steimitz play, he found peace, imagining himself as the Swan Knight, the guardian of the Holy Grail. That was his destiny, to be like Lohengrin, New Hohenschwangau his Montsalvat. To protect everything that was good, not waste his time on petty government squabbles over money.

It was four o'clock before the kapellmeister, slumping with exhaustion at the keyboard, was allowed to finish and return to his home. Ludwig retired to his bedroom and sat for a moment gazing at the mural on the wall, another Wagnerian tribute – this one Tristan on his deathbed, Isolde looking on in distress. The painting affected him more than usual. It seemed to emphasise the loneliness he felt, that was becoming more acute as he aged. He listened. The palace was silent. So silent he might have been the only person in it. He was entirely alone. Entirely friendless. Wagner was dead. Ludwig had never had an Isolde. He had never married, never wanted to, despite the pressure put on him by those around him. But he had loved. And he felt guilt for that love, guilt for his desires, for sins that the Catholic church – *his* church – would savagely condemn. Was it so wrong?

Ludwig sat there on the edge of his bed, the quiet wrapping itself around him like a shroud, and the tears trickled down his cheeks as he wept for what he had lost.

NINE

Nine o'clock in the morning was inconsiderately early to be visiting a brothel, the fact evidenced by the number of times Lothar Beck had to hammer on the door before it was answered, and the dishevelled state of the maid who did the answering. She was barely half awake, her dress unfastened and slipping off her shoulders, her hair unbrushed, the strands dangling over her face. Her mouth opened, about to spit out a protest at this untimely intrusion, when she saw who it was and reconsidered.

"Captain Beck, sir. What brings you here?"

Beck pushed past her into the hall. Neumann followed.

"Where is Frau Kuhn?" the captain asked curtly.

"She's still in bed, sir. Everyone's in bed."

"Wake her. We'll wait in the parlour."

Beck led the way to a spacious room at the rear of the house. He seemed to know his way around the place, Neumann thought. And the maid had recognised him. Did he come here on business, or pleasure?

The parlour was lavishly furnished in a florid style. Thick Turkish rugs on the floor; soft couches and ottomans covered with cushions; red velvet curtains over the windows; porcelain vases and other china ornaments in a glass display case; cheap paintings in vulgar gilt frames on the walls and a crystal chandelier hanging from the ceiling. It smelt of stale cigar smoke, spilt wine and women's perfume – bordello scents, Neumann thought, the stench turning his stomach.

The madam of the house, Hannelore Kuhn, was with them in ten minutes. Long enough for the maid to have wakened her, but not long enough for Hannelore to have done much to her appearance. She hadn't dressed, just thrown a silk peignoir over her nightgown. She hadn't put on any make-up, either. Her face looked all of her fifty-six years: blotchy skin, bags under her eyes, a double chin that was sagging over her turkey neck. She'd had no time to wash, but she'd freshened herself up with a liberal application of cologne. Was this the scent Geissler's landlady had detected on his clothes? Neumann wondered as the madam walked into the parlour, her feet encased in gold slippers, her coarse, reddish hair hanging loose around her shoulders.

"Captain Beck," she said, smiling and exposing her yellowish teeth. "What a pleasure to see you. And so early. This must be important."

She sat down on an ottoman and pulled her peignoir close across her chest. The fire had not yet been lit and the room was unpleasantly cold.

"My apologies for the hour," Beck replied. "But this couldn't wait. Allow me to introduce Major Reinhardt Neumann, of the Berlin police. He's conducting a murder investigation and would like to speak to you."

"To *me*?" Frau Kuhn's eyebrows rose enough to furrow her already wrinkled forehead. "A murder? What would I know about that?"

"Have you seen this young man before?" Neumann asked.

He showed her the photograph of Christoph Geissler. Hannelore studied it for a while.

"A handsome man. He would always be most welcome here, but no, I've never seen him before."

"You're sure?"

"Yes."

"What about your girls? I'll need to ask them, too."

"That won't be necessary, major. I know all the gentlemen who come here. Many are regulars. And that young man isn't one of them."

"How many girls work here?"

"Five."

"Do any of them have male friends? Outside their work."

"Lovers, you mean?" Frau Kuhn's eyes narrowed and Neumann caught a glimpse of the real woman behind the cordial public façade. "If they did, they wouldn't be here long. I don't allow any kind of personal relationships with men. The girls are here to work, to entertain the clientele. Nothing more."

"Nevertheless, I want to speak to them."

"I told you, that won't be –"

"*Now*," Neumann interrupted. "Get them down here."

Frau Kuhn glared at him, then her eyes flicked across to Beck who nodded almost imperceptibly, the exchange not going unnoticed by Neumann. The madam's mouth tightened with anger, but she forced an insincere smile.

"As you wish. Anna!"

The maid was summoned and instructed to wake the girls and bring them down to the parlour. They arrived as a group, all of them bleary-eyed and semi-dressed, irritated to be woken so early but careful not to show it. Neumann saw the wariness in their young faces, none of them older than about twenty, the nervous way they glanced at both Beck and the madam. He tried to put them at their ease, assuring them that they weren't in trouble, then he asked Frau Kuhn if there was another room he could use to interview them.

"What's wrong with here?" she demanded.

Neumann just looked at her. He didn't have to justify himself. The madam shrugged.

"You can use the dining room."

Neumann spoke to the girls one by one, and alone. Beck wanted to join him, but the major refused. He said it was more important for him to stay with the group in the parlour, to make sure the girls didn't confer with one another and Hannelore didn't try to influence their answers.

Four of the girls looked at Geissler's photograph and shook their heads, they'd never seen him before. Neumann watched them closely and was sure they were telling the truth. The fifth, a pale blonde named Ursula, who couldn't have been more than seventeen years old, showed a flicker of recognition and the major jumped in immediately.

"You know him?"

"No, no," she replied hurriedly. "I don't know him."

"But you've seen him. Is that it?"

"Frau Kuhn," Ursula said anxiously. "You won't tell her?"

"This conversation is confidential," Neumann said gently. "Frau Kuhn will hear nothing of it. You've seen him?"

Ursula nodded. "Not here. I've never seen him in the house."

"Where then?"

"On the street."

"In Füssen?"

"Look, we're not allowed out. Frau Kuhn makes us stay in the house all the time. If we need anything from the shops, she sends one of the maids to get it. But there was a day, a few weeks ago, I wanted a present for my sister's birthday. And I wanted to choose it for myself. So I…" She glanced uneasily towards the door and lowered her voice. "...sneaked out one morning when everyone was still in bed. That's when I saw him. With the captain."

"Captain? Captain Beck?"

"No, Captain Schirmer. He's a soldier. He works for the king, I think. He comes to the house fairly often. A lot of soldiers do."

From her expression, Neumann got the clear impression she didn't like the adjutant.

"You saw this young man with Captain Schirmer? What were they doing?"

"Just standing on a street corner, talking. I passed by them, that's all. I don't know anything more." Her voice took on a frightened note. "Please don't mention this to Frau Kuhn. She'll throw me out."

Neumann regarded her sympathetically. "How long have you been here, in this house?"

"Seven, eight months."

"Where were you before?"

"In Munich."

"Doing what?"

"I worked for a dressmaker, as a seamstress."

"How did you end up here?"

Ursula hesitated, then she shrugged, her thin shoulders shifting beneath her flimsy nightgown.

"Things... happened. There was a man. I thought he... you know. I was wrong."

Her voice trailed off and she looked away, uncomfortable with the conversation. Neumann didn't press her. He'd seen a lot of girls like her in Berlin. Pretty, vulnerable young women ruined by men. Exploited, abused by pimps and madams who saw them as ripe fodder for the brothels of the city. Ursula looked fragile, the kind of girl who could be snapped in two by a brutal man. Or by a callous woman like Hannelore Kuhn. Neumann wanted to tell her to get out, to find some other way of earning a living, but he kept his peace. It was easy for him to say, much harder for her to actually do it.

"Do you have family?" he asked.

"No. My parents are dead. I have no one, nowhere to go. That's why Frau Kuhn mustn't know I've said anything to you."

"You have my word this will go no further."

"And Captain Beck? Will you tell him? He and Frau Kuhn, well, they're... close."

"This is just between the two of us, Ursula. Thank you for your honesty."

"You get anything out of them?" Lothar Beck enquired casually on the walk back to the police station.

"Not a thing," Neumann replied. "Whatever Geissler got up to in his free time, he obviously didn't go to the brothel."

Beck nodded. Then he waited a moment before asking, "Anything else you've found out?"

"Nothing of any consequence, I'm afraid." Neumann glanced at the captain, knowing that he couldn't trust him, and the feeling was mutual. "But there's something you could do for me. Have you ever heard of a man named Norbert Ziegler?"

"Ziegler? Writes books, gives lectures?"

"That's the one."

"I think we have a file on him."

They went into the police station and upstairs to Beck's office where he removed a folder from a cabinet and handed it to Neumann

"That's it."

"You keep tabs on the man?" the major asked. "Does that mean you have suspicions about him?"

"Nothing definite," Beck replied. "But you know how it is. A man like him. Teaches some course at the university in Munich." The curl of his lip made it clear what he thought about that kind of activity. "Writes books and pamphlets about peculiar stuff. You know, myths and gods and religion. Intellectuals." His mouth twisted again. "We keep an eye on all of them."

Neumann wasn't unduly surprised. The force in Berlin did the same, although not his department. Monitored anyone who seemed to be a free thinker, particularly academics. Independence of thought, intelligence, a questioning mind – few things were more terrifying to the state.

He leafed through the file. It contained a brief biography of Ziegler, mentioning his childhood in Füssen, his studies in Munich and later Berlin and his current occupation as a freelance author and visiting lecturer at his old alma mater, the Ludwig-Maximilian University of Munich. There was a long list of his publications – on Bavarian history, folklore and Norse mythology – and various reports on his character and activities, all recognisable to Neumann as the typical product of paid informers: short on substance, long on uncorroborated rumour and gossip. He noted down Ziegler's address. Beck looked at him inquiringly.

"Why are you interested in him?"

"The mistletoe around the spear," Neumann replied. "I'm looking for an explanation." He handed the file back. "One other thing. Could I see Geissler's possessions again?"

The cloth bag was brought out from the cabinet and Neumann examined the gold pocket watch and chain. There was a maker's label on the watch face – Hartmann and Stein, Munich – the name also engraved on the inside of the back cover. Neumann could see hallmarks on both the chain and the small golden swan attached to it, but they were too tiny to read.

"Do you have a magnifying glass?"

The marks became clearer under the lens.

"WG?" Neumann asked.

"Werner Graf," Beck replied. "He's a local jeweller. Excellent reputation. He makes some fine stuff."

Neumann replaced the items in the bag and pulled the drawstring tight.

"I'll hang onto these for a while."

Werner Graf's workshop was in a gloomy courtyard accessed via a narrow alley from Brunnengasse. There was no sign on the frontage, just a discreet metal plaque by the door giving his name and occupation: Goldsmith and Jeweller. The door was unglazed, a solid looking piece of varnished timber that would be difficult to break down. The small side window beside it was protected by stout iron bars.

Neumann knocked and heard footsteps inside, the sound of a bolt being drawn. The door eased open a fraction on a chain. Two eyes peered out at him quizzically, the face around them a young boy's – presumably an apprentice.

"Police," Neumann said. "Is Herr Graf there?"

The boy scrutinised him carefully, taking in his uniform and cap before he unhooked the chain and let him in. The front part of the premises was a small shop: a glass-fronted counter showcasing the jeweller's wares, two more glass cabinets displaying rings and necklaces and various items of silverware. Neumann peered into one of the cabinets. Compared to the glittering jewellery stores in Berlin this was a modest affair, but for a town the size of Füssen it was impressive. The work looked to be well designed and crafted.

He gazed at one of the diamond rings and felt a sudden pang, like the prick of a needle in his chest. The ring was almost identical to the one he'd bought Kristina for their engagement – only a small stone, it was all he could afford on his salary, but a symbol of their commitment to each other, of their lifelong love that in the end had lasted only two years. The ring had been returned to him by the hospital, along with Kristina's clothes and other possessions, a watch, an ivory hair-clasp and a pair of earrings that were now gathering dust in a drawer in his apartment, tangible reminders of his wife to add to his other memories.

"Sir?"

He realised the apprentice was waiting for him and roused himself from his momentary distraction. They went through a door into the rear part of the building which had been set up as a workshop. Werner Graf was at his bench, inspecting a ruby bracelet he was making through a large magnifying glass. He was a squat, gnome-like man in his fifties with pale skin, liver spots on his balding pate and jowls like molten wax. He looked up and the flame from the gas lamp on the worktop flared in the lenses of his spectacles, making it look as if his eyes were on fire. Neumann introduced himself.

"I wonder if I might ask you about a customer of yours, a young man named Christoph Geissler?"

"Geissler?" Graf repeated with a frown. "That doesn't ring any bells."

He got up from his stool and shuffled across to the shelf on the wall where a row of thick ledgers was arranged in alphabetical order. Lifting down one of the volumes, he leafed through it.

"No, I've never made anything for a Geissler."

Neumann showed him the gold watch and chain and the jeweller gave a start.

"Where did you get those?"

"Christoph Geissler had them. Those are your hallmarks on the chain and the swan, aren't they?"

"Oh, yes, it's my work."

Graf took the chain from Neumann and studied it

closely, nodding with satisfaction.

"A fine piece, though I say so myself."

"If not Geissler, then who?" the major asked. "Whom did you make it for?"

Graf suddenly became more reticent. He licked his lips and looked away furtively.

"I'm not at liberty to tell you that."

"Herr Graf," Neumann said sharply. "I'm conducting a murder investigation. This gold chain, made by you, was found on the victim's body. Either you cooperate with me, or I arrest you for obstruction, then get a court order to go through your records. Which is it to be?"

Graf went back to his workbench and sat down again. He looked at Neumann with shifty, calculating eyes.

"I have the greatest respect for the police," he said obsequiously. "If called upon, I would always do my utmost to help them. But you place me in a very difficult situation. Very difficult. If I give you the information you are asking for, I will be breaking a confidence and that is something I am most reluctant to do. My business, you see, it is built on trust."

"I understand that," Neumann replied. "But this is a matter of the greatest importance. Geissler was a diplomat at the German legation here in Füssen. It is not just a question of homicide, serious though that is. There are wider implications that are critical to the relations between Berlin and Bavaria. That is why I have the full support of both the chancellor and King Ludwig."

Graf's head jerked up abruptly, his brow furrowing. "His Majesty?"

"It's in everyone's interests for this to be cleared up as soon as possible."

The jeweller hunched forward over the bench, his face hidden. His hands picked up tools and toyed with them distractedly, his thoughts elsewhere. Neumann gave him time. Graf lifted his head to look directly at him.

"The king, you say?"

"I saw him yesterday."

The jeweller hesitated. There was something untrustworthy about him, Neumann thought. He was an unprepossessing specimen. His legs were too short for his body, his head too big. His face was soft and flabby, eyes set too deep, his complexion pitted with smallpox scars. It seemed ironic that such a coarse looking man could craft such beautiful pieces of jewellery.

"I suppose it's all right then," Graf said. "I made it for him."

Neumann stared at him, wondering if he'd misunderstood.

"For the king?"

"Yes. The swan, that's his special symbol. The Swan King."

"So how would Geissler have got hold of it?"

"I don't know. Perhaps the king gave it to him. I make a lot of jewellery for the palace. His Majesty gives much of it away as gifts, he's a very generous man."

"When did you make it?"

"The exact date?" Graf returned to the shelf and consulted another ledger. "January the eighteenth. That's when the order came in. I delivered the finished piece on February the second."

"Delivered? You took it to the palace?"

"Well, no. His Majesty sent someone to collect it."

"Who?"

"His adjutant, Captain Schirmer. He always picks up the items."

Neumann took back the chain and stowed it away in the cloth bag. Then he produced the 'W' ring and showed it to the jeweller.

"You didn't make this, too, did you?"

Graf leaned across to get a better look and stiffened. Was it his imagination, Neumann wondered, or did the jeweller suddenly turn pale? It was hard to tell in the glare of the gas lamp.

"No… no, I didn't make it."

"Might it be connected to the king? His family name is Wittelsbach, after all."

"I wouldn't know. Now, if we're finished, major, I have work to do.

"Take a closer look. I'd value your opinion."

Neumann thrust the ring forward and, somewhat reluctantly, Graf took it. He gave it a perfunctory inspection.

"It's just a simple ring. Eighteen carat gold, enamel decoration. Well enough made, but nothing special."

"There's no hallmark on it."

"That's not unusual. A lot of jewellery is unmarked."

"Can you hazard a guess as to who made it? Another goldsmith in Füssen, perhaps?"

"There are no other goldsmiths. It must have come from somewhere else. Maybe Munich. A piece like this, it could have come from anywhere, really."

He passed the ring back quickly, as if he didn't want to hang on to it any longer than necessary.

"Thank you, Herr Graf. You've been most helpful."

Neumann paused to look back as he reached the door. The jeweller was bent over his bench again, but he wasn't doing any work. He was staring down at the worktop, the light reflecting off his spectacles, concealing the expression in his eyes. Neumann continued on into the shop and took another look in one of the display cases before the apprentice unlocked the door and let him out into the courtyard.

Interesting, the major thought as he walked away along the alley. There were items of jewellery in Graf's shop – mostly brooches, but also a couple of rings – that featured the same kind of colourful enamelwork as the 'W' ring. He had a strong suspicion that the goldsmith had either made that ring himself, or knew who had? So why was he lying about it?

TEN

Sophie looked at herself in the mirror. Her face was pale from the long, dark months of winter, but the skin was clear and unblemished. There were wrinkles next to her eyes and lines curving down from her nose to the edges of her mouth, but they were still faint and relatively undefined. She didn't mind that. She was thirty-five years old. She didn't want the face of a sixteen-year-old girl. She wanted the years to show, for time and experience to leave their marks on her body.

That wasn't, however, the conventional view of her sex. Women were supposed to prolong their youth – or, at least, the appearance of it – for as long as possible. They were supposed to hide their imperfections, paper over their faults with cosmetics. Sophie loathed make-up, the rouge and the powder and lipstick that turned a woman into a doll for the appeasement and pleasure of men. But there were times when even she felt obliged to apply some.

She was going into town. She had visits to make, a meeting with her banker who, though robust enough in financial matters, was woefully frail when it came to feminine custom. He would be shocked, perhaps need salts and a lie down, if she showed up in trousers and riding boots, if her face was allowed to remain in its natural state. Sophie didn't want to distress him unduly, so she was prepared to make a few concessions, albeit within limits. A kohl pencil added a bit of definition to her eyes, then she brushed on a touch of colour to her cheeks. Too much, she decided, and rubbed some of it off with a handkerchief. Her mouth was already pink, but she paid lip service to the male gaze – literally – by reddening them further with lipstick. That, too, was deemed excessive and partially removed with the handkerchief. She inspected herself in the glass and judged she'd gone far enough. Her bank manager's blushes would be spared, even though hers had had to be artificially applied.

The dress was next. She didn't usually wear dresses, certainly not around her house and estate. They were ridiculously impractical garments intended to restrict women's movements and activities. They might have been suitable for drinking tea in a salon, but for doing anything more energetic they made no sense at all. But people – women as well as men – were very conservative about dress. A woman in trousers unnerved them, made them uncomfortable. Sophie didn't really care what anyone thought about her, but she was astute enough to know when to make compromises. There was already enough gossip about her in town. The label "independent", even "eccentric", she could cope with. "Peculiar" or "unhinged" were a different matter. She didn't want to shut herself away from society. Her estate was remote, but she wasn't a recluse. She liked company, needed friendship. You could flaunt convention only so far before you risked ostracising yourself, and she didn't want that.

So she put on a dress – a navy blue gown with a modest neckline and a bodice embroidered with white lace. No corset. She quite liked breathing and drew the line at encasing herself in a whalebone cage. Black, ankle-high leather boots and a warm black cloak completed the outfit, then she went out to the stables and saddled her horse: a side saddle today, another abhorrent female custom, but unavoidable if she was wearing a dress. It didn't stop her riding fast, however. Half an hour and she was across the River Pöllat, trotting up the drive towards the von Breckendorf mansion. It was a big stone house with turrets, a black slate roof rimmed by crenellations, and grounds sweeping down to a frozen lake.

Anneliese, the Baroness von Breckendorf, was Sophie's cousin. She was waiting for her in the drawing room at the back of the house. The room was high ceilinged and bright, French windows giving onto a paved terrace framed by a stone balustrade, and beyond that a snow-covered lawn that ended at the water's edge. The ice on the lake was beginning to melt a little in the sunshine, cracking along the shoreline and providing a sliver of open water on which the swans could feed.

A maid brought a tray of tea and ginger biscuits and the two women sat down together by the fire. Anneliese was two years older than Sophie. She was a tall, statuesque woman with a full figure, blonde hair and a beautiful face that had attracted her husband almost as much as her considerable dowry.

"How are you, cousin?" Sophie asked her.

"I'm well. And you?"

"Well, too." Sophie studied Anneliese's face. "You look tired."

"Do I?"

"Is something troubling you?"

"No... Well, yes."

"Friedrich?" It was always her husband, Sophie reflected. A wealthy, sheltered, childless woman, Anneliese had nothing else to worry about.

"Yes, I suppose so."

"What is it this time? Another woman?" *Yet* another woman, Sophie thought, for the baron was a serial adulterer.

Anneliese gave a resigned nod. "There's someone, I can tell. There are all the usual signs. He stays out a lot in the evenings, comes back smelling of perfume. He says he's been working, but I know that's not true. But that's not my main worry. I think he's gambling again. I fear he's losing a lot of money."

"You have evidence of it?"

"He keeps it secret, but I spoke to our banker when I was in Munich last week. You know, Herr Richter. He hinted that things were not well with our finances."

"Not well in what way?"

"He wouldn't be specific. You know how it is. Money isn't a matter for women, even the dowry I brought with me."

"It's *your* money, Anni."

"That's not how Friedrich sees it."

"Have you spoken to him?"

"Of course. He just brushes it away, says I'm being silly."

"He *did* promise to stop. Maybe he has."

Anneliese looked at her and shook her head. "You know his promises are worthless."

"Can you find out? Write to Herr Richter, tell him how anxious you are."

"He won't tell me. He speaks only to Friedrich." Anneliese's lip trembled and she blinked away tears. "I'm so worried, Sophie. He's reckless, stupid. He could do anything."

Sophie reached out and took her cousin's hand.

"I'm sure it's not as bad as you think. Friedrich isn't that foolish."

"Isn't he? I hope you're right."

"I'm seeing Herr Bauer later this afternoon. Maybe he

could talk to Herr Richter, one banker to another, find out what the situation is."

"No, I couldn't allow that. Friedrich would be furious."

Sophie hesitated, wondering how to find a tactful way of putting this.

"Look, you know you can always call on me. I could give you something, I have plenty. Or a loan if you prefer."

"Oh, no, no," Anneliese said firmly. "That's very kind of you, but I couldn't. No, we must resolve this ourselves."

She sipped her tea, her eyes still moist, her make-up slightly smudged where a tear had welled over onto her cheek.

"Let's talk about something less gloomy. What about you? What've you been up to?"

"Don't change the subject, Anni. This is important."

"There's nothing you can do, Sophie. Things are what they are."

True, Sophie thought, but they didn't have to be that way. Why did Anneliese put up with it? The mistresses, the whores, the gambling, the drinking. And Friedrich a minister in the government. The public would've been appalled if they'd known his proclivities. But she knew the answer. Loyalty to the man she'd married, a stoic resignation, fear of his response if she confronted him, all conjoined with a naïve optimism – so far unjustified – that he would change his ways. He never would, Sophie knew, but she couldn't tell Anneliese that. She couldn't tell her something that, in her heart, her cousin already knew but was unwilling to acknowledge.

"Take my mind off it all," Anneliese pleaded. "What've you been doing? What's all this about a man being murdered on your land?"

"You've heard about that?"

"Everyone's heard about it. It's Friedrich's department, remember, now he's at Justice. It's caused a massive diplomatic stink. Prince von Auerswald insisted on bringing in a policeman from Berlin to investigate it and that, of course, caused outrage. Friedrich was beside himself with anger at the insult to Bavarian pride. But Baumgartner made him comply. Under pressure from the thugs in Wilhelmstrasse, no doubt, but he wouldn't admit that."

"I met him," Sophie said. "The policeman from Berlin."

Anneliese's eyes opened wide with interest. "Really? Tell me more."

"I was out in the forest, chopping wood. He mistook me for a servant."

Anneliese gave her a disapproving look. "You were dressed like one, I suppose. And chopping wood! Honestly Sophie, no wonder people talk about you."

"I admit it gave me a certain amount of amusement. I took him to the house to meet the mistress. You should've seen the look on his face when I walked into the room and he realised who I was."

"That was naughty, Sophie. He's only doing his job."

"He was bossy and arrogant."

Anneliese shrugged. "A typical Prussian."

"A typical man."

"He's supposed to be very good. That's what Friedrich says, anyway. A former army officer, apparently, drafted in to the police to root out corruption and incompetence."

"He should have a field day here. Let's hope he's not too good or the government won't last long."

"Now, now, don't get political. Politics is men's business."

"That's the problem."

Anneliese took a ginger biscuit and dipped it delicately into her tea – something she would never have dreamt of doing with anyone but Sophie. Her cousin brought out the rebel in her. Rebel? she thought, laughing inwardly at herself. Dunking a biscuit in tea? That was about as daring as she got. She sometimes wished she were more like Sophie, that she had her strength, her freedom to do as she pleased. But their circumstances were different. Sophie was unmarried. She was a freiherrin which meant her estate and her income were allodial, free of the feudal ties that bound a lot of landowners to a superior nobleman. She had no lord to answer to. Her money was hers to do with as she chose. Unlike me, Anneliese thought ruefully. I had my own money once, but now it belongs to my husband. What's left of it, anyway. Was there much left? She didn't know. She put the thought out of her mind; it was too depressing.

"What did he want with you, this policeman?"

"He asked me questions. He wanted to interrogate the servants too, but I refused to allow it."

"You *refused*? Was that wise?"

"I said I'd do it for him."

"So you're a policeman now, as well as a servant," Anneliese said dryly. "Shouldn't you be a little more cooperative?"

"I know. I feel a bit bad about it. That's one of the reasons I'm going to town. To invite him to tea."

"To tea? Don't frighten the poor man."

Sophie smiled. "I don't get the impression he's easily frightened."

Neumann paused outside the three-storey building on Drehergasse and checked the address for Norbert Ziegler he'd written down on a slip of paper. This was the right number, yet from the sign hanging outside on a wrought-iron bracket, it appeared to be the workshop of a lute-maker named Ignatz Weber. He pushed open the door and went inside. A man in a soiled apron was working at a bench, bending thin strips of wood around a hot iron to form the curved back of a lute. The room smelt of wood-shavings, pine and the wet rag he was using to dampen the strips to make them more pliable.

"I'm looking for a Doctor Norbert Ziegler."

The lute-maker didn't reply, didn't even look up from his work. He just jabbed a grubby thumb at the open staircase that ran up the side of the workshop to the floor above. Neumann climbed the steps and knocked on the door at the top. The man who answered was big and solid, in his early sixties. He had a head of thick, curly hair that had originally been black but was now mostly grey. He wore it long, the locks curling over the shoulders of his jacket which were liberally sprinkled with dandruff. His face was fleshy, the upper half covered by his fringe and a pair of bushy eyebrows, the lower half by a luxuriant beard and moustache. In between, his eyes gazed out, dark hazel and sparkling with curiosity and intelligence.

Neumann showed his police identity card. "I'm investigating the murder of Christoph Geissler. I wonder if I might take up a moment of your time, doctor?"

"Please."

Ziegler ushered him along the hall into a study that was cluttered with papers and files and more books than Neumann had ever seen outside the precincts of a public library.

"Take a seat, please," Ziegler said amiably. "Can I offer you a drink? A brandy? A glass of wine? I keep an excellent cellar, you know – although it's not actually a cellar, it's more of a cupboard. I have a fine selection of Riesling and Moselle, or a Bordeaux if you prefer a red."

"Thank you, but no," Neumann said.

"You don't mind if I do?"

The question was rhetorical for Ziegler was already dipping beneath the mound of papers on his desk and extricating a bottle of cognac and a dirty glass. He poured himself a generous measure, then sat back, his hands cupped around the glass, warming the amber liquid inside it.

"I'm intrigued, major. I've read about the case in the paper, of course. It's caused quite a stir. But I'm puzzled as to why you should come knocking on my door."

Neumann explained why he was there. Ziegler's caterpillar eyebrows rose a little when he mentioned the spear and the mistletoe and he nodded with understanding.

"And you think I might have some insight into the meaning of that?"

"Exactly, doctor," Neumann said. "I believe you're something of an expert on folklore and myth and pagan practises."

Ziegler smiled drolly. "Put like that, it doesn't sound much of a recommendation, does it? But yes, I have a certain knowledge in that area." He took a sip of his brandy and swallowed it slowly. "Do you know much about Norse mythology?"

Neumann shrugged. "The names of the gods, maybe a few myths half remembered from childhood story books. Nothing more than that."

"What you have to bear in mind is that those stories originated in a time when nothing was written down. They were part of an oral storytelling tradition, the tales passed down from generation to generation by word of mouth. The first written record we have of the ancient Germanic religious beliefs was made by Tacitus in his *Germania*, in the first century AD, but it wasn't until the thirteenth century that we got a fuller, more detailed account of them. Have you heard of a man named Snorri Sturluson?"

"No, I don't think I have," Neumann replied, bracing himself for a pedagogic lecture of the kind the doctor no doubt gave his students at the university.

"He was an Icelandic man of letters. A great poet, scholar and historian who brought together a number of sources when he wrote his *Prose Edda*. Some of those sources are likely to have been oral, others were already in literary form, mostly as poems. Snorri merged all those sources and retold the stories in a much more comprehensive way. But he may well have embellished them to make them more coherent – the original sources are not always consistent with one another. He may have filled gaps, even made things up. He was a writer, after all, and they have a tendency to do that.

"The next thing you need to know is that Snorri was a Christian writing about pagan beliefs so his own faith may well have influenced the *Edda*. Some of his prejudices, his biases, may have crept in, to give a particular slant on the myths. Having said that, there are obvious similarities between the two religions. The Norse myths, like Christianity, are a narrative response – an explanation really, or an attempt at one – for all the big questions we have to face as humans: Where did we come from? What is the meaning of life? What happens when we die?"

Ziegler paused to drink some more cognac and Neumann took the opportunity to bring him back on topic.

"The spear, the mistletoe, where do they fit in?"

"I'm coming to that," Ziegler replied, unwilling to deviate from his own narrative response. "You've heard of Ragnarök, have you? The end of the world for the Norse gods, when they are all doomed to die?"

"Yes."

"Well, the lead-up to that final, apocalyptic event is the death of Odin's son, Baldur."

Neumann froze, recalling his conversation with the king.

"What did you say? What was that name?"

"Baldur," Ziegler repeated. "The god of light, the most radiant and beautiful of all the gods. He has a dream of his own death, summoned by Hel, the goddess of the underworld, to follow her down to Helheim. This disturbs his parents so much that Odin – Wotan, in the old Germanic tradition – goes down to the land of the dead and rouses the prophetess, Wala, from her grave. She predicts that Baldur will indeed be killed. Frigg, his mother, is so distraught at the prophecy that she travels the world, making every living creature, and every thing on the earth, in the ocean, in the air, swear not to harm her son. All animals and birds and fish, all plants, water and fire, the rocks and mountains, metals and minerals, even all illnesses, poisons and diseases, they promise to leave him alone. Baldur becomes untouchable, indestructible."

Ziegler leaned back in his chair and folded his hands across his ample paunch. His mouth moved, as if he were savouring one of his fine wines, and Neumann foresaw some digression, some academic pontification, that would be of no conceivable interest to him. He was right.

"What you have to remember about the Norse gods – about the Greek and Roman, too – is that they are fundamentally different from our Christian God. At least, the God of the New Testament, the God of love and forgiveness and compassion. Our God created Man in his own image, but the Norse gods were created in human form, with the same vices and weaknesses as Man. They are all too human. Jealous, greedy, violent, angry, fearful, lecherous. The male gods enjoy fighting, fornicating, drinking and playing games; the females do their hair and deck themselves out in jewellery and rich clothes and plot against each other. They are cruel and vain and lazy. All Man's faults are embodied in them. They know that their end is coming, but they are incapable, or unwilling, to do anything to stop it. They have resigned themselves to their fate and the story of Baldur presages their eventual destruction."

"But you said he was indestructible," Neumann said.

"And at this point he is. The gods, being very human and prone to boredom, amuse themselves by challenging his immortality. They throw things at him. Spears, daggers, arrows, even Thor's mighty hammer, Mjollnir. All of them are turned away, as if there's an invisible wall protecting him. Then an old woman comes to see Frigg and she hears the gods whooping with delight at their games and asks what is going on. Frigg talks to her of a mother's love for her children and explains how everything has promised not to harm Baldur. Everything? asks the old woman. Well, not everything, Frigg confesses. There was one living thing that didn't – mistletoe – but that was such a weak, flimsy thing it didn't worry her. What could a plant like mistletoe, a feeble parasite with no branches, just soft, pliable stems, do to a god? But the Norse gods are subject to the same inexorable fate as Man. A prophecy must come true."

Old women in Norse mythology are rarely what they seem and this one, it soon transpires, is the wicked, shapeshifting trickster, Loki, who immediately goes off and finds some mistletoe on an ash tree. He murmurs a spell over it, touching it with his crooked stick until the stem thickens into something more substantial, into a branch from which he crafts a spear. Then he goes to Asgard and finds the gods still laughing and hurling weapons at the invulnerable Baldur. All except one: Baldur's brother, Hödur, the god of darkness who is blind, standing on the sidelines unable to join in the fun.

"Let me help you share the entertainment," says Loki and he puts the mistletoe spear in Hödur's hand and guides his arm as he hurls it at his brother. Baldur is struck in the breast and falls down dead. And before anyone can see him, Loki is gone, transforming himself into a tiny gnat that flies away unnoticed. Baldur is given a great funeral, attended by the gods and the Valkyries, the light elves, the wood and water sprites, the mountain and frost giants and even the black elves. Baldur's wife, Nanna, dies heartbroken and her body is placed alongside her husband's on a dragon ship laden with so much wood and gold and jewels that no one, not even Thor, can push it down into the water. A frost giant says there is a female giant in Jotunheim named Hyrokkin who can move mountains, so she is sent for and arrives riding a monstrous wolf with living vipers for reins. She pushes the boat into the sea so fast that the friction ignites the rollers beneath it and the vessel catches fire. The flames burn more fiercely as the ship floats out from the shore, the funeral pyre reflected in the water, leaving behind a wake like crimson blood.

Frigg, overcome with grief, asks who will go down to Helheim to ask Hel to return Baldur to the living world. Her son, Hermondur, the herald of the gods, volunteers. Odin lends him his eight-legged horse, Sleipnir, and for nine days and nine nights Hermondur rides through Nifelheim, the land of mists, to the River Giöll, the frontier between the lands of the living and the dead. Guarding the golden bridge spanning the river is the gigantic porteress, Mödgud, who confirms that Baldur has passed over into Helheim. She lets Hermondur pass, although he is not one of the dead, and he rides on until he reaches the high iron fence around the kingdom of Hel. He can find no entrance, but Sleipnir leaps over the barrier into the realm of shades and they make their way past the fiery cauldron, Hvergelmir, where the dragon Nidhøggr feasts on bad men, to the house where Hel holds court.

She sits on a throne in a hall bedecked with gold and silver, her flesh black and dead, her head crowned with gold and diamonds which sparkle in the candlelight. Baldur is seated next to her, Nanna beside him. Hermondur pleads with Hel to release the god of light back to the gods in Asgard and she consents, but only if every living thing on earth, and every inanimate object, too, weeps for Baldur. If one refuses, he must remain in the land of the dead.

Hermondur rides back to Asgard and messengers are sent out to all the corners of the world, calling on everyone and everything to weep. And almost all of them do. The fish, the birds, the animals weep. The rocks drip water like tears, the forests steam, the clouds rain. Only one creature says no: a giantess named Thöck, meaning darkness, as fearsome as Hel herself, who lives in the depths of a cave, her face lined and ancient, her eyes dark pitiless sockets, her mouth full of blackened teeth. The messengers beg her to reconsider, but she will not move. So sweet, golden Baldur is condemned to eternity in the underworld. But once again the mischievous hand of Loki is directing affairs, for Thöck, it turns out, is no giantess but Loki in disguise, his wicked tricks leading the gods towards their appointed fate.

Ziegler ended his story and for a moment there was silence as Neumann tried to understand its implications for his investigation. Was Christoph Geissler Baldur? He was young and beautiful and golden haired. The spear inserted into his chest had not been made of mistletoe, just wrapped in it, but it was surely intended to symbolise the weapon from the Norse myth. But why? Why go to all that trouble when Geissler's life had already been taken by a knife blow to the heart? Was it a message to the police, a clue to help them? Or was it the opposite, a deliberate attempt to muddy the waters and mislead them?

Neumann was confused. Troubled, too, his thoughts returning to his audience with Ludwig. What had the king said? "My Baldur. My beautiful Baldur." The words hadn't been clear at the time, but now he'd heard the myth, Neumann was pretty sure that was what Ludwig had said. Did he know the story? It looked as if he did. But was that relevant, and if so, how? Baldur was Odin's son. The son of the king of the gods. Ludwig was a king. He wasn't married, had no children – at least, none that were known or acknowledged. Was it possible that Geissler had been his son, an illegitimate potential heir to the throne?

"From your face, major, I fear I may not have been of much assistance to you," Ziegler said. "Let me give you something."

Easing himself out of his chair, he went to a shelf and took down a book – one of several in a row with identical spines.

"One of mine," he explained. "At risk of appearing immodest, I'd say it's probably the definitive academic work on Norse mythology. You may find it useful."

Neumann took the book, glancing at its title: *From Asgard to Ragnarök: the Norse Gods Explained.*

"Thank you, doctor. I hope I haven't taken up too much of your time."

"It's been my pleasure. Is there anything else I can help with?"

"No, I don't think..." Neumann stopped, suddenly remembering. "Actually, yes, perhaps there is. Would you be good enough to look at these and give me your opinion?"

He took out the wad of notes he'd found hidden in Geissler's lodgings, and the additional note found on the young man's body, and passed them to Ziegler.

"It's been suggested to me that they might be runes."

Ziegler leafed through the bits of paper.

"They certainly look like it."

"Can you transcribe them for me?"

Ziegler pursed his lips. "I could try. It might take me a bit of time."

"I'd be most grateful."

"The problem is... I have other work, you see."

Neumann took the hint. "I would, of course, pay you for your trouble."

Ziegler hesitated, considering his response, then he nodded. "I'll try to look at them tomorrow."

Neumann walked back to the Gasthaus Hoffmann, his mind preoccupied by the myth he'd just been told in such loving detail. He hadn't known the story of Baldur. None of it had been familiar to him from the books he'd read as a child, although he recognised some of the names: Odin, obviously, and Thor, the thunder god. Every schoolboy had heard of them. Frigg, too, had brought back vague memories, but the figure that stood out most from the tragic tale was Loki. Neumann knew the name. Loki was important in the Norse myths. Not really a god, but an outsider, a slippery, untrustworthy character who could change shape and loved nothing more than creating mischief and chaos. If Geissler was Baldur in this modern murder mystery, Neumann wondered, then who was Loki?

ELEVEN

At breakfast the following morning, Johanna came across to his table while he was peeling a hard-boiled egg and put a copy of the *Füssener Blatt* down in front of him.

"Just to get your day off to a good start, major," she said ironically.

The article, by-lined Gunther Krämer, was on the front page under the headline: *"Geissler Murder Link to Pagan Rites"*.

The journalist had his facts right, at least. He knew about the spear and the mistletoe, he knew the results of the autopsy. Where had he got it all from? Neumann wondered. Who had that kind of detailed knowledge? Von Auerswald? He couldn't see the legate leaking information to an insignificant provincial newspaper. It had to be the police, almost certainly Beck. He'd have close relations with the local press, probably make a few extra marks on the side in tip-off fees and other services.

Neumann could see the captain's hand, his voice, too, in Krämer's description of the investigation. *"Why has this Prussian policeman been sent to lead the enquiry?"* he asked. *"Are Bavaria's officers not considered good enough for Berlin? What qualities can this Major Neumann bring that our valiant local bobbies don't already possess? The major refuses to comment. He may be a decorated war hero, but he seems out of his depth with this murder investigation. A week has gone by since Christoph Geissler's body was discovered. But no significant progress seems to have been made in the hunt for his killer. When is Major Neumann going to show us what he is made of?"*

Neumann wasn't the only person under attack in the article. The freiin also came in for some not-so-subtle innuendo. *"It appears that there are dark, possibly satanic, forces at work in our peaceful province,"* Krämer had written. *"Can it be a coincidence that the young diplomat's body was found on land belonging to the Freiherrin Sophie Hals von Wildenstein?"*

Neumann tossed the paper to one side and sliced some of his egg onto a bread roll. It was irritating, but he wasn't going to let it worry him. He knew his arrival was going to upset the locals. Krämer – as journalists did – was merely articulating their resentment, giving it a public platform. The core of the article, in any case, was accurate. He's right, Neumann thought. I haven't made any obvious progress. I haven't found out why Geissler was killed. I haven't identified any potential suspects. It wouldn't be long before von Auerswald, too, would be asking when he was going to show what he was made of.

He finished his breakfast and went back upstairs to his room, taking the paper with him. Another article on the front page had drawn his attention: a rally in Munich by the Bavarian Freedom Party that had been broken up by the police, with ten people arrested for public order offences. He'd never heard of the group, but they appeared to be campaigning, agitating even, for Bavaria to break away from the empire – in essence, from the hated Prussians – and become an independent, self-governing state again.

He was reading through the piece when there was a knock on the door. "Come in," he called, thinking it was one of the maids arriving to clean or make his bed, and went back to the paper.

"I beg your pardon, sir."

It was a deep male voice, a mature voice. Neumann swivelled round in his chair and saw a tall man standing on the threshold. He must have been in his mid-fifties. He was clean shaven, his hair blond, the paleness of his complexion accentuated by his clothing. He was dressed all in black – trousers, jacket, waistcoat, tie – a black felt hat clutched in his hands. Mourning clothes.

"My apologies for the intrusion," he said. "My name is Geissler. Ehren Geissler. I'm Christoph's father."

"Of course."

Neumann stood up and stepped forward, offering his hand.

"Come in, Herr Geissler. Please."

He gestured at the armchair, then went to close the door.

"My sincere condolences, sir. You must feel the loss deeply."

"Thank you," Geissler replied.

He perched himself on the edge of the chair, fiddling nervously with his hat. He seemed at a loss for words.

"I'm… I'm sorry to interrupt you, major. The legation… they told me where to find you."

"You're not interrupting. Not at all. I will be glad to be of service to you."

"I've come to… you know. Take Christoph's body home. To Berlin. For the funeral."

Neumann could see the strain in his face. The tight mouth, the anxious eyes that spoke of sleepless nights, of tears that even now were only just below the surface. The family likeness was striking. The hair, the blue eyes, the handsome face that thirty years ago would have been the spitting image of Christoph.

"If there's any way I can help. The requisite authorisations, I believe, have all been signed."

"Yes, yes, everything is in order." Geissler looked around the room, still toying with his hat. "His mother is... very upset. As you might imagine."

No mention of himself, Neumann thought, though he was clearly distressed.

"It must have been a great shock."

"Yes, yes, it was..."

He petered out. Neumann sat back down on his chair, sensing that Geissler needed a little time to get to the point of his visit and that some trivial small talk might put him more at ease.

"You arrived yesterday, I assume?"

"Yes, I did."

"And when do you go back?"

"This afternoon."

"You've been to Füssen before?"

"This is my first time. It seems an attractive town, though I haven't seen much of it. Christoph had to relocate to Munich when he took up his post with the legation. We visited him there, his mother and I. A charming city. We'd never been to Bavaria before. Then the king moved down here, so the prince – and, of course, Christoph – had to follow him."

"You must have been very proud of your son."

"Yes, we are... were." The change of tense perturbed him. He swallowed hard and continued talking, as if it would take his mind off his emotions. "Of course, we never expected it. Christoph didn't either. He was just a clerk, a very junior clerk at the chancellery when the appointment came out of nowhere. I won't deny we were surprised. But, naturally, delighted. For Christoph to suddenly be attached to the prince's staff, well, it was a great honour."

Geissler paused, then he looked directly at Neumann and his next words were an anguished cry of bewilderment.

"*Why*? Why did this happen? To our son? Why, major?"

"I don't know," Neumann said gently.

"That's why I came to you. I need to know. His mother needs to know. We can't make any sense of it. Christoph was such a lovely boy. Such a good, kind, talented boy. Why would anyone want to... to... do this to him?" There were tears in his eyes that he was fighting hard to suppress.

"That's what I'm tasked with finding out, Herr Geissler."

"You have made progress?"

"It's still very early. But as you're here, perhaps you could help me."

"Help you how?"

"Did Christoph write to you?"

"Regularly. He was very conscientious about that. He knew how much we looked forward to hearing from him. In Berlin, you see, we were used to seeing a lot of him. That stopped when he moved to Bavaria."

"How did he seem in recent weeks? Was he happy?"

"He certainly said he was."

"No worries?"

"Not that we were aware of."

"And his work? Did he ever write about that?"

"Not in great detail. A lot of that would have been confidential, of course."

"But, in general, his work was going well?"

"Very well. He enjoyed it."

"What about friends? Did he mention anyone?"

"No one in particular."

"Any young ladies?"

Geissler flushed. "He didn't talk about things like that. His work kept him very busy, I think. His only recreation, apart from the odd walk, was music. He loved music, especially Wagner. He was a member of some society here that celebrates his music. He wrote very enthusiastically about their meetings."

"Did he ever mention the king?"

"The king?" Geissler's brow wrinkled with puzzlement. "King Ludwig, you mean? Oh, no. He was far too junior to have anything to do with him, although he did occasionally attend functions at the court. Diplomatic affairs, you know. Work, I suppose."

He paused. The light from the window caught his face as he turned his head, emphasising his cheekbones, the shadows beneath his eyes.

"You think this had something to do with his work?"

"I don't know, Herr Geissler. But I want to reassure you that I will catch whoever did it and see them answer for the crime."

"Yes, yes... thank you, major."

The conversation had run its course. Geissler nodded, as if he understood everything, though his expression conveyed the exact opposite.

"Well, I must get on. I have things to do."

He stood up, stiffening his backbone, letting practical matters override feelings that might otherwise have overwhelmed him.

"Thank you again, major."

They shook hands. Geissler gripped his hat tight, like a child's comfort blanket, and walked stiffly out of the room. Neumann closed the door after him. The man was gone, but he'd left behind a lingering, poignant residue of grief.

Von Auerswald fixed him with his intense blue eyes, his gaze direct, challenging. Neumann felt a sudden qualm of unease, recalling memories – not pleasant ones – of his encounters with the headmaster of his high school in Brandenburg, an institution where discipline had always been more important than learning.

"You've seen the king, I understand."

It was a statement, not a question. Neumann suppressed a start of surprise, then wondered at his own naivety. Of course the legate would know. If the information hadn't come through official channels, he would undoubtedly have a network of informers in the Bavarian government, one of whom would have told him.

"Yes, sir."

"What did he want?"

Neumann felt himself on the spot, his inferiority all the more obvious from their respective positions, von Auerswald behind his desk, Neumann standing, almost at attention, before him.

"He wanted to know about the investigation, sir."

"Know what?"

"How it was going."

"And what did you tell him?"

Neumann hesitated and the legate immediately leapt in, giving him no time to filter his answer.

"Don't tell me what you think I want to hear, major, just give me the facts."

"That's what I gave His Majesty, sir. The facts."

"Which facts?"

"The finding of the body, the circumstances surrounding it."

"You told him about the spear?"

"Yes, sir."

"And how did he react?"

"He seemed shocked, upset."

"Well, yes, who wouldn't be? It's a shocking thing. What else?"

"That was it, sir."

"Did you mention the runic note that was found on Geissler's body?"

"No, sir. I didn't think it appropriate to share that."

"Good. Keep it that way. He might be a king, but the details of this investigation must be kept confidential. You don't tell His Majesty anything more, do you understand?"

"Yes, sir."

"His discretion cannot be relied on."

It was an astonishingly frank remark, Neumann thought. But the prince was secure enough to say what he liked. He was Bismarck's man: a diplomat who didn't need to be diplomatic.

"Where are we with that note, by the way. And the others?"

Neumann described his visit to Norbert Ziegler: showing him the notes, Ziegler undertaking to attempt a transcription of them, his recounting of the tale of Baldur.

"What *is* this?" von Auerswald demanded, his tone more aggressive. "Some ritual pagan killing. Is that what you're saying?"

"It's an explanation of the mistletoe, sir. *One* explanation, at least. I won't say more than that."

The prince reached across to the corner of his desk and picked up a *Füssener Blatt*.

"You've seen this?"

"Yes, sir."

"They've made a great deal of the pagan angle. Where did they get their information?"

"Not from me, sir."

"So, the local police, then?"

"That would be my guess, sir."

"It doesn't make us look good. Doesn't make *you* look good, major. You need to get a move on. Have you any leads?"

"There is something…" How do I put this? Neumann wondered. I'm not a prince with the right friends in Berlin. I probably need to be a little more circumspect.

"Spit it out, man. Don't waste my time."

"There appears to be a connection between the king and Christoph Geissler."

Von Auerswald stared at him. "A connection? What're you talking about?"

"Geissler had a gold chain on his pocket watch. A chain with a golden swan attached to it. I've spoken to the local jeweller whose hallmark is on the items. He said he made them for King Ludwig."

"For the *king*?" The legate was incredulous.

"He thought perhaps His Majesty had made a gift of the chain to Geissler."

Von Auerswald shook his head. "That's highly unlikely. They never met. There must be some other explanation."

"Also… the king, in my audience with him, I didn't quite catch his words, but I think he said something about Baldur."

The prince leaned forward over his desk, his eyes boring into Neumann.

"Do I understand you correctly, major? You think King Ludwig is involved in the murder?"

Spelled out so starkly, it did sound ludicrous, Neumann thought. He'd already ruled out the illegitimate son idea. Meeting Ehren Geissler, it was clear beyond doubt that he was Christoph's father. But what of the king's words. "My Baldur. My beautiful Baldur." How did he explain those?

"I don't know what to think, sir," he said, evading the question, an equivocal stance that did not go unnoticed by von Auerswald.

"Let me tell you what to think, major," the prince said icily. "His Majesty is *not* involved. This murder is the work of some deranged lunatic. And it is your task to find that madman. Do I make myself clear?"

"Yes, sir."

"I expect to see some tangible progress very soon. I

don't want any more newspaper articles like this one. You may go."

Neumann left the office feeling chastened and bruised. Confused, too, and not a little angry. Von Auerswald – for the purposes of this investigation, at any rate – was his boss. But that didn't give him the right to dictate how Neumann conducted it, let alone to push him towards a particular outcome if the evidence didn't lead him that way. He hadn't joined the police force to become a nobleman's lapdog.

On the steps outside the legation, he took a long, deep breath of the frosty air. He'd had two awkward interviews already that day. A third, possibly even more uncomfortable, was yet to come.

TWELVE

"Major, please, take a seat. It's a pleasure to see you again."

The freiherrin was so welcoming that Neumann was instantly on his guard. She seemed genuine enough, but after their previous encounter, he was going to take nothing at face value.

"Thank you, ma'am," he said, sinking down into a corner of a sofa.

Sophie took the armchair nearest the door. She was herself again, back in trousers, shirt and jacket, no trace of cosmetics on her face. There was no need to make a show, to make any concessions to appearance with this policeman from Berlin, an outsider who would soon be gone.

"It's another cold day," she said easily. "You are warm enough?"

"Yes, thank you." Neumann glanced at the blazing fire, the logs stacked neatly beside the hearth. "You have an excellent supply of wood, I see."

Sophie eyed him, suspecting some pointed jibe in the remark, but Neumann returned her gaze with inscrutable innocence. He'd removed his coat and cap, revealing his navy-blue uniform. He looked quite smart, Sophie thought, even dashing. No, where did that come from?

Not dashing at all. Rather, plain and understated, which she found much more preferable. She hated showy men, had suffered the attentions of far too many cocksure, fancy suitors. A drab detective made a pleasant change.

"How are you finding Füssen?" she asked.

"I haven't given it much thought, really," Neumann replied.

"It must be rather dull after Berlin."

"I haven't come here to enjoy myself."

It was politely said, but Sophie sensed a rebuke in his words.

"Quite so," she said. "I'll get to the point, shall I? I've questioned all my staff, as I told you I would do. None of them has any information that would be relevant to your enquiries."

"Nothing?" Neumann said.

"They are house servants. None of them had any cause to be out in the forest last Monday or Tuesday. I've also spoken to an elderly lady who lives in a hut not far from the place you found the body. Gisela Winter. She usually knows everything that occurs in the surrounding area, but not this time. She saw nothing, heard nothing."

Neumann nodded his thanks. "That was very good of you, ma'am. Do you have many servants?"

"Seven. A cook, two scullery maids, three housemaids and a groom."

"All women, I understand."

Sophie's eyes narrowed. "Do you have a problem with that?"

"Not at all. It seems a modest number for a house this size."

"I live alone. How many servants do I need?"

"What about outside staff? Do you have a game-keeper, for instance?"

"No. My estate is open to all – as I believe I told you last time. I don't impose any restrictions on the local people, providing they only take game or wood for their own needs."

"That's a very enlightened attitude."

Sophie shrugged. "I am fortunate. I have a lot. Why wouldn't I share it with those who have less?"

"And gardeners? Who looks after your grounds?"

"They come in from Schwangau. They don't live on the premises. And they haven't been here for weeks now. All the snow, there's nothing for them to do. I'm sorry not to be more helpful."

"You've been most kind, ma'am. Could I show you something?" He passed her his copy of the *Füssener Blatt*. "I wondered whether you'd seen this?"

"No, we're a little out of touch with the news out here."

"You might find it interesting."

Sophie read through the front-page article, then handed the paper back to him with a dismissive shrug.

"It's a rag looking for sensation to attract readers. I wouldn't believe everything you read in it."

"What does Krämer mean? No coincidence that the body was found on your land?"

"As you've already noted, major, we're an all-female household. To a gutter journalist like him, what else could we be except a coven of witches? Dancing naked around bonfires, casting spells, killing people with mistletoe spears. That's what women do, isn't it, when you let them gather together?"

"He doesn't like you?"

"It seems we have something in common. He doesn't appear to like you, either. With me, he's had plenty of time to come to that conclusion, but why so quick with you?"

"I didn't give him the information he was seeking."

"Aah. Poor strategy with a journalist."

"And you? May I ask how *you've* upset him?"

"Nothing terrifies a man more than an assertive woman."

"Not all men," Neumann said.

"No? You think you're different?"

"Are you trying to provoke me, freiin?"

Sophie smiled. "I don't know. If I am, I sense I won't succeed."

"My wife was a strong, assertive woman. She didn't scare me. I respected it."

"'Was'?"

"She died."

"I'm sorry. But you surely don't take Krämer seriously? Pagan rites, dark satanic forces? Whatever killed that young man, it wasn't magic."

"May I show you something else?" Neumann rummaged in his pocket and brought out the 'W' ring. "Have you seen this before?"

He walked across to her chair and gave her the ring, then returned to the sofa and watched her examine it.

"I wondered if it belonged to someone in the von Wildenstein family. A male relative perhaps?"

Sophie shook her head. "I have an uncle and a few male cousins, but I've never seen any of them wearing a ring like this. Where did you get it?"

Neumann didn't answer the question. That was a detail she didn't need to know.

"There's a Wagner Society here, I gather. Do you know anything about it?"

"I'm a member."

"Do any of the men wear rings like that?"

"Not that I've seen."

"Christoph Geissler was also a member of the society."

"I know. I recognised him from the photograph in the paper. It was quite a shock."

"Did you know him? Did you ever speak to him at the meetings?"

"No. They're mostly musical, rather than social, occasions. We listen to singers, we don't sit around talking. Perhaps Herr Steimitz –"

She broke off as the door to the drawing room clicked open and one of the maids entered carrying a tea tray. Sophie put the ring down on the table beside her.

"Ah, Amalie, thank you. Just here will do."

The maid approached the table. She looked down and went suddenly rigid, her eyes fixed on the ring. She seemed to be a trance for a moment. Then the tray in her hands began to shake – so violently that the cups and saucers rattled hard enough to break. All the colour had drained from her face. She took a step back, her mouth gaping in horror. Neumann leapt to his feet, strode across the room and grabbed the tray from her just before she dropped it.

"Amalie?" Sophie said in alarm. "What is it? What's the matter?"

The maid gave a sob, her face crumpling with distress, and rushed from the room. Neumann put down the tray and made to go after her, but Sophie was on her feet now. She put a hand on his arm to restrain him.

"No."

"She was looking at the ring," Neumann said. "I need to speak to her."

"Let me."

"No, this time I have to question her."

"I said no."

Sophie stepped in front of him to block his path to the door. Her fingers were still on his arm. He could feel the strength of her grip, see the determination in her eyes.

"This is police business," he said.

"Amalie is *my* maid. This is *my* house. I will speak to her."

"She knows something. I have to find out what."

"You won't find it by running after her and yelling at her."

Her fingers dug deeper into his arm. Neumann winced and pulled her hand away. For a moment, their fingers were entwined. Their faces were close enough for him to feel the warmth of her breath. Then she backed away from him, still blocking the door.

"What do you think I am?" Neumann asked indignantly. "I'm not going to yell. I'll be gentle with her. You think I can't be gentle?"

"She will not speak to you," Sophie said.

"How do you know?"

"Because she hasn't spoken to anyone since she came here."

"What are you talking about?"

"Wait here, major. Pour yourself some tea. You must leave this to me."

She glared at him pugnaciously, squaring up for a fight. She was breathing heavily. Her jaw was set tight. A strand of dark hair had come loose and was straggling across her forehead. Neumann thought suddenly of his wife. How Kristina would flare up and confront him on the rare occasions they'd quarrelled. A woman's anger: there was only one way to deal with it. He took a pace back, holding up his hands in a gesture of appeasement.

"Very well. I'll leave it to you."

The sensations flooded back through her mind in a torrent that took her breath away. She gasped for air. Her pulse was racing, her heart pounding in her chest. She felt nauseous. Her stomach churned over and over. The sounds, the smells, they came back in a wave that engulfed her. The dank, musty odour of the chamber, the chill air that made her think of a cave, of a hollow in a mountain, even though she'd never caught more than a glimpse of her surroundings. The quiet, the echo of voices, of chanting like a religious order, the darkness all around her. She could feel the cloth over her face, over her eyes, in her mouth. She could taste it. Taste her own fear.

Everything was black. They were hidden from her, the men. They had no form, no identities. They were just indistinct sounds, pungent scents of hair oil and sweat. She felt the necklace being placed around her again, the metal cold on her skin. She felt the hands touching her, the bodies pressing down and into her, her throat gagging, her voice choked off in a scream that she knew nobody could hear.

It was always the same: the ritual, the fear, the pain. Always the same sounds and smells, always the same darkness. Except for that moment when the blindfold slipped and she saw his face, saw the ring on his finger. The ring. The symbol of everything that hurt her, that in her mind was the encapsulation of evil.

"Amalie? Amalie, it's me."

She curled herself deeper into a ball, her legs pulled up, her head tucked into her knees, eyes tight shut to close out the world.

"Amalie? It's Sophie."

The voice, the darkness, she let them envelop her, hoping that somehow, they would wash away her memories. A hand touched her arm and she flinched.

"No! No!"

This time the scream escaped. The shrill cry reverberated around the house, echoing painfully through her head. She clasped her hands over her ears, trying to still the vibrations.

"Trudi, help me here!"

More hands grasped her. Firm, but also gentle. She tried to resist. She pressed her head hard into her knees, her muscles tense, unyielding. She felt the hands pulling her arms, soothing female voices murmuring, and her body gave up the fight. She went limp and allowed herself to uncurl. Her eyes opened and she saw the freiin's face, saw the maid, Trudi, beside her, both gazing at her with tender concern. They lifted her to her feet and half carried, half led her away to the stairs.

Did winter never end here? Neumann wondered as he gazed out at the snowy landscape. Away from the fire, the room was cool. He could feel the cold air seeping in around the window frames and when he touched the glass, it was like a pane of ice. He took a sip of his tea. He'd heard a scream, almost run out to investigate, but stopped himself. He was a man in a women's house. He wasn't needed.

He paced back to the hearth and warmed himself up by the fire. There was a picture above the mantelpiece – a soldier on horseback wearing the blue and yellow uniform of Bavaria, a cocked hat on his head. Neumann studied his face. He could see something of the freiin in the shape of the mouth and chin. The eyes, too, had the same blue-orange tint, the same look of tenacious strength. Her father, he guessed.

He heard footsteps outside in the corridor and turned to see Sophie coming back into the room. Very deliberately, she poured a cup of tea and drank some before she spoke.

"She's calm now. I gave her a sleeping draught."

"The scream?"

"She was frightened."

"Of you?"

"Of the things inside her head. She has nightmares. We hear her crying out sometimes. She sees things which disturb her."

"Like this ring."

Sophie nodded. She sat down in the armchair. She looked pale, Neumann thought. There was a notch of anxiety in the gap between her eyebrows. She scraped back the lock of hair over her forehead and tucked it in under her silver clasp. Then she glanced down at the ring, still lying on the table beside the tea tray.

"What is it? Where does it come from?"

Neumann walked over to the table, picked up the ring and slipped it away into his pocket. He owed her a straight answer.

"It was in the clearing. Where Christoph Geissler's body was found."

"It was his?"

"I don't know."

"You think it might belong to his killer?"

"Or the man who dumped the body. They may be different people."

It was strange, Neumann thought. He'd been carrying the ring around for hours and not noticed it. Yet now he was acutely conscious of it in his pocket. It seemed to be glowing, as if it had suddenly come alive. Don't be absurd. Now you're imagining things like Amalie. Or was she imagining them?

"Do you think Amalie knows something about the murder?" Sophie asked.

Neumann returned to the sofa and sat down before he replied.

"I don't know. She certainly seems to know something about the ring. Did you question her?"

"She was in no state to be questioned. Not that she would have answered, in any case."

"You said she doesn't speak."

"Not a word since she arrived."

"Arrived from where?"

"I found her wandering in the forest." Sophie's face clouded as she recalled the day. "Back in January. She was wearing nothing but a shift and a dressing gown, thin slippers on her feet. She was half frozen to death. I thought she might lose her toes to frostbite, but we got her inside into the warmth just in time."

"How do you know her name's Amalie?"

"There was a handkerchief in her dressing gown pocket. It had the name embroidered on it."

Neumann nodded. "Have you any idea where she comes from? Has she been reported missing by anyone?"

"We know nothing about her. She's obviously had some kind of trauma. Something she can't speak about."

"Has a doctor seen her?"

"The doctor came out. She was terrified of him."

"Of a doctor?"

"Of a man, I think. She wouldn't let him near her. I have a friend, the old lady I mentioned to you. Gisela. She has healing skills. She's been treating Amalie. Drawing her out of herself. The poor child couldn't do anything at the beginning. She just lay curled up in bed all day. But she can do a few light chores now. Help a little in the kitchen, bring tea for visitors." She gave a humourless smile. "At least, I thought she could. Today has been a bit of a setback."

Sophie drank some more tea, then looked away towards the window. Her lip trembled and she bit down on it, a bleakness in her eyes. Amalie's reaction had obviously upset her.

"I'm sorry to have been the cause of this," Neumann said.

"It wasn't your fault. You weren't to know this would happen."

"If you could try to speak to her, I'd be grateful. The ring's important. I don't know exactly why yet."

"I wouldn't hold out much hope, but, yes, I'll try."

Neumann got to his feet. He crossed the room and put his cup down on the tea tray. Sophie stood up. They looked at each other, a slight awkwardness between them that neither could explain.

"Good day, ma'am."

"Good day, major."

He went out to his horse. It was only when he swung himself up into the saddle that he felt the ache just above his right elbow, a bruise where the freiin's fingers had gripped his arm.

Sophie went upstairs to the servants' quarters in the attics and entered a small room that overlooked the garden. Amalie was asleep in bed, Trudi watching over her from a chair.

"How is she?"

"She dropped off a few minutes ago," Trudi said. "She seems peaceful now."

Sophie looked down at Amalie. She did indeed look tranquil, her eyes closed, her breathing soft and steady.

"Did she say anything?"

Trudi shook her head. "Nothing I could understand. She was restless, making strange noises, like sobs. I stroked her hair until she fell asleep."

"Good girl."

"Shall I stay?"

"For a while. I'll get Dagmar to relieve you in a bit."

Sophie went back downstairs, put on her cloak and boots and headed out across the garden into the forest. It was a dismal, overcast day, the black clouds in the east presaging yet more snow. Dusk seemed to be falling early. In the trees, the light was dim, riven with shadows that moved as the branches overhead swayed in the wind.

She walked quickly along the path. Something told her she shouldn't linger. She didn't know what it was. The weather, the heaviness in the air, some sense inside her, they all contributed to her feeling of unease and she was glad when she saw the lantern glowing in the window of Gisela's hut.

The old woman was dozing in front of the hearth, but she stirred as Sophie entered, the draught from the door skittering across the floor and rekindling the embers of the fire. Sophie pulled up a chair and sat down beside her, letting the warmth revive her frigid fingers and toes.

Gisela opened her eyes. "Ah, it's you."

"Don't let me wake you."

"No, it's all right." Gisela turned her head to look at her. "What ails you, child?"

Sophie was used to the old woman's intuition, the way she could pick up signals to discover moods and feelings, but she could still be surprised by it.

"I sense turbulence, anxiety," Gisela went on. "What is it?"

"I need some more of your sleeping draught."

"For yourself?"

"For Amalie."

"Aah," Gisela nodded. "Has something happened?"

Sophie told her. Gisela listened, studying the freiin's face as she described Neumann's visit, the ring and Amalie's reaction to it.

"I've never seen anyone so frightened," Sophie said.

"Did she say anything?"

"No."

"This policeman, was he rough with her?"

"No, not at all," Sophie replied, thinking that, if anything, she had been more aggressive than Neumann. "He did nothing, said nothing that might have upset her. It was all down to the ring."

"It has a letter W on it, you say?"

"Yes. White on a blue enamel background. Does that mean anything to you?"

"No. Where is Amalie now?"

"Sleeping. But I dread to think what state she'll be in when she wakes."

"I will give you something to calm her. You look cold, child. Stay there by the fire."

Gisela levered herself up from her chair and shuffled

over to the table where she got out her measuring spoons and her powders and herbs and mixed a bottle of sleeping draught and a smaller vial of sedative.

"Put three drops of this in water," she instructed. "It will mollify her, ease her fears. And what about you?"

"Me?" Sophie said. "There's nothing wrong with me."

She slipped the bottles into the inside pocket of her cloak and thanked Gisela, then left the hut. Gisela watched the door close behind her. The freiin was a good woman, but perhaps she was not always as strong as she liked to think. Gisela often sensed a loneliness in her and today she'd detected a trace of turmoil inside her that she was sure wasn't entirely caused by Amalie.

This ring puzzled her. How could something so apparently innocuous have aroused such a violent reaction in the maid, a young woman already so troubled by her memories? Gisela went to the shelf and took down her bag of runesticks, then spread out the white cloth on the table. Concentrating hard on the ring and the letter W, she cast the sticks out across the cloth and examined the pattern they formed. Most had landed upside down, the marks on them hidden from sight. But three were the right way up, spaced in a triangle so perfect she might have arranged it that way deliberately. All three were the *purisaz*, the sign of the Devil. Gisela shuddered, an icy hand touching the back of her neck. Rarely had she seen such a clear portent of evil.

She gathered in the sticks and cleared her thoughts, blanking out the ring and focusing instead on the freiin. The pattern was vaguer this time, much harder to interpret, but she thought she could see a glimmering of the future, of an omen that startled her but whose meaning was still slightly unformed, uncertain. She would say nothing of it to Sophie, of course. Sometimes it was better not to know your fate.

*

It was unusual for her to feel nervous in the forest. Sophie looked around her, sensing something watching her, though she could neither see nor hear anything in the waning light. She increased her pace, glancing behind her, peering into the trees on either side of the path. Whatever was there, it moved silently, like an apparition.

But she didn't believe in ghosts. She believed in the tangible, in the real. The imagination might conjure up demons, but not hers. There is nothing there, she told herself, nothing to worry about. But then she heard the faint snap of a twig and her head spun round, seeing a shape in the undergrowth. Or was it just a shadow? Stay calm, she thought. She was on edge, but she felt no danger, no real fear.

She accelerated, half jogging now, her gaze fixed on the path in front of her, then suddenly she burst out of the forest onto the fringes of the garden. She turned and looked back. And saw the eyes glinting in the trees like opals. A wolf. Sophie relaxed a little. The shape had taken on a definite form, one that didn't frighten her. She'd seen wolves before, knew they were seldom a threat, particularly on their own. And this one seemed to be alone. Her eyes grew accustomed to the gloom and she could see a distinctive white blaze on the creature's forehead. It was too dark to make out any more details, but she sensed it was a female. The wolf edged forward and she could see how thin she was, how her ribcage showed through the fur on her flanks. Sophie stared at her for a moment. Some indefinable sensation passed between the two of them, some kind of symbiotic communication, and Sophie knew instinctively what she needed to do.

Scooping up her cloak, she ran across the garden to the house and into the kitchen. There were some scraps of meat in the pantry. Sophie wrapped them up in a cloth and retraced her steps back to the edge of the garden.

The eyes were still there in the undergrowth, luminescent in the twilight. Sophie shovelled away a patch of snow with her boot and placed the meat on the exposed ground.

Then she backed away – twenty, thirty metres – and stopped. A minute passed, then two. Slowly, the wolf emerged from the trees. She was wary, her skinny frame poised to flee if necessary. But she smelt no danger. Her snout came up. The blaze gleamed bright white on her grizzled fur and her eyes locked onto Sophie's, as if they understood each other. Then she snatched up the meat in one mouthful, turned, and vanished into the darkness of the forest.

THIRTEEN

Neumann rode slowly back to Füssen, deep in thought. It was almost dark now, but the moon was breaking through the cloud cover, casting a sheen of silvery light over the snowy ground so he had no trouble seeing the road.

He was agitated. The incident with the maid, Amalie, had disturbed him – not just because of her extreme reaction to the ring, but because of what it might mean for his own investigation. He could feel that small, seemingly harmless piece of jewellery in his tunic pocket and was struck suddenly by the irrational urge to pull it out and cast it away into the furthest reaches of the forest. He didn't want it on his person, contaminating his clothes with... what? What was it about the ring that had so terrified Amalie? What was it that made him anxious to be rid of it? It was just gold and enamel, after all. He wasn't prone to superstition, but something instinctive, almost atavistic, inside him warned him to be wary of it. Not the object itself, perhaps, but of what it signified. And what was that? What import did it have on the murder of Christoph Geissler?

Crossing the bridge over the Lech, he rode up the hill into the town and bypassed the entrance to Brotmarkt to make a detour to the police station. Captain Beck had left for the day, but the constable, Lehmann, was on duty behind the desk. Neumann asked him to check if there had been any recent reports of missing young women, particularly anyone named Amalie. Lehmann examined the logbook they kept under the counter and shook his head. Nothing. Check further afield, Neumann ordered. Telegraph neighbouring police districts to see if they'd had any reports. Then he climbed back on his horse and returned to the Gasthaus Hoffmann.

"A soldier from the barracks came a while ago," Johanna told him. "Left you a message."

Neumann took the sealed note and waited until he was in the privacy of his room before he opened it. It was from Lukas Hafner.

"If you're free this evening, come to the mess. We dine at eight."

Why not? Neumann thought. I could do with a change from the Gasthaus's limited menu and what better company than an old army friend, particularly one as lively and gregarious as Hafner? He checked his watch. He had plenty of time before eight so he pulled off his boots and sat down in the armchair for a short rest. Immediately, he felt the bulge of the ring in his pocket. He took it out and examined it in the light from the gaslamp on the wall. Why had it affected him so badly earlier? he wondered. It was only a ring, not even a very valuable one. Now some time had elapsed since his visit to Waldblick, he could look at it more dispassionately, divorced from all the emotions it had aroused.

What on earth was I doing? he thought. Letting Amalie's reaction influence me. I'm a police officer. Cool, objective, clear-headed. Items of jewellery shouldn't cloud my judgement. He could see the ring now for what it was – a simple piece of embossed metal – but, nevertheless, he didn't put it back in his tunic. He stowed it safely away in the drawer of the desk, locked the drawer and put the key in his pocket – annoyed with himself because the process gave him a definite, but illogical, feeling of relief.

Shortly after he heard the bells of Saint Magnus strike seven, he washed his face and hands in the bowl on the washstand, then went out to the stables next to the inn, saddled his horse and headed across the town. The barracks were a few hundred metres beyond the northern edge of Füssen – the old defensive wall in this section of the perimeter long gone. Functional, ugly wooden buildings, they'd been thrown up on the cheap in an area that only a few years ago had been fields and was still mainly agricultural. The soldiers' parade ground was rimmed with market gardens and smallholdings that in summer were knee-deep in potatoes and cabbage.

The guards on the main gate took Neumann's name and sent word to the commanding officer's quarters and, shortly afterwards, Hafner himself came out to greet him.

"Reinhardt, this is a real pleasure!" he said effusively, shaking Neumann's hand.

He gave orders for the major's horse to be taken care of, then led the way across the yard. The barracks weren't big by military standards: just a modest two-storey block housing the administration offices and armoury and a few long, single-storey dormitories for the soldiers and officers. The snow had been cleared from most of the open spaces, but patches still remained in shadowy corners. Wind gusted along the narrow corridors between the buildings, the grim, institutional bleakness of the site reminding Neumann why he didn't miss the army.

"It's not exactly luxurious," Hafner remarked dryly. "But it's all we have to call home."

"How many men have you here?" Neumann asked.

"Just a couple of hundred. Split between Füssen and Hohenschwangau, where we have a bunkhouse and canteen for the men on duty there. There are more in

Munich, of course, but most of our work is down here now that the king has taken against the city."

"He doesn't like Munich?"

"Hates it. Too many people, too much noise, too many politicians. Time was we'd spend the winter in Munich and only come to Füssen in summer, but that's all changed. His Majesty shuts himself away now, rarely goes out, sees only a few ministers and those as infrequently as he can. Makes our job a lot simpler. We only have to guard him at Hohenschwangau and the new palace. And, occasionally, Linderhof, his residence over near Oberammergau."

Hafner pulled open a door and they went through into the officers' mess where a soldier took Neumann's coat, then showed them to a table in a small, private room off the main dining hall.

"I'll introduce you to the officers later," Hafner said. "But I thought we'd dine alone. We've a lot to catch up on."

The table was set with starched white linen and silver cutlery and crystal glasses, evidence, Neumann noted wryly, that the depressing austerity of the buildings didn't extend to every aspect of the barracks, at least as far as the commanding officer was concerned. Champagne was uncorked and Hafner proposed a toast to his guest.

"Your health, Reinhardt. It's good to see you after all these years."

"You too, Lukas. You've barely changed since I last saw you."

It was a compliment, but there was a lot of truth in it. Hafner had retained much of the clear, fresh-faced look of his youth, when the two men had first met, Neumann a lieutenant in the Prussian XI Corps, Hafner the same rank in the Bavarian II Corps. His waist had thickened a little, his jowls lost some of their firmness, but he was wearing his thirty-eight years well.

"Where do we start?" Hafner asked, smiling affectionately at Neumann.

"With you. How are you?"

"I'm well."

"Your own command now. That must feel good."

"It does, I admit."

"Is Charlotte with you?"

Hafner shook his head. "Alas, no. I have married quarters here – she visits regularly – but she prefers to stay mostly in Munich. The children, you know. It disrupts them, their education, to come down here too often."

"How many do you have now?"

"Five."

"*Five*? You *have* been busy."

"Well, as domestic duties go, it's one of the best," Hafner said and Neumann laughed.

The CO drank some of his champagne and his face took on a more serious look.

"I'm sorry about your wife. And your baby. You have my sincere condolences."

"You heard?"

"Not till a long time afterwards. That's why I didn't write. It seemed, I don't know, insensitive. As if I would just be reviving painful emotions that you were trying to forget."

You never forget them, Neumann thought, but he didn't want to dwell on the subject so he said, "I'm over it now," knowing that he would never be over it. He saw Hafner's sceptical glance and added, "Well, as much as you can be. Time heals and all that."

"Of course." Hafner nodded, not fooled by the remark. He turned his head, hearing the door click open. Both of them were relieved to see a soldier come in with their starters – two bowls of steaming goulash soup, the cue to talk of other things.

Of Füssen, of Munich, of Berlin and, inevitably, the war, the event that had brought them together and done so much to shape their development as young, inexperienced soldiers. One a Prussian, the other a Bavarian, countries which only four years earlier had been on opposite sides in the Austrian War, but were now allies in the conflict against France.

The whole thing had been a shambles from the start, the war deliberately provoked by Bismarck to unite the German nations against a common external foe – but cunningly, so it was the French who first mobilised, allowing Prussia to play the innocent victim.

That the Germans had eventually triumphed was a miracle considering the quality of their senior officers. Von Steinmetz commanding the First Army in the north, the seventy-four-year-old hero of the '66 war who ran his own private campaign, disobeying orders and making the kind of reckless decisions that would have got a junior officer court-martialled and shot, but in a distinguished general were regarded as merely eccentric. The Prussian king's nephew, the headstrong Prince Frederick Charles, in charge of the Second Army in the centre who sent the IX Corps to its destruction at St. Privat-la-Montagne, eight thousand officers and men slaughtered in barely twenty minutes. Then the Third Army in the south under the crown prince, Frederick William, with his two Prussian corps outnumbered by Bavarians, Württemburgers and Badeners whom he regarded as incompetent and untrustworthy until their valour on the battlefield proved him wrong. And tagging along, playing at soldiers, the ludicrous figure of Bismarck himself with his self-awarded rank of major-general and his spiked helmet and thigh-high cavalry boots – a joke, but a dangerous one, to the military in whose affairs he liked to meddle.

It was at Wörth, on the Sauer River in Alsace, that

Neumann and Hafner had first encountered each other, Hafner's Bavarian regiment pinned down by heavy French fire until Neumann's XI Corps came to their aid, the artillery bombarding the enemy positions before the infantry swept in to finish the job. But at a high cost. Ten and a half thousand Germans killed or wounded, even more on the French side. Liaising between their respective units, Neumann and Hafner had become staunch allies, their friendship strengthened as they moved on to the victory at Sedan, the Third Army marching fifty miles in three days through the treacherous lanes of the Argonne forest before routing the French and capturing their emperor, Napoleon III.

"Happy days," Hafner said, with just a hint of sarcasm. "I can't think why you left. No, seriously, why did you?"

Neumann shrugged. After what they'd just been discussing, did his decision really need an explanation? Was there anything about being a soldier that was honourable, that was worthwhile? To kill or to be killed – were those worthy ambitions for a man? But there'd been other factors at play by then. He was married and Kristina had begged him repeatedly to change career. She hated the army, the prospect that she might lose him in some conflict. Ironic, really, considering it was he who'd lost her. But he'd been ready for a change himself, disillusioned with military life. It was bad enough in war, but what was the point of it in peacetime? The regimental dinners, the parading, the drilling, it all seemed so futile. But he couldn't say that to Hafner. It seemed insulting to a friend for whom those rituals were still an important part of his life. So he framed it instead as a matter of thwarted ambition, a male preoccupation that Hafner would understand.

"I was going nowhere," he said. "Stuck at captain with no real prospect of promotion. Every time a majority came up, I was overlooked. Then I heard that von Richthofen, the Berlin police commissioner, was looking for new blood. For senior people to come in and help clean up the force, to eradicate the waste and corruption. And he was looking particularly for men with a military background. Well, it seemed an ideal opportunity to do something different."

"But *police* work?" Hafner said, unable to conceal his distaste. "Isn't it all rather..." He searched for a word that wasn't too derogatory. "Mundane?"

Neumann wasn't going to be defensive. He wasn't going to be a victim of the snobbery, the condescension, that was an integral part of the army mindset.

"Not at all. It's interesting, varied, challenging and very rewarding. I feel I'm doing something useful." Unlike in the army, he didn't say. The pawns in the manoeuvrings of so-called "great men", the impotent dupes whose loyalty was rewarded with either worthless ribbons and medals or a bloody death.

More food arrived, brought in by two soldiers trained in the fine military art of silver service who dished it up with well-honed efficiency and then quietly left, having also opened and poured a bottle of red wine – a "rather interesting claret" as Hafner described it, liberated from the French during the Siege of Paris in 1870.

"The cook likes a chance to show off occasionally," the CO explained. "These are two of Bavaria's most celebrated specialities – *Schweinshaxen*, roast knuckle of pork with potato dumplings and sauerkraut, and *Käsespätzle*, noodles mixed with spicy Allgäu cheese and topped with fried onions. *Bon appetit!*"

They ate and drank – the bottle of wine disappearing so rapidly that Hafner had to summon reinforcements – and soon the talk got around to Neumann's investigation.

"A messy business," Hafner said, shaking his head. "I don't envy you."

"Messy in what way?" Neumann asked.

"Well, it's not just an ordinary murder, is it? If there's such a thing. This one has political dimensions. A Prussian diplomat killed in Bavaria. You could be opening a nasty can of worms."

Neumann ate some more of his *Käsespätzle*. The noodles were tasty, but heavy on the stomach. He was reaching the limit of his appetite, but he didn't want to offend Hafner by leaving anything on his plate.

"Why do you say that? Have you heard something?"

"No, not at all. If I had, I'd tell you. But it won't be news to you that Prussia isn't exactly popular in these parts. People have long memories. They haven't forgotten the Austrian War. They haven't forgotten the way their independence was taken away, the way they've been subsumed into an empire in which they are very much a junior partner."

"You think this was a political killing?"

"I don't know what it was. But there are certainly factions here that would shed no tears for a dead Prussian. I'm sorry, that sounds terribly harsh, but I'm being honest with you."

"I appreciate it, Lukas. Have you come across any of these 'factions'?"

"Have you heard of the Bavarian Freedom Party?"

"I saw something about them in the local paper. A rally in Munich."

"That's them. They've been around for a few years, used to be a fringe group of nutcases and cranks, but they're becoming more mainstream now, attracting more followers. They're vocal, well-funded. They could be dangerous."

"Violent?"

"Certainly, if necessary. Their aim is independence for Bavaria, with Ludwig as ruler. God help us if that ever came to pass."

"Do I sense a lack of enthusiasm for your king?"

Hafner guffawed. "Well, let's just say he's difficult. He doesn't make our task of protecting him straightforward. He keeps strange hours, for a start. Has his breakfast at six in the evening, his dinner at midnight and his supper at eight in the morning, then goes to bed. His moods swing unpredictably, too, veering from the kind and solicitous to the downright medieval."

"Really?"

"One occasion, we were at Nymphenburg and he came out for a walk in the grounds and thought one of the guards on duty was looking a little tired, so he ordered a sofa to be brought out from a salon so the poor fellow could have a lie down. Another time, he discovered it was a soldier's birthday and he showered him with gifts – wines, cigars, an enormous cake. At Linderhof, he once invited his favourite mare to dinner and had her served a six-course meal on the best Sèvres porcelain which the animal cleared then proceeded to smash with her hooves. Yet sometimes he can go the other way. Have violent tantrums when he screams and throws things and orders that the soldier, or servant, who's offended him should be flogged or even executed."

Neumann stared at him in astonishment. "Which you surely don't carry out?"

"Of course not. We just ignore him and take the soldier off duty for a couple of days, by which time His Majesty has forgotten whatever it was that upset him."

Hafner poured the last of the wine and held up the bottle. "Another?"

"Not for me, thanks."

"You liked it?"

"It was very good."

"What were the French reparations after the war? Five billion francs, Alsace-Lorraine, Strasbourg and Metz ceded to us? Plus a few hundred thousand bottles of wine that somehow found their way to Berlin and Munich. What it is to be the victor."

Hafner rang a bell and the dessert course was brought in. Nothing too substantial, Neumann was glad to see. Just *marillen*, an apricot cake topped with crumble, and vanilla ice cream. Accompanying it was a bottle of sweet Provençal wine, another trophy of the Siege that Neumann remembered as a time of intense privation – for the German soldiers encircling Paris, but particularly for the starving residents of the city who were forced to eat rats, cats, dogs and anything else with four legs bar their dining tables. Even the two famous elephants in the zoo, Castor and Pollux, ended up as steaks medium rare.

"The other day, when I met you at New Hohenschwangau," Hafner said. "What were you doing there?"

"Meeting the king."

Hafner glanced up sharply from his dessert, surprised. "You were honoured. He meets almost nobody. Even the cabinet ministers struggle to see him."

"He was interested in the Geissler case. Did they know each other?"

"I suppose they may have met," Hafner conceded. "Geissler was with the German legation, after all. But 'know', that's a stretch."

"Did Geissler ever go to the palace?"

"I don't know. I'm not over there all the time."

"You know what I mean, Lukas. Your men keep a log of everyone who visits, don't they? Could you check it for me?"

"Is this an official request? If it is, it will have to go through the proper channels."

"Can we keep it informal for now?"

Hafner hesitated for a moment, then nodded. "I'll see what I can do."

"Thank you."

They ate their *marillen* in silence for a while. Neumann's head was clouded by alcohol, his stomach so full he was starting to feel nauseous. He'd forgotten how indulgent mess dinners were. He took a sip of water.

"The king isn't married, is he?" he said.

Hafner knew this wasn't a casual question. He understood the unspoken subtext, but took his time answering.

"There *are* rumours about his... private life."

"What kind of rumours?"

"Not flattering."

"Are they true?"

Hafner took a sip of wine and looked at Neumann over his glass.

"Where is this going, Reinhardt?"

"Wherever it takes me."

"You think Geissler...?"

"I'm exploring all avenues."

"Maybe the king was, too." Hafner gave a coarse chuckle, then put his inhibitions aside and opened up more. "They say he's close to some of his servants, though there's no evidence of any impropriety. There's also been talk in the past about troopers being invited to his rooms. You know the cavalry – anything for king and country."

They both laughed, then Hafner suddenly turned more serious, as if he regretted his indiscretion.

"I think it's best if I don't say any more." He drained his glass and pushed back his chair. "Let's go and meet my officers."

FOURTEEN

There were four of them around the table playing *Siebzehn und Vier*: Count Walther Ehrenbeck zu Freudenberg, Baron Friedrich von Breckendorf, Baron Leopold von Sturm and Ritter Albrecht von Mühlbeck. All of them were ministers in the Bavarian government and all were unwinding after another challenging meeting with the king – this one, fortunately, not in the bleak environs of New Hohenschwangau but in the more congenial setting of the old palace where there were a few luxuries, like heating, and no workmen hammering away outside the windows.

Not that this had stopped the main focus of the king's attention being the building work up the hill. He'd set up a telescope in one of the rooms, the lens directed at the site, and every few minutes he would break off and leave the meeting to check on progress, despatching a messenger each time to the foreman of works, exhorting him and his team to greater efforts on pain of dismissal, or worse.

Even when he was actually present in the cabinet discussions, his mind was still on his construction projects. Once again, he was advocating breaking treaties with the rest of Germany in order to retain more money in the Bavarian treasury for his fantastic palaces. Another five million marks for New Hohenschwangau, another ten million for Herrenchiemsee and even more for a new site he'd found at Falkenstein, in the mountains to the west, where he planned to erect yet another monstrous edifice. A theatre designer was already at work on plans so lavish they would make the king's other palaces look like dog kennels.

"He's going to bankrupt the state if we're not careful," von Sturm said.

Von Mühlbeck checked his cards. "Not if we don't give him the money."

"He spends it, anyway, just runs up massive personal debts that, in the end, the state will have to settle. We'll have no choice, and His Majesty knows that."

"Your call, Leopold," zu Freudenberg said.

Von Sturm lifted the corner of the card he'd just been dealt and saw that it was a nine of acorns.

"Buy," he said.

Zu Freudenberg dealt him a second card.

"I've had letters from eight tradesmen in the last month, all working on Herrenchiemsee, all wanting to know when they're going to be paid," he said. "Friedrich?"

"Buy," said von Breckendorf.

"Bills amounting to more than two hundred thousand marks. Albrecht?"

"Buy."

Zu Freudenberg dealt more cards, then they went through another round. Von Mühlbeck and von Sturm went bust, von Breckendorf stuck on twenty. Zu Freudenberg turned over his three cards – an ace, a nine and an *ober* that scored one, making a total of twenty-one. He raked in the stakes and passed the role of banker to von Mühlbeck.

"I don't suppose we can look to Berlin for help," the ritter said.

"Spiritual, or financial?" zu Freudenberg asked dryly.

"I don't think Bismarck does the former, and as for the latter, well, he might consider it but he'd exact an onerous price for his assistance. Do we really want to deliver Bavaria even deeper into the clutches of the Prussians?"

Von Mühlbeck dealt the cards and they made their bets. Von Breckendorf threw in the last of his chips and topped up his glass from the bottle of brandy in the corner of the table. The lounge of the club was crowded – ministers, both senior and junior, government officials, a handful of retired politicians who still clung to the fringes of power for the gossip and the perks. A few others were also playing cards, but most were chatting and enjoying a post-dinner cigar and brandy.

Von Mühlbeck dealt another round. Zu Freudenberg stuck on two cards, von Sturm took a third and went bust. Von Breckendorf had a ten and an eight in his hand. Rashly, he bought a third card and drew a seven – bust! Zu Freudenberg revealed his cards: a ten and an ace – twenty-one. Von Mühlbeck showed his: a nine and an eight. He considered sticking, but took a chance and drew a third card – another eight – and went bust. Zu Freudenberg collected in all their stakes. Von Breckendorf scowled at him. The count had the devil's own luck. He must have won at least twenty thousand marks this evening, most of it from von Breckendorf.

"Von Auerswald is getting anxious," zu Freudenberg said, arranging his chips into neat little piles in front of him.

Is he rubbing it in? von Breckendorf thought angrily. Flaunting his winnings. How can he win so consistently? He must be cheating.

"Anxious in what way?" von Sturm asked.

"He's heard rumours. About the king wanting to renege on our commitments to Berlin."

"That's not going to happen. He must know that."

"And the Bavarian Freedom Party is making him nervous. He wants us to ban it."

"That would only bring them more support."

"That's what I told him. They're getting bolder, more outspoken. The last thing we want is the king getting ideas of changing the constitution and acquiring more powers."

"Would the people back that?" von Mühlbeck asked.

"Well, the ones he doesn't owe money to," von Sturm interjected and they all laughed. All except von Breckendorf, who was downing his glass of cognac and topping it up with more.

"Are we going to play?" he demanded. His eyes were slightly bloodshot, his voice slurring a little.

"Maybe we should call it a night?" zu Freudenberg suggested.

"Now you've cleaned me out, you mean? I want a chance to win some of it back. Deal the cards, Leopold."

"Are you sure that's wise?"

"I'll decide what's wise. Deal the damn cards."

The others looked at one another and shrugged.

"If that's what you want."

"It is. My luck's got to turn some time."

Von Sturm glanced at the count and the ritter. They'd all heard that remark before and could see it for the wishful thinking it was. Von Breckendorf's luck might indeed change, but even if it did, he never knew when to stop. He never knew when a winning streak was suddenly going to turn back into a losing one.

Von Sturm dealt the cards. Zu Freudenberg took a suck on his cigar and turned his head to blow the smoke away from the table. Von Breckendorf signalled to a waiter to bring them another bottle of brandy. He was settling in for a long evening. The fifteen thousand he'd already lost was just a blip. Give him time and he'd soon win it all back.

"He's asked me – von Auerswald, that is," zu Freudenberg went on, "Whether the king is in need of medical attention. Just an informal enquiry, of course. Nothing official."

"Medical attention?" von Mühlbeck asked.

"A psychiatric evaluation."

"Good God! Is he serious?"

"That's hard to tell. He might just be playing games, trying to unsettle us, put doubts into our minds. But His Majesty *is* becoming, well, more erratic, more unreasoning. We've all seen that."

"But mad?" von Sturm said. "We're getting onto very dangerous ground here."

"Look at his uncontrolled spending, his tantrums."

"Uncontrolled spending isn't necessarily an indication of insanity," von Mühlbeck said. "Or my wife would have been locked up years ago. And the tantrums, that's just the royal prerogative, isn't it? Normal for a king."

"Maybe," zu Freudenberg said. "But look at his brother."

Otto, three years younger than Ludwig, who had been certified insane in his twenties and kept in secure confinement ever since.

"You think he's going the same way?"

"All I'm saying is we need to be vigilant. Bear in mind that if things continue the way they are, or get worse, we may need to think about some kind of medical assessment."

Von Breckendorf tore a page from his pocket book and scribbled an IOU on it for five thousand marks. Then he tossed it impatiently into the middle of the table.

"Buy!" he said.

Anneliese woke with a start and rolled over in bed, listening. She was a light sleeper. Even slight noises in the night disturbed her. And the house – *her* house, inherited from her father – was big and echoey, every sound amplified by the stone walls and high-vaulted spaces.

She could hear noises downstairs in the hall – footsteps, two voices, one louder than the other – and could piece together what was happening from long experience. Friedrich coming home from his club, so drunk he could barely walk. His manservant, Helmut, waiting up for him, dozing on a chair by the front door, helping his master inside, then removing his coat and hat, his voice soft and deferential in contrast to Friedrich's sharper, more aggressive tones.

Then she heard them coming upstairs and could picture the scene. Helmut – fortunately, a strapping young man of twenty-eight – half supporting, half carrying the baron up to the first floor, Friedrich complaining and whingeing all the time, his words just an incoherent ramble. They went past the door to her room and paused for a second. Anneliese stiffened. For one horrific moment, she thought her husband might knock and demand entry, might attempt to take her even though his inebriation usually made him incapable of anything more than a clumsy fumble. But then, to her relief, they moved on along the landing to Friedrich's own bedroom.

How could I have thought otherwise? she wondered. It was a long time since her husband, drunk or sober, had come to her at night. It was a long time since there'd been any affection, let alone desire, in their marriage. The attentive lover the baron had once been had vanished into the arms of other women and the brandy and gaming tables of his clubs.

A door clicked open. Feet scuffed on a wooden floor. Friedrich's voice rose in anger, cursing his manservant for some unspecified transgression, then there was silence, Helmut no doubt laying his master out on the bed, not troubling to undress him, just covering him with a quilt and leaving him to sleep off his intoxication. The door clicked again, this time closing, and Anneliese heard Helmut padding away to his room in the attics.

She lay awake for a long time afterwards, wondering how much her husband had lost this evening.

Mess life, Neumann thought. It was supposedly an opportunity for army officers to bond and share experiences and insights that would make them better soldiers, that would make them better leaders. But all it really was was an excuse to over-eat and get drunk.

He'd stayed late at the barracks, drinking port and brandy with Hafner and his fellow officers. He'd tried to be sensible, to limit his intake, but he'd still absorbed far more alcohol than his system was used to. By midnight, when the officers finally turned in, he was unsteady on his legs, unsure whether he was fit enough to ride back to Füssen. Hafner offered him a bed for the night, but Neumann refused. He went outside and walked up and down a few times, letting the cold air clear his head. Then he retrieved his horse and headed slowly back to the Gasthaus Hoffmann.

Sleep came easily at first, but it was a troubled sleep. The conversation at the barracks, his reunion with Hafner, had brought back disturbing memories of the war. It had revived the nightmares that he had thought, had hoped, were a thing of the past. He'd had them badly in the immediate aftermath of the conflict, but they'd become less frequent after he'd married Kristina, her presence in bed beside him somehow soothing his mind as he slept. Following her death, they'd come back with a vengeance, then eased off in the years since. But tonight, they'd returned with vivid force. The noise of gunfire, the crash of artillery shells, the bodies sprawled over the blood-soaked battlefield and the recurring image of him leading his men towards the enemy positions and watching everyone around him dying, the trauma exacerbated by the feeling that he was responsible for it all. Those men died because of him.

It was a relief when he woke up, when he broke free of the nightmare. His pulse was racing, his head spinning. He stared around in the darkness, unable to work out where he was. Then he took in the faint light penetrating the curtains, the shapes of the furniture in the room, and calmed down. His breathing relaxed. He felt dizzy, but that was more the effect of the alcohol than the nightmare. He was hot. His stomach was overfull with pork knuckle and noodles and potato dumplings. He wondered whether he was going to be sick. Throwing back the covers, he sat up and sipped some water from the glass on the bedside table. He took a few deep breaths, then got out of bed and lit the oil lamp. The soft yellow glow reassured him, calmed him further.

He pulled back the curtains and opened the window to let in the cold night air. Outside in the square, a flickering gas lamp cast a garish light over the surrounding buildings, illuminating the mist that drifted up from the river and swathed the rooftops in its pale, damp embrace. He inhaled, letting the fresh air drive away his nausea, then, after a while, when his body began to cool, he closed the window and returned to the warmth of the bed.

He was tired, but he didn't want to go back to the darkness of sleep, to the demons that lurked in his dreams, so he gazed around the room, wondering how he could keep himself awake. There was the book on the desk – *From Asgard to Ragnarök* – that Norbert Ziegler had given him. It was thick and intimidating and would no doubt be a difficult read, but there was nothing else to distract him.

Getting out of bed again, he picked up the book,

weighing it in his hands for a moment, as if gauging its contents, before he slipped back beneath the covers and made himself comfortable on the pillows. The chapter headings didn't exactly encourage him to dip deeper into the book: *The Aesir and the Vanir*; *The Norns and Yggdrasill*; *Ginnungagap, Audumla and the Creation of the World*; *Freyja and the Necklace of the Brisings*. It all looked incredibly tedious, and probably pompous and self-important too, if Ziegler's writing was anything like his speech.

Neumann leafed idly through the pages and something caught his eye – a section entitled, *Valhalla and the Heroic Warriors*. That struck a chord with him. Isn't that me? he thought. A heroic warrior. Isn't that how the soldiers who returned from the war were described by the gushing German press? By the politicians who hadn't been there but wanted to appropriate the courage of others to burnish their own reputations. Neumann hadn't felt heroic. He'd felt angry and misled and exploited. Guilty and inadequate and ashamed by the senseless carnage. Was that heroic? Let's see what Norse mythology tells us, he thought, and began to read.

The realm of the gods, the home of Odin, Thor, Frigg and the others, Ziegler had written, was Asgard, a mighty citadel encircled by high walls that had been built by a giant. Within those walls lay Valhalla, a vast hall with five hundred doors and a ceiling lined with golden shields that housed the Einheriar, warriors who had been slain on the battlefield and brought to Asgard by the Valkyries, the ferocious shield-maidens who chose the heroes deserving of an afterlife with the gods.

And what an afterlife it was. The Einheriar started each day with a battle, fighting each other to the death. Then in the evening, they were brought back to life and celebrated with copious draughts of mead and feasting on the roast flesh of the boar, Sährimnir, an unfortunate creature who was resurrected each night so he could be eaten again next day after yet another battle. Neumann read the description of these events and was sickened by them. It seemed obscene to him, this worshipping of the warrior who wanted only to kill his fellow man, to revel in slaughter. He'd seen the battlefield and knew there was no honour in it, no glory. The Einheriar, to him, were not heroes, they were brutal psychopaths. And as for their home, Valhalla seemed a dark, grim place because there were no women there and thus no love. Only men indulging their taste for violence.

He flicked through another few pages and saw the story of Baldur that Ziegler had recounted to him. Refreshing his memory, he read it, thinking of Christoph Geissler, of how little progress he was making in his search for the man who'd killed him. And then his thoughts turned to his dead wife and daughter. In the Norse tale, the gods sent out messengers to ask the whole world to weep so Baldur could come back from Hel. Neumann had wept for Kristina and Julia, but all his tears had not brought them back.

FIFTEEN

The knock on the door woke him. Neumann came round slowly from a deep sleep, thinking the noise was inside his head, just part of a dream. Then it came again, louder, more insistent. A hammering rather than a knock now. He rolled over and sat up.

"Yes?" he called.

The door opened and Constable Lehmann walked in.

"Sir."

Neumann squinted at him, still half asleep.

"What is it?"

"There's been another murder. The jeweller, Werner Graf."

That jolted Neumann, cleared his fuzzy head immediately.

"*What*? Graf? Where?"

"In his workshop. His apprentice found him there dead this morning."

Neumann checked his watch. It was ten-past eight. What would Lehmann think of him, still in bed at this hour?

"Wait for me downstairs," he said. "I'll be right there."

He threw on his clothes and splashed cold water on his face from the jug on the washstand. No time to shave. Then he glanced at himself in the mirror. He looked the way he felt: a man with a stinking great hangover.

It was another freezing day outside. The wind howled through the narrow streets of the town, the gusts strong enough to knock an unwary pedestrian off balance. As they walked, Neumann probed Lehman for more information. The apprentice, Bruno Roth, had come in to work as usual at half-past seven and found Graf slumped over his workbench, his head in a puddle of blood. It appeared that the jeweller's throat had been cut.

"Who's there now?" Neumann asked.

"Everyone," Lehmann replied with almost gleeful enthusiasm. Something as exciting as this, no one wanted to be left out. "Captain Beck, Sergeant Krause, the apprentice, of course. Doctor Busch has been sent for. He might be there, too, by now."

The entrance to the alley off Brunengasse was half blocked by curious locals, drawn to the location by the police activity. Neumann ordered Lehmann to disperse them, on pain of arrest for obstruction, and headed through to the jeweller's premises. The front door was wide open, the retail part of the business deserted. Neumann looked around, automatically observing and noting the details of the scene: no sign of forced entry on the door, the glass display cases all intact, the jewellery inside them apparently undisturbed.

He went through into the rear workshop where Beck, Krause and Roth were waiting. The police officers were seated on stools and made no effort to stand up or look busy when Neumann entered. The apprentice was standing to one side, his eyes averted from his dead master.

Lehmann hadn't been exaggerating. Werner Graf's head *was* lying in a pool of blood on his workbench. It was twisted to one side, his left cheek resting on the wooden surface, his right eye staring lifelessly out across the room. Close by, on the worktop, was a bone-handled hunting knife with a long blade that was rust-red with dried blood.

Neumann gazed at the dead man and the knife for a few seconds. From the pallor of Graf's face and the condition of the blood, he estimated he must have been dead for several hours. Then he noticed another shape further along the worktop: a strange black object that resembled a crumpled umbrella. He took a closer look and recoiled in surprise. It wasn't an umbrella, it was a bird. A dead raven.

"What the devil is this?" he asked.

Beck shrugged. "Puzzled us, too."

"A raven?"

"Looks like it."

Neumann turned to the apprentice. "Does this mean anything to you?"

Roth shook his head. "Nothing, sir. It was there when I came in."

"Have you touched anything?"

"No, sir. I just came in and... saw...saw the master there, then went straight to the police station."

"Was the front door open when you arrived?"

"Yes, sir."

"Was that usual?"

"No, sir. Herr Graf usually arrives before me and locks the door behind him. For security, you know. I have to knock for him to let me in."

The apprentice was a callow youth of about sixteen or seventeen, his cheeks pink and spattered with acne. There was a tremor in his voice and he was gripping his hands together to prevent them shaking. He was clearly upset by his master's death, unable to look at the body by the workbench. Was he involved in this in some way? Neumann wondered. Consider everyone a potential suspect until proven otherwise. But he didn't think it likely. The boy didn't appear to be faking his distress, and he didn't look like someone with the stomach to cut a man's throat.

A figure came in through the door from the shop. Tall, thin, a black medical bag dangling from a bony hand. He peered around, his eyes dark sockets in his cadaverous face. His gaze lingered enquiringly on Neumann for a second before it moved on to someone he recognised.

"Ah, Beck. You sent for me."

The captain didn't bother to explain, just jerked his head towards Graf's body, which the doctor appeared not to have noticed. Busch turned and gazed at the corpse with phlegmatic indifference. He put his bag down on the worktop and opened it to pull on a pair of rubber gloves.

"Let's go next door," Neumann said to the apprentice. The boy was looking pale and sickly. Having to witness the medical examination of his master was not going to be pleasant for him.

Neumann waited until they were in the shop, the door to the workshop pulled to, before he resumed his questioning.

"How long have you worked here?"

"About two years, sir."

"Was Herr Graf a good master?"

Roth's hesitation told him all he needed to know, but the boy wasn't about to be disloyal, not with the jeweller lying dead just a few metres away.

"Yes, sir, he was good to me."

"You want to be a jeweller and goldsmith yourself?"

"Yes, sir. I'm apprenticed until I'm twenty-one. *Was* apprenticed," he corrected himself. He swallowed and glanced uneasily towards the workshop. "I'm not going to... get into trouble over this, am I?"

"You did the right thing, going to the police," Neumann said. "When did you last see Herr Graf alive?"

"Yesterday evening."

"What time?"

"When I left for the day. Between six and seven o'clock."

"Herr Graf stayed on in the workshop?"

"Yes, sir."

"Was that something he always did?"

"Not always, sir. But fairly often he would work late."

"Do you know why he stayed on yesterday? Was he working on something in particular? Something that had to be finished? Was a client coming in to see him perhaps?"

"I don't know, sir."

"He had an appointments' book or a diary, I take it? Where he made a note of commissions and customers."

"Yes, sir. It's on the shelf in the workshop. Shall I get it?"

"Not now," Neumann replied. He looked around the shop. "You serve in here sometimes?" Roth nodded. "So you know the stock well. See if anything's missing since yesterday."

The apprentice leaned over the glass front of the counter and examined the jewellery laid out on velvet-lined trays inside. Then he moved on to the other display cases, checking each of them carefully.

"I can't see anything, sir. It all seems to be here."

"Who has the keys to these cases?"

"Herr Graf. He keeps them in his pocket."

Neumann made his own inspection of the cases. The locks hadn't been broken and there were no obvious gaps on the shelves. That seemed to rule out robbery as the motive for the murder. What about the front door? That was undamaged, too, so whoever the killer was, it looked as if Graf had let him in.

"Your master was a successful jeweller," Neumann said. "No doubt a wealthy man. Had he fallen out with anyone recently? Was there anyone who might have wanted to harm him?"

Roth screwed up his face, thinking hard for a moment, then he shook his head.

"Not that I know of, sir. His reputation was excellent, his work always very fine. We never had any customers who weren't completely happy with the jewellery they bought."

"That's all for the time being," Neumann said. "Stay here. You'll need to make a formal statement to one of the other police officers."

He returned to the workshop and introduced himself to the doctor, who had just finished his examination of Graf's body.

"What can you tell us?"

Busch pulled off his rubber gloves and stowed them away in his bag.

"Cause of death, pretty obvious," he replied laconically. "His throat was cut – with that." He nodded towards the knife on the worktop.

"Time?"

"From the state of the body, I'd say some time yesterday evening."

"Any other signs of violence?"

"A slashed throat not enough for you? No, nothing obvious. No other wounds or bruises that I can see. Of course, an autopsy will give you a fuller picture."

"Thank you, doctor."

Neumann waited for him to leave, then turned to Beck and Krause, both of them still sitting there like spectators at a theatre, rather than police officers with a role to play.

"Do we know who Graf's next-of-kin is?" he asked.

Beck shook his head. "Don't know anything about him."

"Well, perhaps we ought to find out."

"We were waiting for you, major." The same excuse, the same insolent smirk on his face that Neumann wanted to slap away. "Aren't you in charge of the Geissler case?"

"You think this is connected?"

Beck shrugged. "That's for you to decide, isn't it... sir?"

"Roth!" Neumann called.

The apprentice came cautiously back into the workshop.

"Was your master married?" Neumann asked him.

"No, sir."

"Any family?"

"I don't know. He never spoke of any."

"You know where he lived?"

"Yes, sir."

"Give the address to Sergeant Krause. Sergeant, go over there and make enquiries. Find out all you can about him. Captain Beck, the body needs to be moved to the morgue and an autopsy arranged. Then question the neighbours around here, find out if anyone saw or heard anything yesterday evening. And bag up the knife as evidence, see if we can identify where it came from."

"I think we can manage that," Beck said, sliding lazily off his stool and strolling out of the workshop.

Neumann walked over to the worktop. The doctor had moved Graf's body to examine his neck and chest, but then put it back in a slightly different position. The jeweller's head was now angled more towards the ceiling. To Neumann, it seemed as if Graf's eyes were gazing accusingly at him, saying, "If you hadn't dragged me into your Geissler investigation, this wouldn't have happened. I would still be alive."

Stepping round the body, Neumann took another look at the raven. It was a beautiful creature, its eyes bright and shining, its feathers glossy and iridescent, the black tinged with rainbow hues. Its neck appeared to have been snapped. But why had it been placed there? Was this another touch – like the mistletoe around the spear – that had some kind of symbolic meaning? But what?

Neumann didn't waste time on speculation. There

were more practical matters to be dealt with – like a thorough search of the crime scene. This was something he would normally have delegated to a junior officer, but none was available. Beck and Krause had left and Lehmann was nowhere to be seen. Besides, Neumann didn't trust any of them to do it properly.

He started with the body. Went through Graf's pockets and found a handkerchief, a bunch of keys and a wallet containing some business cards and two hundred marks. The worktop and floor were next. Neumann examined them closely, looking for anything that seemed unusual, anything that the killer might have accidentally left behind. There was nothing.

"Look around," he said to Roth. "Is there anything missing in here, anything that's out of place?"

The apprentice did as he was instructed, his eyes skirting rapidly over Graf's corpse.

"It all seems to be in order. No, wait a minute..." His gaze was fixed on the shelves on the far wall. "That's not right."

"What isn't?"

"The record books. They're out of order."

Neumann looked at the shelves, at the row of thick, identical black books he'd seen last time he was here. Each had a group of letters of the alphabet embossed in gold on the spine: A-C; D-F; G-I and so on. One of them – D-F – had been put back in the wrong place.

"Is that strange?" Neumann asked.

"Herr Graf was most particular about his record keeping," Roth replied. "He would never have done something like that."

Neumann took down the wayward volume and opened it. Clients' names were listed, along with information about the jewellery they'd bought or commissioned: the date, a description of the item and the price. He turned over the pages – and paused. Two of them had been torn out, leaving behind jagged edges of paper. The entry before was for a Herr Ebner, the one after Herr Emmerling. He showed it to Roth.

"Do you know which customer, or customers, are missing?"

"I'm sorry, sir. Herr Graf kept the records himself. He never allowed me to go near them."

"Can you think of anyone beginning with the letter 'E'?"

"Well, there's Herr Epstein. I know we've done work for him. And Herr Eulenburg."

Neumann checked the book. "It's not them. Their pages are still here."

"I can't think of anyone else."

Neumann put the volume to one side.

"Where's the appointments' book you mentioned?"

"This is it."

Roth lifted down a leather-bound tome and handed it to him. Inside, it was a diary, each page a separate day of the year. Neumann turned to the previous day. There was a ten o'clock appointment in the morning listed – a Herr Zimmerman – and one for three o'clock in the afternoon – a Frau Drechsler. There was nothing for the evening.

"Did anyone else visit the shop yesterday?"

"No, sir. Just those two."

Neumann replaced the diary on the shelf. The apprentice, summoning the nerve that had thus far evaded him, was gazing directly at Graf's body.

"What happens now, sir?" he asked anxiously. "To me, I mean. What happens to me? To my apprenticeship?"

"I don't know," Neumann replied. "Go to the police station. Tell them I sent you to make a statement about this morning. You understand?"

"Yes, sir."

"Don't worry. A young, fit lad like you, you'll find work somewhere else."

Neumann took the jeweller's keys and locked up the premises. Lehmann was still outside in the alley, keeping idle gawkers away from the scene. Neumann gave him the keys and told him to wait until someone came to take away the body. Then he went back to his room at the Gasthaus Hoffman and checked the index of Ziegler's book, finding an entry that read: "Ravens, Odin's two, 61" He turned to page sixty-one.

"Odin is the Allfather, the Allseer, but he cannot know everything that goes on in the nine worlds of the universe: in Asgard, Vanaheim, Alfheim, Midgard, Jotunheim, Nidavellir, Svartalfheim, Nifelheim and Hel. For that, he relies on his two ravens, Huginn – Thought – and Muninn – Memory. These two indefatigable birds are Odin's spies. Each morning, they fly out from Asgard and visit every corner of the universe in their search for information and news. They observe the world, eavesdrop on conversations, picking up intelligence, both important and trivial – for the gods, like humans, have a fondness for gossip. Then each evening, they return and perch on Odin's shoulders and whisper into his ears the news they have discovered. More than any other creatures, they know the secrets of the universe."

Neumann closed the book and stared pensively at the wall. The precise meaning of the dead raven left beside Graf's body was still not clear to him, but there were a few possible interpretations. The jeweller was a spy, he knew too much, he talked too much. However you looked at it, he had been murdered to silence him, to ensure that whatever secrets he harboured went with him to the grave.

SIXTEEN

The horsemen gathered on the shores of the Alpsee. The water was still frosted with ice, the peaks around the lake encrusted with snow that glistened in the bright morning sun. There were twelve men present, all wrapped in thick cloaks against the cold, all armed with hunting rifles and pistols. By the side of the lead rider, Count Ehrenbeck zu Freudenberg, two shaggy, muscular wolfhounds strained at their leashes, desperate to begin the day's business.

Wolves had been seen again on the outskirts of Schwangau. A bolder male had even been spotted creeping around the yard of one of the outlying farms. Livestock were at risk, the cows in the barns, the pigs in their sties. Something had to be done about it. When nature and money collided, there was only going to be one winner.

Goblets of wine were brought out from the inn and passed up to the riders, then zu Freudenberg made a toast to the hunt, his words echoed around the group as they lifted their goblets and downed the wine. There hadn't been an occasion like this for more than two years. There'd been no need. The wolves had stayed in the forest, restricted their movements to the wild, uninhabited regions along the foothills of the mountains. But now they'd strayed dangerously close to civilisation, the situation had changed. Man had to reassert his dominance.

The men were animated, cheeks flushed with excitement at the prospect of the chase. All were local gentry, many of them, like zu Freudenberg, also ministers in the government. They were tired of being cooped up in their homes and offices during the long winter. They were bored, looking forward to the fresh air, the camaraderie of the hunt and the thrill of a kill.

Friedrich von Breckendorf was there, and his gaming companions Leopold von Sturm and Albrecht von Mühlbeck. The opportunity for such sport was so enticing that they even had a guest from outside their normal circle. Prince Ernst Heinrich von Auerswald had joined them for the day, invited by zu Freudenberg and Rolf Bergmann, the Bavarian foreign minister, who was always keen to cement relations with Berlin. The prince was mounted on a tall black stallion, the skirts of his long riding coat draped over the sides of the horse, almost covering his saddle and the leather holster in which he kept his rifle. His face was pale, his duelling scars even more noticeable than usual. The other men treated him with the respect his rank merited, but tempered with a degree of wariness. He was an outsider, after all. A Prussian. They were honoured by his presence, but a little resentful that he was intruding on their recreation.

Zu Freudenberg checked that everyone was there, then gave the signal to move off. The riders headed away from the lake past Schloss Hohenschwangau, turning their gazes away from the foot of the road up to the new palace where a team of horses was struggling to pull a sled of stone blocks up the steep hill. The last thing they wanted to be reminded of, particularly on this day of leisure, was the king and his preposterous building projects.

They rode due north towards Schwangau, then northeast along the road to Bannwald See. They crossed the River Pöllat, but before they reached the lake, turned off across the snowy fields, onto land belonging to the von Wildenstein estate. Their pace was little more than an easy trot. They were saving their horses' energy for later, for when the wolfhounds picked up the scent. *If* they picked up a scent. Wolves were notoriously elusive, the forest deep and full of hiding places. But the hounds, Bergelmir and Skrymir – named after giants in Norse mythology – were renowned for their tracking abilities. If any creatures could find a wolf in this vast wilderness, it was they.

Most probably, they weren't looking for a pack. The wolves that had been sighted near human habitation had been lone animals: a scavenging male, almost certainly excluded from the group by the alpha leader, and a female driven away for some reason. They would still be close by, drawn towards the villages by their hunger and the tempting scents of the domesticated livestock.

The overnight mist had lifted and it was a clear, crisp day. The Säuling, the rocky, ice-covered peak that dominated the mountain range, stood out stark against the blue sky. The men rode two abreast, zu Freudenberg at the front, the wolfhounds loping along easily beside him. As they neared the fringes of the trees, he stopped and dismounted for a moment to unleash the dogs. Well-trained and experienced, they knew their role. For a few minutes, they criss-crossed the terrain, snouts down, the snow deep enough to graze their bellies. Then Bergelmir paused. He'd found something. The men could see tracks in the snow where some animal had crossed the fields, but the hound wasn't using his eyes to identify exactly what kind of animal, he was using his nose. And this was the scent he was after. Free of restraint, he took off in a straight line, Skrymir right behind him. The riders followed, their horses cantering now. The men were suddenly alert, aroused. The hunt was on.

For half a kilometre, they charged across the open

fields, the forest a green line to one side. They'd split up, the bolder ones taking the lead. Zu Freudenberg was joined at the front by von Auerswald, a horseman whose expertise was matched by his nerve. They glanced at each other as they pulled slowly away from the others, vaulting a wide drainage ditch side by side, vying with one another to jump the furthest, then spurring their horses on. Behind them, the line was strung out, the more timid riders straggling along fifty metres back.

Bergelmir and Skrymir veered slightly to the right, haring up a track that led into the forest. It was wide enough for a cart, this area harvested commercially for its timber. Felled trees, their trunks stripped of branches and cut up into logs, were stacked in neat piles, awaiting collection. After three or four hundred metres, the track narrowed. The men had to ride single file, but they still had a clear run, the branches of the trees far enough away not to impede their passage. The hounds still had the scent and were running with definite purpose. They emerged into a clearing and stopped, momentarily confused, giving the riders time to regroup, their horses a moment to catch their breath. Von Breckendorf nodded at von Auerswald, but no one spoke. No one wanted to break the silence of the forest, to alert their intended prey to their presence.

It was Skrymir who rediscovered the scent, nosing around on the edge of the clearing. He cocked his head towards zu Freudenberg, as if to say, *Guess what?* Then he was off through the trees, Bergelmir tight on his heels. The riders went after them. In the air above, an eagle circled, a dark silhouette like a gash in the sky.

Deeper into the forest, the trees closed in on the path and the men had to slow down. They had to duck under overhanging branches, even dismount in places. But the hounds, fast and low to the ground, kept going, the smell of wolf in their nostrils. The wind was from the east, blowing the scent of man and dog back the way they'd come. If it had been the opposite way, the wolves would have been long gone, vanished into the impenetrable interior of the forest. As it was, they had no warning. They were by one of the many springs that sprouted from the earth all the way along the range, drinking from a pool that hadn't frozen. There were two of them, both thin and scrawny, a mangy male and a female with a white blaze on her forehead.

They didn't smell the wolfhounds until it was too late. Until Bergelmir and Skrymir burst out from the undergrowth behind them, snarling and barking. The wolves took off down the hill. No thought, no plan, just pure panic, the instinct to flee from danger. The hounds knew what they were doing, what *their* instincts and their breeding had taught them. They split up, not chasing directly, but circling round, cutting off the escape routes so the wolves were forced to run towards the approaching horsemen.

Von Auerswald saw them first, dark shapes in the distance weaving between the trees. He reined in his horse and reached for his rifle. The male wolf was less than thirty metres away when the prince fired. The bullet hit the creature in the shoulder, the impact sending it reeling across the forest floor. The hounds pounced, ready for the kill, but the final blow was man's privilege. Zu Freudenberg, pulling up behind von Auerswald, whistled them off, leaving the wolf bleeding and immobile on the ground.

The prince swung down from his horse and walked over to it. Half hidden in the thickets, the female wolf cowered in terror and watched. Her male companion was mortally injured, blood pumping from the bullet wound. Von Auerswald stood over it. The other riders looked on from their horses as the prince took out his pistol and delivered the *coup de grace*. He wanted the head undamaged for the wall of one of his residences, so he put the bullet into the wolf's throat. Then, when the creature was still, he leaned down, dipped his finger into the wound and anointed his own forehead with blood.

The female wolf backed away quietly, taking the opportunity to escape. The wolfhounds were under control by the horses, panting with fatigue, the men were preoccupied with von Auerswald's trophy. Now was her chance. She kept low, concealed by the bushes, then broke suddenly from cover and raced away across the slope. Zu Freudenberg saw her and released the hounds. The other men spun their horses and went after her, too.

Sophie was coming down the hill from Gisela's hut when she heard the scrabble of paws in the undergrowth and a wolf suddenly erupted out of the bushes in front of her. The creature skidded to a halt. Its jaw gaped. Its mouth was flecked with white foam. It was panting noisily. *She* was panting, for Sophie recognised the animal from the blaze between her eyes – the female she'd encountered the previous evening. They stared at each other. The wolf was clearly terrified. Exhausted, too. Sophie could see that in her posture, her eyes.

Sophie looked up, a far-off movement catching her attention: horsemen in the distance, riding fast through the trees. And she knew immediately what was happening. She gestured to the wolf, pointing, showing her the rocky outcrop behind her that concealed the opening to a narrow gulley and beyond that a cave. The creature didn't move. She was still staring at Sophie, wary and unsure, but not frightened of her. Sophie gestured more forcefully, using her arms to shoo the wolf towards the gulley. The creature got the message and darted away through the gap in the rocks.

The horsemen were closing in rapidly, now less than a hundred metres away. Sophie knew the hunt, knew the men weren't the most pressing threat to the wolf. Reaching inside her cloak pocket, she took out the flask of lavender bath oil she'd just bought from Gisela, unstoppered it and quickly sprinkled the contents on the ground around her, then slid the flask back into her pocket. Only just in time, for seconds later, two slavering wolfhounds streaked out and pulled up short in front of her, their paws slipping on the icy path. They snuffled around, bewildered by the pungent scent of lavender which was all they could smell.

Sophie waited for the horsemen to rein in and stop. Her eyes roved over them: Von Breckendorf, Zu Freudenberg, von Sturm, she knew them all. One rider came in after the others – von Auerswald, the Prussian legate she'd encountered at a number of social occasions. Draped over the back of his horse, roped to the saddle, was the carcass of a wolf. Sophie saw the blood on the legate's forehead and her hackles rose. They disgusted her, these men taking pleasure in killing wild creatures for sport.

Zu Freudenberg touched a finger to his hat. "Good day, freiin."

"Gentlemen."

"Have you seen a wolf?"

"Apart from the one hanging from the saddle over there, you mean?" She made no attempt to conceal the contempt in her voice.

Zu Freudenberg looked her over from the lofty heights of his horse. The freiin was a handsome filly, he thought. But insolent, way too sure of herself for a woman. If she'd been his wife, he'd have taught her to behave like a lady. Stripped off those trousers she wore and showed her some discipline. He'd have enjoyed that.

"There was a second one," he said. "It came this way."

"Not past me," Sophie replied. "Maybe further down the hill."

Zu Freudenberg nodded. The wolfhounds were still nosing around the area, trying to pick up the scent they'd lost. The count snapped out a command, "Come!", then rode off through the forest, the hounds and the other horsemen trotting after him.

Sophie waited until they were out of sight before she squeezed around the rock outcrop into the hidden gulley. The she-wolf was crouching inside the mouth of the cave, but she rose to her feet as Sophie approached. She was still nervous, ready to defend herself. Sophie held out her arms, trying to look unthreatening, then backed away out of the gulley, beckoning to the wolf. It took a few minutes, but before long the creature crept cautiously out from behind the rock. Sophie stepped to one side, giving her space. The wolf hesitated, sniffing, looking around for danger. Then she glanced briefly at Sophie and pelted away into the trees.

SEVENTEEN

Neumann heard the distant sound of a piano as he walked through the main entrance of the Monastery of Saint Magnus. The building was no longer used for its original purpose. The last of the monks had left in 1803 and most of the rooms around the vast cobbled courtyard had lain empty ever since. Only the rear part of the complex was still in regular use – the church and some of the larger chambers, like the magnificent Emperor's Hall in which the rehearsals and concerts of the Wagner Society were held.

The piano grew louder as Neumann progressed along the corridor, the sound luring him deeper into the building. Then it was joined by two male voices singing, two resonant bass-baritones booming out through the high stone vaults just as the chants of the Benedictines must have done a century earlier.

On the threshold of the hall, Neumann paused to take in the scene inside: the marble pillars, the gilt Baroque decoration on the walls, the polished wooden floor inlaid with a marquetry star. To one side was a black grand piano, a repetiteur seated at the keyboard. Standing next to the piano were the two singers being conducted by a bespectacled man whose tiny stature was more than redressed by his energetic style and the long baton in his right hand which he wielded like a sorcerer casting spells.

Neumann didn't know the music the two men were

singing. Wagner, he assumed, but he couldn't be certain. The composer was famous throughout Germany – infamous, in some people's books – but Neumann had never seen any of his operas. Whatever it was, it had a certain dramatic power, even with just a piano accompaniment. The men were singing, but they were acting, too, moving around the room as if in a theatre, though there was no scenery, no lights and only one prop – a ring. A golden ring, which the men appeared to be arguing over, both desperate to possess it.

Neumann slipped onto a chair at the back of the hall and watched. Apart from the musicians, he was the only person present. His arrival had aroused no attention. The conductor and singers were so absorbed in their tasks they hadn't noticed him come in. Only the repetiteur, a young man in his early thirties with shoulder-length black hair and a dark, saturnine complexion, glanced briefly in his direction before resuming his focus on the piano score in front of him.

From time to time, the conductor brought the proceedings to a halt to make some point. To comment on the singing, to emphasise or explain a particular phrase in the music. Neumann caught only fragments of the exchanges and could understand little of it. One of the men, he gathered, was playing a god – Wotan – the other, he wasn't sure who he was. The name Alberich emerged, but it meant nothing to the major.

He waited patiently for five or ten minutes, and just when he thought he ought to interrupt – he was there on official police business, after all – the conductor put down his baton and called a short break. Neumann went forward and introduced himself.

"You are Doctor Hubert Steimitz, I presume."

"At your service, sir." Steimitz peered at him through the thick lenses of his spectacles. "A police officer, you say? How may I help you?"

"I'm interested in the Wagner Society you run."

"Indeed? Then you have come at the right time. We have a meeting this evening. You are most welcome to join us. This is our final rehearsal, you know. We are running through a scene from *The Rhinegold*. You are familiar with the work, perhaps? The first part of Wagner's superb *Ring* tetralogy."

"I don't know it, I'm afraid."

"Then it will be a revelation to you. This is the scene in which Wotan, the king of the Norse gods – Herr Voigt, over there." Steimitz indicated the taller of the two singers. "Takes the ring from the Nibelung dwarf, Alberich. That's Herr Oberdorf, another very fine singer." A nod towards the second bass-baritone. "Forces Alberich to hand it over, although the gold from which the ring has been crafted, of course, belongs to neither of them. It has been stolen by Alberich from the Rhinemaidens."

"That's very interesting…" Neumann began, but the kapellmeister hadn't finished.

"It's one of the key moments of the music-drama. Indeed, one of the key moments of the whole cycle. When Alberich puts a curse on the ring, a curse that will bring not only death to anyone who possesses it, but unhappiness to everyone connected with it. But Wotan doesn't listen, he doesn't care. He wants the absolute power he thinks the ring will give him. It is tremendous stuff, major. It should really be seen on a stage with a full orchestra, but we do our best with our limited resources."

Steimitz's eyes shone with enthusiasm. With his plump, rosy cheeks, round glasses and benign air, he reminded Neumann of a character from a fairy tale. A shoemaker, perhaps, or a friendly elf.

"I'm sure you do," Neumann said politely, "But what I really – "

"There will be more tonight. Scenes from *Lohengrin* and *Tannhäuser*, too. You don't have to be a member of the society to attend."

"Actually, it's a member of your society I'm interested in. An ex-member, I should say. A young man named Christoph Geissler."

Steimitz frowned. "Geissler? Isn't he the one who was killed? I saw it in the paper."

"Yes. Did you ever meet him?"

"Meet him?" Steimitz frowned again, searching his memory. "Not that I recall. But then there are so many members of the society. More than two hundred, I believe, although they don't all come to every meeting. Perhaps my assistant can help you. I leave the administration to him. My time is entirely taken up with the musical side of things. Schäfer!"

He called out to the repetiteur, who came out from behind the piano and walked over to them.

"Sir?"

"This is Major... I'm sorry, I've forgotten your name."

"Neumann."

"My assistant, Karl Schäfer. The major would like to ask you some questions, Schäfer."

The assistant kapellmeister didn't seem at all perturbed by the prospect. He merely gazed quizzically at Neumann and said, "Yes?"

"The young man who was murdered recently, Christoph Geissler, he was a member of the Wagner Society. Did you know him?"

Schäfer shook his head, his hands clasped together. There was something obsequious about his manner, something insincere, Neumann thought.

"I'm sorry, sir. I know the name, of course, but I don't think I ever spoke to him. At most of the meetings, you understand, I am occupied at the piano. And even during the intervals, well, there are more... distinguished...

members who demand my attention."

"People like the king, you mean?"

"Well –"

"His Majesty, I attend to personally," Steimitz broke in. "When he comes, that is."

"Is that often?"

"Alas, he has not been for some time. He is passionate about Wagner, you know. *Passionate*. I go over to the palace regularly to play for him. *Palaces*, I should say, for I go to both old and new Hohenschwangau. His Majesty is building a Singers' Hall in the new palace which he intends to use for recitals, but it's not quite ready yet. When it is, it is my fondest hope that we may go over there to perform Wagner for him."

"When did the king last come to a meeting?" Neumann asked.

"Oh, not since the autumn."

"Would he have met Christoph Geissler?"

"They may have been introduced. I couldn't say for certain. Our meetings are very informal, you see. Music, it is such a universal language. It brings together people from all stations of life."

"Have you seen this before?"

Neumann took out the enamel 'W' ring and showed it to the kapellmeister. Out of the corner of his eye, he saw Schäfer give a start. Steimitz looked at the ring.

"No, what is it?"

"Your society doesn't have an insignia like this? The letter 'W'? I wondered whether it was a sign of membership."

"Oh, no, we don't have anything like that. Jewellery, badges, membership cards. We are joined together by our love of Wagner."

"And you?"

Neumann turned to Schäfer, who shook his head.

"I've never seen it before."

Neumann put the ring back in his pocket. "Thank you for your time, gentlemen."

"Tonight, remember," Steimitz said, waggling his finger at him. "It should be a most enjoyable occasion. Shall we get the women in now?" he said to Schäfer, stepping over to his conductor's stand and changing the score.

The assistant kapellmeister disappeared through a side door. Neumann lingered for a while at the back of the hall until Schäfer returned, followed by a group of about a dozen young women. They arranged themselves into two neat lines while Schäfer resumed his position at the piano. Steimitz picked up his baton.

"Thank you, ladies. Let's take it from the top, shall we?"

Neumann went back out into the corridor. As he headed for the exit, a chorus of female voices echoed around him like a heavenly choir.

The *Füssener Blatt* reporter, Gunther Krämer, was loitering on the pavement outside the police station, collar of his coat turned up, hat crammed down over his ears, eyes watering in the frosty air. Neumann couldn't tell whether he was about to go into the building or had just come out.

"Major," the journalist said brightly. "Just the man. About the Werner Graf case…"

Neumann held up his hand. "I can't comment on that, except to say that we are shocked by the killing and doing our utmost to track down the perpetrator."

"As you are in the Geissler case, you mean?"

"Exactly."

"Are the two murders connected?"

"I can't say any more."

"The dead raven, what do you make of that? Very peculiar, don't you think?"

Neumann suppressed his annoyance. "Who told you about the raven?" he asked, though he could guess the answer.

Krämer grinned insolently. "I have my sources."

"Then you don't need me, do you?" Neumann said and pushed past him into the police station. The reception area was deserted, the fire in the hearth behind the desk burning fiercely, filling the room with the scent of woodsmoke. He removed his greatcoat, already feeling the heat, and slung it over his arm. Through the open doorway, he could see Krause and the two constables, Lehmann and Böhm, in the back room. They were at their desks, enjoying their regular afternoon snack of *bratwurst* with sweet mustard and rye bread. Neumann went through to join them.

"Where are we with the Graf investigation?" he asked.

Krause looked up from his sausage, wiping the grease off his lips with the back of his hand.

"Well advanced, sir, well advanced," he said. "Captain Beck will be able to give you the details."

"He's upstairs?"

"Yes, sir."

Neumann turned to Lehmann. "Have you had any response to your telegrams?"

The constable looked at him blankly, chewing on a chunk of rye bread.

"About missing young women," Neumann prompted him.

"Ah, yes, sir." He kept chewing, a dribble of mustard escaping from the corner of his mouth.

"And?"

"What? Oh, nothing. Well, there *was* one – a girl who disappeared a week ago in Pfronten – but she turned up two days later."

"No others?"

"No, sir."

Neumann headed for the exit. Krause, moving very fast for a man of his impressive girth, scrambled up from his chair and hurried out into the reception area.

"I'll let the captain know you're here, sir."

The stairs, requiring a degree of exertion that the sergeant deemed excessive, were out of the question, so he just yelled up them. "Captain Beck, sir! Major Neumann to see you."

A clearer warning – subordinate tipping off his superior – was hard to imagine. Neumann went quickly up the stairs and into Beck's office without knocking, just in time to catch the captain closing a cupboard door. But too late to see the glass of beer he was concealing, although the tell-tale odour of ale still lingered in the room.

"Ah, major," Beck said, sitting back down at his desk. "What a pleasure to see you."

"What did you tell Gunther Krämer?" Neumann asked bluntly.

Beck wasn't stupid enough to fall for that. He looked shocked. "Me, sir? Nothing."

"He seems suspiciously well informed about our investigations."

"Does he? Well, you know how it is with reporters, they have their –"

"Sources, yes, I know. Let me make myself clear, captain. We do not give any information to the press without my authorisation."

"No, sir. Of course not, sir."

"Now, the Graf case."

Beck gave his report and it turned out that Krause's "well advanced" was something of an exaggeration for no real progress had actually been made. Graf's body had been removed to the morgue and a telegram sent to Doctor Jaeger in Munich. The pathologist would be down to carry out the autopsy as soon as he was free, although, in Beck's view, that was just a formality. There was no question as to the cause of death. A slashed throat was pretty conclusive evidence.

Böhm had been trawling around all the knifemakers and hardware shops in the area, but had not, so far, managed to find a link to the hunting knife that killed the jeweller. Nor was he likely to, Beck said. The knife was a very common implement with no particularly unusual features. Probably half the adult male population of Bavaria had something like it in their homes. As to any witnesses who might have seen the killer arrive or leave Graf's premises, well, the captain and Krause had spent *hours* interviewing neighbours without finding anyone who could provide any salient information.

What about the jeweller's private life? Neumann wanted to know. He lived alone, Beck replied. In some comfort, too. A big house in its own grounds out on the Hopfen road, a cook, a housekeeper and two maids who came in every day, but no live-in servants. What about next-of-kin, or any relatives who would inherit his considerable estate? There didn't appear to be any.

Beck shook his head in an insincere show of sympathy.

"This is going to be a difficult one for you to solve, major," he said, and Neumann didn't miss the pronoun, the apportioning of responsibility. "If it's really linked to the killing of Christoph Geissler, I can't see how."

Nor can I, at the moment. Neumann thought. But I have absolutely no doubt it is.

EIGHTEEN

For the first time since his arrival in Füssen he put his uniform away in the wardrobe and changed into civilian clothes. He was off-duty, going to a social event where a policeman would not be welcome. His greatcoat he kept on – it was going to be another cold night – but his peaked cap was left on the desk in his room before he ventured out into Brotmarkt and made the short walk across Lechhalde to the monastery.

Other people were arriving on foot, but the courtyard was also crowded with carriages lining up to disgorge their passengers outside the main entrance. Lamps burned inside the building, throwing out strips of light onto the cobbles which were rimed with frost.

The Emperor's Hall was filling up fast with guests: men in suits and ties, women in evening gowns, the cream of the local society. Neumann found a seat in the corner furthest from the door, where he would be unobtrusive. He was a stranger here, among people who knew one another, and he didn't want to draw attention to himself. The room was brightly lit, gas lamps on the walls, candles flickering in the chandeliers suspended from the painted ceiling, their flames reflected in the glossy lid of the piano at the front.

He watched the guests coming in, recognising no one until a trim, middle-aged man with a beard entered. Neumann had seen him before, at New Hohenschwangau after his audience with the king. He tried to recall his name. Baron Something. Von Breckendorf, that was it. The Minister of Justice. He was accompanied by a tall ash-blonde woman, presumably his wife, and a second woman – shorter, slim and dark haired. This woman turned her head as they went to their seats. Neumann caught a glimpse of her face and jolted back in his chair in surprise. It was Sophie Hals von Wildenstein. But not as he'd ever seen her before. The trousers, plain white shirt and jacket were gone. She was wearing a rich royal blue gown, cut low at the front, and matching jewellery: sapphire earrings and a sapphire necklace that complemented the colour of her eyes. The three of them sat down on the far side of the hall. Sophie adjusted a silk shawl over her shoulders, her earrings glinting in the candlelight. There were more obviously beautiful women in the room, Neumann thought, but none quite as striking as Sophie.

The audience settled down, their chatter fading away as the performers came out into the hall – the chorus of young women Neumann had seen that afternoon. Karl Schäfer slipped quietly onto his seat behind the piano, another young man stationed by his shoulder to turn the pages of the music. Then Hubert Steimitz appeared to a brief round of applause. He introduced the first piece – a chorus of flower maidens from *Parsifal* – and explained a bit about its context in the opera, then the singing began.

It was a new experience for Neumann. He knew very little about opera, or Wagner – at least, not his musical achievements. He did know the composer had been a revolutionary, a leading participant in the 1849 uprising in Dresden, which led to a long exile before his deeds were forgiven and he was allowed to return to Germany.

He knew he was still a hugely controversial figure, particularly in Bavaria, where his relationship with King Ludwig had attracted widespread criticism, Wagner portrayed by his detractors as a scheming, spendthrift sponger who had ensnared the young monarch and extracted vast sums from him to support his dubious operatic endeavours. But he'd never actually heard any Wagner until today. And, as Steimitz had predicted that afternoon, it was a revelation to him.

He listened raptly as the concert unfolded, the chorus of women giving way to solo arias from a soprano and a tenor before the two bass-baritones he'd seen rehearsing earlier came on to perform their scene from *The Rhinegold*. The music was captivating, absorbing his full attention, but in between the numbers, he found his gaze being drawn towards Sophie. He could see her only in profile: her straight nose, her high cheekbones, her pale neck, the edge of her mouth above a chin that was firm and determined. Once, she caught him in the act. Turned her head unexpectedly and saw him staring at her, too late for him to look away. She acknowledged him with a slight gracious nod, then looked back towards the front of the hall.

At the interval, wine was served in an adjoining chamber. Neumann contemplated remaining in his seat, avoiding the awkwardness of mingling with people he didn't know, people who would almost certainly not deign to speak to him. Then he changed his mind. Why not have a drink? Why not make the most of the evening? Going out through the double doors into a plainer, whitewashed room, he helped himself to a glass from the table and looked around. The audience had divided itself naturally into groups: husbands and wives together, a few single-sex clusters of the unattached, unmarried or widowed, one or two more gregarious individuals moving easily between them, smiling, greeting, exchanging the platitudes that passed for conversation at social events like this. No one took any notice of Neumann. He stood apart from everyone else, an observer rather than a participant. A pariah, he thought wryly. Like all policemen. Except most people here didn't know his profession, and he wore no uniform to apprise them of it.

He sipped his wine, watching Steimitz doing his round of the subscribers, glad handing, chatting, keeping everyone sweet. Over in a corner, Schäfer was talking to a large, balding man who glanced briefly in Neumann's direction, as if they were talking about him. He looked vaguely familiar. Neumann took a moment to place him: like von Breckendorf, he'd also been there in the Throne Room at New Hohenschwangau, one of the bureaucrats or politicians in attendance on the king.

"Good evening, major."

Neumann turned. Sophie was looking up at him. He could smell her perfume, feel the unsettling gaze of her blue eyes on his face.

"Ma'am," he said politely, unable to think of anything more.

"I didn't expect to see you here."

"I didn't expect to *be* here."

"You are a music lover?"

"Not exactly."

She took in his dark suit and tie.

"But you're not on duty?"

"No, ma'am."

"Even policemen need to relax occasionally. You like Wagner?"

"This is the first time I've heard any."

She raised an eyebrow. "Really? What do you think?"

"I'm enjoying it."

"He's a divisive figure. People either love or hate him."

"You love him, I assume, or you wouldn't be here."

"His music, yes. His writings, less so. As for his portrayal of women, well, let's just say it leaves a lot to be desired. But then that's opera for you. Pretty much every heroine is doomed to die tragically. Lucia, Aida, Violetta, Gilda, Desdemona, Carmen, the list goes on and on. The male perspective, you see. Wagner's women are no different. They are passive vessels with no lives or wills of their own. They are there to serve the men in the story, to help them find redemption before quietly expiring. It's not a life story I intend to emulate."

Neumann half smiled. "No, I can believe that."

Sophie drank some of her wine.

"You will forgive me, major. I don't want to spoil your evening by reminding you of your work, but I have done as you asked. I have tried to speak to Amalie about what occurred the other day. About the ring. I cannot get a word out of her, I'm afraid. Whatever has happened to her, the trauma is clearly too great for her to speak of it yet."

"Thank you for trying, ma'am. I will have to find other ways of pursuing my enquiries. How is she, by the way?"

Sophie pursed her lips. "Not well. She has withdrawn into herself again, almost gone back to the state in which I first found her. She keeps to her bed and refuses to engage with anyone. The other maids say her violent nightmares have also returned."

"I'm sorry to have been the cause of that."

"It was not you, major. It was that ring."

"I've been trying to find out who she is and where she might have come from. But with no success. I can find no reports of any missing young women. At least, not in the immediate area."

"It's strange, I know. Perhaps she has come from further afield."

"Or perhaps no one cares about her enough to seek her out."

Sophie looked at him pensively. "Yes, perhaps. She would not be the first – or the last – young woman to be abandoned by her family."

"We have a new face among us, I see," a soft voice broke in suddenly from the side. Neumann turned and saw the ash-blonde woman regarding him intently.

"Aren't you going to introduce us, Sophie?"

"My cousin, the Baroness von Breckendorf. This is Major Reinhardt Neumann."

"Ah, the police officer from Berlin."

It was accurate – how else would she describe him? – but Neumann couldn't help feeling he was being defined by his negatives. A policeman, a Berliner, neither of them things to celebrate in Bavaria

"Ma'am." He took the hand she offered and bowed over it.

"My husband has mentioned you to me. I believe you've met."

"Yes, ma'am. The baron was good enough to introduce himself at New Hohenschwangau."

"You were in the army, I understand?"

"That's correct."

"An honourable profession."

The baroness didn't say it, but Neumann sensed a clear implication that police work wasn't quite so distinguished.

"Our fathers were both in the army," Anneliese went on.

"Is that so?" Neumann glanced at Sophie, "I saw the portrait above the mantelpiece in your drawing room. Is that your father?"

Sophie nodded. "He was a colonel in the light cavalry. He was killed at Kissingen in sixty-six."

It was blunt, and intended to be so. One of the decisive battles of the war between Prussia and Austria in which Bavaria – to its great cost – had sided with the losing Austrians.

"I'm sorry to hear that," Neumann said, and meant it.

"It wasn't your fault, major. You weren't there."

It was pleasantly enough said, but there was an underlying feeling of hurt in her words. Understandable, Neumann thought. Yet another reason for her to dislike Prussians.

"Mine, I'm glad to say, had a rather less dramatic end," Anneliese said. "A heart attack on a hunting expedition to the Black Forest. So, major, how goes your investigation? Or is that something a lady shouldn't ask?"

"It's early days," Neumann replied evasively.

"That's what my husband says. But then he adds the caveat, 'early days quickly become late days'." Anneliese glanced around. The throng was breaking up as everyone returned to their seats. "Excuse us, major, I believe the second half is about to begin. It was a pleasure to meet you."

"Baroness, freiin."

Neumann bowed again and watched the two women walk away. Anneliese slid her arm into Sophie's and gave her an arch look.

"What a handsome man," she whispered. "You know, I believe our policeman from Berlin is rather taken with you."

Sophie's head jerked round. "*What?*"

"I saw the way he looked at you. Men are so obvious."

"Don't be ridiculous," Sophie said, feeling the heat rising in her cheeks.

"Why not?"

"He's a policeman."

"Well, you haven't exactly been enamoured of any of the many men who've tried to court you, have you? The ambitious, grand, titled men on the make. Why not a policeman? Think of him as an army officer."

"Don't tease me, Anni. It's not funny."

"No, of course not. Not funny at all."

Anneliese smiled and squeezed Sophie's arm. Sophie glared at her.

"He's just a dull, boorish Prussian."

"He didn't seem at all dull or boorish to me," Anneliese said. "Why must you always be so severe with men?"

"It keeps the bad ones away."

"Maybe it also keeps the good ones away."

Sophie was distracted as they sat back down. She resisted the temptation to see if Neumann was staring at her again. The nerve of the man! Who did he think he was? Yes, perhaps she'd been a little hard on him. He wasn't really dull or boorish. And handsome, as Anni had said? Well, maybe. But she was hardly going to fall for a policeman. That would be absurd.

Across the hall, Neumann was also paying little attention to the music. He was thinking about Sophie. Her face, her hair, her eyes, her lips, her figure that her evening gown had revealed to him with a disconcerting allure. Not since Kristina had he felt such a strong physical attraction. He stole another look at her, annoyed with himself for his presumption, for his naïve stupidity. She is a freiin with her own estate, he told himself. And you are... what? Nothing.

Then his thoughts turned to the Baroness von Breckendorf and what she'd said. "Early days quickly become late days." At what point did that transition happen? he wondered. How much time do I have? So far, he'd been given the freedom to conduct his investigation in his own way. Yet he'd made no meaningful progress. Indeed, the whole business had been made more complicated by the murder of Werner Graf. Von Auerswald wasn't a patient man. Sooner or later – probably sooner – he would want to see the culprits identified and caught. But Neumann was nowhere near that point at the moment, and couldn't see a path forward that would help him get there.

Out at the front of the hall, a rotund tenor soloist was taking a bow and Neumann realised he'd listened to barely a note of his aria. In the soloist's place came a mixed chorus, the young women now joined by a group of young men. They sang the pilgrims' chorus from *Tannhäuser*, a moving piece of vocal writing, but Neumann's mind was wandering again. He kept looking at Schäfer, half hidden away behind the piano, recalling the moment that afternoon when he'd brought out the 'W' ring. Steimitz had reacted innocently; he'd clearly never seen it before. But Schäfer? Neumann hadn't been looking directly at him, but he's seen a definite start of recognition. The assistant kapellmeister knew something about the ring.

Neumann's gaze switched to the chorus, particularly the female half. The women were all young, in their early to mid-twenties, he guessed. And not one of them was plain. He watched them singing and slowly a line of thought began to take shape inside his head. Vague and incomplete, most of it speculative. But he knew from experience that informed guesswork could be an important part of police work.

At the end of the concert, he stayed in his seat while the rest of the audience left. He saw Sophie and the Baroness von Breckendorf in the heart of the crowd, but neither looked his way. When the hall was empty, he went out through the antechamber and along a corridor, looking for the green room where the performers assembled. The sound of voices drew him towards an open door through which he could see the male singers slouching on chairs, unwinding after the concert. Some were putting on coats and hats, getting ready to leave. He asked where he might find the women and got a knowing leer and directions to a room further along the corridor. Two other audience members were already waiting outside: middle-aged, respectable-looking men whose motives for being there, he suspected, were not as honourable as his.

Neumann kept his distance from them, watching the door. The first few women emerged – in a group, perhaps for safety – and the two men immediately made overtures to them, all smiles and gallant attention. Neumann heard compliments, "so good", "such beautiful singing", "perhaps champagne and dinner?" – but the women, no doubt accustomed to predatory admirers, brushed them off politely and went on their way.

More women came out. More approaches from the two men. More unequivocal rejections. Neumann bided his time, then selected a couple who appeared less hostile than the others and stepped forward as they passed him by.

"I beg your pardon," he said. "I wonder if you could help me?"

He'd toyed with the idea of identifying himself – if only to distinguish himself from the lechers by the door – and decided against it. A policeman asking questions might just alarm them, make them less likely to speak freely.

"I'm making enquiries about what may be a missing young woman."

Perhaps it was his appearance, his manner, or simply the novelty of the advance, but the two singers stopped.

"Missing?" one of them said.

"Her name is Amalie. That's all I know. Has there ever been a singer in your group named Amalie?"

"Well, yes, there was."

Neumann felt a sudden inner surge of excitement, of striking gold.

"Do you know what happened to her?"

"She left. Went back to her home."

"When was this?"

The two women exchanged glances, conferring.

"I think it was last autumn some time. She was only with us for a couple of weeks. October, was it?"

"No, earlier. Probably September."

"What was her surname?"

Another conferral.

"I can't remember."

"I think it was Sommer. Yes, Amalie Sommer."

"And her home?" Neumann asked.

"That I do remember. Out east like me. Deggendorf. It's only a small town, not far from my home in Straubing."

"You've come a long way. Are none of you local?"

"Well... no, I suppose we're not. We come from all over, don't we, Lena?"

Lena nodded. "That's how we're recruited."

"Recruited?"

"You know, selected for the chorus. Herr Schäfer – you know Herr Schäfer, the assistant kapellmeister? – he travels all over Bavaria, listening to local choirs, auditioning, picking the best singers to come here to the Wagner Society."

"And Amalie returned to her home, you say?"

"Yes. As far as we know."

"You don't seem certain."

"Well... I think so."

"That's what we were told."

"Told by whom?"

"Herr Schäfer. We were rehearsing one day and Amalie didn't turn up. Herr Schäfer said she'd had to go home suddenly. I think her mother had been taken ill."

"Can you describe her for me? Age, height, hair colour."

"Early twenties, like us," Lena replied. "Dark brown

hair, about the same height as me."

"Thank you, ladies. I'm much obliged to you."

Back in the Emperor's Hall, Steimitz and Schäfer were clearing up after the concert, collecting in the scores and checking the vocal parts.

"Ah, major… major…" Steimitz stuttered to a halt. He'd forgotten his name again. "I'm glad you could make it. Did you enjoy the evening?"

"I did," Neumann replied. "You have some excellent singers. Where do you get them from?"

"The soloists have to come down from Munich. Musicians of that calibre you just can't find locally. The chorus, however – whose vocal roles are less onerous – we recruit ourselves. We find promising singers and train them up. Well, Herr Schäfer here does. I cannot really take much credit for the chorus. It's mostly down to Schäfer."

"You had a chorus member named Amalie Sommer, I believe?" Neumann said.

He addressed the question to the kapellmeister, but it was the assistant he was watching for a reaction. Schäfer glanced up abruptly, then quickly went back to organising the scores.

"Amalie?" Steimitz replied. "Indeed, we did. A charming young lady. A fine soprano."

"What happened to her?"

"She had to leave. Family reasons, if I remember correctly. Schäfer?"

"Yes," the assistant kapellmeister confirmed. "An illness. She had to return home to care for her mother."

"Do you get much turnover with your chorus members?" Neumann asked.

"Oh, yes. They are generally young and you know how young people are. They get restless, they move on, they get other jobs, get married. But we are used to it. What matters is that the quality of singing doesn't diminish. We have standards to maintain, you understand."

"Of course. And most impressive they are. I will not detain you further, Herr Steimitz. I see you have things to do."

Neumann went out of the hall and back along the corridor to the exit. The building was quiet. The singers all appeared to have left and the last of the carriages for the audience members was just clattering out of the courtyard. The caretaker was hovering in the entrance hall, impatient to lock up.

Neumann walked across the courtyard, treading carefully on the icy cobbles. The air was cold and damp. He could see tendrils of mist creeping in over the surrounding roofs, drifting down over the windows like spiders' webs. Outside on Lechhalde, he paused for a second, looking for a suitable place to station himself. Then he crossed over the road into Brotmarkt and backed away into a shadowy doorway from where he had a clear view of the arched gateway to the monastery.

He didn't have long to wait. Ten minutes later, Steimitz and Schäfer came out together, both huddled inside their cloaks, too cold to linger, let alone look across to where Neumann was hiding. They turned left and hurried up Lechhalde. Neumann followed them. At Stadtbrunnen, the small square where the locals could draw water from a well, the two men split up, Steimitz forking right along Reichenstrasse, Schafer going left into Ritterstrasse. Neumann stayed with the assistant kapellmeister who walked fast, not once glancing back.

At the far end of Ritterstrasse, Schäfer stopped outside a door in between two shops, unlocked it and went inside. Neumann slid into another dark doorway diagonally across the street and watched the building. A lamp went on in the first-floor apartment and Schäfer appeared briefly at the window to draw the curtains.

Neumann pressed himself deeper into the doorway. After fifteen minutes, the light was extinguished. Neumann waited, but the assistant kapellmeister didn't come out again. He must have gone to bed. Neumann gave it a further twenty minutes, just to be sure, then, when his feet were starting to go numb, he slipped out of the doorway and strode rapidly back to his lodgings.

NINETEEN

Neumann woke early the following morning. Too early for the maid to have brought him his hot water, so he dressed and went downstairs without washing or shaving. Johanna was already bustling about the kitchen and dining room. Neumann wondered at her stamina. Rarely in bed before midnight, up again at six, she had the energy of a half dozen women. She glanced at him, noting the stubble on his jowls.

"You'll be wanting your hot water, will you, major?"
"All in good time. I'll have breakfast first."
"Eggs?"
"Just bread and coffee, please."

Johanna reverted to dialect. "Liesl! Breakfast for Major Neumann, then hot water to his room. Jump to it, girl."

There was a copy of the *Füssener Blatt* on one of the tables. Neumann picked it up, dreading what he was going to find. The Bavarian Freedom Party had another mention on the front page – a group of supporters besieging the central police station in Munich to protest at the detention of the party members who'd been arrested at their rally in the city. But the main story was the murder of Werner Graf. Gunther Krämer had done his job well, Neumann had to concede. He had all the facts, no doubt courtesy of Lothar Beck. The jeweller slumped over his workbench, his throat cut, the murder weapon next to him; the dead raven dumped close by; the untouched cases of jewellery in the shop. The reporter had spoken to Bruno Roth, who'd been forthcoming about finding the body. Neumann had only himself to blame for that; he should have warned the apprentice not to talk to the press.

Krämer hadn't made any specific connection between the raven and Norse mythology, but he had speculated that it might be part of some peculiar pagan rite, like the mistletoe spear in the Geissler killing – thus making a direct link between the two cases. For Neumann, the most telling line came towards the end of the story. *"Major Neumann, the distinguished police officer from Berlin* (he could imagine the sarcasm that was intended to accompany that description) *now has two murders on his plate. But is he any closer to solving either of them?"*

More pressure I could do without, Neumann thought ruefully as he had his rolls and coffee, then returned to his room to wash and shave. When he was downstairs again, he accompanied Tobias to his workplace.

"Is there a telegraph office in Deggendorf?" he asked.

Tobias nodded. He knew every office in Bavaria, no matter how small. "You want to send a telegram?"

Neumann wrote out his message and paid the fee.

"Could you have the reply delivered to the police station? Thank you."

It was still early when he went back into the centre of town. The tradesmen were just opening their shutters, the shopkeepers scraping the ice from their front steps. Wind funnelled along Reichenstrasse, bringing with it a stab of glacial mountain air. Is it ever going to warm up here? Neumann wondered as he turned into Ritterstrasse and walked along to Schäfer's apartment.

The first-floor curtains were still closed. It didn't look as if the assistant kapellmeister was up. Neumann wasn't surprised. Musicians weren't renowned for keeping regular hours and Schäfer had worked late the previous evening.

The major surveyed the area. There was nowhere he could really loiter outside without being obvious, but a few doors away, conveniently situated on the opposite side of the street, was a coffee house. He went inside, ordered a coffee, then sat at a table in the window which afforded him a good view of Schäfer's apartment.

It was gone nine o'clock when the assistant kapellmeister emerged. He was wearing the same black cloak as the night before, but he'd changed his footwear. His smart town shoes had been replaced with knee-high black leather boots, implying to Neumann that he was going somewhere out of Füssen. Somewhere muddy or snowy. Schäfer headed towards Stadtbrunnen, then took Lechhalde down past the monastery and across the bridge. Neumann followed at a discreet distance. The Lech was an icy green torrent, like melted mint ice cream. Neumann glanced over the parapet thinking, fall in and you would be lucky to last a minute.

At the far side, Schäfer turned right and headed upstream along the main road towards the Austrian frontier. Below them, built on a patch of flat land by the river, was the rope-making factory, a huge, long, three-storey building which had its own water-generated electricity supply to power its thousand-plus spinning machines and the lights that illuminated the work rooms. Even up here on the road, the noise of the machines was deafening, Neumann thought. What it must have been like inside was unimaginable, but then that wasn't something that was of great concern to the local people. The workers, after all, were mainly immigrants from Austria and Bohemia - the people that Captain Beck blamed for most of the crime in the area, although how they found the time or energy after their exhausting twelve-hour shifts was a bit of a mystery.

Schäfer continued along the road. There was very little traffic – just a few carts and wagons and almost no pedestrians. Neumann held back, conscious that if the assistant kapellmeister looked round he would be very conspicuous. Fortunately, the visibility wasn't good. The mountains were covered with dense low cloud and even in the valley the mist made it difficult to see much more than fifty metres.

The road followed the river. Away to the right, hidden from sight, Neumann could hear the fierce roar of the water going over the Lech Falls, the noise almost as loud as the spinning machines in the rope factory. He wondered where Schäfer was going. There was no real settlement out here, just a few houses tucked along the edge of the road, the land behind them too steep for building, too wooded for agriculture.

They were getting close to the border, Neumann beginning to think Schäfer was going to cross over into Austria, when the young man suddenly turned off to the left, taking a path that led up the hill through thick forest. Neumann waited a moment, then followed him. The path was rough and stony, just wide enough for a person – or a horse. To one side, set deep into a gulley, a fast-flowing stream cascaded over boulders and tiny falls on its way down to the Lech. Mist rolled through the pine trees, clinging to the branches, imbuing the air with a moisture that Neumann could feel in his lungs as he climbed up the slope. It was hard going. The path was steep and slippery with compacted snow that indicated it was in regular use. But where did it go?

Neumann was breathing heavily, trying to suppress the noise, and the sound of his feet, so Schäfer wouldn't hear. The assistant kapellmeister was fifty metres ahead of him. Neumann caught glimpses of his cloak through the trees, the young man never looking back, unaware that he was being tailed.

After fifteen minutes of tough ascent, the path went over a lip and the terrain suddenly levelled out into a shelf that had been largely cleared of forest. The area was about twenty metres wide and forty metres deep, hemmed in by steep wooded slopes to the sides and, at the rear, a sheer cliff that rose vertically up the mountain face, its top lost in cloud.

At the base of the cliff, seemingly half set into the rock, was a single-storey wooden building about the size of a family home. Except it didn't look like a home. The corrugated iron roof gave it an industrial feel and the metal bars over the windows certainly didn't look like a domestic dwelling. From the overgrown mounds of earth along the edges of the clearing, that could have been spoil heaps, Neumann wondered if the building had once been connected to quarrying or mining.

He concealed himself behind the trunk of a tree and watched Schäfer approach the building and rap on the door. Bolts snapped back – three of them – loud enough for Neumann to hear, and the door swung open. He caught sight of a middle-aged woman inside. She was wearing an apron like a servant, her grey hair pulled back in a tight bun. Schäfer went inside the house. The bolts clicked back into their slots.

What was this place? Neumann wondered. Bars on the windows, multiple bolts on the door, it had the appearance of a prison. And the woman? Who was she? Anywhere else, a single man visiting a woman, Neumann might have suspected a sexual motive. But not here. You wouldn't keep a mistress somewhere as remote and inaccessible as this. And the woman was surely too old for Schäfer.

Using the trees as cover, Neumann clambered higher up the slope to give himself a better view. He could now see one side of the building as well as the front. There were three windows in a row, all covered with stout wooden shutters secured with iron straps. And a side door that looked as solid as the one at the front. Why was Schäfer here? A musician, assistant kapellmeister to the king. What business did he have in this strange, forbidding location? Neumann shivered. The place unnerved him.

Less than ten minutes had elapsed when the front door opened again and Schäfer came out. Neumann strained to see deeper into the building, but the grey-haired woman blocked the view, then she closed the door and rammed home the bolts. Schäfer walked back across the ledge and disappeared from sight onto the path down the mountain. Neumann stayed put, thinking about what he did next. He could go and knock on the door, force his way inside, if necessary, but he had no legal authority to do that. If something suspicious was going on inside the building, and he had no real evidence of that, showing himself would take away any element of surprise, warn the occupants that the police were taking an interest in them. Better to leave now, then come back later with a warrant and reinforcements.

He waited five minutes, to give Schäfer plenty of time to get clear of the area, then made his way back down the path.

Two messages awaited him at the police station. One was a telegram from the Deggendorf police, the reply to the message he'd sent earlier.

AMALIE SOMMER NOT HERE. HER MOTHER DIED FIVE YEARS AGO

The other was a note from Norbert Ziegler: "*I've done what you asked. Please call on me at your earliest convenience.*"

Neumann was torn. Did he go back to the house in the hills with a warrant? Or go to see Ziegler? He chose the latter. That was simpler, easier to get out of the way first.

The author was in his rooms above the lute-making workshop, already nursing a glass of wine although it was barely mid-day. He offered Neumann the same, but the major refused.

"What have you got?" he asked, trying to speed things up.

But Ziegler was in no hurry.

"Please," he said, gesturing at a chair. "You recall you asked me to look at those strange runic notes for you?"

"Of course. You know what they mean?"

"It's not quite as straightforward as that," Ziegler replied and Neumann's heart sank. He braced himself for a long-winded explanation.

"Do you know much about runes?" Ziegler asked.

Neumann had to admit he didn't, even though he knew this was playing into the author's hands.

"Well," Ziegler said and paused, running a hand through his long, curly hair. He looked even more dishevelled than the last time they'd met. Hair a mess, shirt unpressed, traces of what looked like scrambled egg in his beard.

"The name is derived from *rûna*, an ancient word meaning 'mystery' or 'secret'. They probably had their origins in the North Italic Alps in the first two centuries before the birth of Christ and gradually moved further north through Germany and into Scandinavia some time before the third century AD.

"They were almost certainly derived from pictures and pictorial symbols initially carved into pieces of wood. That's why they are largely composed of straight lines and angles, rather than curves, which would have been harder to cut against the grain of the wood. But they were also inscribed onto stone and it's the stone runes which, for obvious reasons, have survived, although one or two inscriptions on wood have been found preserved in Danish peat bogs."

"Very interesting," Neumann said. "Now, about the notes."

"I'm coming to that," Ziegler replied, lubricating his mouth with a sip of wine. "Runes were closely linked with the religious beliefs and ritual practises of pagan Germany and their main use may have been for divination or casting lots, their signs being interpreted by a priest or other initiated person. They weren't primarily used for communication among people, but to invoke higher powers to affect and influence the lives and futures of men. Like praying to our Christian God for good luck or good fortune. An eternal hope of all men, that some supernatural being can make our lives better.

"They were epigraphic rather than cursive, being superseded by the Latin alphabet for writing, but, nevertheless, there *was* a runic alphabet. We call it the 'futhark', after the first six letters – the sound 'th' being just a single letter. There were twenty-four runes in the Germanic futhark and they were used until about the eighth century when modifications began to appear in Scandinavia which resulted in two closely-related Northern runic alphabets of only sixteen letters each. In England, however, it went the other way as the Anglo-Saxons settled in the country and increased the number of runes to thirty-three." Ziegler permitted himself a dry smile. "The English, as prolix then as they are now."

He took another sip of wine. "You're sure you won't have a glass?"

"No, thank you. I'm on duty."

"A commendable attitude, major. You will forgive me if I show no such restraint." He leaned over the desk and topped up his glass. "Now, each individual rune had its own meaning and, as with most early alphabetic scripts, there was no division between words. The inscriptions could also read from right to left, or left to right, and sometimes from bottom to top."

"That must make them difficult to understand," Neumann said, hoping to get the author back onto the purpose of the meeting.

"It does indeed," Ziegler replied.

He searched around the clutter on his desk and found a pen and piece of paper. Then he looked for the ink, eventually locating a pot on the windowsill behind him. He wrote a letter on the paper.

"This is *uruz*, which means auroch, a species of wild ox found in many parts of Europe until the eleventh century. The animals were used in sacrifices to the gods and had great status because they were huge beasts and very difficult to kill. Young boys were initiated into manhood on auroch hunting expeditions so the rune symbolises manly strength."

He wrote another letter.

"This is *teiwaz*, meaning the Norse god Tyr, the bravest of the gods. He had one of his hands bitten off by the giant wolf, Fenrir, who would go on to kill Odin himself at Ragnarök. The rune has been found engraved on ancient swords as an invocation to Tyr to bring victory in battle."

Ziegler put down the pen and picked up his glass, enjoying himself with all the relish of the born pedagogue.

"What I'm saying is that every rune has a symbolic meaning. *Ansuz* – god; *algiz* – protection; *dagaz* – light; *kaunaz* – fire or torch, and so on. But they can also be used in conjunction with one another to form words – modern German words."

He put down his glass again and shuffled through the stacks of papers on the table beside the desk, extracting the thin sheaf of notes that Neumann had given him. *At last*, the major thought.

"Which brings me to those messages. Do you want an exact breakdown of their contents, or will the gist suffice?"

"Just the gist," Neumann replied quickly. "At least, to begin with."

"Well, you gave me eleven notes. Ten of them are very similar in content. They all begin with what appears to be a greeting – 'My B' – the letter B being the *berkana*, which symbolises life, but may also be the first initial of someone's name."

Baldur? Neumann thought.

"They are, essentially, invitations, almost love letters. This one, for example." He chose one of the notes. "Reads, '*I miss you, my dear friend. I miss your company, I miss your...*' Here, the writer uses the *uruz*, so we can infer 'manly strength'. '*I miss your love. Come to me tonight.*' They are all signed with a single letter, 'P'."

"You said one was different."

"This one."

Ziegler showed it to him. It was the one that had been found on Geissler's body.

"The tone of this message is very different. The others are affectionate, happy. But this one is angry. '*Where are you? Why do you not come to me? Why do you reject my love? You have abandoned me, betrayed me, deserted me. I hate you. Odin's curse upon you.*'"

"Odin?" Neumann said.

"King of the Norse gods, of course, but also the one most strongly linked to runic magic. You have heard of Yggdrasill, the mighty ash tree usually known as the Guardian or World Tree?"

Neumann hadn't, but he had a feeling Ziegler was going to enlighten him.

"It is a key part of Norse mythology. I wrote about it in detail in my book, the one I gave you. It's fascinating stuff. Let me find the relevant chapter for you." Ziegler stood up and took down the book from the shelves, then riffled through it.

"I don't need the detail, doctor," Neumann said. "Just

give me the general picture. What about this tree?"

"Oh. All right." Ziegler sounded disappointed. He sat back down and gathered his thoughts. "Well, Yggdrasill is so vast its branches spread out over the whole world, even up to heaven. It has three roots, the first sunk into Asgard, the home of the gods. Under that root is the Well of Urd, or Fate, where the three Norns meet to spin the destinies of both men and gods. Another root lies beneath Nifelheim, the land of the dead, and the third below Jotunheim, the home of the giants. By this last root is the Spring of Mimir, whose waters are the source of wisdom. In exchange for one of his eyes, Odin was allowed to drink from the spring to obtain immense knowledge."

"This is all very well," Neumann said, starting to lose patience. "But what does it have to do with the notes?"

"Everything," Ziegler replied, looking a little hurt. "It was from the branches of Yggdrasill that Odin later hung, his side pierced by a spear, without food or drink for nine days and nights. He gazed on the world below and learned eighteen runes that gave him the magical power to heal, to thwart evil intentions, to calm stormy seas, to seduce and other things. The parallels with Christ are striking, don't you think? Jesus on the cross, Odin hanging from a tree, both with their sides pierced by a spear. Snorri Sturluson – you remember I mentioned him last time, the Icelandic scholar who wrote down the Norse myths – he was a Christian, but modern commentators don't think he was influenced by that. This story about Odin hanging from Yggdrasill comes from a long pagan tradition that predates the birth of Christ."

"And his curse?"

"He was the god of war and death. His spear, Gungnir, forged by the dwarves, never missed its mark. Odin's curse brings certain death."

Ziegler passed the notes across the desk.

"And this extra sheet," he said, "is a transcription of

all the messages, as far as I can understand them."

"Thank you, doctor. You've been most helpful."

Neumann stowed the papers away in his coat pocket and went back down the stairs. So Geissler had been having what appeared to be an affair, an affair that he seemed to have ended. But with whom? The notes were all signed 'P'. Neumann had so far encountered no one with that initial. Who was P? he wondered as he walked out onto the street. Something else occurred to him. Runes weren't exactly a common form of communication. So how had Geissler managed to read them?

TWENTY

It was the meat pies that made the decision for him. Returning to the police station, he found Krause, Lehmann and Böhm enjoying a light lunch of bread, cheese and steak and ale pie, each man with his own individual pie the size of a dinner plate. Captain Beck was no doubt upstairs in his office, having a similar meal.

Neumann studied the men, taking in their plump, pink faces and prodigious bellies. He'd never seen such a bunch of overweight, out-of-condition police officers. In Berlin, where annual fitness tests had been recently introduced for the rank-and-file membership – although not senior officers – they would have been put on diets and enrolled in exercise classes to improve their fitness. He pictured the task he had ahead of him and judged that not one of these men was going to be up to it.

He asked for a map of the area and unfolded it on a desk while the sergeant and constables concentrated on their stomachs. The house in the hills was marked, just a tiny black square, but it had no name or other label to identify it. Neumann showed it to Krause, who was chewing a mouthful of pie, gravy trickling down his various chins.

"Do you know what this building is?"

Krause peered at the map, getting his bearings.

"That's the other side of the Kalvarienberg. Never been there, never noticed it before."

"Who issues your search warrants?"

"Herr Krüger, the cloth merchant. He's one of the magistrates."

"Where do I find him?"

It was only a short walk to Krüger's premises in Schrannenplatz, a three-storey building with a draper's shop on the ground floor, storage space on the second and the magistrate's business office in between. He was a small, ferret-faced man with buck teeth and wispy grey side whiskers. A clear friend of the police – not always the case in Berlin – he was more than happy to issue Neumann with his warrant, few questions asked. All he needed was the address. Neumann showed him the map.

"Hmm," Krüger mused. "Strange. I don't think I've ever heard of a building out there. What is it?"

"I'm not sure. It could be an old mining or quarrying place. Would that make sense?"

"Maybe. There are old quarries all over the mountains. I'll call it Number One, Kalvarienberg, shall I?"

"That will be fine."

Next stop was the barracks and a request to Lukas Hafner for half a dozen of his best men.

"You don't want to use the local police?" Hafner asked.

"Have you seen them? They'd get ten metres up the hill and collapse with exhaustion."

"I'll come, too."

"You don't have to do that, Lukas."

"Do you know how tedious my job is? A bit of action like this, damn it, man, you're not leaving me out."

They rode through the town and over the Lech, Neumann at the front with Hafner, thinking how long it was since he'd last been out with an army troop, reassured by the five soldiers and a lieutenant behind, all young, fit and armed. Whatever awaited them on Kalvarienberg, he was confident these men would be able to handle it.

"I had the logbooks checked for you, as you asked," Hafner said. "We have no record of Christoph Geissler visiting either of the Hohenschwangau palaces – old or new."

"Thanks, Lukas. That was good of you."

"Is it a setback?"

"I don't know," Neumann admitted. "It certainly doesn't make anything clearer."

At the foot of the track up the mountain they dismounted. One soldier was deputed to stay with the horses while the rest climbed up the path. On reaching the ledge, they stayed well back in the trees, surveying the building beneath the cliff.

"No sign of activity," Hafner said. "One woman inside, you say?"

Neumann nodded. "She's the only person I saw. But I think there may be others."

"Bars on the windows. What kind of place is it?"

"That's what I want to find out."

Hafner gave his instructions. Lieutenant Feldt and two soldiers were to cover the side door, everyone else would go to the front. Drawing their pistols, they made their way guardedly across the ledge. Neumann hammered on the door. He heard the shuffle of footsteps inside, then the bolts were withdrawn. The door swung open a little and the grey-haired woman peered out through the gap.

"Police!" Neumann said.

She gaped at him in shock, then turned and bolted away along the hall. Neumann raced after her, but she hadn't got far. Feldt had apprehended her as she tried to flee through the side door and dragged her back inside the building.

The rear room was a large kitchen, a wood fire burning in the hearth, a blackened cooking range beside it on which a pot of broth was bubbling. There was a table and four chairs to one side and a soft armchair drawn up close to the fire.

"Reinhardt!"

Neumann stepped back out into the hall. Three of the doors opening off it had small flaps in them at eye level – like the observation slits found in prison cells. It was through one of these that Hafner was peering.

"Look at this."

He moved aside to let Neuman see. Inside the small room was a single bed and no other furniture. The shutters were closed, but there was just enough light to make out the shape huddled beneath the blanket on the bed, to see the pale glimmer of a face. Neumann tried the handle. The door was locked.

He checked the slits in the other two doors. The scenes inside were the same: a bed, closed shutters, an unidentified shape hidden under a blanket, the doors locked. Only the fourth room was different. Comfortably furnished, it had a quilt on the bed, a rug on the floor, a wardrobe and chest of drawers against the wall. A suitcase was open on the bed, clothes piled beside it waiting to be packed. We were only just in time, Neumann thought. Any much later and the grey-haired woman would have been gone. What was she, some kind of gaoler?

He went back into the kitchen. The woman was sitting on one of the chairs, Feldt and another soldier standing guard over her.

"What's your name?" Neumann asked.

The woman didn't reply. She stared down at the floor, her hands clasped tightly in her lap.

"What is this place? Who are the people locked in the rooms? Answer me!"

Still no reply. Neumann looked around. Hanging from a nail on the wall was a large bunch of keys. He lifted it down and returned to the cells, trying the keys until he found one that fitted the first door. The lock clicked open and he went warily in. The shape beneath the blanket shifted and gave a whimper that was more animal than human. From the pitch, he could tell it was female. He approached the bed.

"My name is Neumann. I'm a police officer."

The shape curled up into a ball. He could see a face, but the eyes were screwed shut, long dark hair straggling over the cheeks. A woman, but it was too dark to see any details.

"I mean you no harm. Who are you?"

He crouched down and reached out his arm, pulling back the blanket a little to get a better look at the woman's face. She gave a sharp cry of fear and curled up more, pulling her knees up protectively to her chest, her arms wrapped around them.

"I'm here to help," Neumann said gently. "Don't be frightened."

He touched one of her hands and she flinched, pressing herself back against the wall. Her skin was cold. No wonder. The room had no heating and the woman had only the one thin blanket to keep her warm.

"A woman?" Hafner said from the doorway.

"Help me, Lukas."

They eased back the blanket. The woman was wearing a white linen shift and nothing else. She squirmed away from them, her eyes opening wide in terror.

"We are friends," Neumann murmured. "Friends. Let's get you somewhere warm."

Together, they lifted her off the bed. Neumann had expected resistance, but the woman went suddenly limp and passive. They wrapped the blanket around her shoulders and carried her through into the kitchen.

"A chair by the fire," Neumann called out and one of the soldiers placed a dining chair in front of the hearth. Neumann and Hafner lowered the woman onto it. She was shivering, whether from fear or cold it was hard to tell.

"She needs food," Neumann said. "What's that on the stove? Broth? Get her a bowl."

In the light from the kitchen window, he could see her more clearly now. She was young – in her early twenties – and pretty, though her skin was chalk white, her face showing signs of stress and malnourishment. She glanced at the grey-haired woman and Neuman saw the anxiety in her eyes.

"Get her out of here," he said to Feldt. "Put her in her room and keep an eye on her."

The grey-haired woman was led out. Then Neumann and Hafner opened up the other cells and found two more young women in a similar condition. Cold, frightened, clad only in shifts. They were helped through into the kitchen, put in front of the fire and given broth and bread to warm them up. They didn't speak, but they seemed to find comfort from being with one another.

Neumann and Hafner went out through the side door to confer. The mist had lifted and weak sunlight was filtering down through the trees, dappling the forest floor. Another place, another time, it might have felt peaceful, but not here, not now. Both men could sense something malign in the air.

"What the hell's going on here?" Hafner asked.

"I don't know."

"Those women – who are they?"

"We have to get them away," Neumann said. "They need medical help, but they're in no condition to walk. Can you send one of your men to bring a carriage?"

"Of course. I'll send Feldt."

They went back inside the house. The women were

consuming their broth greedily, as if they hadn't eaten in days. Two of them kept their eyes fixed on their bowls, but the third – blonde-haired, older than the others – looked tentatively at Neumann. He saw weariness in her face and a brief flicker of something like hope that was quickly replaced by suspicion. Whatever had happened to these women, they were not going to easily trust anyone ever again.

"You are safe now," Neumann said. "We are here to protect you."

The blonde woman looked at him again. In the circumstances, a smile seemed inappropriate so he just nodded at her, trying to convey a whole raft of emotions: understanding, concern, reassurance. He had questions he needed to ask, but they would have to wait till later.

"Reinhardt?"

Hafner was trying the handle of a door set into the rear wall of the kitchen – a door that, until now, Neumann hadn't noticed.

"Where does this go? It doesn't look like a cupboard."

Neumann observed the three women look up and glance at the door, shuddering visibly before swiftly averting their eyes. He went over with the bunch of keys and found one that unlocked the door. Beyond it was a tunnel cut into the rock face, about a metre wide and two metres high, presumably a remnant of the mining and quarrying that had once taken place here. An oil lantern hung from the wall just inside the entrance. Neumann lifted it down and lit it, then he and Hafner ventured cautiously along the passage.

After four or five metres it opened out into a chamber that must originally have been a natural cave but had been enlarged by man. The ceiling was still rough, jagged rock, glistening with moisture, but the walls and floor had been tooled to a smoother finish. More lanterns hung from brackets on the walls. Neumann lit them all and in the soft yellow glow of their light, he and Hafner gazed around the chamber.

On a cursory inspection, it looked a little like a chapel. There were embroidered cloth hangings on the walls, a large stone table like an altar at one end and, above it, the painted image of a figure who had a strong religious appearance. But the impression didn't withstand closer scrutiny. The image on the wall wasn't Christ; it was an old man with a spear, the brim of his hat tilted over to one side to conceal his missing eye. Odin. The tapestries depicted scenes from Norse mythology: Odin, again, Thor with his hammer, giants and dwarves and the great ash tree, Yggdrasill. The cloth draped over the stone table was white, with a large royal blue oval patch woven into it. In the centre of the oval was a white letter W – an exact, magnified replica of the ring Neumann had found. Underneath the W were three words embroidered in gold: The Wotan Brotherhood.

Hafner wandered around the table. At each of the four corners, an iron ring had been fastened to the stone. Hanging from hooks nearby were ropes and manacles and grim implements that wouldn't have been out of place in a medieval dungeon.

"Dear God," he breathed. "What is this place? A pagan temple?"

Neumann was over to one side of the chamber, examining a heavy golden necklace that was laid out on a velvet-covered shelf and clearly had some ritual purpose. He could feel his flesh crawl as he tried to imagine what ghastly ceremonies had been conducted in this sinister heathen cave.

Hafner obviously felt the same for he said, "I don't like it here. You think those women...?" He didn't finish the question and neither of them wanted to think about the answer. "What is The Wotan Brotherhood? I've never heard of it. Let's go, Reinhardt."

They extinguished the lanterns and went back along the tunnel into the kitchen. Neumann locked the door behind them and felt a surge of relief, as if they'd shut away some evil spirit.

He went through into the bedroom where the grey-haired woman was being held. She was perched on the edge of the bed, gazing down at the floor.

"What is that chamber in the rock?" Neumann demanded. "What is The Wotan Brotherhood?"

He might not have spoken. The woman ignored him.

"Do men come here? Is that what this is about? If you've been holding those young women against their will, you'll go to prison for a very long time. Are you listening to me?"

The woman looked up at him. He saw no fear in her face, just a calm defiance. He'd taken an instant dislike to her – which he knew was bad professional practise – but he couldn't help it. She had the hardest eyes he'd ever seen – cruel, icy, devoid of empathy. He could recognise a wicked woman when he saw one, but she was only a small part of this. Men were involved, too. Men who were just as complicit – or more so – in the crimes that he was certain had been committed here.

He could feel the anger seething inside him. Fearing he might lose control, he strode out of the room and out through the front door where he paced up and down on the rocky ledge until he calmed down. One thing at a time, he said to himself. The grey-haired woman could wait. Karl Schäfer, too. The young women came first. They had to be taken away from here to some place of safety where they could be properly cared for. He thought of Amalie. He was sure now that she had also been held prisoner in this hideous building, been subjected to the same unspeakable treatment as the three women they'd just released. And he knew exactly where he was going to take them.

TWENTY-ONE

To her credit, Sophie asked no questions, though there were plenty reverberating around inside her head. She knew when talking could wait and action was the imperative.

"Show me," she said to Neumann and he took her out to the front of her house where the carriage was parked, Lieutenant Feldt and his men arranged in protective formation around it. Sophie took in their blue and yellow uniforms and paused, suddenly reminded of her father, of the last time Bavarian soldiers had been seen at Waldblick.

She pulled open the carriage door and looked inside, her gaze passing gently over the three pale young women, assessing them and deciding what needed to be done.

"We can carry them in for you," Neumann said, but Sophie shook her head.

"No, we will take it from here. Go and wait in the drawing room."

She called her maids out – Dagmar and Trudi – and together they helped the women out of the carriage and into the house. They'd been dressed in clothes and shoes Neumann had found in a wardrobe in the house on Kalvarienberg, then wrapped in blankets and brought down the hill on the soldiers' horses. They were weak and disorientated. Despite Neumann's calm reassurances, they'd found the carriage ride distressing, the soldiers' presence – their good intentions notwithstanding – threatening. But now they were among other women, they relaxed a little. Perhaps they really were safe.

Sophie put them all in one bedroom, the biggest in the house that contained a double and a single bed. They'd been alone for too long. She ordered food and tea to be brought up and sent Dagmar to fetch Gisela. Then she went downstairs to the drawing room. Neumann was standing by the window, gazing out over the garden.

"Major, please."

She sat down in an armchair near the fire. Neumann took the sofa opposite, suddenly remembering her the previous evening in her silk gown and sapphire earrings. She was back in trousers, shirt and jacket today, but it made no difference to him. It was the woman beneath the clothes that attracted him.

"Tell me," she said.

He gave her the full story, from his suspicions about Karl Schäfer through to the raid on the house that had discovered the captive women and the pagan temple.

"What is The Wotan Brotherhood?" she asked.

"I don't know. Some perverted cult which worships the old gods, I think."

"A religious cult?"

"It would seem so, from the images of Odin – Wotan – and the other Norse gods we found in the chamber."

"You're sure it's not simply sexual? The women held prisoner there, what do you think they were used for?"

Neumann hesitated. "I don't know. I will have to question them at some point. When they're ready, of course," he added quickly.

"But you must have formed some opinion based on what you've seen."

He chose his words carefully. "They may have had some ceremonial role in the activities of this Brotherhood. Or it may have gone further."

"Further?"

"They may have been physically abused."

"You don't need to spare my blushes, major. I know what the world is like. They've been raped, you mean?"

"Yes," he admitted. "I believe that's quite likely."

"Repeatedly?"

"Probably."

He looked away, ashamed for his sex, but Sophie wasn't going to let him off the hook.

"So these women were abducted and kept for the sexual pleasure of a group of depraved men."

"That would appear to be the case."

"Appear to be the case?" she repeated, almost mockingly. "Is that a yes?"

"Yes."

She was angry and he didn't blame her. Not all men, he wanted to say, but he knew that wasn't a defence, wasn't an explanation or a justification. Not from a woman's point of view. The guilt, the shame were communal.

"And Schäfer?" Sophie asked. "What is his role in this? Is he a member of the Brotherhood?"

"I don't know. But I think he procured the women for them. Part of his job is to scout for singers for the Wagner Society. I think he singled out particular young women to be abducted. On what basis I'm not sure. Maybe their appearance, or their vulnerability, or simply ones who wouldn't be missed by their families. I believe Amalie was one of them."

"Amalie?"

"I spoke to some members of the chorus last night. An Amalie Sommer was part of the group until last autumn when she disappeared. Schäfer told them she'd had to return home, but I know that was a lie."

Sophie stared at him. "Amalie was in the chorus? And I never recognised her?" She took a moment to reflect. "How blind is that?"

"She was only there for a very short time. You may never have seen her perform. And she was part of a group where the soloists are the centre of attention," Neumann said. "She would have been easy to overlook. I think she was held prisoner and somehow managed to escape into the forest where you found her. That would explain her reaction to the ring, the symbol of the Brotherhood."

"And the men behind it all? Who are they?"

"That I have to find out. The older woman in the house, the gaoler, she's in a cell at the police station. Schäfer should also be under arrest by now." He stood up. "I have to go. Thank you for your help, freiin. I could think of no better place to bring those women than here. I know you will look after them. They have been through a terrible ordeal, suffered a great deal, but the sooner I can interview them, the sooner we may be able to identify the men responsible."

Sophie got up from the armchair.

"I will talk to them myself," she said. "And send word to you when they are well enough to be questioned."

"Thank you. The soldiers will stay here for a few days."

"That won't be necessary."

"Their commanding officer is an old friend of mine. He has authorised them to remain."

Sophie's mouth tightened. "I won't have soldiers in my house."

"They do not need to be in the house. You have outbuildings where they can bunk down and they will only stand guard outside."

"I said no."

Neumann stepped forward. "Freiin," he said earnestly. "You must trust my judgement on this."

He realised he'd taken both her hands in his and was gazing fervently into her eyes. Embarrassed by this uninvited familiarity, he let go swiftly and backed away.

"I'm sorry, I shouldn't have done that. Forgive me. But these women are important witnesses, and they may potentially be in danger. The men who subjected them to their maltreatment may want to harm them, to silence them. They need to be protected."

Sophie looked at him pensively. She could still feel the touch of his hands. Warm, firm, squeezing her fingers. And the intense look in his eyes. Her heart was beating a little faster than normal. Her mouth was slightly dry. She thought about what Anneliese had said at the concert. It was still ludicrous, but perhaps it was true. She nodded.

"Very well. They may stay."

The door to the room swung open without warning and Gisela hurried in.

"Sophie, my dear, I came as soon…" The words petered out as she saw Neumann. "Excuse me, I didn't know you had company."

"This is Major Neumann. Gisela Winter. The healer I told you about. She will help look after the women."

Neumann turned to Gisela. He felt her eyes probing him, knowing him, although this was the first time they'd met. It made him uncomfortable.

"Frau Winter." He bowed. "I was just leaving. Good day to you both."

Gisela stood aside to let him exit.

"So that is the policeman from Berlin. Are you all right, child? Your face is flushed. I sense some agitation inside you."

"Not at all," Sophie replied quickly. "I'm just a little warm, nothing more. Come, we have work to do."

*

"We can't find Schäfer," Beck said, with a shrug that implied he wasn't unduly concerned.

"Where've you looked?" Neumann asked, trying to conceal his irritation. He'd given the local police one simple task and they couldn't even carry that out successfully.

"His apartment, the monastery. The kapellmeister fellow, I forget his name – "

"Hubert Steimitz."

"Yes, him. He said Schäfer never showed up for work today. And there's no sign of him at his apartment."

"Did you check inside it?"

"Not without a warrant."

"Where else does he frequent?"

Another shrug. "I don't know."

With admirable restraint, Neumann said, "Perhaps you could find out. Does he have family, friends, a mistress? Are there inns or coffee houses he goes to regularly? Talk to his neighbours, ask if they've seen him today, if they know where he might be. Send one of the constables to watch his apartment and one to check the stagecoach station. He may have left Füssen."

"What's this all about, anyway?"

"Just find Schäfer," Neumann replied. He didn't trust Beck, didn't trust any of his men. This was a small town, with small town connections, debts and obligations. Someone somewhere would know what The Wotan Brotherhood was, would know – or be able to guess – its membership. Neumann had no intention of showing his hand before he was good and ready.

Going downstairs into the main office, he got the key to the cell from Krause and went out into the yard to unlock it. The grey-haired woman was reclining on the slatted wooden platform that served as a bed, a blanket over her legs. The only other items in the room were a hard wooden chair and a slop bucket which the woman had already used. The cell reeked of urine.

Neumann sat on the chair. Shafts of dusky light lanced down through the barred window above him. The woman glanced at him indifferently, then looked away. She didn't appear concerned that she was locked in a police cell.

"What's your name?" Neumann asked her again.

She ignored him, her gaze fixed on the blank brick wall at the foot of the bed.

"You don't seem to be aware of the seriousness of your situation," Neumann went on. "You're accused of kidnapping three young women and holding them against their will. Not to mention the other crimes that may well have been committed in that house where we found you. If convicted, you'll get a lengthy jail sentence."

The woman showed a brief flicker of interest. Her eyes turned to look at him. The cold, pitiless eyes of a monster who felt no remorse for what she'd done.

"If convicted," she said and Neumann felt a sudden qualm. She wasn't frightened of her situation, or him, because she was confident nothing was going to happen to her. She had powerful protectors who would ensure it didn't: the men of The Wotan Brotherhood.

"The evidence against you is considerable. If I were you, I'd cooperate as fully as possible. The judge will take that into account in his sentencing."

"But you're not me, are you?" she said insolently.

At least she was engaging with him now, Neumann thought. Keep her talking and she might let something slip.

"Listen Frau… Why don't you tell me your name? It will have to come out eventually."

She considered for a moment and could obviously see no reason not to.

"Frida. Frida Messer."

"Whom do you work for, Frida? Who pays your wages?"

That was too direct for her. She looked back at the wall. Neumann changed tack.

"I realise you're only a small cog in this vile machine. Why should you take all the responsibility for it? You didn't kidnap those women, did you? That was Karl Schäfer. But you kept them under lock and key."

"That's all I did," she said defiantly. "I just fed them, nothing more."

"Is that right? You want me to believe that's all you did? It's not credible, Frida. And no court is going to believe it either. Why do you think the women were there?"

"That was no concern of mine."

"What's The Wotan Brotherhood?"

"I've never heard of it."

"The name's in the cave at the back of the house. In their temple."

"What cave? I've never been in any cave?"

"What about the men who visited?"

"What men?"

"The Brotherhood."

"I've just told you, I've never heard of any Brotherhood."

"I'll talk to the women, you know. They'll tell me what went on. They'll tell me what you did."

"Let them."

"I know men came to the house. Who are they, Frida? Tell me their names. You must have seen them. You know what The Wotan Brotherhood is, don't you? Do you want to pay the price for their crimes? Do you want to spend the next fifteen years, or more, in prison while they walk free? Be sensible. Think of your own future."

She'd given as much as she was going to. Neumann persisted for a while, hoping to break down her resistance, asking the same questions over and over, but Frida just stared at the wall as if he wasn't there. Finally, he gave up.

"Think about your position," he advised her as he headed for the door. "No one's going to come to your rescue, you know. They'll let you take the blame. They'll get on with their lives while yours is ruined. Is that what you want? Think about it, Frida."

He went out, locking the door behind him, and back into the main building. Krause was alone in the office.

"Where is everyone?" Neumann asked.

"Lehmann's gone to Schäfer's apartment, Böhm's at the stagecoach station."

So Beck had taken some notice of his instructions, Neumann thought. That was something. He left the station and walked over to Ritterstrasse where he found Lehmann loitering in the street.

"I've talked to the neighbours, the shopkeepers," the constable told him. "No one's seen Schäfer all day."

"Wait here," Neumann ordered.

He headed over to Schrannenplatz and caught the magistrate, Krüger, just as he was about to lock up for the night.

"My apologies, sir. I need another search warrant."

"You *are* having a busy day, major. Where is it this time?"

Neumann gave him the address. Krüger filled in the details on the warrant and handed it to him. Neumann walked back to Ritterstrasse.

"Break down the door," he said to Lehmann.

The constable applied his sizeable weight to the task. The door crumpled like cardboard. Neumann led the way up the stairs. There was a living room at the top, open to the roof to expose the timber beams that held the building together. Hanging from one of the beams, a noose around his neck, was Karl Schäfer. Close by, overturned on the rug, was a wooden chair.

"Jesus Christ!" Neumann exclaimed. "Help me here."

Lehmann grabbed hold of Schäfer's body, supporting it, while Neumann scrambled up onto the chair and cut through the rope with his pocket knife. They lowered the body to the floor. Neumann knelt down beside it. Schäfer's face was white and grotesquely contorted, his tongue sticking out from the corner of his mouth. Neumann felt for a pulse, though he knew it was too late. Schäfer had clearly been dead for several hours.

TWENTY-TWO

The pile of IOUs had been getting steadily larger all evening. Most of them were on the table in front of zu Freudenberg, but one or two belonged to von Sturm and von Mühlbeck. All of them had been written out by von Breckendorf, who had run out of cash early on and was betting money he didn't have in the hope of making good his losses.

Desperation begat recklessness and von Breckendorf was gambling like a man possessed, all caution long thrown to the wind. With each loss he doubled down and bet higher, scribbling out another note for five, ten, sometimes twenty thousand marks, huge sums which he would never be able to repay. But he didn't care. He was lost in a madness that had overwhelmed his reason, an insanity that saw a loss as a temporary blip, a losing streak as an aberration that he could overcome by throwing away even more money.

The others watched him, not spectators but participants in his downfall. They could have stopped, called an end to the proceedings, but they didn't. They played on, one hand of cards after another, driven by their own greed but also by a fascination – like a scientific experiment into human behaviour – for just how far a man could go to bring about his own ruin.

Von Mühlbeck drew another card to add to the eight and seven he already held – a nine of bells. Bust. Von Sturm, playing prudently, stuck on seventeen. Von Breckendorf had the same, but he took a chance and bought another card – a seven of leaves. Bust. Zu Freudenberg, the banker, turned over his cards. He had a ten of hearts and an eight of acorns.

"Damn you!" von Breckendorf exclaimed angrily as zu Freudenberg raked in his winnings. "Again? You had a ten and an eight before."

"And I'll have them again," zu Freudenberg replied mildly. "There are four of each in the pack, after all."

"But what are the odds, eh? What are the odds on you winning so often?"

"The same for me, as for you, as for anyone else. Chance has no favourites."

"Doesn't it? It looks that way to me. Unless you're doing something to influence it."

"What do you mean by that, Friedrich?"

Zu Freudenberg's eyes took on a steelier cast that von Breckendorf was too drunk to notice. Von Sturm, however, had a clearer head and he stepped in immediately.

"Nothing, Walther. He means nothing. Let's move on. Albrecht, you're the banker now. Deal the cards. Friedrich, are you in?"

"Of course I'm in," von Breckendorf snapped. "I'm in until I get back the money I've lost."

He topped up his glass with brandy from his second bottle of the evening and downed half of it in one gulp. His eyes were glassy, his hands shaking. Von Mühlbeck dealt him an ace of bells, von Sturm had an *unter* of acorns, zu Freudenberg an eight of leaves. All three bought a second card, von Breckendorf with another IOU, this one for five thousand marks. Von Mühlbeck checked his card – a king of hearts which counted for only two points. He bought a second, an *ober* of leaves worth just one. Von Breckendorf's second card was an *unter* of hearts – another one, giving him a total of twelve. He bought a third card – an *ober* of bells – with a second IOU for five thousand marks. The others looked at each other. Maybe enough was enough and it was time to end the game.

"You're sure about that?" von Mühlbeck asked.

"Don't patronise me," von Breckendorf shouted. "Give me a goddamn card!"

Heads turned across the room, gentlemen looking up from their newspapers or conversations. Raised voices were unusual in a club that prided itself on its manners. Members did not swear, they did not argue, they did not yell at one another, even in the most extreme of circumstances. Curious to see what the fuss was about, a few men got up from their armchairs and wandered over to the gaming table to watch.

It was the worst thing that could have happened. Von Breckendorf had an audience now and his male pride swelled up to distend a head that was already bloated with alcohol and resentment. He wasn't going to throw in the towel. He couldn't. He was going to fight back, even if all that meant was another IOU.

He had thirteen in his hand. He bought a fourth card, a seven of hearts and stuck. Zu Freudenberg also stuck. Von Sturm drew an eight of acorns and went bust. That left just the banker. Von Mühlbeck bought another card and went bust.

"Friedrich?"

Von Breckendorf turned over his cards.

"Twenty."

"Walther?"

Zu Freudenberg turned over his.

"*Siebzehn und vier.*"

Zu Freudenberg reached out to collect in the pot, but

von Breckendorf grabbed his hand to stop him.

"No, no, that cannot be. You cannot have twenty-one."

"But I have. You can see the cards."

"I can see something else, too. Something that should be obvious to everyone."

Von Breckendorf pushed back his chair and rose unsteadily to his feet, glaring at zu Freudenberg. Von Sturm stood up quickly beside him and put a restraining hand on his arm.

"Let's call it a night, Friedrich. I think we've all had enough."

"Get your damned hands off me."

"Let's go, come on. Albrecht, help me."

"Twenty-one?" Von Breckendorf yelled, leaning over the table to confront zu Freudenberg. His face was flushed with fury, spittle flecking his mouth like a rabid dog. Zu Freudenberg's expression of calm detachment didn't change and that only infuriated von Breckendorf even more.

"*Twenty-one?* Never. You, sir, are a damned –"

Von Sturm jerked von Breckendorf back abruptly before he could say the word that would inevitably call for a challenge, a demand for satisfaction. It was in no one's interests for two ministers to fight a duel.

"Take no notice, Walther," von Mühlbeck said. "He's had too much to drink. He doesn't know what he's saying."

"Let go of me, damn you," von Breckendorf bawled. "Zu Freudenberg, you are a –"

Von Sturm's hand clamped over his mouth just in time. Von Mühlbeck took hold of von Breckendorf's other arm and they dragged him out of the room, von Breckendorf barely able to stand, let alone walk.

Zu Freudenberg remained seated, apparently undisturbed by the scene. He waited for the commotion to die down, for everyone to return to their places. Then he calmly swept up his winnings, the cash and stack of IOUs, and tucked them away in his pocket.

It was the noise of shouting that woke her. Anneliese sat up in bed and listened. One of the voices was Friedrich's, the other his manservant, Helmut's. She was accustomed to the disturbance – it happened nearly every time her husband went to his club – but something about this evening was different. Friedrich's voice was louder, angrier. Helmut's, usually calm and soothing, contained a clear note of alarm.

Slipping on dressing gown and slippers, Anneliese went downstairs. The gas lamp in the hall was burning. Friedrich's coat and hat were draped over the chair by the front door. The voices were coming from her husband's study at the back of the house. Still loud and heated, as if an argument were taking place. But menservants didn't argue with their masters. Something else was going on. Something that she sensed required immediate intervention.

Anneliese hurried along the corridor and threw open the study door. Friedrich was standing by his desk, swaying on unsteady legs, a revolver in his hand which he was waving around recklessly.

"Sir, please put it down," Helmut was pleading. "Sir, just put it down."

"I'm going to do it," Friedrich shouted. "I have to. It's the only way."

He raised the revolver and tried to press it to his temple, but he was too drunk to hold the gun up. He overbalanced and toppled onto the desk. Anneliese strode forward fearlessly and wrenched the revolver from his grasp.

"Help me, Helmut."

They half dragged, half carried Friedrich to the sofa and forced him down onto the cushions. He sprawled back in the corner, semi-supine, trying to pull himself up like a floundering turtle, but too weak with alcohol to manage it.

"Wait in the hall, Helmut," Anneliese commanded.

"Ma'am, are you sure? Wouldn't it be –"

"Wait in the hall! I will call when I need you."

Anneliese waited for the manservant to leave, then she broke open the revolver. It was unloaded. It had all been a show, an empty gesture, like so many of Friedrich's actions. A cry for help, if you were inclined to be sympathetic, but Anneliese wasn't. She'd seen too many of her husband's drunken antics to have any time for his maudlin self-pity.

She put the gun away in the desk drawer and went over to the sofa.

"What's happened?" she asked bluntly. "Why all this fuss?"

Friedrich looked up at her. His eyes were glazed, unfocused. He stank of brandy. He began to whimper.

"We are ruined," he said and Anneliese's blood ran cold.

"What do you mean?"

"Ruined. I have destroyed us, Anni. There is nothing left."

"Nothing? What are you talking about?"

Friedrich didn't reply. Tears welled up in his eyes and he began to cry.

"Friedrich, pull yourself together," Anneliese said, her stomach knotting. "Tell me what's happened."

"That devil, zu Freudenberg," Friedrich sobbed.

"What about him?"

"He has taken it all. He cheated me. He rigged the cards."

"How much did you lose?"

"All gone, all gone. Zu Freudenberg took it all."

"How much, Friedrich?"

"I don't know. The IOUs. I lost track of them."

"How many IOUs?"

"I don't remember. Forgive me, Anni. It wasn't my fault. He cheated. He always cheats."

"How much?" Anneliese repeated.

"I don't know. Thousands. More."

Tears were running down his cheeks into his beard. He couldn't look his wife in the eye.

"You can't have lost it all," Anneliese said, trying to find a tiny glimmer of hope in the darkness. "Not in one evening."

"There were others before," Friedrich admitted. "Other IOUs."

"To zu Freudenberg?"

"Yes. I don't know how many."

She felt the anger surging up inside her, red hot like molten lava.

"You said you'd stop."

He looked away for a moment, then his gaze came back to her face.

"It's not my fault," he whined. "He cheated. I could've won it all back, but he cheated, I tell you. Nobody can win the way he does. I'm sorry, Anni. Forgive me." He held out his arms, imploring her. "Please, Anni. I need you."

She wanted to slap him, this pathetic weeping creature wallowing in self-pity, but amid the contempt there was still a vestige of love in her heart – the love that had joined them as man and wife fourteen years earlier and had sustained their marriage despite Friedrich's many flaws and infidelities.

"Forgive me, Anni. It's not my fault. It's not."

She went to him. She couldn't help herself. Her sense of duty as a wife was too strong to resist. She put her arms around him and drew him to her breast, his tears dribbling onto her nightgown. Staring bleakly across the room, she comforted him like the feeble child he was.

*

The first light was just creeping over the eastern horizon when Anneliese left the house. The groom and coachman had been up before dawn to prepare the carriage and horses, but the rest of the household was still asleep. Friedrich was in his room. Anneliese hadn't seen him since she and Helmut had put him to bed. She knew he wouldn't be up for hours and, even then, he wouldn't notice she'd gone.

They drove north, changing horses at Weilheim and Starnberg, and by early afternoon they were in Munich, clattering over the Isar and along Kaufingerstrasse to Herr Richter's office in the shadow of the Frauenkirche. The banker wasn't expecting her, but he immediately rearranged his appointments to create a short window in which he could see her.

"Baroness, this is indeed a pleasure," he said in his obsequious way, ushering her into his spacious suite. "And so soon after our last meeting."

"I apologise for intruding," Anneliese said. "But something has come up that requires your urgent attention."

"Of course. Can I offer you some refreshment? Tea, coffee, a glass of wine?"

"No, thank you." She was thirsty, but a drink would have to wait. Her business could brook no delay.

"I'm sorry to be so blunt, Herr Richter, but I need to know how much money we have."

The banker was adept at concealing his emotions, but even he couldn't help but wince slightly at the directness of the question. Money was his profession, his vocation even, but his clients were generally more circumspect in their dealings with him.

As Anneliese had expected, he evaded a straight answer.

"May I ask what has prompted your enquiry?"

"My husband," Anneliese replied candidly. She

wasn't going to give any details of the previous evening's events – that would have been too mortifying – but nor was she going to doctor the facts. "Last night he gave me to understand that all our money is gone. Is that true?"

Richter shifted in his seat. He was a big man, immaculate in tailcoat, black trousers, waistcoat and grey cravat. His face – well-fed, slightly pink and perfumed from his morning shave – took on a look of sincere concern, his banker's bedside manner.

"This is rather difficult, baroness. As I believe I mentioned last time, I regret that I cannot discuss financial matters with you. Only with your husband."

"But it is *our* money."

"In law, it is your husband's."

"Even the dowry I brought?" Anneliese asked. She knew the answer, but was somehow hoping that this time it might be different.

"All your property, including your dowry," the banker explained patiently, "passed to your husband on your marriage."

"But I need to know our situation. Friedrich said we are ruined. That he…" She hesitated. This was painfully embarrassing, but there was no avoiding the issue. "… has gambled it away."

Richter winced again, knowing what courage it had taken for the baroness to say that.

"I understand your concern," he said smoothly. "But you must talk to your husband about it."

When he's sober, Anneliese thought. Even then, he's unlikely to be honest with me. I need to find out now.

"You say you understand, Herr Richter, and I'm grateful for that. So I'm sure you can appreciate just how worried I am. Yes, the law says my property is my husband's, but it doesn't say that I am to be excluded from all discussions about it. Not when our very future may be at stake."

"As I said, baroness, I can deal only with the baron."

What, the feckless drunk lying snoring in bed, having frittered away a fortune? Anneliese thought bitterly. You can deal only with *him*? But she wasn't going to give up.

"Has it all gone? You must see why I have to know. Has my dowry gone, the two million marks I brought? What about our house? That was mine, too, before our marriage. Is it still ours?"

"I can tell you nothing, I'm afraid. I am bound by a bankers' code of confidentiality."

"Then tell me in confidence. Are we ruined?"

She leaned over the desk, her eyes fixed on his, a distraught woman appealing to his sense of decency. But he was not to be swayed.

"I'm sorry, baroness. As I keep saying, these are matters for your husband."

"No," Anneliese said forcefully, trying a different approach. "They are matters for *me*. It was *my* dowry, *my* house. If they are gone, do you not think I have a right to know?"

Richter held out his arms in a gesture of helplessness.

"Baroness, I would like to help…"

"Then help. Can you not see my distress? Friedrich said he had written IOUs. He didn't know how many, but probably a great number. Most seem to be to the Count Ehrenbeck zu Freudenberg. Do we owe the count a lot of money?"

"Baroness –"

"I know – you said – but I don't care about legal niceties. I care about what is right. So must you, Herr Richter. You have a reputation as a man of integrity, of honour. You must tell me. Please."

She didn't intend it, but the tears came naturally into her eyes, a few droplets trickling down her cheeks. She saw a flicker of dismay in the banker's face. Nothing made a man more uncomfortable than a weeping woman. Anneliese didn't try to hold it back. They treat me like a helpless female, she thought. Well, I'll behave like one.

The tears were flooding down her face now, smudging her make-up, the kohl and rouge blending together in ugly smears. She took out a handkerchief and dabbed at her eyes. Richter didn't know what to do. All he wanted was to bring this unsettling scene to an end.

"Baroness, please. Look, can we... Don't agitate yourself so. Please, this isn't necessary."

"We are ruined," Anneliese sobbed. "Everything is gone, everything. Friedrich told me so himself. But you will tell me nothing. You see my torment, but you will not alleviate it, even though it is in your power to do so. You are not that callous, Herr Richter. You are a better man than that."

"Baroness, please, stop crying." He held up his hands, leaning back in his chair as if he were surrendering. "It pains me to tell you this, but yes, your wealth is much diminished."

"How much?"

He hesitated, still unsure how much to tell her. But she was right. Most of the money was hers.

"You are greatly in debt. The count has a lien on your estate to cover the money he is owed by your husband."

"A lien?"

"A legal charge that effectively means he owns the estate."

Anneliese stared at him through her tears.

"Count Ehrenbeck zu Freudenberg *owns* our house and land?"

"And perhaps more if you are right about those IOUs."

"And my dowry?"

Richter grimaced. "All gone."

Anneliese couldn't speak for a time. It felt as if her

throat had suddenly swollen up and was choking her. She glared at him accusingly, finally finding her voice.

"You let my husband squander my dowry, my inheritance, and didn't say a word to me?"

Richter coloured. Even a banker could feel shame, but he had his excuses ready to hand.

"That was not my place, baroness. I advise my clients, but I do not make their decisions for them."

No, Anneliese thought, that much is true. I can blame no one else for this but Friedrich. My husband. What were their vows? For richer or poorer. For better or worse. Well, she knew now which options were going to be her fate.

TWENTY-THREE

Neumann spent the morning in Karl Schäfer's apartment, searching the premises for anything that might tell him more about The Wotan Brotherhood. The assistant kapellmeister's body had been removed, taken to the makeshift morgue in the yard behind the police station. An autopsy would have to be carried out, although there was no doubt in Neumann's mind about the cause of death. What troubled him was whether it was suicide, or something more sinister. On the face of it, Schäfer appeared to have taken his own life. The rope around his neck, the overturned chair – it all seemed pretty clear-cut. But was it? The scene would have been the same if someone had murdered the young man, strung him up and staged it to look like suicide.

There was no note, no final message from Schäfer to explain his death. In some ways his sudden end, if self-inflicted, made sense. He must have suspected that the Brotherhood – and his role in it – was in danger of exposure. Neumann mentioning Amalie after the Wagner Society concert would have alerted him to that possibility. That was surely why he'd gone out to the house in the hills the following morning – to see Frida Messer and warn her to get out as soon as she could. But homicide also made sense. Schäfer knew too much. What if the men behind the Brotherhood had decided to silence him?

Neumann went through every room, looking in cupboards and drawers, lifting rugs, checking floorboards and roof spaces, but he found nothing of interest. The assistant kapellmeister had had few possessions. Some clothes, a piano, a large stack of sheet music, but, apparently, no personal papers – although, from the large quantity of ashes in the living room fireplace it looked as if he might recently have burnt them.

Frustrated by the situation, Neumann slumped down in an armchair to gather his thoughts. Things were not looking good for him. Another violent death to add to the list. Christoph Geissler, Werner Graf and now Karl Schäfer. All linked, he was sure about that, but linked in what way? He didn't know where to go next. Lehmann and Böhm had been knocking on doors, checking whether neighbours had seen anyone visiting Schäfer, so far without success. Krause was trawling hardware stores, trying to identify the source of the rope from which Schäfer had been hanged, but Neumann didn't hold out much hope of him finding anything significant. That particular rope was no doubt in widespread use throughout the area, given that a factory making it was just across the river.

Neumann was aware that the clock was ticking. Ticking loudly. Others were, too. At their morning conference at the police station, Captain Beck had made no effort to conceal his glee at the new turn of events. Another body, another puzzle. Not so clever now are you, Mr Detective from Berlin? It wouldn't be long before von Auerswald got wind of it and then Neumann would really have some explaining to do. There was an abyss by his feet, and it wouldn't take much to send him toppling over the edge.

Sitting there passively in an armchair, however, wasn't going to get him far. He had to *do* something. Rousing himself, he left the apartment and walked across the town to Geissler's lodgings near the Franciscan Monastery. Frau Seidel, the landlady, was pleased to see him, though for purely self-interested reasons.

"I've been meaning to contact you, major," she said, showing him into the house and cornering him in the hall. She'd been scrubbing the kitchen floor and smelt strongly of disinfectant. "Herr Geissler's rooms. When will I be able to let them again? I don't want to sound insensitive, the poor man is barely cold in his grave, but, well, it *is* my income. You understand that, I hope. And at the moment they are just lying empty."

"You haven't touched anything, have you?" Neumann asked sharply.

"No, no, nothing. I haven't been in since you were last here."

"I appreciate your concerns, Frau Seidel. I hope it won't be long before you can get a new lodger. In the meantime, the rooms must remain sealed off."

"Of course. Whatever you say, major."

"Now, I have a question for you. Did Herr Geissler have any friends or acquaintances whose name began with the letter P?"

"P?" Frau Seidel repeated. "Is that the Christian or surname?"

"It could be either."

She thought for a moment. "As I said before, he didn't have many visitors, didn't go out that much. No, I can't think of anybody."

"Thank you. I won't be long."

Neumann squeezed past her and went up the stairs to the first floor. The rooms were unchanged since his previous visit, but they seemed somehow emptier, more desolate, as if the links to Geissler had grown weaker, their memory of him slowly fading away.

He'd searched the place thoroughly already, but had he missed something? He started again with the secret cavity where he'd found the runic notes. Removing the loose windowsill in the sitting room, he checked beneath it in case there was something hidden deeper in the wall, but the stonework was solid. There was nothing there.

He replaced the sill and looked out of the window. The river below was still in full flow, still that icy turquoise green. What created such a striking colour? he wondered. Some mineral in the water? Beyond the Lech, the wooded slopes of the Kalvarienberg rose steeply up into the mist. He thought about the house on the other side of the mountain, about the young women they'd freed and, inevitably, that brought him to Sophie. She was on his mind a lot at the moment. For professional reasons, he told himself. Because she'd taken in the rescued women, because with her help he might extract information from them that would move his investigation forward. But he knew that wasn't the only reason. There were personal feelings there, too. Feelings that he tried to suppress. They weren't helpful. They were a distraction that stopped him focusing on more important matters.

Like now. Where else in Geissler's rooms was he going to look? Drawers and cupboards he'd checked before. Likewise, the floorboards and bed. What did that leave? The bookcase. But he'd also examined that last time, taken out all the books and riffled through them, looking for love letters from a possible lady friend.

Wait a minute. He ran his eyes over the shelves, noting the titles, but recognising very few of them. How come? he thought, considering he'd inspected each one. But he hadn't. He hadn't been interested in the books themselves; he'd been interested in what they might potentially have been concealing. Crouching down, he scrutinised the spines. Schiller, Goethe, Hegel, he remembered those. Also, the foreign novels in English and French. But what was this? A thin little pamphlet tucked away between *Germinal* and *David Copperfield*. He pulled it out and took in the title: *Runes: A Study of the Ancient Germanic Alphabet*, by Doctor E.W Grossmeyer. It had been hiding in plain sight.

Making himself comfortable in the armchair, he opened the cover of the pamphlet and the first thing he saw was the inscription on the title page.

To my beloved B with the deepest affection, P

B and P again, Neumann thought. The same as in the runic notes. He leafed through the rest of the pamphlet. It covered much of the same ground that Ziegler had already explained to him. The source of runes, their use in pagan ritual, the meanings of the individual letters. There were no other inscriptions, but on the pages listing the letters and comparing them to the Etruscan, North Italic and Latin alphabets, someone had made ink marks beside some of the letters, as if they'd been selecting them for a reason. To transcribe messages written in runes? Or to write messages in runes? Perhaps both. If Geissler had received runic notes, it stood to reason that he might well have sent similar notes himself. But to whom? To P? Always, he kept coming back to the mysterious P.

Neumann slipped the pamphlet into the pocket of his greatcoat and went back downstairs. Frau Seidel accosted him again, still anxious about her rental income, and he reassured her once more that soon she would be able to take in a new lodger. Soon? he thought. Is that wishful thinking? It had better be soon or I'll be going back to Berlin in disgrace.

There was a note waiting for him when he got back to the police station.

"Come whenever you are free. We have something for you."

It was signed, *"Sophie"*. No title, no full name. Just

Sophie. Neumann studied the signature, finding something intensely intimate about that one word, that one name. Then he put the note in his pocket and went out to get his horse from the stables.

She took him into the drawing room first. To lay down the ground rules for him – he being a Prussian and a policeman and thus, by definition, a brute and a bully, a man who yelled at witnesses, or worse, and certainly could not be trusted with a young, vulnerable woman without simple instructions about how to behave. And Neumann listened, trying not to feel offended – or, at least, not to show it – whilst wondering how this intelligent, perceptive, sensitive woman could misjudge him so badly. Yet the answer was there in the room, the portrait of her father above the mantelpiece, the soldier killed at Kissingen, which meant she would never be able to look at him as anything other than a foe.

"Do I make myself clear, major?" Sophie asked, addressing him as if he were a servant – which I suppose I am to a freiherrin like her, Neumann thought.

"Perfectly, ma'am. You can rest assured that the young lady's welfare is of paramount importance to me."

Sophie shot him a probing glance, as though she suspected insolence, or amusement at her expense. Have I been a little condescending? she wondered. That was not my intention. I just want to protect the girl.

They went upstairs to a sitting room where the blonde woman from the house on the hill was sitting in an armchair in front of a blazing fire. Her name, Sophie had told him, was Magdalena Hahn and she was twenty-six years old. She was wearing a thick quilted dressing gown and fur slippers. On the low table beside her was a cup of tea and a plate of biscuits.

Neumann pulled up a chair and sat down. Sophie took the sofa, sitting next to Gisela who was already there, watching over Magdalena, ready to intervene if things got too much for her.

Neuman looked at the young woman. She was pale and drawn, but when her gaze turned towards him, he saw a spark in her eyes that hinted at an inner resilience – a strength that enabled her to speak to him so soon after she had been freed from her captivity. He kept his voice low and gentle. He knew from Sophie that Magdalena spoke only dialect, no High German, so the freiin would act as interpreter for them.

"Fräulein, I'm grateful for your cooperation. I know this is not going to be easy for you, but any information you can give me will help us find the people who imprisoned you. If at any point you want a break, or to stop entirely, just say so. Do you mind if I take notes?"

Magdalena shook her head. "No, I want it written down. I want people to know what they did to me, and the others."

"In your own time, then. Perhaps you could begin by telling us a little about yourself. Your background, where you come from, how you came to be in this part of Bavaria."

Magdalena nodded, preparing herself. Then she told her story. Her home was in Zwiesel, a small town in the east of the country, just a few kilometres from the border with Bohemia. An only child, her parents both died when she was young and she was brought up by an elderly widowed aunt who ensured she had a good elementary education, then found her a position as a maid in the home of the local doctor whose wife was a keen amateur musician – a pianist and singer. It soon became apparent that Magdalena had a promising singing voice. The doctor's wife encouraged her, taught her to read music and allowed her to join the choir of the nearby convent, singing for the services on a Sunday.

Then word came that the king's kapellmeister was

looking to recruit new singers for the Wagner Society at Füssen and Karl Schäfer showed up in Zwiesel.

At this point, Magdalena broke off for a moment to compose herself. For this was the fateful event that would shape the next few years of her life and lead to her eventual incarceration and maltreatment.

Bored with domestic service and small-town life and looking for new, more interesting opportunities, Magdalena auditioned for Schäfer and was delighted to be chosen. Her travelling expenses paid, with a generous bonus on top, she moved to Füssen and into lodgings with the other female members of the Wagner Society chorus, including the two other young women who'd been imprisoned alongside her.

For almost two years, her new career went well. She rehearsed and performed regularly, enjoying both the singing and the camaraderie with the other girls. Then one day, Schäfer collected her from her lodgings, saying that she'd been selected for extra coaching that would enable her to step up to the next level, to sing small solo roles for the society.

Magdalena was pleased, flattered. She suspected nothing. The assistant kapellmeister was well regarded by the chorus. He was a fine musician, a hard taskmaster at times, but his behaviour towards the female singers was always perfectly proper. Even when they went out to the Kalvarienberg, a strange location for singing lessons, Magdalena continued to put her trust in Schäfer. He was taking her to a special school, he said. A remote centre where there were no distractions and she could receive intense one-to-one tuition to improve her vocal skills. It was only when she entered the building that a few alarm bells started to ring inside her head. But by then it was too late. She was seized by Schäfer and Frida Messer and bundled into a cell. The nightmare began.

Magdalena paused, clearly discomposed. Neumann

asked if she'd like a break, but she shook her head. Now she'd started, she wanted to finish. Taking a sip of tea, she continued her story.

For the next few weeks, she was kept locked in the cell. She was given only basic rations – water and a tiny amount of food. At intervals, Schäfer would return and she was bound with rope and beaten by Frida Messer. The plan was clear: to weaken her and break down her resistance. She wasn't allowed out of her cell, wasn't allowed to see anyone other than Schäfer and Frida, although she knew other girls were also being held prisoner because she could hear their cries as they, too, were beaten.

Neumann listened in horror, wondering how she could recount these appalling events with such stoic calm. At one point, he glanced at Sophie and Gisela and saw the shock, the revulsion, in their faces – particularly Sophie's, as she was having to listen to the harrowing details and then repeat them to him in a language he could understand.

Finally, one evening, Magdalena was brought out of her cell, too cowed and debilitated to fight back. She was bathed by Frida, her hair washed and her body anointed with perfume. Then, still naked, her hands were tied behind her and a blindfold placed over her eyes and she was led along the tunnel into the chamber behind the house – the temple of The Wotan Brotherhood – where the men were waiting for her.

She paused again and Neumann saw a change come over her. Her unnatural calm fractured and she showed the first clear signs of distress.

"Do you need a break, fräulein?" he asked again. "We can continue at another time."

Magdalena didn't reply. Neumann looked at Sophie, who was regarding the young woman with intense concern.

"Perhaps we should stop," she said.

"Has she told you any of this already?"

"We're hearing it for the first time, like you."

"Fräulein –" Neumann began, but he was cut short by Magdalena.

"No, I must tell you now. Let me finish."

She closed her eyes for a few seconds, steeling herself for the next part of her account. Then she went on, speaking softly but more rapidly now as if she just wanted the ordeal to be over.

She never knew how many men there were in total. From their voices, she guessed it was around half a dozen. There was always a ceremony involved. First, a necklace was placed around her neck. The Brisingamen, the men called it. It was made of metal and was cold on her skin. Neumann nodded. That had to be the gold necklace he had found in the temple. Then Magdalena was led to the stone table – the altar of the Brotherhood – and tied down on top of it. A gag was fastened around her mouth and the men went through a series of ritual chants, all invocations and prayers to Wotan.

Then... Magdalena choked on her words and she gave a shudder that seemed to vibrate through the floorboards and up through the chair into Neumann's body, chilling his flesh, sending icy shivers up his spine and out along his arms and legs.

Then...

Magdalena and Sophie conversed briefly in dialect and Sophie translated for Neumann.

"She says the men raped her. One after the other."

"Were those her exact words? Rape?"

"'Did things to her'. That's what she said. But rape is what she meant. She's just too ashamed to say it, though why she should feel shame God only knows. God and those despicable men."

"If that's what happened," Neumann said. "Then I

need to hear her say it."

Sophie's eyes flashed angrily. "Haven't you put her through enough already? Can you not see how traumatic this is for her? And yet you want all the gruesome details."

"Freiin, this is a formal legal process. I am taking down evidence. What kind of man do you think I am? Of course, I don't want to cause her any unnecessary pain, but she has to be specific. I need to establish what crimes have been committed. A court will need that information, too."

Sophie glared at him, but she took his point. She had another exchange in dialect with Magdalena, then the young woman began to speak. Haltingly, pausing at intervals, obviously fighting back tears. And it was a grim, sickening tale she had to tell. Neumann wrote it down in his notebook, feeling a range of emotions: horror, shame, sympathy, anger, disgust and admiration for Magdalena's courage in reliving experiences that must have wounded her deeply, perhaps irrevocably.

"Thank you, fräulein," he said at the end. "I know how difficult that must have been for you. I'm afraid I have a few more questions to ask you, but shall we take a break first?"

"Questions?" Sophie asked before she relayed his words to Magdalena. "Is that really necessary?"

"It's essential," Neumann replied. "The men who did this, I need to identify them."

Sophie spoke again to Magdalena and her reply was unequivocal.

"Ask your questions now. Get this finished."

"These ceremonies..." Neumann began. No, call them what they are. "These violations... how often were you subjected to them?"

Every few weeks, Magdalena replied. There were three girls held captive in the house and they were rotated, a different one chosen each week. It became more frequent for a time after Amalie managed to escape, but she was soon replaced by another girl and the routine resumed.

"So The Wotan Brotherhood met every week?"

"Yes."

"And was it always the same men?"

"I think so. I recognised their voices, the smell of their bodies."

"What did they smell of?"

"Perfume, eau de cologne. They were gentlemen."

"What makes you think that?"

"Their hands when they touched me. They weren't rough like a workman's hands. They were soft and pampered."

"Did you hear any names mentioned?"

"No."

"Or see their faces?"

"Twice. The blindfold slipped and I caught a glimpse of two of them."

"Can you describe them?"

"One was clean shaven. A big, balding man. He was always rough, one of the nastiest. The other had a beard and moustache. I only saw them very briefly."

"Would you recognise them if you saw them again?"

Magdalena nodded, suppressing another shudder.

"I will never forget their faces."

"I'm nearly done," Neumann said. "May I show you something?" He produced the enamelled 'W' ring from his pocket and held it out. "Have you ever seen this before?"

He recalled Amalie's violent reaction and braced himself for something similar, but Magdalena just squeezed her eyes shut for a second, then nodded.

"The men I saw, they both wore a ring like that."

"Thank you, fräulein."

Neumann brought the interview to a close. He could see how distraught Magdalena was, how spent by his questions. Gisela helped her to her feet and took her away to her bedroom, leaving Neumann and Sophie alone in the sitting room.

"Will you find these men?" the freiin asked.

"I will do my best."

"Her descriptions are very vague."

"I know, there's not much to go on, but I have Frida Messer in custody. I will question her."

"And Schäfer, too?"

"Schäfer's dead," Neumann replied, embarrassed by the admission.

"*Dead*?"

"He was found hanging from a beam in his apartment."

"Suicide?"

"We're keeping an open mind."

"You heard what Magdalena said. They are gentlemen, perhaps powerful gentlemen. And powerful gentlemen are not often held to account for their crimes."

She was right, Neumann reflected. He didn't want to give her false hope, but nor did he want to sound defeatist.

"I will do my utmost to catch them," he said. "Now I must go."

They both stood up.

"How are the other girls?" Neumann asked as he walked past Sophie to the door.

"Not good, as you might expect. They are more traumatised than Magdalena. Like Amalie, they cannot speak about the torments they have had to endure, but with help they may eventually recover. That is my fervent hope, anyway."

"Mine, too," Neumann said. "And I cannot think of anyone better able to achieve that aim than you, freiin.

Thank you for taking them in and looking after them."

Impulsively, he took her hands in his own again. This time he didn't apologise, didn't step away. Sophie looked startled. She made no attempt to withdraw. Neumann sensed that she was as drained as he was by the interview with Magdalena. As appalled and revolted. He felt a compelling need for some kind of human contact that would wash away the sick depravity of The Wotan Brotherhood. That would show the tenderness, the warmth, the love that was possible between men and women. He was tempted to pull her into his arms and hold her, but he restrained himself. He gave her fingers a final squeeze and let go.

"I will be in touch."

He bowed and strode quickly out of the room. Sophie remained rooted to the spot, staring at her hands, and that was how Gisela found her when she returned a few minutes later.

"Magdalena is resting," she said. "I have given her something to calm her... Freiin? What's the matter? You look troubled."

"No, no, I'm fine."

Gisela gave her a searching look. "The major has gone?"

"Just now."

"Do not be too hard on him, child. He's a good man."

"You think so?"

"I know it. I can see it in his face, his eyes, the way he conducts himself. He is a policeman. He is just doing his job."

Sophie nodded, rubbing her palms on her jacket to erase the memory of his touch.

"Yes, perhaps you're right."

The ride back to Füssen gave Neumann the time to get a hold on his emotions, to cool the anger that Magdalena's brutal treatment had aroused in him. Anger was not good in a policeman, but rarely had he felt such a white-hot fury, such an overpowering loathing for a group of his fellow men. This Wotan Brotherhood, whoever they were, were viler and more evil than any criminals he had ever encountered before, and beneath his simmering hatred was an equally burning determination to track them down and bring them to justice.

He was calmer when he reached the police station. Lehmann was on duty, though he looked half asleep slumped in a chair in the back office. Neumann gave him a prod and asked for the key to the cell.

"When was the last time you checked the prisoner?" he enquired.

"Me?" Lehmann said, yawning.

"Anyone."

"Böhm took her some supper before he went home."

"Supper?"

"Just some bread and soup from the inn across the street."

Neumann went out into the yard and flipped down the observation hatch on the cell door. Frida Messer was sprawled on her bed, apparently asleep. One arm was beneath her, the other hanging limply over the side. Her face was turned away, half hidden by her hair. On the floor beside the bed was a bowl of soup that looked almost untouched. Neumann felt a sudden stirring of alarm. Something wasn't right.

He turned the key in the lock, whipped open the door and hurried inside, stopping as he drew closer to the bed and got a better view of Frida's face. Her skin was ashen, her eyes wide open but lifeless. Her mouth gaped, the corners flecked white with dried foam. Neumann reached down carefully and felt her neck for a pulse that wasn't there.

TWENTY-FOUR

Sophie wrapped up warm – a thick cloak with a hood, mittens and fur-lined boots – and went out through the drawing room French windows onto the terrace at the back of the house. She needed to clear her head. The interview with Magdalena had upset her greatly. Not just the horrific facts about the young woman's imprisonment and rape, but the way in which Neumann's questions had had to be relayed through her so she felt as if Magdalena's answers were somehow also her own. Every distressing detail she had had to hear twice: Magdalena's words in dialect and then the translation into High German.

It was pitch dark outside, but enough light spilled out from the drawing room for her to make out the shadowy figure of one of the soldiers keeping guard around the building. She was glad that Neumann had overcome her objections to the extra security – particularly now that she knew what violence the men of The Wotan Brotherhood were capable of. Having sentries to protect both her and the young women upstairs was immensely reassuring.

The soldier looked towards her. "Ma'am. Is everything all right?"

"Yes, thank you. I'm just getting some air."

"Would you like me to accompany you?"

"Thank you, but that won't be necessary. I'm not going far."

She went across the lawn and stopped at the fringes of the forest. She peered into the blackness. Are you there? she wondered. If only I had your sense of smell, your keen eyes, I would know. Pulling a bag from beneath her cloak, she tipped out the contents onto the ground – some scraps of meat and fat and a pig's bone. Then she stepped back. She knew there were all manner of reasons why she shouldn't do this. But there were even more why she should. It was an act of kindness, communion with another creature that was in need of assistance.

Like the young women she'd taken in over the years – the vulnerable, the damaged, the defenceless women who had had no one else to turn to. Like Amalie and the three girls who'd just arrived. She had a duty of care towards them, but she also wanted to help them, if for no other reason than it was the right thing to do.

Neumann understood that. A good man, Gisela had said. A good man doing his job, but he was doing more than that. He didn't need to have brought Magdalena and the others here, but he did. He knew I would look after them. He thanked me for it. He seems to understand me, too. That was rare in a man in her experience. He'd gone too far, of course. Taking the liberty of holding her hands again. She should have rebuked him for that, but she was quite glad she hadn't.

Something moved in the undergrowth. She saw eyes gleaming, the flash of white on fur. The she-wolf she thought of as White Blaze edged cautiously out of the forest. They looked at each other for a moment. There was no fear. They were at ease together. Then the wolf gobbled down the meat and fat, picked up the bone in her jaws and trotted back into the trees.

Sophie retraced her steps across the garden and back

into the house, locking the French windows behind her. She was in the hall, preparing to go upstairs to bed, when she heard the rattle of wheels outside on the forecourt. Peering out through the narrow window beside the front door, she saw a carriage coming to a halt and recognised it immediately. She rammed back the bolts, disengaged the lock and pulled open the door. One of the soldiers was already at the carriage window, talking to the occupant. Sophie dashed down the steps and called out to him.

"It's all right, it's a friend. I'll deal with it."

Anneliese was huddled inside the carriage, wrapped in a cloak and blankets, but still shivering with the cold.

"Anni? What is it?"

"I've been to Munich. I saw Herr Richter. Sophie –"

"Let's get you inside. You must be half frozen."

Anneliese stumbled out of the carriage, her legs struggling to support her. With the soldier's help, Sophie guided her up the steps and into the warmth of the house.

"You look exhausted, Anni. Have you eaten?"

"Nothing all day."

Sophie rang for the maids and gave orders for food to be brought from the kitchen. It didn't matter what so long as it was hot.

"And my coachman, he'll need something, too," Anneliese said with typical selflessness.

Sophie stoked the fire in the drawing room herself, blowing the embers back to life and adding more wood until it was burning fiercely, the heat radiating out to enfold Anneliese in a reviving embrace.

The food arrived quickly: a pot of strong tea and a bowl of heated-up pork stew and dumplings. Sophie poured Anneliese a cup of tea and made her eat some of the stew before she allowed her to speak.

"Why is there a soldier outside?" Anneliese asked.

Sophie explained. Anneliese stared at her, aghast.

"The Wotan Brotherhood? There are men who still worship the old gods?"

Sophie shook her head.

"There is nothing religious about it, in my view. It's merely a cover for them to gratify their most base desires."

"And the policeman, Neumann, he thinks those men might come here and harm the women?"

"He fears it, yes. He insisted on posting a guard around the house, just in case."

"And you? Are you not frightened, too?"

"I can protect myself, you know that. I have pistols, rifles, and know how to use them."

"And the women themselves, how are they?"

"Deeply traumatised. Who wouldn't be after what they've been through? But we are looking after them."

Sophie studied her carefully. Anneliese was pale, her eyes puffy and red, as if she'd been weeping.

"What's happened?"

Anneliese took a moment. She'd had the six-hour carriage journey from Munich to collect her thoughts, but now she was asked to express them, words failed her. She drank some tea. The warm liquid was soothing, the fire in the hearth roasting, but still she felt a core of ice inside her, a desolation that would never thaw.

"It's Friedrich," she said eventually.

Of course, Sophie thought. What else? She waited, giving Anneliese time.

"He has gambled away everything."

Sophie took it as a figure of speech, an exaggeration, but then she saw that her cousin meant it literally. Anneliese's composure disintegrated and she burst into tears. Sophie pulled her into a tight embrace and held her while she wept.

"I'm sorry," Anneliese said, pushing Sophie away

gently and reaching for a handkerchief to wipe her eyes. "I shouldn't burden you with my troubles."

"That's exactly what you should do," Sophie replied. "We are family, we are friends. I'm here to listen and help. How bad is it?"

Anneliese sniffed, a tear glistening on her cheek.

"Very. I don't know the full extent – I don't think Herr Richter knows either – but it's serious. Walther Ehrenbeck zu Freudenberg has a charge on our estate, a lien, whatever that is. Herr Richter says it effectively means he owns it unless we can pay off the debts Friedrich owes him."

"How much is that?"

"I don't know. But I think there are more IOUs. Friedrich could owe hundreds of thousands. My dowry is all gone, our bank account is virtually empty. Herr Richter was very understanding, but he said that only Friedrich can sort it out. It's not my place as a woman."

"Damn your place as a woman," Sophie snapped. "It's your money that's gone, your house that Friedrich has thrown away. Have you spoken to him?"

"Last night. He came home from his club, drunk as usual, and tried to kill himself."

"*What*?"

Anneliese held up her hand. "Not as alarming as it sounds. He keeps a revolver in his study desk drawer, but it was unloaded. He was waving it around, making threats to end it all. Poor Helmut was trying to restrain him. The whole incident was hugely embarrassing."

"Anni, embarrassment is the least of your worries. We need to establish exactly how much Friedrich owes and then work out a plan to deal with the situation."

"'We'?"

"I'm not going to leave you to sort it out by yourself. If needs be, I will lend you the necessary money."

"You will do nothing of the kind," Anneliese said firmly.

"I'm a rich woman."

"This is *our* problem, Sophie, not yours. I won't have you compromising your own estate to help us. Besides, the amounts involved may be too much even for you. I didn't come here to ask for your help. Well, not your financial help. I just needed to talk to you."

"Talking is good," Sophie said. "But talking won't solve the problem. If you won't take anything from me, how do you propose to handle it?"

"That's what I've been thinking about all the way home. I have only one course of action. I must throw myself on the count's mercy. Ask him to tear up Friedrich's IOUs."

"Surely Friedrich should do that, not you?"

"He would only make matters worse. He is angry, humiliated. He says zu Freudenberg cheated him. He would probably do something rash."

"And will the count listen to you?"

"I think so. He is an honourable man. He will do the right thing."

TWENTY-FIVE

It was gone midnight when Neumann returned to his room at the Gasthaus Hoffmann. He was exhausted, both mentally and physically. Frida Messer's death had been a shock, a body blow that had left him reeling. Was it murder? It might conceivably have been natural causes, a heart attack or a stroke, but he doubted it. The colour of her skin, the foam around her mouth; it looked like poisoning to him. The second murder since he'd arrived in Füssen. Possibly the third if Karl Schäfer's end hadn't really been suicide. And Frida's demise inevitably cast suspicions over Schäfer's. The two key witnesses to the activities of The Wotan Brotherhood, both dead before they could be seriously interrogated. That was too convenient to be a coincidence.

Only an autopsy would establish the exact cause of Frida's death. The pathologist had been informed, although when he might actually show up wasn't clear, given that he hadn't yet come down from Munich to carry out the post-mortem examination of Werner Graf's corpse. Doctor Jaeger was, apparently, a very busy man.

Neumann was furious with himself. He'd been unforgivably remiss with both Schäfer and Messer. He should have arrested the assistant kapellmeister as soon as he returned from the raid on the house in the hills, rather than putting the welfare of the young women first. With Messer, he should have questioned her more forcefully when he had the chance, then made sure she was closely monitored in her cell. He'd assumed she would be safe in the police station. In hindsight, a woefully negligent decision.

He'd spent the evening trying to establish what had happened to Frida. In the absence of any autopsy evidence, he had worked on the assumption of foul play, most probably poison. The soup and bread she'd been given had come from the Wild Hart, the inn across the street from the police station. All the food served to prisoners came from there as the police station had no cooking facilities, let alone anyone capable of using them. Had someone interfered with the meal, slipped poison into it before it reached Frida?

Neumann had questioned the staff at the inn: the cook who'd made the soup, the scullery maid who'd helped, and the kitchen boy who'd delivered it to the police station. All denied adulterating it in any way and Neumann could find nothing suspicious about their testimony or, indeed, the soup itself which had also been served to several customers of the inn with no ill effects. Frida's portion, he discovered, had been left unattended on the saloon bar for a few minutes while the kitchen boy went to fetch his overcoat. The bar had been crowded and it was possible that someone had taken the opportunity to covertly add poison then. But there was no hard evidence to support that theory.

That left only the police. The kitchen boy had brought the soup to the police station and deposited it on the front counter where any of the officers could have had access to it before Böhm took it through to the cell. A policeman? Neumann wondered. It didn't bear thinking about.

He went to the window and looked out across

Brotmarkt. The square was deserted, illuminated by a single streetlamp that cast a sickly yellow glow over the frosty cobbles. He recalled the day he'd arrived, his first meeting with Prince von Auerswald, his first briefing about the murder of Christoph Geissler. He'd had a bad feeling about the case from the very start, and those misgivings had been entirely justified. A straightforward homicide investigation had metamorphosed into something much more complicated. Into multiple homicides, into kidnapping and rape, into a perverted cult that appeared to worship the old Norse gods.

He thought back over his interview with Magdalena Hahn, remembering a detail she had mentioned – the gold necklace that had been a key part of the ceremony in the temple to Wotan. The Brisingamen. The name had rung a bell with him and it was only now that he recollected why. Sitting down in the armchair, he opened Norbert Ziegler's book on the Norse gods to the contents page. There it was, a chapter heading: *Freyja and the Necklace of the Brisings* – p162. He turned to page one hundred and sixty-two.

In Norse mythology, Ziegler had written, the male gods were dominant. Odin, or Wotan, the most powerful of all, was the God of Battle and also, somewhat incongruously, the God of Poetry. Wise, all-seeing and terrifying, he was a god to be respected rather than loved. In contrast, his son, Thor, second in the pantheon, was the god held in the greatest affection by both men and the other gods. A huge, red-bearded figure, the God of Thunder, he was the champion of farmers and the common people, the strongest, most dependable of the gods who held the giants at bay with his mighty hammer, Mjollnir.

Third most important was Freyr, the God of Plenty, lord of the sun and rain and harvests who controlled the prosperity of men. There were other male gods, nine of them, including Heimdall, Tyr and Baldur, but they featured only intermittently in the myths. The female gods fared even worse. Apart from Frigg, Odin's wife, only one had much prominence: Freyr's sister, Freyja, who, like her brother, was a deity associated with fertility, although in her case, because of her sex, she was also portrayed as the Goddess of Love and the Earth Mother, the protector of women in childbirth.

Compared to the male gods, the females were given little substance and only minor supporting roles in the tales. While the male representation was not always flattering – they were shown to be violent, dishonest and lustful – the goddesses were invariably trivialised as vain, greedy and promiscuous, these characteristics exemplified no more clearly than in the myth of Freyja and the Necklace of the Brisings.

Freyja, the most beautiful and sexually alluring of all the goddesses, had a love for gold, silver and jewels. Early one morning, she left her home in Asgard and walked over Bifrost, the flaming rainbow bridge, into Midgard, the land of men. For a day she picked her way across a hostile terrain, past glaciers and frozen rivers and rocky, barren outcrops until, as dusk fell, she reached the entrance to a dark cave. Venturing into the opening, she went down and down into the bowels of the earth and found herself in a huge dank cavern, the walls dripping with water, the air damp and fetid. In the distance, she could hear the sound of hammering. Continuing on along a narrow passage, she emerged into another rock chamber where a group of dwarfs was labouring over a blazing smithy. On a shelf to one side, shimmering in the firelight, was a gold necklace whose beauty took Freyja's breath away. Burnished, incised with almost magical patterns, it was the most enticing object she'd ever seen. She knew she had to have it.

The dwarfs stopped work. There were four of them –

Alfrigg, Dvalin, Berling and Grerr – dirty, ugly and cunning, as dwarfs in Norse mythology always were. Freyja asked if they had made the necklace and they nodded. How much did they want for it? It's not for sale, they replied. I will give you silver and gold, Freyja went on. As much as you want. We have gold and silver aplenty, the dwarfs said. I must have it, Freyja insisted. What do you want for it? The dwarfs looked at her with unconcealed lust. They conferred for a while, then Alfrigg said, "We want you." Freyja demurred. She wasn't for sale either. She tried to bargain with them, but the dwarfs would not be moved. "The necklace belongs to all of us," Alfrigg said. "If you want it, you must lie one night with each of us."

Freyja was appalled at the idea. The dwarfs were deformed and repulsive. Just looking at them made her shudder. But the necklace was exquisite. Was it too high a price to pay for something she desired so desperately? She agreed to their terms. For four nights she remained in the cavern, sleeping with each of the dwarfs in turn, and on the final morning they presented her with the necklace, the Brisingamen.

No one knew where the name came from, Ziegler explained. The Old Norse word *men* meant necklace, but what the prefix Brising denoted was uncertain. Were the Brisings an ancient tribe? Were the dwarfs the Brisings? Or was the name derived from the Old Norse *brisingr*, meaning fire, because of the golden brilliance of the object?

Neumann didn't care. Etymology was of no interest to him. But he wondered why the men of The Wotan Brotherhood had replicated the necklace. Was it purely for aesthetic or sexual reasons – the adorning of a naked woman with jewellery? Or was there something more symbolic about it? Freyja didn't come out well from the myth, a goddess who was prepared to sell her body for an ostentatious ornament. Was the message here, all women are whores? Is that what the Brotherhood wanted to believe, to justify their abuse of them?

Neumann was pretty sure of one thing: the necklace had been made by Werner Graf – as had the 'W' rings – and the missing pages in his record books identified the client who had commissioned them. He was mulling over the significance of that when there was a sudden, loud rap on the door.

At this hour? he thought tetchily. It had better be something urgent. The king's adjutant, Captain Wilhelm Schirmer, was outside.

"Ah, you are still up. Good," Schirmer said, striding in.

He was dressed in his usual finery, his polished helmet tucked under one arm, the feather finial poking out over his elbow, as if he were concealing an ostrich under his jacket.

"My apologies for disturbing you so late, but His Majesty wishes to see you."

"Now?" Neumann asked, and immediately saw the foolishness of the question. Why else would the adjutant have called at this time of night?

Schirmer nodded. "The carriage is waiting outside."

For a fleeting moment, Neumann thought about refusing. He wanted nothing more than to go to bed. But that would not have been prudent. When a monarch summoned you, the wise man obeyed. He was already in enough difficulties with his investigation. The last thing he needed was a formal complaint from the palace to von Auerswald. He accompanied Schirmer out to the carriage.

He expected to be taken to New Hohenschwangau, as before, but they went up the drive to the old palace instead. Although it was one o'clock in the morning, the building was ablaze with lights. Gathered in the courtyard were various household servants and a group of cavalrymen who were harnessing four gleaming white stallions to an ornate sleigh. At the rear of the sleigh was an upholstered seat and, at the prow, entwined in a rococo gold decoration, a golden mermaid, her breasts exposed, her hands holding aloft two glass lanterns.

"Wait here," Schirmer instructed and disappeared into the palace.

Neumann paced up and down, trying to keep warm. The courtyard was sheltered, but it was still bitterly cold. To one side was the main building, an impressive construction in the Romantic style, with yellow stucco render and turrets and battlements on the roof. Painted on the wall of the nearest tower was a heraldic emblem featuring the Palatinate Lion, the Imperial orb and the Bavarian lozenges. The leonine theme was continued on the fountain at the end of the courtyard where a carved lion's head would normally have spouted a jet of water into a stone basin, but in the sub-zero temperatures it was now just a frozen trickle drooling from the creature's lips.

Two figures came down the steps from the palace. At the front was Ludwig, wearing an overcoat and a black bowler hat, looking more like a mid-rank civil servant than a monarch. Behind him came Axel Hoffmann, carrying a hemp sack over his shoulder.

The king looked vaguely at Neumann, frowning as if he recognised him but couldn't remember from where. Axel leaned over and whispered something in his ear.

"Ah, yes, Major Neumann," Ludwig said. "The policeman from Berlin. You are ready, I trust?"

Neumann nodded automatically, although he had no idea what he was supposed to be ready *for*.

"Well, get in then," the king continued, an edge of irritation in his tone. "We haven't got all night. Actually, we have." He gave a high-pitched bark, as if this were a tremendous joke, and everyone around him laughed sycophantically.

"If you please, sir," Axel said to Neumann, gesturing at the sleigh, then lowering his voice. "We're going for a ride."

A ride? Neumann thought. A ride where? But he did as he was bid – what choice did he have? – clambering into the sleigh and settling down in the seat. Ludwig climbed in next to him. He was a big, corpulent man. Neumann found himself squeezed tight into the corner. Axel stowed the sack in the well of the sleigh, then servants came forward and wrapped thick blankets around the legs of Neumann and the king. Axel took the perch behind them, less a seat than a padded protrusion which he had to straddle precariously, his toes tucked into a couple of insulated footrests.

"The lights, Hoffmann!" Ludwig commanded.

Axel flicked a switch and the two lanterns on the prow burst into life, illuminating the mermaid's golden tresses and scaly tail.

"What do you think?" the king asked Neumann. "Impressive, eh? Electricity, you know. There are batteries under the seat to store it. Who knew you could do that? But I've always been ahead of my time. The day will come, I vouch you, when everyone will have electric lights in their homes. Well, perhaps not the common people, but certainly the gentry. What're we waiting for? Let's be off."

The cavalrymen mounted their horses, two riding postillion on the stallions pulling the sleigh, two more acting as outriders at the front. They pulled off down the icy drive, descending in a curve past the frozen Alpsee, through the village of Hohenschwangau and out onto the plain, heading east past Schwangau.

It was a cloudless night. The moon was almost full, bathing the landscape in a brilliant silvery light. Urged on by the king, who seemed to get a thrill from speed, the postillions spurred the horses into a gallop and the sleigh raced across the snow, its shadow chasing along beside it.

"I love a sleigh ride, don't you, major?" Ludwig cried, pressing his bowler hat down over his ears to stop it blowing off. "Have done since I was a boy. Faster! Faster! Wheeee!"

Neumann was crushed against the side of the seat, his nostrils filled with the pungent scent of the cologne the king was wearing. The sleigh was swerving dangerously from side to side, but Ludwig didn't seem concerned. He reached beneath the seat and pulled out a flask and two crystal glasses. He poured them each a generous measure of honey-coloured liquid.

"Mead," he said, taking a sip and smacking his lips. "The drink of the gods. The old gods, I mean. Odin, Thor and the rest. Are you familiar with Norse mythology, major? I've always been fascinated by it. I read the tales avidly as a child. In secret, of course. I was brought up a strict Catholic and my parents disapproved strongly of what they regarded as heathen nonsense. But I didn't find it nonsense. I loved it. I wanted two ravens of my own, like Odin. A Huginn and a Muninn to sit on my shoulders and tell me the secrets of the world. But my father wouldn't allow it."

Ravens? Neumann thought, suddenly paying more attention.

"I wanted to see Yggdrasill, the World Tree," the king went on. "And visit the Norns, the old women who lived beneath it, spinning the fates of men. Urd, who saw the past; Werdandi, the present and Skuld, the future. I used to wonder whether they would determine my fate too. Did you think about that when you were a boy? Did you wonder what your destiny would be?"

Did I? Neumann thought. Of course. But he'd never considered that the answer might have come from a bunch of imaginary crones living under an ash tree.

"Norse mythology was so much more interesting to

me than Christianity," Ludwig continued. "That's probably blasphemy, but what's one more sin among all my others? The stories were just so entertaining. You know their version of the Creation? In the beginning there was nothing except a great gulf named Ginnungagap, to the north of which was Nifelheim, the land of mists and cold and ice. Sounds a bit like Prussia to me."

He let out another high-pitched laugh. Neumann hadn't expected him to have a sense of humour. He seemed to be on good form tonight.

"To the south was Muspellheim, a hot place of smoking fires and raging volcanoes. When an iceberg from Nifelheim floated down into Muspellheim, it was melted into steam from which a huge creature of pure white clay was shaped – the giant, Ymir. He was the father of the frost giants who budded from his body like leaf buds from a tree. They were Burr and Bor and a giantess named Bestla who gave birth to three sons, Wili, We and Odin. These three set upon Ymir and killed him and from his body they made the world. The mountains from his bones, the heavens from his skull and the sea from his blood. A gory image, don't you think? But so apposite for our world where men slaughter each other all the time."

Neumann couldn't have agreed more. The Old Testament God was forbidding and vengeful, but his creation of the world was gentle in comparison to the Norse version. Ludwig was right: the pagans knew better just how violent and cruel the human species was.

Neumann tried some of his mead. It was cloyingly sweet, almost undrinkable to his palate, but he could hardly tip it away. Ludwig was gulping his down, waving the glass around as he continued talking. Neumann had heard that he was shy and reclusive, reluctant to socialise, but tonight he was positively garrulous.

"I used to think the frost giants were like my father. He was a cold, distant man who frightened me, hardly ever spoke to me. Did your father speak to you?"

"I don't remember," Neuman replied. "He died when I was three."

The king didn't respond with the usual platitudes, the sympathy and condolences. He just nodded thoughtfully, relating Neumann's loss to his own unhappy childhood experiences.

"That might have been no bad thing. Fathers, you know, they can be harsh. Mine used to beat us mercilessly – me and Otto – for the smallest transgression. And he starved us, too. Fed us so little that we had to sneak down to the kitchens and beg for bread from the servants. I suppose that's partly why I liked to read the Norse tales. It was my way of defying my father, of finding a world inside my head that was more congenial than the one outside."

Neumann only half listened as Ludwig rambled on, talking now about how the gods created men and women from two logs, an ash and an alder, they found lying on the seashore. There were still three gods. Wili and We for some reason had gone, replaced by Hönir and Lodur, but Odin remained, a trinity like Christianity. The Father, the Son and the Holy Ghost. But Odin was always the most important.

"He had a palace in Asgard called Gladsheim – Shining Home," the king said. "That's where Valhalla was, the hall of the slaughtered warriors. I used to read about it and imagine my own shining hall, my own palace, although not a hall for dead warriors. That would have been going a bit too far, don't you think? Haw, haw." That high-pitched laugh again. "And now I've got it – New Hohenschwangau." His face clouded for an instant. "Well, when it's finished. When those penny-pinching ministers have given me the money I need."

And he went off at a tangent, ranting about miserly, short-sighted politicians who couldn't see that the palace was intended to be a home fit not just for a king, but for a god.

"Odin was a father figure to me, as my own was so aloof and unloving. This all-powerful, colourful deity who ruled over the universe, who roamed the world on his eight-legged steed, Sleipnir, and carried a magic spear carved with mystic runes that held the secret to all knowledge. I wanted a spear like that. I wanted to learn the runes, to be able to communicate in them like Odin."

Suddenly, Neumann was listening intently.

"And did you, sire?"

"Did I what?"

"Learn to write in runes."

"Oh, yes. It's not difficult. I had a book about it. My governess, Sibylle Meilhaus, a wonderful, affectionate woman, got it for me in Munich. On the sly, of course. My father would never have allowed such a pagan practise. He wasn't keen on Sibylle either. Got rid of her when I was eight and replaced her with this ghastly old major-general who knew nothing about children and taught me as if I were an army cadet."

"Can you remember the title of the book?"

"Not offhand. It was written by some learned doctor fellow."

"Grossmeyer?"

"Maybe. Do you know it?"

Neumann didn't reply. He was piecing together fragments in his mind. Runes, Baldur, spears, mistletoe, ravens, even the cologne the king was wearing, and coming to the logical conclusion.

The sleigh was slowing, entering a small village – no more than a dozen ramshackle wooden huts with pigsties attached. One of the outriders had galloped on ahead to rouse the inhabitants and they were emerging reluctantly from their homes, coats pulled on over their nightclothes, bare feet thrust hastily into tatty boots. The sleigh came to a halt in front of them.

A beaming Ludwig greeted them in High German – a language they couldn't understand – then proceeded to give a long speech about kingship. About his authority being bestowed on him directly by God. About his duty to them as their ruler and their duty to him as subjects. The villagers listened in silence, shivering in the cold, their gazes fixed on Ludwig, their expressions bemused, unable to believe that this strange fat man in a bowler hat was their king, not some absurd impostor.

After ten minutes of this incomprehensible waffle, Ludwig signalled to Axel, who lifted the sack out of the sleigh and opened it. One of the cavalrymen – speaking in dialect – ordered the villagers to line up, then Axel pulled out gifts from the sack and passed them to the king to give to the villagers. Copper ornaments, trinkets, small framed photographs of Ludwig that the recipients stared at in utter bafflement. It was an old, flattering picture that looked nothing like the king today – so they didn't know who it was. And what were they supposed to do with it? Hang it in their pigsties? Finally, Axel produced a bag of coins and Ludwig gave each of the villagers five marks. At last, something they could use. They bowed and touched their forelocks, about ready to sing the Bavarian national anthem – if any of them had known the words.

Axel replaced the sack in the well of the sleigh and climbed back onto his perch, then the king raised his bowler hat.

"Farewell, my loyal subjects," he cried. "Never forget this night when your king called on you in your humble shacks and showered you with gifts. Let it live on in your memories and in the folklore of your village, passed down from generation to generation as an example of your king's love for his people. Next!"

This last command for the postillions who immediately remounted and urged their horses forward. The sleigh slid slowly out of the village, Ludwig waving magnanimously to the villagers who waited politely until he disappeared from sight, then dashed back to their beds.

Three more stops followed for the royal sleigh. Three more villages in which the inhabitants were roused from their slumbers and dragged out into the icy night to be treated to the same pompous speech from the king, the same gracious bestowal of gifts and coins. Neumann watched the ceremonies with wry amusement, Ludwig's self-absorption astonishing, the peasants' faces pictures of puzzlement, resentment and incipient frostbite.

As dawn broke, the sleigh descended a slope into a basin surrounded by snow-capped mountains. In the centre of the basin was a modest – by Ludwig's standards – palace surrounded by formal gardens. Linderhof, the villa that the king had transformed into his favourite country retreat – in fact, the only one of his ambitious building projects that was currently fully habitable.

The household must have had advance notice of his arrival for the servants were waiting on the front steps when the sleigh pulled in outside. Ludwig disembarked, Neumann and Axel following him into the palace where the king doffed his bowler hat to the bronze statue of a mounted Louis XIV that occupied pride of place in the middle of the vestibule. On the ceiling above the sculpture was a stylised golden stucco sun, two white plaster cherubs bathed in its rays beside the Sun King's motto, *nec pluribus impar* – I stand above the others.

Through a doorway flanked by red marble pillars was a second hall with a double flight of marble stairs rising up at one end. Ludwig headed up the stairs. Neumann made to follow, but Axel grabbed hold of his arm and whispered in his ear, "Only His Majesty is permitted to use the main stairs. This way."

The footman led him through a door into the kitchen and servants' quarters. The staff were busy setting out dishes on a gold dining table that was situated in the centre of a curious metal structure – skeletal steel pillars at each of the four corners with a steel panel above at ceiling height.

"We call it 'The Table That Lays Itself'," Axel explained. "The food is placed on it down here, then it's winched up into the king's dining room so he never has to see any of the servants."

"I notice it's set for four. Is His Majesty having guests?" Neumann asked, wondering if one of the places was intended for him.

But Axel soon disabused him of that notion.

"No, he never has guests here. There's only one bedroom and he always eats alone. The other three places are for his… friends."

Neumann picked up the hesitation. "Friends?"

Axel pulled a face, embarrassed not for himself, but for his master.

"His Majesty has imaginary friends. He likes to talk to them while he eats."

"Aah."

Neumann made no further comment, just watched the servants at work. It was breakfast time, but in keeping with the king's nocturnal habits, he was being served supper: a beef broth with pastries on the side, a beef ragout, fish in a wine sauce, boiled beef with sweet chestnut purée, apple strudel, sorbet and coffee, all accompanied by white wine and arrack. There was enough for at least four people but, presumably, Ludwig was having the imaginary friends' share, too.

The dishes were laid out carefully, like a work of art, the desserts nestling in trays of ice, the other courses hidden under silver domes in silver bowls with candles burning beneath them to keep the food warm. The chef ran his eye over the arrangement, making a few minor adjustments, then he stepped back and gave a nod of approval. Two kitchen boys took hold of a long crank handle and began to turn it, the effort obviously taxing their strength. Slowly, the table began to rise up the steel pillars. As it got higher, the metal panel in the ceiling split in two and slid aside to allow the table to ascend into the king's dining room.

Ludwig was waiting for it. He was ravenous, his appetite stimulated by the long sleigh ride. But he hadn't forgotten his manners. He allowed his friends to sit down first before he took his own place at the table. Opposite him was his most frequent guest, Louis XIV, and to either side the Sun King's second wife, Madame de Maintenon, and Louis XV's legendary mistress, Madame de Pompadour, both looking extremely elegant this morning.

The influence of the French kings was visible all over Linderhof. The statue in the vestibule, of course, but also further sculptures of Louis XIV in the Music Room and the Audience Room and a painting showing his glorification in the King's Bedchamber. Louis Quinze and his mistress were honoured with portraits in the Lilac Cabinet and the extravagant gilt décor of the whole palace owed much to the Bourbon court.

Ludwig helped himself to the beef broth and launched into a conversation with the Sun King whom he admired, and envied, as an autocrat and absolute monarch who had never had to cede power to anyone, least of all pettifogging politicians.

"You won't believe what's happened now, Your Majesty," he said. "They've refused again to give me the money to complete New Hohenschwangau, not to mention Herrenchiemsee and Falkenstein. It's an outrage! How dare they! Madame de Pompadour, I'd be obliged if you would pass me the salt. Do they not realise what great monuments to the Bavarian people they will be? And to me, naturally. Let's not forget, they are my palaces. So what would you advise me to do…?"

Downstairs in the servants' quarters, Neumann was feeling as bewildered as the villagers he'd encountered during the night.

"What happens now?" he asked Axel.

"His Majesty will dine and then he will retire to his bedchamber to sleep."

"Are we going back to Hohenschwangau today?"

Axel shrugged. "That will be up to the king. We may go straight back tonight, or we may stay for longer."

"What? You mean I might be stuck here for days?"

"That is possible, sir. Let me show you where you can get some rest."

They went back across the hall into a room containing bunkbeds stacked three high against the walls. Neumann took off his greatcoat and boots and lay down on a thin mattress. He was frustrated and angry. He'd given up a whole night, travelled forty kilometres across the country, and he still had no inkling as to why the king had invited him on this trip.

TWENTY-SIX

Anneliese took her time over her preparations. She wanted to – *needed* to – look her absolute best for this meeting. She had a leisurely bath, the water perfumed with rose oil, then got her maid to braid her long blonde hair and fasten it up with a diamond-encrusted clasp. She applied her make-up meticulously, taking particular care with her eyes and lips, then slipped into a low-cut crimson gown that she knew showed off her figure in all its enticing fullness. It was calculated, and she hated herself for it, for resorting to what she regarded contemptuously as feminine wiles, but what choice did she have? She had nothing left to bargain with. A diamond necklace and diamond earrings completed her ensemble. At least she still had her jewellery. That was something Friedrich had not yet managed to gamble away.

The carriage took her north-west from Füssen, out into the countryside near Eisenberg where Count Walther Ehrenbeck zu Freudenberg had a vast estate – five thousand hectares of rich farmland and forest. His house was large, but ugly – like its owner, Anneliese reflected as they drove up the tree-lined avenue to the front door. All blank, austere stonework and grim battlements, the building's original style – if it had ever had any – long since swamped by new additions.

The interior was equally severe. Bare stone-flagged floors and dark masculine colours, except in the drawing room where vestiges of the count's late wife could still be seen in the soft Turkish rugs and the sofas upholstered in cream and gold. Zu Freudenberg received her politely, but brusquely, a busy man who had pressing business to complete with his estate manager.

"Baroness, this is indeed a pleasure." He took her hand and bowed over it, his gaze lingering on her décolletage. "What brings you out here?"

"A delicate matter," Anneliese replied. "I wonder now how I might broach it with you."

"Delicate in what way?"

Anneliese hesitated. There was no subtle way of putting it. "My husband, I understand, owes you a lot of money."

Zu Freudenberg didn't reply. He strolled over to the fireplace and stood with his back to it, warming his legs. He was a tall, hefty man with broad shoulders and a torso that had thickened with age, the muscle turning to fat. His neck was wide, but short, his jaw heavy, sagging a little, his high, balding forehead and eyes of steely cold blue giving him a forbidding appearance.

"With all respect, baroness, that isn't really your concern."

"But it *is*," Anneliese blurted out. "It is if we are ruined."

"You exaggerate, I think."

"Do I? I think you know our position only too well. You have a charge on our estate and IOUs from Friedrich which will be enough to finish us – should you call them in, that is."

"Did Friedrich tell you that?"

"No. But I have it on good authority."

"These are not matters for a woman."

"Count, please, leave my gender out of this. Speak to

me as if I were a man. It is *my* future, *my* prosperity that is at stake here, too."

Zu Freudenberg's face remained impassive. "They are debts of honour. Your husband is bound to pay them or face shame and social ostracism."

"But we will lose everything."

"Friedrich should have thought of that before he wagered so recklessly."

"I will not disagree with you on that point, but am I to be made to suffer, too? To lose my home, which was my father's before me. To lose the land that was also my family's."

"What are you asking me for, baroness?"

"To tear up the IOUs, to cancel the debts."

"You ask a lot."

"You say they are debts of honour. Could you not waive them as a matter of honour? It's not as if you need the money."

She regretted the words the moment they left her mouth. The count's face darkened. His eyes glinted angrily, tinged with malice. Anneliese tried desperately to recover.

"I'm sorry, that was not what I meant. Forgive me, I spoke without thinking."

"But you spoke, nevertheless," zu Freudenberg said icily. "This isn't about money, it's about integrity and principle. A man must pay his debts, however they are created."

"Friedrich has been foolish, I concede that. But I beg you to reconsider."

Anneliese gazed at him imploringly. Tears had swayed Herr Richter, but she knew they wouldn't move zu Freudenberg. He was an altogether harder, more implacable man. The count returned her gaze and she fancied she saw a hint of sympathy in his expression.

"And what are you prepared to give me, my dear

Anneliese?" he asked gently.

She felt a sudden chill on the back of her neck. A premonition. The abrupt change in his tone, the familiarity of his address, they sent a shiver of warning through her.

"My gratitude," she replied. "The knowledge that through your generosity you have saved us from destitution."

"Hmm." He considered that for a moment. When he spoke again, he was almost sneering.

"Gratitude is such an... an amorphous concept, don't you think? Isn't there something more tangible you can offer me?"

"I have nothing," Anneliese said. "My money, my dowry, it all went to Friedrich when we married. I have my jewellery, that's all, but I will give you that willingly."

"I'm not talking about money, or jewellery, my dear."

That intimate word again. Except with zu Freudenberg it sounded more threatening than affectionate.

"What do you mean?"

"I mean, what are you prepared to *give* me?"

She stared at him, wondering if she'd misunderstood. She'd come here dressed to impress, to beguile, but she hadn't expected this.

"You ask for... that?"

"Those are my terms."

"And in return, you will tear up the IOUs?"

"I will." He looked pointedly at his fob watch. "I have business to attend to. Your answer?"

Anneliese swallowed. She couldn't say the word. She just nodded.

"I have a slot in my timetable this afternoon," the count said. "I will see you back here at four o'clock."

*

Neumann slept intermittently for a few hours, the bunkbed too uncomfortable for uninterrupted rest. When he opened his eyes, he was aware of the other people sharing the space with him. He could see Axel asleep across the room, two maids in the bunks above him. He could hear the kitchen boys snoring, all the servants keeping the king's hours – sleeping when he slept, serving him when he was awake, whatever the time. Have I deprived someone of their bed? Neumann wondered guiltily as he swung his legs off the mattress and stood up. He was still tired, but he knew he wasn't going to get back to sleep again.

Slipping on his boots and greatcoat, he crept quietly out into the hall. The palace was silent, apparently deserted. He glanced at the staircase. Somewhere up above, Ludwig was in bed. How easy it would be for me to sneak up and confront him, Neumann thought. To put to him all the questions that are bouncing around inside my head. But he went out through the vestibule instead. A sentry was standing guard outside at the front of the building, a rifle slung over his shoulder, his breath condensing in the cold air. He took no notice of the major, just stared out across the gardens. His posture was stiff, as if his spine were frozen – which it probably was, given the frigid conditions.

Neumann put on his gloves, walked across the forecourt and down a flight of steps to a large ornamental pond flanked by rows of neatly-pruned lime trees. In the centre of the pool was a golden statue of Flora, the Goddess of Flowers, surrounded by cherubs. In milder weather, a fountain powered by a gravity pump would send a jet of water thirty-five metres up into the air above the goddess's head, but today it was quiescent, the pool around it glazed with ice.

He went round the pool and up some steps to a broad terrace broken up by flowerbeds. In front of the terrace was a tall lime tree containing a series of dog-legged stairs leading up to a tree house in which the king had played as a boy and in which he still liked to take the occasional meal in summer. Further flights of steps took Neumann past a niche containing a bust of the unlucky Marie-Antoinette, of whose life – though not her end – Ludwig was a great admirer, and up to the Temple of Venus crowning the top of the hill. From the temple he had a fine view of the whole area: the ring of craggy mountains that encircled Linderhof, their lower slopes hidden by thick forest, and the palace itself nestling in the valley bottom. Compared to New Hohenschwangau, it was tiny. It had only two storeys, the ground floor given over to entrance halls, servants' quarters and the kitchen, the first floor divided up into just six principal rooms, all for the sole use of the king.

The exterior was built of white stone in a neo-rococo style that in the bright winter sunshine made the palace look like a gigantic iced cake. Statues and the Bavarian coat-of-arms adorned the front and, on the roof, was the figure of Atlas holding aloft a globe – a symbolic choice for Ludwig who had always felt he had the weight of the world on his shoulders. Neumann gazed around. It was remote, peaceful. He could see why a monarch wanting solitude would build a palace here.

He lingered a while until he started to feel the cold, then went back down the steps. Axel was coming out through the front entrance of the palace. Neumann greeted him.

"It's beautiful here, isn't it?" he said. "So tranquil."

"You've been exploring the gardens, sir?"

"Just this part. The pool and the terraces. Are the grounds extensive?"

"Not particularly. A few formal areas and some wilder parkland, but it's all quite contained. Would you like me to show you around?"

"The king doesn't need you?"

"He will sleep until late afternoon now."

They walked round the building through the West Garden, Axel pointing out the statue of Fama in the centre of another ornamental pool.

"Fama?" Neumann asked.

"I didn't know either, until one of the gardeners told me. She's the Goddess of Rumour. That trumpet she's holding, she uses it to inform the world of true and untrue events."

"I've never heard of her."

"But she's quite appropriate, I think," Axel said. "Considering all the rumours about the court that circulate."

Neumann glanced at him sharply. The remark seemed very unwise for a footman, but Axel appeared unconcerned by his indiscretion. They continued round to the back of the palace where there was yet another pool and statue – this one an elaborate composition of a bearded bronze figure on horseback, accompanied by two more horses and two youths.

"Neptune and the Tritons," Axel explained. "And above it you can see the cascade coming down the hill. Dry now, of course, but very cooling in summer. The king's bedroom looks out this way." He nodded up at a line of three windows, behind which dark blue drapes were drawn. "And that building beyond the cascade is called the Music Pavilion, although no music is ever played in it. His Majesty likes to sit there in the middle of the night and read books by moonlight. Do you want to see the Venus Grotto?"

Axel led them through the East Garden and up the hill on the north side of the palace to a strange construction that was more earthworks than a building. Passing through a short tunnel, Axel flicked a switch on the wall and they emerged into what appeared to be a cavern illuminated by hidden lights: a rock chamber with stalactites hanging from the roof and a vivid turquoise pool in the centre.

"Is this a natural cave?" Neumann asked, suspecting something artificial about the place.

Axel shook his head. "It's all fake, made from cement and canvas on an iron frame."

Neumann took in the cavern. On the back wall, behind a small stage, was a large painting of a man reclining dreamily on a rug, surrounded by attractive young women, most of whom were wearing very few clothes. The picture looked familiar.

"That's very similar to the painting in the king's study at New Hohenschwangau," he said.

"Yes, sir. It's the same scene from *Tannhäuser*, his seduction by Venus and her nymphs. His Majesty has a passion for Wagner."

"And that?" Neumann asked, nodding at a gaudy coracle that was moored at the side of the pool. It was shaped like a large gilded mussel shell, with a figurehead of Cupid on the prow.

"His Majesty likes to float around the pool, listening to Wagner. The singers stand over there on the stage and the orchestra – only a small one – squeezes in by those rocks. Sometimes he dresses up as Lohengrin or Parsifal."

After the previous night's excursion, nothing much about Ludwig could surprise Neumann. But Axel seemed very free with personal information about the king. That boded well for the questions the major wanted to put to him.

"He's very fond of the Grail legends," Axel went on. "He sees himself as one of the Grail knights. When he used to write to Wagner, he often signed his letters 'Parsifal'."

Parsifal? Neumann thought. P.

"Let me show you something, sir. If you'd wait here."

Axel disappeared into the shadows, presumably to a control panel of some sort, for the lights began to change colour, glowing red and orange and green and yellow across the vault of the cavern. At the same time, the water in the pool started rippling, the waves lapping gently onto the rocky shore.

"Clever, isn't it?" Axel said, returning to Neumann's side. "There's a light show and wave machine, all powered by electricity. His Majesty has a wonderful imagination."

He does indeed, Neumann thought. And the money to indulge it.

"Axel," he said. "You know I'm in Bavaria to investigate the death of Christoph Geissler?"

"Yes, sir. Everyone knows that."

"Did you ever meet him?"

"Me, sir? Why would I have met him?"

Neumann sensed a change come over the footman, a wariness that hadn't been there before.

"You visited him in his lodgings."

"Who told you that?"

"His landlady. Why did you go there?"

"One moment, sir. I'd better turn off the machines before they overheat."

Axel vanished again. Giving himself time to think, Neumann suspected. He prepared himself for an evasive conversation when the young man reappeared. The waves in the pool slowly petered out, the surface returning to a limpid calm. The lights dimmed, back to just one colour. Neumann tried to picture Ludwig in here, dressed as a Grail knight. He seemed an unhappy, perhaps lonely man. Lohengrin, Parsifal, even Odin with his ravens. He wanted to be anyone other than the king of Bavaria.

"We should leave now, sir," Axel said, coming back into the grotto.

"In a minute," Neumann said.

"The king might wake, sir. I need to be there when he does."

"After you've answered my questions. Why did you visit Christoph Geissler? Was it for the king?"

He expected a denial, but Axel had obviously worked out how much he was prepared to admit – and perhaps also how much he was going to conceal.

"Yes, sir," he replied. "For the king."

"You took him messages, didn't you?"

"Yes, sir. Just a few."

"What was in the messages?"

"I don't know, sir. They were sealed."

"Were they invitations to the palace?"

"As I said, sir, I don't know what they were. They might have been official diplomatic business."

Neumann shook his head. "There are proper channels for that. No, they were personal messages. Did Geissler and His Majesty have a… friendship?"

"I don't know anything about that, sir. Now, if you'll permit me, I really need to be getting back."

Neumann put a hand on his arm.

"Did Geissler ever visit the king in his palaces? In his private quarters?"

"Oh, no, sir," Axel said firmly. "Never."

The footman turned away, heading for the exit. Neumann followed him back out into the gardens, sure that Axel was lying to him.

Anneliese was more nervous than she'd ever been in her life. More even than on her wedding night when a similar – though less repugnant – ordeal had awaited her. She wondered whether she could go through with it. Did she have the stomach, the resolve? It was a long time since she'd slept with a man. After an initial flurry, the physical side of her marriage had waned and then ceased altogether. Friedrich took his pleasure elsewhere these days.

She thought about what lay ahead. Would it be painful, would it be brutal? Zu Freudenberg wasn't a gentle man. He was hard, selfish. Perhaps it would all be over with quickly. All she knew for certain was that it would be unpleasant and humiliating. Perversely, the duties of a wife, of a woman, were so deeply imbued in her that she was most worried that the count would be disappointed with her. Have some pride, she chastised herself. But, really, what pride did she have left?

Did her coachman know what she was about to do? she wondered as he dropped her off outside the house. How could he? And the maid who showed her upstairs? She must surely have known, even if Anneliese's flushed face didn't tell her. An unaccompanied woman going to a man's bedroom; there was only one conclusion to draw.

Zu Freudenberg kept her waiting – as she had suspected he would. He was that kind of man. A man who relished wielding power – whether over men or women it didn't matter so long as he was the master. And he was certainly that here. She was entirely at his mercy. He held her future – and Friedrich's – in the palm of his hand. He would want to rub that in, to make the most of his advantage. She was the supplicant. He would enjoy forcing her to submit to him.

Anneliese walked around the room, trying to calm her throbbing heart, to ease the knot in her stomach. There was still time to change her mind, but she knew that wasn't an option. That would mean ruin. It was unmistakably a man's bedroom. Brown curtains on the windows, a brown leather armchair in one corner, a plain grey quilt on the bed. No bright colours, no frills, no woman's touch. She distracted herself by speculating about what she would have done to the room, had it been hers. The wallpaper she would have chosen, the rugs on the floor, the furniture. Then she laughed. Part nerves, part disbelief. I'm about to be – what? Not raped in the legal sense for she had given her consent, but certainly taken against her will from any kind of moral standpoint. And I'm thinking about interior decoration.

The door opened and the count came in. No greeting, none of the common courtesies she would normally have expected – and would normally have received. He walked over to the dressing table and removed his jacket. Then he took out his silver cuff-links – a task, Anneliese thought, that would usually have been undertaken by his manservant. At least I've been spared that, she reflected. No valet here to witness my shame.

Zu Freudenberg opened a small onyx box and dropped the cuff-links into a velvet-lined compartment that contained shirt and collar studs and other bits of jewellery. At one end of the box, nestling in its own separate slot, was a gold ring embossed with a white enamel letter 'W' on a blue background.

The count came over to Anneliese and, without warning, pulled her to him and kissed her roughly, his hands pawing at her breasts. He smelt of brandy and tobacco. Anneliese pushed him away.

"The IOUs," she said.

Zu Freudenberg laughed. "You're a practical woman, baroness. I like that. Your husband doesn't deserve you."

He went to the desk and took out a sheaf of papers from a drawer. As many as that? Anneliese thought. He held them out to show her, then tore each one in half and tossed the pieces onto the desk.

"Satisfied?"

Anneliese nodded.

The count pulled off his shoes and started to undo his shirt.

"Take off your clothes and lie down on the bed," he ordered harshly.

He's treating me like a whore, Anneliese thought. But then that's what I am.

By late afternoon, Neumann's frustration was mounting. He'd killed time exploring the garden and park around Linderhof and had a meal with the servants in the kitchen. "Breakfast", they'd termed it, even though it was 5pm, because that was what the king had at that hour of the day. But where was he? There was still no sign of Ludwig.

"Is he up?" Neumann asked Axel.

"No, sir. Not yet."

"Can you wake him?"

The footman looked horrified at the idea. "Certainly not, sir. His Majesty is never roused before he's ready."

"And what time will that be?"

"I don't know, sir. But he will ring the bell when he wishes me to attend on him."

Neumann hadn't seen much of Axel since their visit to the Venus Grotto. He hadn't had the opportunity to probe him further and suspected, in any case, that he wouldn't get any more out of him. The footman was probably realising he'd already said too much. He made sure he was either out of the way or in the presence of the other servants so the major could never catch him alone.

It was clear to Neumann, however, that Christoph Geissler and the king had known each other. The perfume Geissler's landlady had detected on his clothes after his nocturnal absences hadn't come from a lady friend: it had come from Ludwig. The runic notes had also come from the king. From Parsifal to his Baldur. What was the nature of their friendship? Axel had denied that Geissler had ever visited the king. The official logbooks appeared to confirm that, but perhaps there were other, more discreet, entrances to the royal palaces.

Lukas Hafner had hinted at the monarch's proclivities.

Had the young diplomat and Ludwig had a sexual relationship? They had certainly been close; the runic messages showed that. At least, until the last one. The tone there had changed markedly from affection to hatred. A love affair gone sour? Ludwig, apparently angry at his betrayal, had put the curse of Odin on Geissler – effectively a sentence of death. The question was: had that sentence been carried out on the king's orders? And by whom?

TWENTY-SEVEN

Could Friedrich tell what she'd done just by looking at her? Anneliese wondered. Was there some mark of infidelity on her? She'd had a bath on her return to remove the smell of zu Freudenberg from her body, but she could still feel his loathsome touch, feel his hands, the weight of him, hear the sound of him taking what he wanted from her. Those were memories that she would never be able to erase. But would Friedrich notice? He barely glanced at her most of the time, showed no interest in her appearance, no warmth let alone passion. He wouldn't see anything different about her. He wouldn't see the guilt and revulsion eating away inside her.

"What's this?" was all he said when she presented him with the torn-up pieces of paper.

"Your IOUs from Count Ehrenbeck zu Freudenberg."

"My IOUs?"

"He's cancelled the debts you owe him."

Friedrich stared at the papers, then he riffled quickly through them to check they were genuine.

"Where did you get these?" His tone, his expression, was accusatory.

"He gave them to me."

"You've seen him?"

"This afternoon."

"You knew about them? How?"

"You told me."

"What? When?"

"Two nights ago. Don't you remember? When you came home from your club."

Drunk, she could have added, but he clearly had no recollection of their conversation. He was gazing at the IOUs again, his brow furrowing.

"He's cancelled the debts, you say? Why?"

"Because I asked him to."

"You didn't beg, I hope? It would be unbearable for me if you stooped so low with that man."

"I had to do something, Friedrich."

"I would have won the money back from him, anyway. You didn't have to do this. You didn't have to humiliate me by going to him."

Humiliate *you*? Anneliese thought. If only you knew.

"What did you say to him?" Friedrich snapped. "What pathetic female artifice did you use on him? Tell me!"

"No artifice," Anneliese replied.

She'd already thought through her explanation. It wasn't credible for zu Freudenberg to have been sympathetic to their plight. He'd never done anything altruistic in his life – and Friedrich knew that. She had to frame it purely in terms of his own self-interest.

"It wouldn't have looked good for him to ruin us. A wealthy man like him, you a fellow minister in the government. He had to think of his reputation."

"His reputation!" Friedrich sneered. "What reputation? The man is a damned cheat."

"But we are saved now," Anneliese said. "We can stay in our home, pay our bills."

She was bewildered. She'd expected some gratitude from him, not this simmering anger. She hesitated. She had to say this. "But Friedrich, you must give up gambling for good."

"Don't tell me what to do," Friedrich exploded. "You shouldn't have interfered. This was none of your business. I will do exactly as I please, damn you."

He threw the torn-up IOUs into her face and stormed out of the room.

Friedrich sensed people staring at him the minute he walked into the lounge of the club. Gazes focused on him, then quickly turned away as he glanced in their direction. Covert looks of pity and contempt from the other members. Heads leaning towards one another in whispered exchanges, as if they were sharing secrets to which he was not a party.

Zu Freudenberg and a group of other men were standing at the bar, drinking champagne. They saw him approaching and one of them said something under his breath. The others laughed and von Breckendorf knew they were laughing at him.

"Ah, Friedrich, join us in a glass of champagne," zu Freudenberg said with a bonhomie that sounded forced.

"Are we playing tonight?" von Breckendorf asked bluntly.

If the count expected his thanks for the IOUs, he was sorely mistaken. He didn't need his charity. He wasn't going to abase himself in front of him; he was going to restore his pride and take his revenge at the gaming table.

"The count has been telling us all about your wife," von Sturm said, smirking. "What a wonderful, devoted woman she is."

"The sacrifices she's prepared to make for you," von Mühlbeck added and the comment seemed to give the others licence to join in.

"A toast to the baroness," one of them said, raising his glass.

"You're a lucky man, von Breckendorf."

"Run up a debt with me, old man, and I'll look forward to your wife paying it off."

"She must be one hell of a lay."

Friedrich felt his head spinning. The faces around him seemed to close in, crowding him, suffocating him. Red, grinning faces, lips curling, moist with champagne, eyes glinting with malicious amusement. He couldn't breathe. A cold sweat swept up his body, then a hot flush that made his skin tingle. The comments kept coming. Crude, ribald, offensive. Men in a pack losing all sense of control and decency. Von Breckendorf turned and fled, the men's mocking laughter burning like acid in his ears.

Anneliese had never seen him so angry before, so incandescent with rage. She was at her dressing table, her maid, Eva, brushing her hair, when Friedrich burst into the bedroom, already red in the face and shouting incoherently.

"Get *out!*" he yelled at the maid.

Eva backed away. She glanced anxiously at her mistress, intimidated but reluctant to leave her alone. Anneliese nodded, giving her permission. The girl scurried out of the door.

"What on earth is going on, Friedrich? What's the matter?" Anneliese asked, countering his fury with calm composure.

"Don't play the innocent. You know damned well what's going on."

He knew. She could tell. But perhaps she could brazen it out.

"I have no idea what you're talking about."

"Haven't you? Zu Freudenberg does. Half the members of my club do. He's been boasting about it."

Anneliese went cold, a wave of nausea rippling suddenly through her. Men, was there nothing they wouldn't brag about? She couldn't admit it. At all costs, she had to deny his accusations.

"Friedrich, I don't know what you've been hearing, but –"

"Don't lie!" he broke in aggressively.

He leaned down towards her, his eyes bulging. She could feel his breath hot on her face.

"He fucked you, didn't he?"

The obscenity was like a blow – as he'd intended. Anneliese flinched. Friedrich hit her with it again.

"Fucked you. And you didn't just let him, you gave yourself to him. You whore. You harlot. You slag. You…" The stream of invective spewed from his mouth. So many different words to shame and defame a woman.

"You're mistaken, Friedrich. I assure you that –"

He hit her once more. Not with a word this time, but with his hand. An open-palmed slap that almost knocked her off her chair.

"You have brought shame on me, dishonoured me," he shouted. "I'm a laughing stock, a cuckold, and you have disgraced the name of von Breckendorf. I will never be able to hold my head up here again."

Anneliese touched her cheek where the slap had landed, her eyes watering. He'd never hit her before. For the first time in their marriage, she was frightened of him, of what he might do.

There was no point in maintaining her denials.

"I did it for us," she said. "To save us from penury."

"Not for me," Friedrich retorted. "You think I wanted my wife to prostitute herself?"

"You think *I* wanted to? It was what the count demanded. It was his price."

"And you paid it."

"I had no choice. It was that or lose this house, lose this estate."

"Better to lose my fortune than to lose my honour."

"But it wasn't *your* fortune, was it?" Anneliese fired back. She wasn't going to submit meekly to his anger. "It was mine. And you frittered it away."

He raised his hand again. Anneliese faced him down.

"Go on. Hit me. Hit me like the coward you are. The reckless coward who has ruined us."

Friedrich pulled back and took a deep breath. Then he walked away across the room, getting back control of his emotions. When he turned to look at her, his face was set hard, his eyes cold and pitiless.

"You are no longer my wife. You disgust me. In the morning, you leave this house."

She stared at him. "What do you mean?"

"This is no longer your home."

"But it's *my* house."

"In law, it's mine. You leave first thing tomorrow. And if you don't, I will physically throw you down the steps. You understand?"

He spun on his heels and marched out. Anneliese gazed after him, the room misting through her tears.

The summons came late in the evening, just as Neumann was resigning himself to spending the night at Linderhof.

"His Majesty will see you now," Axel announced, coming into the servants' quarters where the major was sprawled on a chair, bored and irritated by the long wait. Relieved that something was happening at last, he followed the footman up the dark, narrow servants' staircase and out through a concealed door into a small chamber decorated in shades of pink and rose. From there they went into the king's dining room. Ludwig was seated in a gilt, throne-like chair by The Table That Lays Itself, the surface of which was littered with the detritus of his breakfast – dirty bowls and plates, fragments of bread and a half-finished cup of coffee.

"Ah..." the king said, looking at Neumann and

waving his hand vaguely in the air as he tried to remember his name.

"Major Neumann, sire," Axel prompted helpfully.

"Yes, of course. Major, good evening. You are rested, I trust?"

"Yes, thank you, Your Majesty."

"Good, good. What is the weather like, Hoffmann?"

"Cold, but clear, sire."

"You can see the stars?"

"I believe so, sire."

"Then we must go out. The Music Pavilion, I think. You will accompany me, major."

"As you wish, sire."

Ludwig's outdoor clothes were brought up from his wardrobe on the ground floor – his coat, gloves, boots and bowler hat – and Neumann stood by while Axel dressed the king. Then they went downstairs – Ludwig using the main staircase, Axel and Neumann the servants', the major picking up his own coat en route before they all trooped round to the rear of the palace and up a covered walkway of pleached lime trees to the Music Pavilion at the top of the cascade.

Two servants were placing two armchairs in the centre of the pavilion – an octagonal, latticework iron structure, almost entirely open to the elements – while a third arranged a tall silver candelabrum and a fourth lit a log fire in a wide metal dish on the floor. They hurried out of the way as the king arrived, but remained close by, out of sight in the darkness, in case they were needed again. Ludwig eased himself down into one of the armchairs, his belly spreading out around him, and invited Neuman to take the other.

"This is one of my favourite places at night," the king said. "The moon, the stars, the fresh air. It makes me feel a part of nature. It brings me closer to God. Do you feel that, major?"

"Well, sire," Neumann began, lost for an answer. "I suppose I've never thought about it."

"That's the trouble with the world. We don't think about things. The things that matter, I mean. We spend our time squabbling over trivialities, over money, when we should be concentrating on creating things that are beautiful. Like music. And art. And buildings."

Neumann feared that this was the prelude to another disgruntled rant about politicians frustrating his grand palace schemes, but Ludwig changed tack, leaning back in his chair and gazing up at the sky through the skeletal roof of the pavilion.

"Look up, major."

Neumann looked up. Axel had been right: it was a fine cloudless night, the stars clearly visible, the moonlight glowing on the circle of snowy peaks so the palace appeared to be surrounded by a heavenly halo.

"We don't look up nearly enough," the king went on. "How can you find inspiration if you keep your eyes fixed on the ground? Do you know your constellations? I learnt them all when I was a boy and now I have a telescope to see them better, but I've never really understood them. That one there. It's called Ursa Major, but it looks nothing like a bear. Why did they call it that? And that one. Pegasus. He was a winged horse, wasn't he? How could you ever think that random arrangement of stars resembles a winged horse? Were the ancient astronomers idiots? And how about that one, Cygnus? The swan star. You know they call me The Swan King? So I know a lot about swans and I can tell you that that constellation does not look like a swan. What do you think?"

"I'm inclined to agree with you, sire," Neumann replied, then wondered if he could use this as a pretext to divert the conversation onto something rather more interesting to him.

"Now you mention swans, sire, may I ask you a question? Christoph Geissler had a gold watch chain with a gold swan attached to it. Did you give it to him?"

"I did," Ludwig replied without hesitation. "It was a first-rate piece of craftsmanship. I like to give gifts to people. I don't think we give enough gifts."

"Was he... a friend?"

The king didn't appear to hear the question. His gaze was fixed on the sky.

"Are you a Christian man, major?"

The change of subject momentarily perplexed Neumann. "Well, sire, I was brought up a Lutheran."

"I'm a Catholic. We have more sins. So many sins. It's very hard to be virtuous, don't you think? Or maybe it's easy for you, you're a policeman. I suppose you never do anything wrong."

"I've done plenty wrong, sire."

Ludwig nodded, still staring up at the stars. Then he became more reflective.

"I wonder if he's up there."

"Sire?"

"My beautiful Baldur. Is he in heaven?"

"You mean Christoph, sire?"

"He should be. If anyone should be in heaven, it's him." The king's eyes swung round onto Neumann, suddenly more focused. "Have you found him yet?"

"Found who, sire?"

"The killer, of course. Pay attention, major."

"No, sire."

"What are you doing? Why's it taking you so long?"

"It's a complicated case, sire," Neumann said, aware how feeble the reply was. "Did you know Christoph well?"

"He was such a beautiful boy. Why would anyone want to kill someone so beautiful, so good? Answer me that, major."

"I don't understand either, sire. You sent him notes, didn't you? Written in runes."

"It was our little secret. No one else could read them."

"But then you fell out with him."

"What?"

"Am I wrong?"

"Fell out?" Ludwig frowned and his voice became agitated, angry. "You forget yourself, major. You talk of matters which are none of your concern. I believe you are insolent, sir."

"Forgive me, sire. It was not my intention to offend you."

"I bring you here to Linderhof. I take you into my confidence and this is how you repay me? You are insolent, major. And incompetent. That much is clear to me. If you were a member of my household, I would have you whipped. Can you not see what is in front of your eyes? Can you not see the men who are responsible for this? The men who hate beauty, who hate me, who want to make me unhappy."

"What men are you talking of, sire?"

"Begone! I cannot bear your presence a moment longer. Begone, I say!"

The king waved his arms wildly, as if he were repelling a swarm of hornets.

"Go! Go now!"

Neumann got to his feet, nonplussed by the sudden change of mood, by the king's violent outburst.

"Sire, I assure you –"

"Out of my sight! *Now!*"

Neumann backed away across the pavilion and out into the garden where the servants were waiting.

"What happened, sir?" Axel asked.

"I don't know.

"Hoffmann!" Ludwig yelled. "Bring me biscuits!"

*

For the second time in as many days, Anneliese took extra care with her morning ablutions. Only this time it wasn't for a man, it was for herself. She rose early and summoned her maid to run her a bath, soaking in it indulgently until the water began to cool, then sitting at her dressing table in a towelling robe while Eva did her hair. She put on her make-up and got Eva to lace up her corset before donning her favourite dress – a rich yellow silk gown that complemented her hair. Jewellery was next. The same diamond necklace and earrings she'd worn for the count. Dipping her hand into her jewellery box, she lifted out a sapphire bracelet and offered it to Eva.

"This is for you, my dear. A token of my appreciation for all your years of loyal service."

Eva gazed uncertainly at the bracelet, then her eyes went to her mistress's face. She was puzzled, slightly fearful. Was she being dismissed? This felt like a parting gift.

"Ma'am, is everything all right? Are you not happy with my performance?"

"Quite happy. Take it. Put it somewhere safe."

"It's too much, ma'am. I don't deserve it."

"On the contrary. Please, take it."

Anneliese thrust the bracelet into Eva's hand.

"Wait a moment, please. I need you to do something for me."

The baroness took paper, pen and ink from a drawer and wrote a short note, the message fully formulated in her head earlier so the words flowed easily. Then she slid the note into an envelope and sealed it, wrote a name on the front and handed it to Eva.

"Ask one of the footmen to deliver this immediately to the Freiin von Wildenstein."

"Yes, ma'am."

Anneliese waited for the maid to leave, then slipped on a pair of yellow shoes, to match her gown, and wrapped a cloak around her shoulders. She took a last look in the mirror. She looked good, she knew that. A woman in her prime who would never grow old.

No one was around when she went downstairs. No sign of her husband, thank God. She couldn't have borne another confrontation. Outside in the grounds there was a feel of spring in the air. The snow was melting, dripping off the eaves of the house. Tiny green shoots were emerging tentatively through the soil. Even the lake was thawing, the ice breaking apart, leaving pools of open water.

Anneliese walked along the path beside the lawn. She was tired. She'd had a sleepless night, lying awake in a turmoil, reviewing what had happened and pondering what to do next. Her marriage was over. She'd lost her home – she knew Friedrich was too proud and intransigent to change his mind about that. Even if he did, what future was there for her here? By now, everyone would know what she'd done. The shame, the condemnation, would all fall on her, not zu Freudenberg. It was her reputation that was destroyed, not his. That was how things worked.

She had nowhere to go. Sophie would have taken her in without question, but she couldn't impose on her, couldn't take her shame into her cousin's house. She would be forever a pariah, shunned by the society of which she had been such a distinguished and well-regarded member. Her fall was too great to bear. She'd been foolish to think that her actions would have no consequences. There was only one way out.

She paused on the edge of the lake to take a final look at the house and grounds she loved so much: the swing in the trees she'd played on as a child, the paddock where she'd learnt to ride on her first pony, the ballroom where she'd danced and fallen in love with Friedrich von Breckendorf. So many happy memories to take with her.

She stepped into the lake. The water lapped over her feet. I'm ruining my shoes, she thought. That brought a smile to her lips. A lady to the end. She walked out through the shallows. The cold took her breath away, then mellowed into a dull numbness. She was surprised how calm she was. The anxiety of the night had fallen away. She felt no fear. A swan foraging nearby raised its head and looked at her curiously, as if it were wondering what she was doing. Such a beautiful, graceful creature, Anneliese thought. If I were to be reincarnated, I'd like to come back as a swan.

The water crept over her knees and then her thighs. She stopped and tugged off her wedding ring and gazed at it for a moment, recalling her marriage vows: till death us do part. Then she hurled it out across the lake. It skittered across a patch of ice, then splashed into an open pool. Anneliese kept walking.

My dear Sophie,

I cannot go without sending you one final note to say thank you. Thank you for being my dearest, most loyal, most loving friend. For being you. You will not yet know my shame, but you will hear of it soon enough. I thought I could solve our difficulties, but have brought only dishonour upon myself and the family. Please know that I felt I had no choice and did not think for one second that it would turn out this way. Everything I did I thought was for the best. Friedrich has rejected me and I see no hope for the future. I know you, of all people, will not judge me harshly, but I hope you will forgive me.

Goodbye, dear cousin. Keep me in your thoughts.
With all my love, Anneliese

Sophie read the message at the breakfast table and took a moment to absorb its implications. Surely not? Not Anneliese? Dear God, no! Then she was on her feet, dashing out into the hall to pull on her riding boots and cloak before racing out to the stables and saddling her horse.

She rode like a winter gale – faster, more recklessly, than she'd ever ridden in her life. Through the forest, across the fields, over the Pöllat, jumping hedges and fences, ignoring the hazards, the risks, until at last the von Breckendorf house came into sight. She rode straight up to the front door, abandoning her horse on the forecourt and running up the steps and into the house, startling the maid who was polishing the brass stair rail in the entrance hall.

"Where is your mistress?" Sophie asked breathlessly.

"My mistress?"

"The baroness. Where is she?"

"I think she went out into the grounds."

Sophie sprinted through the house, taking the most direct route to the garden. She unlatched the French windows in the sitting room and hurried out onto the terrace, staring around desperately.

"Anni! Anni!" she called.

She rushed down onto the lawn and along the path through the trees, calling out her cousin's name. Then she burst out onto the lakeshore.

"Anni! It's Sophie. Anni, where are you?"

She saw the shape out on the water and knew she was too late.

"No! No!" she screamed, wading out through the shallows, then swimming the final few metres. Anneliese was floating face down, her cloak and gown billowing out around her. Sophie turned her head over. Anneliese was beyond help. Her face was ice cold, as beautiful in death as it had been in life.

Sophie grabbed hold of her arms and towed her towards the shore, struggling against the weight of her waterlogged clothes. When she reached the edge of the lake, she sank to her knees and held Anneliese in her arms, cradling her, protecting her, the tears coursing down her face.

TWENTY-EIGHT

It was late evening when Neumann got back to Füssen. He crossed the bridge over the Lech at walking pace, his horse even more tired than he was. He'd just ridden the forty kilometres from Linderhof, over terrain with which he wasn't familiar, a large part of it in the dark. Inevitably, he'd got lost several times and had to stop to ask the way – on one occasion, ironically, in one of the villages he'd visited with the king on their sleigh ride two nights earlier. The inhabitants hadn't been able to understand his High German, but sign language and repeated mention of the word Füssen had eventually put him on the right track.

He wasn't in a good mood. He was furious with Ludwig, and with himself – although why *he* should be responsible for any of this was questionable. Perhaps he should have handled the conversation in the Music Pavilion better, but how? The king's reaction had taken him by surprise. It seemed completely irrational and over the top. What was he so upset about? Neumann had spent the rest of the night trying to work out where he'd gone wrong. By morning, he was sure of only one thing: he was in disgrace.

A quiet word with Axel when the king finally retired

to his bed at 7am had confirmed that. Ludwig had made his displeasure known to his staff; Major Neumann was no longer *persona grata* at the palace and was not to be afforded any kind of hospitality. The servants, of course, accustomed to their master's moods, would not be enforcing that instruction too rigorously. With Ludwig safely out of the way upstairs, they gave Neumann a meal in the kitchen and use of a bunk bed in their sleeping quarters. What was clear beyond doubt, however, was that Neumann would not be returning to Füssen in the royal sleigh.

So how would he get there? He could hardly walk, and it soon became apparent that finding an alternative means of transport would not be straightforward. The horses in the palace stables were all reserved for the king's use. He might call on them at any time and no one wanted to risk letting Neumann have one. That left only the security detail. The outriders who'd accompanied the sleigh were not going to part with their mounts, but there were other soldiers stationed at Linderhof to protect Ludwig. They had a pool of horses they could draw on. Neumann asked the lieutenant in charge if he might borrow one. The lieutenant was reluctant to help. What if there was an emergency and he needed them himself?

Neumann tried to persuade him to change his mind without much success until he mentioned he was an old army friend of Lukas Hafner. That broke the lieutenant's resistance but, a stickler for correct procedure – otherwise known as covering his backside – he insisted on telegraphing the barracks in Füssen for official permission. The reply, when it eventually arrived several hours later, was unequivocal. Major Neumann was to be given every possible assistance. But by then he'd already lost most of the day, the second he'd wasted at Linderhof when he could have been getting on with his investigation.

He dropped the horse off at the barracks, then walked back into the town. The kitchen at the Gasthaus Hoffmann had officially stopped serving food, but Johanna got him a plate of lukewarm *bratwurst* and leftover potatoes and brought it to him in the bar with a glass of beer.

"I haven't seen you for a while, major," she said. "Have you been away?"

Neumann told her about his visit to Linderhof – though not the ignominious way in which it had ended – including the sleigh ride with Ludwig.

"Axel was with us," he said. "Sitting behind, working the lights."

"And freezing his arse off," Johanna said. "He hates those sleigh rides. He puts on every bit of clothing he possesses, but it's still bloody awful."

"How long has he worked for the king?"

"Four years now."

"Does he enjoy it? Ludwig seems, well, a demanding employer."

"Demanding? He's a bloody nightmare. I don't know how Axel sticks it. I keep telling him to come home and work here, but he won't. Too loyal to the king, although why I can't fathom. The pay's terrible and he's treated worse than the lowest skivvy. On call all the time and only a half day off every week. You wouldn't catch me putting up with conditions like that."

"He seems very fond of the king, very devoted to him."

"More fool him. He doesn't get any thanks for it, I can tell you. But that's royalty for you. Taking advantage of everyone."

"You don't seem overly keen on Ludwig."

"Why would I be? What does he do for us except spend our money on stupid palaces? Axel's described them to me. All that gold, all that luxury. What's he done to deserve that, eh? Kings, princes, they're all the same, aren't they? Yours has been looking for you, by the way."

"Mine?"

"Prince von Auerswald. Young fellow in livery, looks as if he needs a square meal, was here this morning asking for you. Carriage parked outside. Fancy black thing."

"What did you tell him?"

"Said I didn't know where you were. You staying much longer?"

"I don't know. Do you need the room?"

"Not at all. So long as the bill's paid, you can have it as long as you like."

Neumann finished his food and went upstairs, wondering how long he could avoid von Auerswald. And what he'd tell him when the legate caught up with him – as he undoubtedly would. That Ludwig and Christoph Geissler had been friends? That they may have had a sexual relationship? That the king may have been involved in the young diplomat's death? That wasn't going to go down well, particularly as von Auerswald had expressly declared that the king couldn't possibly have had anything to do with it. What do I do? Neumann thought. I have to follow the evidence. But where did that lead him?

He pondered Ludwig's reaction again, picturing the king in the pavilion, the candlelight on his plump face, the logs burning brightly in the iron fire pit by his feet. What emotion exactly had he been expressing in his furious outburst? It seemed to Neumann that there were two possible explanations – each diametrically opposed to the other. Was it guilt? Neumann had suggested the king had fallen out with Geissler and Ludwig had reacted angrily because it was true. He had ordered his young lover's murder and the burden on his conscience was unbearable. Or was it outrage? He was angry because it was untrue. He hadn't fallen out with Christoph and Neumann was somehow besmirching them both by asserting that he had.

Yet the runic notes seemed to be clear on the issue. Neumann took them out of the locked desk drawer where he'd been storing them and examined them again, re-reading Ziegler's transcriptions of the messages. There was absolutely no doubt. Ten of the notes were tantamount to love letters from Ludwig to Geissler, their content personal, intimate, intended for no one else's eyes – as the king had confirmed at Linderhof. The eleventh note was the problem. *"You have abandoned me, betrayed me, deserted me. I hate you. Odin's curse upon you,"* Ludwig had written. There was no ambiguity there. The king was angry, vengeful, because Geissler had broken off their relationship.

Neumann put aside the transcriptions and turned to the originals. He spread them out on the desk and studied each of them in turn. The runes were meaningless to him, but he could see similarities between all the notes: the same opening greeting, *"My B"*, the same symbols recurring throughout the messages, the same one-letter signature, *"P"*. Yet... yet... Something about them troubled him. Something didn't feel right, even to his inexpert eye. He couldn't put his finger on what.

Sleep on it, he thought. Look again when you're not so tired. So he went to bed and next morning re-examined the notes. Still, he couldn't identify what it was that concerned him. That was annoying. Perhaps Ziegler could help.

He breakfasted, then put on his greatcoat and cap and went out. He could feel the change in the weather immediately. It was warmer today. The overnight frost on the cobbled streets was thawing in the sunshine. The snow on the rooftops was melting, the pedestrians below keeping clear of the buildings to avoid the mini-avalanches that periodically cascaded down onto the pavements. The atmosphere felt different too. He could see a change in mood in the people. Their smiles were brighter, their greetings more cordial. They lingered longer to gossip and chat to the tradesmen in their shop doorways. The long winter was finally coming to an end.

Even the luthier, Ignatz Weber, was friendlier when Neumann walked into his workshop. He actually said "good morning" and engaged in a brief bout of small-talk about the weather before Neumann went up the stairs to Ziegler's apartment. The front door was ajar. Neumann hesitated. Had the author gone out and forgotten to shut his door, or had he already been out and left it open on his return? He was so chaotic that either was possible. Neumann pushed it open and stepped through into the hallway.

"Herr Ziegler? It's Major Neumann. Herr Ziegler?"

The small sitting room on the left was unoccupied. So, too, was the bedroom next door. Neumann walked along the hall into the study and stopped dead.

Dear God! Ziegler was sitting in his chair, slumped forward over the desk as if he were napping. Except the pool of blood around his head told a different story.

Neumann strode forward and put his fingers on Ziegler's neck, the cold skin telling him the author was dead before he even found there was no pulse. The blood was thick and coagulated. Ziegler had probably been lying there for several hours, perhaps since the previous evening. Neumann edged round the desk, noticing the debris on the floor – the books and papers that had been scattered everywhere. It wasn't Ziegler's usual untidy mess. Someone had searched the room.

There was a wound on the back of Ziegler's head, a deep indentation where his skull had been bashed in with a hammer. Neumann knew that for certain because the murder weapon was there on the desk – a short-handled, heavy iron hammer with dried blood caked on the end. Mjollnir. That was his first thought. It looked like Thor's dreaded hammer.

He averted his eyes, breathing deeply, feeling sick and despairing and angry. He'd barely known Ziegler, but he'd liked him, warmed to him during their brief acquaintanceship. Why would anyone have wanted to kill him? He glanced around the room, more questions springing up inside his head. What had the killer been looking for? And had he found it?

He went back along the hall, moving almost lethargically now. There was no hurry. The scene was cold, the murderer long gone, Ziegler beyond help. The key was in the lock on the inside of the front door. Neumann took a closer look at the door. There was no sign of any forced entry. Either the door had been unlocked, or Ziegler had let his killer in.

Neumann transferred the key to the outside and locked the door before going downstairs. The luthier was at his bench, carving the neck for one of his instruments.

"When did you last see Herr Ziegler?" Neumann asked him.

Weber looked up, the chisel poised in his hand.

"Yesterday afternoon."

"What time?"

Weber shrugged. "I'm not sure. Maybe five o'clock."

"Did anyone visit him after that?"

"Not that I saw. But then I went home about six."

"What did you do all evening?" Neumann asked. Weber didn't seem a likely suspect, but there was no harm in checking his movements.

"Had supper with my wife, then went to bed."

"You didn't go out again?"

"No." Weber frowned. "Why're you asking? What's happened?"

Neumann didn't reply. He went out into the street

and walked to Doctor Busch's surgery in Brunnengasse. As he turned into the entrance, he almost collided with a woman who was coming out.

"I beg your pardon," he said, stepping back. Then he saw who it was. "Freiin! Excuse me."

"Major," Sophie replied.

They looked at each other awkwardly for a moment, both feeling that more should be said, but neither sure exactly what. Sophie felt suddenly flustered, that some kind of explanation was in order. "My cousin," she said quickly. "Anneliese von Breckendorf. You met her at the concert. She has... had an accident. I'm here sorting out the death certificate."

Neumann's eyes opened wide. "I'm sorry to hear that, ma'am. An accident?"

"She stumbled and fell into a lake while out walking," Sophie said, giving him the family line that she'd agreed with Friedrich. The stigma of suicide, its implications for a Christian burial and the baroness's reputation were too great to acknowledge what had really happened.

"My condolences, ma'am. That must be very distressing for you."

Sophie nodded, the emotions she thought she had under control welling up to the surface. She blinked away a tear. Neumann saw the pain in her eyes. For the first time, in his experience, she looked vulnerable.

The awkwardness returned. Neither knew what to do, what to say.

"... You are well, major?" Sophie asked, falling back on banal courtesies.

"Yes, thank you. How is Magdalena? I hope she's recovered from our interview."

"She has. She's a strong young woman. What about Frida Messer? Have you questioned her yet?"

Neumann shifted uncomfortably. Then he told her what had happened and saw her face darken with anger.

"So your two key witnesses, Schäfer and Messer, are both dead? What happens now? How will those abused young women get justice?"

"I don't know," Neumann admitted and was mortified to see the contempt in Sophie's eyes. "But they will, I promise you."

"I hope that's a promise you can keep, major. Good day to you."

She brushed past him and hurried away along the street. Neumann watched her go, feeling crestfallen, ashamed that he'd let her down – and the young women in her care, too. Too late for regrets now, he thought ruefully. You just have to deal with the mess you've made.

He went into the surgery to report Ziegler's death and ask the doctor to come out to examine the body, then headed over to the police station. Captain Beck received his news with a phlegmatic nod and perhaps just a hint of schadenfreude.

"Another body?" he remarked. "My, they do seem to be piling up a bit, major. What are we going to do with it? The morgue is getting pretty crowded. The jeweller fellow, Graf, the musician, Schäfer, the woman, Messer. We've even got a baroness decomposing out there now."

"Von Breckendorf?" Neumann said.

"You've heard about her? Nothing to do with you, you'll be glad to hear." Unlike all the others was the unspoken accusation.

"You're investigating her death?"

"Have to, you know that. Not that there's anything funny about it. She went for a walk in her garden yesterday morning, slipped on the ice and fell in the lake. Either drowned or the cold got her. We'll have to see what the pathologist says."

"Where is the good Doctor Jaeger?"

"On his way. Should be here this afternoon. We'll get him to do all four, plus this new one – Ziegler, was it?

Maybe he'll give us a discount on his fee."

"I'll need Lehmann and Böhm over at Ziegler's apartment," Neumann said.

"I think I can spare them."

"And perhaps Krause could track down Ziegler's next-of-kin."

The two constables accompanied Neumann back to Drehergasse. He briefed them on the way, then got them knocking on doors in the area, asking the neighbours if they'd seen anything, or anyone, suspicious since the previous evening. Doctor Busch was waiting for him in the luthier's workshop. They went up together to the apartment and Busch examined Ziegler's body.

"Nasty," he said, sucking in air between his teeth as he saw the gaping hole in the author's skull. "I don't think you need me to tell you the cause of death."

"An approximate time would be good," Neumann said.

"From the body temperature, its condition, I'd say some time in the last twelve hours." The doctor peered at the hammer. "I can touch it?"

"Go ahead."

Busch picked up the hammer and held it over the cavity in Ziegler's head, comparing the two.

"Looks pretty certain this is your murder weapon. That's one hell of a hammer. It's almost too heavy to lift. You'd have to be very strong to wield something like that."

"Thank you, doctor. Can we move the body?"

"Not much I can do for him now," Busch replied.

Neumann surveyed the scene after the doctor had left, his gaze coming to rest on the giant hammer. Was he being fanciful in comparing it to Mjollnir? Or was this another crude message – like the ravens and the mistletoe – linking the death to Norse mythology. But why? Why Ziegler? Where did he begin? he wondered.

Start with the obvious. Ziegler had been murdered, but that hadn't been enough for the killer. He'd also searched the study, implying that Ziegler had possessed something the killer wanted badly. Had he found it? Maybe, maybe not. Assume it's still here, Neumann told himself. You need to be sure.

He started with the desk, the locked drawers that had been forced open. Nothing there. Then he moved on to the shelves, the cupboards, checking every book, every document – a slow, painstaking process that was going to take him hours to complete.

Mid-afternoon – Ziegler's body removed to the morgue – he broke off and walked over to the police station. Doctor Jaeger was in the outhouse carrying out his first autopsy. Neumann was dismayed to see it was Anneliese von Breckendorf, the least important as far as he was concerned.

"Why her?" he asked the pathologist.

"Captain Beck's orders," Jaeger replied. "Makes no difference to me."

Neumann put the same question to Beck in his office.

"She's a baroness," was his answer. "Wife of a government minister who has a lot of clout round here. The family wanted it out of the way so they can bury her as soon as possible."

Social status, Neumann thought. As powerful in death as it is in life.

"I'd hoped he'd start with Frida Messer. I really need to know how she died."

Beck shrugged carelessly. "What's a couple of hours? He can do her next."

Neumann returned to Ziegler's apartment and resumed his search, checking all the other rooms as well as the study, but finding nothing of any significance. Tired and frustrated, he called it a day, locked up and went downstairs. Weber was taking off his apron and washing his hands at the sink.

"A sad business," he said, shaking his head regretfully. "Such a nice, harmless man like him."

Neumann murmured something non-committal. He didn't want to discuss the case. He headed for the door.

"You'll be wanting the envelope, I suppose?" the luthier said.

Neumann turned. "What was that?"

"The envelope he gave me to keep safe for him."

Neumann felt his heart miss a beat. "What envelope?"

Weber dried his hands on a towel, opened a cupboard and lifted out a metal cash box. Unlocking the box, he handed Neumann a slim manilla envelope.

"When did he give you this?" the major asked.

"A couple of days ago."

"What did he say?"

"Nothing much. Just asked me to take care of it for a while."

Neumann broke the seal on the envelope. Inside was a single sheet of paper with a handwritten message on it.

My B
Where are you? Why do you not come to me? Why do you reject my love? You have abandoned me, betrayed me, deserted me. I hate you. Odin's curse upon you.
P

Disappointment washed over him. It was nothing important – just a copy of Ziegler's transcription of Ludwig's last runic note to Geissler. Why he'd entrusted it to Weber Neumann couldn't comprehend. Yet he *had* entrusted it. It made no sense. Unless...

Neumann took a harder look at the message. Then he thanked the luthier, replaced the paper in the envelope and headed rapidly back to his room at the gasthaus where he took out the transcriptions he already had.

He compared the version Ziegler had provided for him with the one he'd given to Weber. The wording was identical, but the handwriting was different.

TWENTY-NINE

Anneliese was laid to rest in the family vault at her home following a small private service in the chapel that was attended only by relations and a few close friends. Sophie was there, along with Anneliese's uncle and her other cousins who'd travelled down from Munich. The female friends who'd made up the baroness's social circle, and their husbands, completed the funeral party that numbered fewer than twenty.

Friedrich was present, of course, looking sombre in mourning clothes. Sophie could hardly bear to be near him. As Anneliese had predicted in her final, poignant message, the rumours had indeed reached her. Sophie wasn't sure exactly what had occurred between her cousin and her husband, but she knew enough to understand that Friedrich, at least in part, was responsible for Anneliese's suicide. And she hated him for it.

They hadn't spoken in any detail about the death. Sophie hadn't shown him the letter Anneliese had sent her and Friedrich, in any case, was happy to believe in the fiction that it had been an accident. It made things easier for him. It removed the burden of guilt that he might have felt if he'd known the truth, although Sophie was certain he would never have blamed himself for it.

He was too self-centred, too full of self-pity to find fault in any of his actions. He appeared to be grieving, and some of it was genuine, but Sophie suspected that beneath the conventions of mourning he felt no real sense of loss.

After the interment, the party drove over to Hohenschwangau for a larger celebration of Anneliese's life. The king, still absent at Linderhof, had given permission for the old palace to be used – she was, after all, the wife of one of his senior ministers. He wouldn't be present himself, but virtually everyone else in the government and the local high society had been invited. Sophie had brought her carriage, and Magdalena as her maid in attendance, although that wasn't the main reason the young woman was there.

They disembarked in the courtyard – the space too small to accommodate parking – then the carriage went back down the drive to allow other vehicles to unload. Sophie and Magdalena waited in the shelter of the Princes' Building, directly opposite the steps leading up to the palace entrance, watching the passengers emerging from their coaches and carriages. This was the cream of the Allgäu aristocracy: counts, barons, knights, margraves, landgraves, and their wives, though it was only the men Sophie was interested in.

She recognised most of them, had encountered them at society events for many years. Few had been real friends of Anneliese, but they were there because it was expected of them. It was their duty to attend and if in the process they had to drink champagne and get through a sumptuous buffet lunch, well, that was just one of the many trials people in their exalted positions had to endure without complaint.

Magdalena scrutinised every man carefully, looking for those two faces that would always be there with her – in her waking hours and in her nightmares. Not him, nor him, nor him. Half a dozen distinguished gentlemen made their way up the steps, their wives on their arms. Then a carriage door opened and a lone man climbed out. Magdalena stiffened, her eyes fixed on him. Sophie glanced at her, sensing her anguish.

"Him?" she asked softly.

Magdalena nodded, her lip trembling.

"You're sure?"

"Yes, he was one of them. The brutal one."

Sophie watched Count Walther Ehrenbeck zu Freudenberg adjust his black suit and walk across the courtyard. She gripped Magdalena's hand tight in her own. The girl was shaking as if she had a fever.

"You're safe," Sophie murmured. "He can't harm you now."

Magdalena looked away, fighting back tears.

"Just a few more minutes," Sophie went on. "Have courage, we need to do this. Can you manage that?" Magdalena nodded again. "Good girl. You're strong, remember. And I am with you. Together we can do this."

More carriages arrived, more passengers disembarked. Magdalena studied them all, shaking her head occasionally. Then the last vehicle pulled into the courtyard. A footman jumped down from the back and opened the door. A man stepped out and Magdalena gave a start.

"Him," she whispered.

Sophie felt a pulse of shock, like an electric charge, shoot up her spine. No, no. Surely Magdalena must be mistaken. It was Friedrich.

"Are you positive?"

"Absolutely."

"Look again. There must be no doubt."

"I will never forget that face," Magdalena said. "That's him."

Sophie went cold. Friedrich? Friedrich was one of The

Wotan Brotherhood? Zu Freudenberg she could believe. He was a bully with an unsavoury reputation as a womaniser. But Friedrich? That was harder for her to take in. Anneliese's husband – widower now – was a serial rapist.

"Thank you," she said to Magdalena. "It's over. Go and wait inside with the other maids. You've done well."

Magdalena went into the Princes' Building. Sophie followed Friedrich up the steps into the palace, keeping her distance. She didn't want him to see her, didn't want to have to speak to him. She was stunned, revolted, angry, working out what she was going to do next.

The other mourners – guests, really, for this event was more of a reception than a wake – were up on the second floor, in the Hall of the Heroes, the largest room in the palace which had been designed as a banqueting hall – a neo-Gothic ceiling adorned with moulded silver stars, central columns of stucco marble and walls painted with scenes from the Vilkina Saga.

As Sophie ascended the last flight of stairs, she saw a kitchen boy crawling into a small hole in the wall with an armful of wood. The whole building was riddled with hidden passages along which the servants could pass invisibly to stoke the ceramic stoves that kept the place heated. The banqueting hall was warm and crowded, people clustered in groups while maids and footmen circulated with trays of champagne.

Sophie took a glass, though she had no intention of drinking it. It was unseemly. There was nothing here to celebrate. Not for her, anyway. A life that had ended so tragically, so unnecessarily; that wasn't cause for anything other than sorrow. But it gave her something to hold, to make her look as if she were a part of the gathering when inside her, she felt completely detached, a bit of her wanting to scream to all these fine ladies and gentlemen, "*Do you know what really happened?*"

She made light conversation, accepted people's condolences, smiled graciously, all the while her heart breaking. Friends spoke to her of Anneliese's virtues – of her kindness, her selflessness, her good works for charity. All well-meaning, intended to honour and cherish her, but to Sophie they were like knife stabs that only exacerbated her feelings of grief.

Across the room, she saw zu Freudenberg holding court, surrounded by fawning men: followers, would-be acolytes, all looking for his favour. Do you know what he's done? Sophie thought bitterly. Do you know what he *is*? Probably they did, but they didn't care. He was too powerful to cross.

Friedrich came towards her and she knew she could avoid him no longer.

"An excellent turn-out, don't you think?" he said, as if he were assessing attendance at a race-meeting. "Does Anni proud. Lots of top-drawer people, too. I never thought Landgrave von Holzmann would come. Or Margrave zu Brandenstein. Splendid that they could make it. Of course, it helps having the palace. His Majesty has been most kind to us."

Sophie said nothing. She wanted to get away from this place, from all these people who hadn't known Anneliese the way she had, hadn't loved her the way she had. In particular, she wanted to get away from Friedrich. He disgusted her, made her stomach turn.

"I'm glad I have you, Sophie," Friedrich said, taking her hand and squeezing it.

Sophie suppressed a shudder and pulled her hand away.

"This is a very difficult time for me," he went on. "You see that, don't you? Anni was such a great support to me, and I loved her so much. It's going to be very hard without her. But you'll be there for me, won't you?"

What did she say to that? Sophie wondered. She could

hardly be honest, not here at an event that was supposed to bring people together in harmony for Anni.

"Won't you?" Friedrich pressed.

"Of course," Sophie replied.

"I'm going to miss her so much. I'll need help to get through it, Sophie. A lot of help." He made as if to take her hand again, but Sophie ensured it was out of reach. "You know, I've always admired you, despite your peculiar ways. You're a very attractive woman."

Am I really hearing this? Sophie thought. His wife in her grave for only a few hours and he's making a pass at me.

"A man needs a woman," Friedrich continued. "There are comforts that only a loving woman can provide. And you, Sophie, you've always had a special place in my heart. It's early, I know, but I'm deeply distressed by Anni's death. Will you come to the house later?"

"The house?"

"We can talk, share our memories of Anni... perhaps become closer. I'm looking to the future to give me hope. I want you to be part of that future."

It was all she could do to stop herself slapping his face. He was a man with no moral compass, no understanding of right or wrong, good or evil. Magdalena had confirmed that. But amid her revulsion, Sophie was seeing a plan begin to take shape in her mind. She knew what she needed to do.

"Perhaps it would be good to talk," she said. "But we must be discreet. As you said, it's still early."

"Yes, we must keep it a secret," Friedrich said earnestly. "But you will come?"

"After dark. No one must see me. Make sure the French windows in your study are unlocked. I will come through the garden at eleven o'clock."

"At eleven." He nodded. "I will be waiting for you, my dear."

*

Could she do it? Sophie wondered as night descended over Waldblick. Could she really do something so drastic? Surely there were other ways that would be better, that would not place such a heavy weight on her conscience. There were legal channels. There were police officers of integrity like Reinhardt Neumann. Could she not just leave it to them?

Then she thought about the young women she was concerned for – Amalie and Magdalena and the others – and the men they were accusing of the most heinous crimes. The imbalance between the two was enormous. Poor, powerless women, most from working-class stock, with no families to defend them or care what happened to them – the reason they had been chosen by The Wotan Brotherhood in the first place. They were up against titled landowners, men with money and senior positions in government.

Who had more credibility? Who would be believed if it came to a court case? Not that it would get that far. Zu Freudenberg and the others would make sure it didn't. They had influence, the right friends. There was no evidence against them that would stand up to legal scrutiny – just the word of a few women who could easily be tarred as unreliable and mendacious. There was nothing to corroborate their claims. The only witnesses to the activities of the Brotherhood – Karl Schäfer and Frida Messer – had been conveniently removed from the equation. Who was to say that the young female accusers wouldn't suffer the same fate? If they wanted justice, they had to get it another way.

Sophie prepared herself in her bedroom, putting on her usual trousers, shirt and jacket before packing a gown into a small saddlebag. Then she went downstairs, slipped on riding boots and a cloak and headed out to the stables. One of the sentries acknowledged her courteously, but said nothing. It wasn't his place to ask the mistress of the house what she was doing. Sophie saddled her horse, strapped the bag to the back and rode off into the night.

She had plenty of time. No need for any of the shortcuts and reckless risks she'd taken on her last visit to the house. She kept to the main roads, riding steadily, letting the familiar motion of the mare calm her nerves, take her mind off what she was about to do. As she came within sight of the von Breckendorf house, she circled round to the woods at the back. She tethered her horse to a tree, then removed her jacket and shirt and pulled the gown on over her head. The air was cold on the exposed skin of her shoulders and bosom, but the dress was essential. She had to look the part. Friedrich must suspect nothing.

Cautiously, she made her way into the gardens, stopping occasionally to listen, keeping her eyes skinned for people. It wasn't likely that anyone would be out in the grounds at this time of night, but she was taking no chances. No one must see me, she'd said to Friedrich. He'd understood that imperative for his own self-interested purposes. Sophie, however, had different reasons.

She came out onto the shore of the lake. The sight revived distressing memories of finding Anneliese in the water, but it also steeled her resolve. This had to be done. It *needed* to be done. She walked round the lake and paused on the edge of the lawn leading up to the house. There were a few lights on inside the building, but none in either the sitting room or Friedrich's study which faced onto the rear terrace. She checked her watch. Ten forty-five. Exactly on schedule.

Lifting her skirts, she flitted across the lawn and terrace to the French windows of the study. As planned, they were unlocked. She slipped inside and took a moment to remind herself of the layout. Desk to the left, sofa and armchair to the right. She listened. The house was quiet. Most of the servants would already have gone to bed. Friedrich, she guessed, would be in his room, watching the clock and preparing to creep downstairs at the appointed hour.

Crossing to the desk, she lit the lamp and pulled open the top drawer. There it was: Friedrich's revolver and a box of ammunition. She loaded the weapon and put it down on the floor behind the sofa. Then she sat down and adjusted her hair and gown to look suitably alluring. Her heart was racing, her stomach tense. Did she really have the nerve to do this?

On the dot of eleven, the door opened and Friedrich entered. He looked around and saw her. His eyes gleamed with pleasure, and anticipation.

"Lock the door," Sophie said softly.

Friedrich turned the key and strode eagerly over to the sofa, sitting down beside her and taking her hands.

"I'm so glad you came, my dear. You look very beautiful."

"The servants?" Sophie asked.

"All out of the way."

"What about Helmut?"

"I've sent him to his room. No one is around, don't worry. We are quite alone." He lifted one of her hands to his lips and kissed it. "You don't know how happy this makes me. To have you here with me this evening. I found today so difficult, so upsetting."

"We all did," Sophie said.

"I want to put it all behind me now. The sadness, the loss. I want to be happy again, and I know you can help me do that, Sophie. I know you have... feelings for me. I've seen you looking at me over the years. Of course, you were always very proper. Anni was your cousin, your friend. You were very loyal to her. But now she is gone, well, things have changed, haven't they?"

Sophie didn't reply. She was trying to hold down her

disgust, her rising anger, so Friedrich had no hint of her loathing for him. But he wasn't really looking for any signals from her; he was too absorbed in himself. He leaned over and tried to kiss her on the mouth. She turned her head away so his lips only brushed her cheek. Then she stood up, shaking visibly. Friedrich mistook her agitation for desire.

"I have the same feelings for you, too," he said. "But I won't hurry you, my darling. I know you might need more time. But don't be coy. I hate a woman playing the coquette."

Coquette? Sophie thought furiously. You think I'm a coquette? I'll show you what I am. She went behind the sofa, giving herself a few seconds to steady her nerve. Then she leaned over the back of the sofa, reaching down with her right hand to pick up the revolver. Friedrich twisted round to see her. She was deliberately displaying her breasts to him. He leered and stretched out his hand to touch them, but Sophie pulled away. Friedrich chuckled.

"You like the chase, do you, my dear? Well, I'll indulge you for a time. But don't keep me waiting too long. You don't want to make me angry, do you?"

Make *you* angry? Sophie thought. She remembered holding Anni's lifeless body in her arms, remembered Magdalena's anguish as she recounted her brutal violation by the men of The Wotan Brotherhood. By men like Friedrich. And the cold fury gave her all the courage she needed. She edged behind Friedrich and whispered in his ear, "This is for Anni and all those young women you raped."

She put the revolver to the side of his head and pulled the trigger.

The report, the explosion of blood, flesh and bone, stunned her momentarily. Friedrich was slumped sideways on the sofa. Sophie averted her eyes, almost gagging. Then she moved round rapidly and placed the revolver in his right hand, curling his fingers around the grip before she ran to the French windows and out onto the terrace. The servants would certainly have heard the gunshot. How long did she have? Probably a few minutes. She dashed across the lawn, ducking into the trees and pausing to look back. She could see no sign of activity. No faces at the windows, no people coming out into the garden. It would take them a while to break down the study door, in any case. Even then, surely, they would take the scene at face value: a tragic suicide. A distraught widower, unable to live without his beloved wife, takes his own life.

Sophie ran on past the lake and into the woods. Only when she reached her horse did the full enormity of what she'd done hit her. She bent over, retching, and threw up on the ground, the mare watching impassively. It was a couple of minutes before she recovered. She took a few deep breaths, letting the nausea subside, then stripped off her gown, crammed it into the saddlebag and put back on her shirt, jacket and cloak. She resisted the urge to leap onto her horse and race away – the noise might alert someone to her presence. Instead, she led the animal quietly through the trees, listening out for sounds from the house – for a hue and cry that might indicate she was in danger. But she heard nothing.

When she reached the road, she swung herself up into the saddle and maintained a gentle walking pace until they were well away from the house. Then she spurred her mare into a gallop, heading east towards home. The nausea had passed, but she felt light-headed and slightly feverish. There was no elation, just relief that it was over. Relief and guilt and an overwhelming feeling of regret that it had come to this.

THIRTY

Perhaps the ancient Germanic peoples had it right when they believed that their destinies were determined by the Norns. That whatever life had in store for you would not be decided by you, but by remote forces over which you had no control. The thought passed through Neumann's mind as he walked into the dining room for breakfast and saw his fate slouched on a chair in the corner. Not three old women spinning, but a young boy in dark green livery.

"Good morning, sir," Jürgen Keller said, rising to his feet.

"Good morning."

"Sir, I've –"

Neumann raised a hand to silence him.

"I know. Have you breakfasted?"

"I had some bread earlier."

"Join me."

"Sir, I have strict instructions to –"

"*Join me*, Jürgen. Your instructions can wait."

Neumann ushered the boy to a table and made him sit down.

"What else did you have, apart from bread?"

"That was it, sir. Just a bread roll."

"One bread roll? For a growing lad like you? Are you

hungry?" Keller's hesitation gave him his answer. "You'll have a proper breakfast for once. And don't argue with me."

Johanna came out of the kitchen and Neumann ordered for both of them: rolls, butter, jam, cheese, ham, hard-boiled eggs and coffee.

"And plenty of it," he said.

"Sir, I'm not sure –"

"I said don't argue, Jürgen. No one is going to know. You're all skin and bone, for goodness sake. I've seen more fat on a fried potato. Does the prince not feed his staff?"

"Sir, he treats us very well."

"Yes, yes. Your loyalty is admirable, but it won't be much use to you if you fade away from malnutrition."

When the food arrived, Neumann made sure that Keller ate his fill – not that he took much persuading. He started off modestly, still fearful that he was doing something wrong, but soon relaxed as he realised this was a treat that might not come his way again soon. By the end, he'd got through four rolls, three hard-boiled eggs and more ham and cheese than he'd seen in a month. Neumann didn't stint himself, either. The last thing he wanted was to face von Auerswald on an empty stomach.

On the carriage journey out to the prince's residence, he reviewed the progress he'd made in his investigation and prepared his answers to what he could envisage were going to be some difficult questions. He wasn't wrong about that. Von Auerswald's aquiline face was dark, his manner confrontational as Neumann entered the office and stood stiffly before the desk, awaiting his wrath.

"Where the devil have you been?" the prince demanded. "I've been trying to find you for days."

"His Majesty took me to Linderhof, sir."

Von Auerswald wasn't expecting that. He narrowed his eyes. "*What*? Linderhof?"

"Yes, sir."

"Why?"

"As I mentioned before, sir, he has taken an interest in the Geissler case. He wanted to talk about it."

"And you complied?"

"He *is* the king, sir. I didn't feel I had much choice."

"What did you tell him?"

"Well, not a lot, sir. Our conversation was..." He paused, trying to think of a diplomatic way to describe it. "... slightly disjointed."

The prince leaned forward aggressively over the desk.

"And *me*? Perhaps you'd be good enough to share the results of your endeavours with me, major?"

Neumann brought him up to date with the investigation. Von Auerswald took a moment to absorb the information.

"There are a lot of deaths," he said. "You were brought here to investigate one murder, not to create more."

It was an unfair remark, but Neumann didn't try to defend himself. Von Auerswald wasn't interested in excuses.

"Do you have any idea why they were killed?" the legate went on. "Let alone who did it. Let's start with Ziegler, shall we? Enlighten me, major, if you can."

"I don't know why he was killed."

"And the others?"

"Schäfer may have been a suicide."

"May?"

"It could've been murder, though I've no proof of that."

"And Messer?"

"I suspect poisoning. The autopsy was inconclusive, but the pathologist has sent tissue samples off for analysis to the laboratory in Munich. I'm still waiting for the results."

"And Graf?"

"I think he may have made items of jewellery for The Wotan Brotherhood."

"*May*, again? You're fond of that word, aren't you?"

"His records have disappeared from his workshop."

"What items of jewellery?"

"The rings the men wore to denote their membership of the Brotherhood, and a golden necklace they used as part of their perverted ceremonies."

"But you have no proof of this?"

"No, sir."

"You don't have proof of much, do you?"

Neumann remained silent. He could feel von Auerswald's anger, his hostility. He sensed that saying anything would only provoke him further.

"And what about Geissler?" the prince asked.

"I know a little more about that," Neumann replied.

"You *do*?" von Auerswald said with exaggerated emphasis. "Perhaps you haven't wasted your time here, after all. Pray share your insights with me."

How was he going to broach this? Neumann wondered, given the legate's earlier instruction to keep the palace well out of the case. There was no way he could avoid it.

"Well, sir," he began. "I believe the messages Geissler received, written in runes, came from the king. They were addressed to '*My B*', which was His Majesty's pet name for Geissler. After Baldur, the most beautiful of the Norse gods, who was killed by a mistletoe spear. The notes were signed, '*P*', which, I understand from one of the kings' servants –"

"Which one?" the prince broke in quickly.

"Axel Hoffmann. I understand that P – for Parsifal – was how His Majesty used to sign his letters to Richard

Wagner, another of his close friends."

"Parsifal?"

"The knight of the Holy Grail. The king, apparently, identifies strongly with the Grail knights."

"You have evidence for this... speculation?"

Neumann hesitated, but there was no going back now.

"His Majesty himself told me he and Geissler communicated by writing notes in runes. It was their private, secret language."

Von Auerswald sat back heavily in his chair, his jaw dropping a little.

"Good God!" he breathed. "Do you have anything to corroborate this?"

"I found a book on runes in Geissler's lodgings. There's an inscription in the front – *'from P to B'* – which, I'm fairly sure, is in the king's hand."

The legate ran a hand over his face, his fingers stroking his duelling scars.

"Close friends, you said. Exactly how intimate were Geissler and the king?"

Neumann hesitated again. "Very, I believe."

"And the messages? What did they say?"

"Most are affectionate, invitations for Geissler to visit the king in his apartments."

"Most?"

"The last is different. It appears that Geissler has broken off the friendship and the king is angry with him."

"Angry enough to have him killed?"

"That, sir, is the question."

Von Auerswald pushed back his chair, stood up and walked across the room to the window, too agitated to stay still. He gazed out over the garden for a time, then swung round, his eyes burning.

"What did I tell you shortly after you arrived, Neumann? Let me remind you. The king is not involved in this. He *cannot* be involved. The murder of Christoph Geissler is the work of a lunatic. And that madman is the person you must find. Do you remember that?"

"Yes, sir, I remember. But I must go where the evidence leads me. There is no madman." Not unless it's Ludwig, he thought, but didn't say.

The legate paced across the office, shaking his head. The skin on his face looked tauter now, emphasising the sharp bones of his cheeks and jaw.

"This is bad, very bad," he said, talking to himself. Then he turned to glare at Neumann.

"You realise what you've done, don't you, you bloody fool? The king in a... deviant... relationship with a Prussian diplomat who ends up dead. This is going to cause a massive scandal – if it ever gets out. And a dangerous diplomatic problem for Wilhelmstrasse. Well done, major! You may single-handedly have brought down the Bavarian government."

He strode towards the door. "I must telegraph Berlin to advise them of the situation. Wait here."

Von Auerswald left the room. Neumann remained where he was, shifting uneasily, wishing he were anywhere but here. He'd seen enough of power – in the army and in the police force – to know that the men at the top never took responsibility for anything if they could possibly help it. Blame was the only culture they understood.

The prince was right. Neumann had opened a can of worms whose contents had the potential to wriggle into every nook and cranny of the government with untold consequences. Whether it was his fault or not was immaterial. He was the messenger and his superiors didn't like the message. They would find ways to either ignore it, deal with it or cover it up, all of which carried the risk of collateral damage, which Neumann suspected might well be him.

He could feel his stomach cramping. His muscles were tense from standing rigid in front of the desk. He moved away to stretch his limbs, his eyes roving around the room, taking in the furniture, the ornaments on the tables, the pictures on the walls. Then they alighted on the bookshelves. The prince had an extensive collection of books, most of them thick, leather-bound tomes on history and jurisprudence which looked very old and rarely read. But there was a small section of more contemporary books: a few novels and works on current affairs and politics. Neumann saw a spine he recognised – *From Asgard to Ragnarök*. So von Auerswald had Norbert Ziegler's study of Norse mythology. Not in itself surprising, perhaps, but he was curious nonetheless. Had the legate read it?

Neumann pulled out the book from the shelf. A few of the pages were turned down at the top corner to mark particular sections. He flipped to the first of them. It was the chapter entitled *The Death of Baldur*. Nothing strange about that. Neumann had told the prince about Baldur, of course. About the mistletoe spear, about Ludwig mentioning the name. Maybe von Auerswald wanted to know more about the myth so had consulted the book.

He turned to the next bent corner – which marked a passage about Odin and his two ravens, Huginn and Muninn. He felt a slight tingle on the back of his neck, like a warning signal. The prince had been reading about the ravens?

The third marked section was in a chapter about Thor. A passage halfway down the page had been underlined in pencil. It described the forging of the god's hammer, Mjollnir, by the dark elf blacksmiths, Brokk and Eitri, who gave it magic powers and a very short handle. Neumann stared at the words. The tingling sensation on his neck was creeping up into his head and growing more intense. Was this a coincidence? Von Auerswald reading about Mjollnir when a hammer of similar size and shape had been used to kill Ziegler? On its own, perhaps. But in conjunction with the passages about Baldur and the ravens it seemed highly unlikely. There was a pattern here with alarming implications.

Neumann closed the book and quickly put it back on the shelf, walking away across the office just as the legate re-entered the room.

"You may go, major," von Auerswald said. "But keep all this to yourself. Do nothing until I have heard back from Wilhelmstrasse. Do you understand?"

"Yes, sir."

Neumann went out to the carriage, his heart throbbing as if he'd just run up a mountain. Von Auerswald? Was it possible? Surely not. There had to be some other explanation.

THIRTY-ONE

"Thank you for coming, ma'am," Captain Beck said. "I'm very sorry for your loss."

"What happened?" Sophie asked. "Your constable was rather vague on the matter."

"Perhaps you'd like to sit down, ma'am."

They were in the sitting room at the von Breckendorf house. Sophie took one of the armchairs. Through the tall French windows, she could see the gardens, the terrace and lawn across which she'd fled not twelve hours earlier, the smell of cordite in her nostrils, the echo of the single gunshot ringing in her ears. She'd washed thoroughly and changed her clothes since, but still worried that incriminating traces of her actions might somehow be lingering on her person. Beck sat down opposite her and his voice took on the grave tone of a policeman imparting bad news.

"I'm afraid it appears that the baron took his own life."

Appears? Sophie thought, with a sudden jolt of alarm. Did the police suspect something? But she needn't have worried; the captain was only trying to be tactful.

"The details are rather upsetting, ma'am, but it's clear he committed suicide."

Sophie raised a hand to her lips, trying to look suitably shocked.

"Friedrich... Oh, my God! But how? Why?"

"The how isn't difficult to verify. He used a revolver. The why may also be easy to establish. I understand from the servants that he only buried his wife yesterday."

"Yes, that's right."

"You were there, I believe. How did the baron seem?"

"Well, distraught, as you would expect. Losing his wife was a huge blow to him."

"You had no inkling that he might do something like this?"

Sophie shook her head. "None at all. Of course, he may have been putting on a brave face. There was the burial, and then a formal gathering at Hohenschwangau. A lot of people were present. It must have been very hard for him, but he gave no sign that he was in such a desperate state."

"When did you last see him?"

"Let me think... It must have been about three o'clock yesterday afternoon. He seemed all right then. What time did it happen?"

"Around eleven o'clock. The servants heard a gunshot from the study and came rushing downstairs. The door was locked from the inside so they had to break it down. They found the baron dead on the sofa, the revolver in his hand."

"Oh, my goodness! What possessed him? Why didn't he say something to me? He must have been in such distress."

Sophie pulled a handkerchief from her pocket and dabbed her eyes.

"Excuse me, captain. This is quite a bombshell."

"I understand, ma'am," Beck replied, looking away politely while Sophie tended to her imaginary tears.

When she seemed back in control, he said, "His manservant, Helmut Schultz, has told us that the baron threatened to kill himself only last week. He had to be disarmed by his wife."

"*What*? I didn't know that."

"He was apparently depressed about his financial affairs. The death of his wife must have disturbed the balance of his mind even further, so perhaps it isn't surprising that he resorted to something so extreme." Beck eyed her sympathetically. "I'm sorry to have to call on you at such a difficult time, ma'am, but I gather from the housekeeper that you are Baroness von Breckendorf's cousin and very close to the family – closer than any other relation."

"Yes, that's true. Her other cousins live in Munich."

"And the baron's family?"

"He doesn't have much. He was an only child and his parents are both dead. He has a cousin in Nuremberg who is probably his next-of-kin. Would you like me to contact him?"

Beck looked relieved. "That would be most kind of you, ma'am. Bad news like this always comes better from family or friends, rather than the police."

Sophie tucked her handkerchief back into her pocket, giving the impression now of a strong woman putting her emotions aside and turning to more practical matters.

"The baron…" she began. "He is…?"

"The body has been taken to the morgue, ma'am. There will have to be an inquest, but that will just be a formality."

"His affairs are likely to be complicated. I will have to start putting them in order and to do that, I will need access to his papers. The study…?"

"We have finished there, ma'am. But…" Beck hesitated. This wasn't a subject fit for a lady like the freiin. "But you may wish to send the servants in first, to… tidy up."

"Thank you, captain. I am obliged to you for being so sensitive."

Beck stood up. "I will leave you to it, ma'am. Let me once again express my deepest condolences. Good day to you."

Sophie breathed a sigh of relief when he'd gone. To the police, everything seemed clear-cut, unequivocal; just the way she'd planned it. Friedrich's state of mind, the traumatic circumstances, his previous recorded attempt at suicide, it all left little room for doubt that he'd taken his own life. But she was trembling, nevertheless. It had been a perilous few minutes, though the captain would almost certainly have put her agitation down to grief, not guilt.

She waited for her pulse to slow, then went into the study. The sofa and carpet were spattered with crimson. Perhaps she should have taken Beck's advice and got the housemaids to clean up first, but she'd hunted deer and wild boar for years, butchered the carcasses for their meat: a bit of blood wasn't going to bother her.

She went to the desk and tried the drawers. Two were unlocked, but contained nothing of any significance. The others were locked. That was more of a challenge. She had no idea where the keys were. Perhaps Friedrich had carried them with him. Going out into the hall, she found the housekeeper and asked her to get some tools from the groundsman who did odd jobs around the estate. It took the best part of fifteen minutes, but the hammer, chisel and screwdriver the housekeeper eventually brought to the study did the job. There was nothing subtle about it. Sophie simply forced the drawers open, splintering the wood around the locks in the process.

Inside were files of Friedrich's personal correspondence and financial records, including bank statements. There was something else, too: a small black jewellery box of the size and kind used for cufflinks. Sophie flipped it open. On the silk interior lining of the lid was printed the name and address of Werner Graf, Jeweller and Goldsmith. And inserted into a slit in the padded base was a gold ring embossed with a white enamel letter 'W' on a dark blue background.

Sophie stared at it for a moment. She'd never doubted Magdalena, but it was reassuring to have her accusation against Friedrich confirmed. She closed the lid quickly and put the box back in the drawer. Her hands felt soiled merely from touching it. She took out the files and sat down at the desk to examine them. Maybe there would be documentation about The Wotan Brotherhood – an indication of who else was a member. She sifted slowly through the papers.

There was nothing about the Brotherhood. Most were dull and of little interest to her. Letters between Friedrich and his banker, Herr Richter, receipts and invoices for various transactions, some dating back several years. But in a slim cardboard folder she found something that struck her as odd – a brief letter to the baron that read:

My dear von Breckendorf,
The fund is now up and running, as planned. I authorise you to make the following payments: 10,000 marks to Werner Graf; 10,000 marks to Norbert Ziegler; 100,000 marks to Captain Wilhelm Schirmer.

The letter was dated March 2nd, just a few weeks ago, and signed Prince Ernst Heinrich von Auerswald.

Sophie stared at the text. She recognised two of the names – Graf, the jeweller, and Ziegler, the local author, now both dead. She didn't know who Captain Wilhelm Schirmer was, but a hundred thousand marks was a considerable sum. Why was the German legate giving Friedrich permission to distribute money from a fund, and why to those three men?

Sophie put the letter into the pocket of her skirt and replaced the other papers in the desk drawer. Then she went out to her horse and rode to the police station in Füssen and asked for Neumann. He wasn't there, the constable behind the desk said. Try the Gasthaus

Hoffmann. Sophie went to the inn and found the major finishing his dinner in the dining room.

"Freiin, this is a surprise. Please." He pulled out a chair for her to sit down.

"I apologise for interrupting your meal," Sophie said.

"Not at all. May I offer you something? A drink, perhaps?"

"No, thank you. I won't keep you long."

She glanced around the room. It wasn't full – just two other diners, and they were out of earshot over near the bar. Sophie took out the letter and gave it to Neumann. He read the contents, his brow furrowing.

"Where did you get this?"

Sophie explained. Neumann gazed at her sympathetically.

"Your cousin just a few days ago, and now her husband. My condolences, ma'am. That's very sad."

"Anneliese, yes," Sophie said. "Friedrich, less so. I found something else in his desk – a 'W' ring, just like the one you already have."

"A ring? You mean…"

Sophie nodded. "He was a member of The Wotan Brotherhood."

"The Minister of Justice?"

"What did I tell you? Powerful men."

Neumann sat back in his chair, momentarily lost for words. Then he said, "The baron… this letter… I'm not sure I understand." He reread von Auerswald's instructions, looking more closely now at the handwriting.

"Freiin, would you wait here for just a moment? I'll be right back."

He hurried upstairs to his room, removed the collection of papers from the desk drawer and returned to the dining room. He compared von Auerswald's letter with the sheet of paper Ziegler had entrusted to the lute-maker, Weber, for safekeeping. The handwriting on them was identical.

"You seem perplexed," Sophie said. "What are all those papers? May I?" She shuffled them around the table. "What peculiar writing. Is it code?"

"Runes," Neumann replied.

"Runes? What do they mean?"

Neumann riffled through the papers, shaking his head in bewilderment.

"I thought I knew," he said. "Now, I'm not so sure."

"You want help with runes?" Sophie said. "I know just the person."

The hut was filled with the scent of the potion that was cooking in an iron cauldron over the fire. Spearmint and camphor and oil of wintergreen – not unpleasant, but strong, pungent odours that stung the nostrils and the back of the throat. Gisela turned her head as Sophie and Neumann entered. She gave the pot a few vigorous stirs of the spoon, then moved away from the hearth, her eyes looking from one to the other, sensing urgency in their faces and movements.

"What is it, child?" she asked Sophie.

"Would you look at these for us?"

Neumann spread out the runic messages on the table, Ziegler's transcriptions next to them.

"Can you read these? Are the transcriptions an accurate summary of the contents?"

Gisela sat down and studied the papers, reading each message carefully before comparing it to the transcription. Neumann paced restlessly away across the room, impatient for an answer. Gisela glanced at him.

"What will come will come in its own time, major," she said. "It cannot be rushed. Please, sit down."

Neumann pulled out a chair opposite and watched Gisela peering at the pages, her eyes only a few centimetres above them, a bony forefinger moving slowly under the runes as if she were feeling, as much as reading, their meaning. Sophie went to the fire and stirred the cauldron. The contents were thickening into a paste that could be applied to the chest to relieve lung and throat infections. She stepped back a pace. The fumes were making her eyes water.

"I think it's ready," she said.

Gisela nodded, but didn't reply. Sophie wrapped a thick oven cloth around the handle of the cauldron, lifted it off its hook and set it down on top of the range. A cloud of steam drifted up towards the ceiling. Neumann looked around, fascinated by the room: by the bundles of drying herbs and leaves suspended from the rafters, by the jars of powders and oils and other raw ingredients arranged neatly on shelves, the finished medicines labelled and stacked in a separate section like an apothecary's store. The old lady seemed to know what she was doing with her balms and elixirs, but was she equally competent with runes?

"Yes, they are reasonably accurate," Gisela said finally, lifting her head from the last of the messages.

"Reasonably?" Neumann queried.

"You will never get wholly accurate transcriptions because runes aren't like that. They aren't like a foreign language, say, French, or English, where the words have a recognised translation. Runes are symbols. Their meanings can be vague, unformed. They can mean different things in different contexts. That's part of their magic. They are open to interpretation."

"This one, in particular," Neumann said, extracting the note that had been found on Christoph Geissler's body. "Do you agree with the transcription?"

"Broadly, yes. What you have there corresponds well to the original runes, both in tone and meaning."

"Oh."

Neumann felt deflated. He'd hoped for more: for a discrepancy, for something that would explain why he was unsure about that final message from Ludwig to his young lover.

Then Gisela said, "You know it's not written by the same hand, don't you?"

Neumann started. "*What?*"

"These ones here." She grouped together the bulk of the papers. "They are written by the same person. But this one is different."

"You can tell?"

"Of course. Runic writing is like every other kind of handwriting. Everyone has their own individual style. If you have the right eye, you can spot the differences, the idiosyncrasies that mark one writer out from another. Here, for example, see how the *berkana* is written. The main downstroke is longer than in the other notes, which means that the supplementary strokes – those little triangles on the right-hand side – are necessarily stretched out also. You can see it in the other symbols, too. It is clearly a different hand."

Neumann stared at the papers. Now she mentioned it, he could see the differences. The thickness of a pen stroke here, the angle of another line there. They were only slight – easy to overlook – but unmistakable once you knew what you were looking for.

"Thank you, Frau Winter. You've been most kind."

He gathered in the papers. Sophie lingered for a moment, checking that Gisela had all the provisions she needed, then she accompanied Neumann back to her house. They went into the drawing room and Sophie ordered tea.

"I'm grateful to you, ma'am," Neumann said. "Frau Winter is a remarkable woman."

"She has many gifts. Not just reading runes. Her healing powers are greatly valued by the local people, particularly by women who don't trust doctors. She is working wonders with Magdalena and the others."

"I'm glad to hear it. They are recovering, then?"

"Slowly, but, yes. Even Amalie is making progress."

"You must take some credit for that, too. For taking them in, for supporting them, protecting them. I think that you are also a remarkable woman, freiin."

Sophie coloured and covered her embarrassment by pouring them both a cup of tea and changing the subject.

"What are those papers you showed Gisela?"

Neumann hesitated, wondering how much he should reveal, how much was confidential. He trusted her. She was already a party to some of the strands of his investigation, notably The Wotan Brotherhood, and now she'd brought him the letter from von Auerswald to Friedrich von Breckendorf which he sensed was going to be critical in bringing his enquiries to a conclusion. Why not tell her more? He'd felt isolated since he first arrived in Bavaria. It would help him to have someone to confide in.

"They are secret messages from the king to Christoph Geissler," he said. "They wrote to each other in runes."

"From the *king*?" Sophie's eyes opened wide. "They knew each other?"

"They had a... friendship."

"Aah."

"You don't seem surprised."

"People have always talked about Ludwig. His lack of a wife, his close male friends. But didn't Gisela say one of the letters was written by someone else? Who?"

"Norbert Ziegler, I believe. He was given instructions on what to write, then orders to mislead me into thinking it had come from the king."

"Orders from whom?"

"From Prince von Auerswald."

"Von Auerswald? So that payment to Ziegler of ten thousand marks? It was for that?"

"That would be my guess."

"What about the payment to Graf?"

"I'm not sure. Graf was the first person to show me a link between Geissler and the king. It may have been payment for that – another misdirection from von Auerswald."

"And Captain Wilhelm Schirmer? Who is he?"

"The king's adjutant."

"A hundred thousand marks. Why would von Auerswald pay him such a huge sum?"

Why indeed? Neuman thought, though he was beginning to work out the answers. The pieces were starting to fall into place in his mind. He could see how he'd been manipulated by the legate. Told to do everything possible to avoid implicating the king while following a trail that had been deliberately created to lead him to that exact destination. I thought I was an independent actor, but all along my strings were being controlled by someone else. Questions still remained, but one thing was clear beyond doubt to Neumann: he'd found his Loki.

THIRTY-TWO

They met in one of the committee rooms in the government offices at Hohenschwangau, a tiny, wood-panelled chamber far away from the clerks and officials where they could talk without being disturbed. There were three of them: von Auerswald; the cabinet secretary, Konrad Baumgartner, and the finance minister, Count Ehrenbeck zu Freudenberg.

Out of courtesy, the prince addressed his initial comments to Baumgartner, ostensibly the most senior minister in the Bavarian government, though he knew that any decision would not come from the cabinet secretary – a notoriously weak individual. It would be made by zu Freudenberg, a man very much after von Auerswald's heart: cold, calculating and utterly ruthless.

He outlined the progress that had been made in the Geissler murder investigation and took pleasure in seeing the two ministers turn pale.

"The king?" Baumgartner whispered, glancing around nervously, as if they might be overheard. "You're saying His Majesty played a part in this? That cannot be."

"The evidence is there, I'm afraid," von Auerswald said, his face expressing a regret that the cabinet secretary was naïve enough to believe.

"But the king and this... young man? No, it is not

conceivable," Baumgartner insisted. "How could they even have met? The difference in rank... it cannot have happened."

"They met, I believe, last autumn at a reception at the Residenz in Munich," von Auerswald replied smoothly. "September, or October, I think it was." September twenty-third, in fact. He knew the date, even the time, exactly as he'd engineered the encounter himself, right down to the last detail. A beautiful, golden-haired twenty-six-year-old boy and a spoilt monarch with Ludwig's proclivities – the outcome was not hard to predict.

"They continued their... relationship... when the court moved down here to the mountains. We have the notes the king sent Geissler via the intermediary of one of his footmen, Axel Hoffmann. They leave no room for doubt. His Majesty was obviously besotted with Geissler, who visited him regularly at New Hohenschwangau."

"That would not have been possible," Baumgartner said firmly. "The guards would have reported it."

"There is an unguarded postern door, as I understand it," von Auerswald went on. "Close to the staircase to the king's private apartments. Geissler was let in after dark – and let out again at dawn – by the footman, Hoffmann, who has been complicit in the affair from the beginning."

Baumgartner shook his head, bewildered, refusing to believe. "No, no, this is outrageous. These notes you talk about, you are sure they came from the king?"

"Quite sure. He has admitted he sent them to my investigator, Major Neumann. He has admitted his friendship with Geissler."

"Dear Lord!"

The cabinet secretary slumped back in his chair as if the air had been punched out of him. He glanced at zu Freudenberg for help.

"Evidence of a friendship is not evidence that His

Majesty had any part in Geissler's murder," the count said sharply.

"That is true. But we also have evidence that Geissler broke off the relationship and the king reacted badly to the rejection. Very badly, going so far as to wish him dead. And the king's wishes, as you know, have a tendency to be granted."

"You're saying he instigated the murder? Who carried out the deed?"

"Hoffmann. The footman stabbed Geissler, but the – shall we call them 'trimmings'? – the spear, the mistletoe, the clear references to pagan mythology, they were the king's idea, his embellishments."

"You're not making this any better," zu Freudenberg said dryly.

Baumgartner gave him a disapproving glance.

"This isn't the time for levity, count. These are serious allegations. If they can be proven, well, I need hardly explain to you the consequences."

"I couldn't agree more," von Auerswald said. "King Ludwig involved in a deviant – and illegal – relationship with a young man that ends with the violent murder of his lover. That would be catastrophic for the stability of Bavaria... if it were to leak out."

"You mean, if *you* were to leak it," zu Freudenberg said.

Von Auerswald inclined his head in a gracious acknowledgement of the remark.

"I think we understand each other, count."

"What do you mean?" the cabinet secretary asked. "Understand what?"

"My dear Baumgartner," zu Freudenberg said patiently, as if he were addressing a simpleton. "The prince has not come here for justice. He has come to make a deal."

"A deal? What kind of deal?"

"Well," von Auerswald began. "As you've just pointed out, the consequences of this could be very grave indeed. I've been in touch with Wilhelmstrasse. The chancellor is most concerned that any fallout doesn't affect the wider German Empire."

"Spare us the great man's statesmanship, Excellency," zu Freudenberg said. "What does Bismarck want?"

"He believes the best course of action would be for His Majesty to be removed."

"Removed?" Baumgartner echoed. "What are you suggesting?"

"You must be aware, gentlemen, that the king's behaviour in recent years has become more erratic – even by his eccentric standards. Now, with this whole Geissler affair, I think there are very good grounds for questioning his mental balance – and his fitness for remaining on the throne."

"You want him declared insane?" zu Freudenberg said.

"That would be the most straightforward solution. There are precedents in the family, after all."

"And who would take his place, given that we have a constitutional requirement for a monarch?"

"Technically, his brother, Otto, is next in line," von Auerswald said. "But as he is also mentally incapacitated, I would respectfully suggest that a regency should be established under their uncle, Prince Luitpold. He is a Wittelsbach and well regarded, a competent pair of hands to steady the ship of state in these turbulent times."

Zu Freudenberg gazed at the prince with open admiration.

"You have this all worked out, don't you, Excellency?"

"I am just an envoy from Berlin, count," Von Auerswald replied modestly. "But if I can be of service to the country, I would deem it an honour."

He pushed back his chair and stood up.

"Thank you for your time, gentlemen. The matter is now entirely in your hands, but I trust you will come to the right decision."

He bowed deeply and left the room. The two ministers sat in silence for a time after he'd gone. Baumgartner was in a daze.

"Well... what are we to... I mean, this is quite incredible," he blathered, unable to process a coherent thought.

"But, nevertheless, we must do as he says," zu Freudenberg said.

"What, usurp the throne?"

"We have no choice. Von Auerswald, damn his eyes, has us over a barrel. And perhaps it may work to our advantage in the end."

"How so?"

"The king is unfit to rule, we know that. His profligacy already threatens to bankrupt the state. Removing him may be good for Bavaria, as well as Bismarck."

"You make it sound easy. How do we certify a king?"

"The way we certified his brother. We send for Bernhard von Gudden."

"But what if he doesn't find him insane?"

Zu Freudenberg's eyes gleamed with a steely resolution. "The good doctor will do exactly what we tell him."

"What the bloody hell do you think you're playing at?"

Johanna Hoffmann came for Neumann the moment he walked into the inn. Her face was flushed with anger, her fists clenched, ready to throw a punch. He backed away, his arms raised protectively.

"Easy now. I don't know what you're talking about."

"Don't give me that crap. You know, all right."

She pressed closer. She was several centimetres

shorter than him, but formidable in her fury.

"You pack your things and get out of my house," she yelled, flecking him with spittle.

"I don't understand," Neumann said. "What's happened?"

"You know what's happened. Axel. How could you? My sweet, lovely boy, and you do this to him."

"Do what?"

"Out! Before I smash your face in."

"Frau Hoffmann, I assure you... Axel? What about him?"

"Don't tell me you didn't give the order. Major Bigshot from Berlin."

"What order? Believe me, I really don't know what this is about."

Johanna paused. She glared at him, a flicker of doubt in her face.

"You're being straight with me?"

"On my oath. What's happened to Axel?"

"He's been arrested. They're holding him at the police station."

"Arrested?" Neumann said. "Not on *my* orders. There's some mistake here. Let me see what's going on."

He went back out into Brodtmarkt and walked rapidly over to the police station where Krause was manning the front desk.

"You've arrested Axel Hoffmann. On whose orders?" Neumann demanded. "Answer me!"

"Count Ehrenbeck zu Freudenberg, the acting minister of justice," the sergeant replied defensively, taken aback by Neumann's ferocity. "It was all perfectly proper."

"You went to the palace?"

"No, he was brought in by the king's adjutant, Captain Schirmer. Things were found under Hoffmann's bed."

"What things?"

"A knife, some mistletoe."

"How convenient," Neumann said acidly. "Has he been charged?"

"No, not yet."

"Give me the key to the cell."

"Sir, I have orders –"

"Give me the goddamn key, sergeant!"

Axel Hoffmann was huddled beneath a blanket on the wooden platform in the cell. He was shivering, but not just from the cold. He was frightened. Neumann saw it in his face when he came in. His skin was deathly pale, his eyes those of a trapped animal. The major sat down on the end of the platform and wasted no time on preliminaries.

"You're in trouble, Axel. I need you to be absolutely honest with me. Your life may depend on it. Do you understand?"

Axel nodded bleakly. "I don't know why I'm here, sir. I've done nothing."

"I know, Axel. But you're a scapegoat, a pawn in the machinations of some very dangerous men. You lied to me at Linderhof. Don't lie to me now. Christoph Geissler visited the king in his apartments, didn't he?"

"Yes, sir."

"How often?"

"Regularly. Sometimes every week."

"Which palace?"

"Just New Hohenschwangau, sir."

"How did he get in?"

"I let him in. There's a door near the kitchens that can only be opened from the inside. It has no guard on it. He would come upstairs and… stay the night."

"And in the morning?"

"I would let him out through the same door before it got light. So no one saw him."

"Who else knew about this arrangement?"

"Only Captain Schirmer."

"Cast your mind back a few weeks," Neumann said. "To the last time Geissler came to the palace. It was a Sunday evening. He stayed the night. What happened the following morning? Did you let him out, as usual?"

"Yes, sir."

"Did anyone see him leave?"

"Not that I'm aware of, sir."

"How did he get home? Did he have a horse?"

"No, sir. He always came on foot."

"So, after leaving the palace, he would walk back down the road to Hohenschwangau?"

"Yes, sir. Or through the woods. I don't know which way he went. Listen, sir, I had nothing to do with his death. Those things Captain Schirmer found under my bed, I'd never seen them before. They weren't mine."

"I know they weren't." Neumann stood up. "I'm going to do my utmost to get you out, Axel, but you may be here for a while. I will have food and drink brought to you from the Gasthaus Hoffmann, probably delivered by your mother herself. Do not touch anything that hasn't come from her. Not even a sip of water. Do I make myself clear?"

"Yes, sir."

Neumann locked up and went back into the main building.

"I'm arranging for food for the prisoner to be brought in from his mother's inn," he told Krause.

"That's unusual. We generally get it –"

"I know. But last time it didn't work out too well for Frida Messer, did it? We don't want any more suspicious deaths in custody, sergeant. People might start to question whether the officers here are up to the job. And you wouldn't want that, would you?"

He returned to the Gasthaus Hoffmann and took

Johanna into her small private sitting room at the rear of the inn. He explained that Axel was going to have to remain in custody until Neumann could sort out the misunderstanding that had led to his arrest. But she could take him food and water in the meantime. Then he said, "Is Tobias back from work?"

"He hasn't gone yet. He's working the night shift today."

"Can I speak to him?"

"I'll get him, he's down in the cellar."

"I need your help," Neumann said when Johanna came back with her son. "How are things arranged at the telegraph office? Do you keep the forms people have to fill in to send a telegram?"

"Of course," Tobias replied. "We keep them all for six months in the office here, then they're archived in the regional office in Kempten."

"Are they grouped together according to who's sent them?"

"What do you mean?"

"If I wanted to see all the telegrams sent by the German legation in, say, the last four weeks, would they be easy to find?"

"Yes, they'll all be kept in the same file."

"Can you get them for me?"

Tobias stared at him. "Me? I don't have that kind of authority. You'd have to go to the director for something like that."

"I can't do that," Neumann said. "I need them this evening. This is for Axel, Tobias. If I'm to help your brother, I need *your* help."

"For Axel? I don't understand."

"It doesn't matter whether you understand, or not," Johanna interjected forcefully. "Axel's in a police cell, accused of something he didn't do. If the major needs these telegrams, then you give them to him."

"I'll lose my job if anyone finds out," Tobias protested.

"Then make sure they don't find out," Johanna snapped. "This is *family*. Families stick together, no matter what."

Tobias bit his lip, looking apprehensively at his mother. I'm not surprised, Neumann thought. She's a terrifying woman when she's aroused.

"Do you have a break on your shift?" he asked.

"Half an hour at midnight."

"Nothing before? What about toilet breaks?"

"I can take those when I like, provided I'm not away from my desk for too long."

"Does the office have a back door?"

"Yes."

"Unmanned?"

"Yes."

"All right. Here's what I want you to do."

Neumann pressed deep into the shadows in the yard at the rear of the telegraph office. A trickle of light spilled out from one of the ground floor windows, but apart from that the area was in darkness. A horse stirred inside the stable block. A low whinny drifted through the night air and was lost in the wind that gusted between the gates from the street.

He was on edge, though he knew the chances of being discovered were slight. The back door was little used at night, Tobias had told him. A stable boy and a messenger were on stand-by to saddle up and deliver any urgent messages that came in overnight, but they were rarely called on and generally spent most of the shift lounging around the despatch room where there was a fire to keep them warm.

A crack appeared in the back door of the building. A sliver of light cut a yellow line across the steps and Tobias emerged, only his shoulders and head visible.

Neumann stepped out from his cover and took the file Tobias was holding. They didn't speak, barely acknowledged each other. Tobias slipped back inside and closed the door. Neumann tucked the file under his arm and headed rapidly back to his room at the gasthaus.

There were a lot of telegrams in the file. Neumann wasn't surprised. The legation, after all, was a diplomatic outpost of the German Empire. They sent reports on a daily basis to the chancellery in Berlin – all of them encrypted so Neumann couldn't read them without a codebook. A few telegrams, however – to other recipients outside the government circle of secrecy – were not encrypted. Neumann sifted them out and scanned through them. The first to catch his eye was a telegram sent to police headquarters in Berlin, for the attention of Colonel Olaf Wolff.

It read: COME FÜSSEN AT ONCE. URGENT HOMICIDE INVESTIGATION. WILL BE MET ON ARRIVAL. VON AUERSWALD.

It was dated Wednesday March 10th, the day after Christoph Geissler's body had been found in the forest. There was nothing strange about it. Neumann already knew that Wolff had been the first-choice detective to undertake the investigation in Bavaria – and would have done so had he not been caught *in flagrante* taking bribes from a criminal gang.

What was strange, though, was an earlier telegram from von Auerswald to Wolff dated March 6th. This read: BE READY. WILL SUMMON YOU VERY SOON.

Neumann stared at the form. There was no mistake about the date. The telegram had been sent to Wolff on the Saturday – two days *before* Geissler had been murdered. This was confirmation of what Neumann had already worked out. Von Auerswald had planned the whole thing: from the selection of Geissler, an attractive young man plucked out of obscurity in Berlin as bait to tempt a king, through to his actual killing, Schirmer waiting nearby to plunge the knife into his heart when Geissler left the palace, then go through the macabre rite with the spear and mistletoe before he dumped the body in the forest.

The telegram was advance warning to Wolff, who had already been chosen to carry out the investigation: a corrupt detective who was, presumably, either a part of the conspiracy or, more likely, just a useful dupe who could be relied on to do the legate's bidding and come to the 'right' conclusions. But they got me instead, Neumann thought. A more independent police officer. That wasn't part of the plan.

He turned to two of the other non-encrypted telegrams, both sent to Prince Luitpold Wittelsbach, at an address in Munich.

The first, dated March 12th, read: BE PREPARED. EVERYTHING IS IN MOTION.

The second, sent only that afternoon, read: EVERYTHING ARRANGED. BE READY TO STEP IN.

Luitpold Wittelsbach? Neumann thought. He's the king's uncle. Ludwig has no children, no heirs. His only brother, Otto, was certified insane long ago and locked away in one of the more insignificant royal palaces. So Luitpold is next in line for the throne of Bavaria. And von Auerswald is telegraphing him to be ready to step in.

It's happening, he thought. Von Auerswald's plan – and surely, by extension, also Bismarck's – was coming to fruition. But can I do anything about it?

THIRTY-THREE

The delegation from Munich arrived at New Hohenschwangau in the early hours of the morning. It was led by Dr Bernhard von Gudden, Professor of Psychiatry at the University of Munich, and generally considered to be Bavaria's most distinguished alienist. With him was his assistant, Dr Müller, five asylum orderlies and a number of policemen who were there to restrain the king should he try to escape. They had papers from the new regency of Prince Luitpold which authorised their entry into the palace.

Ludwig was in his apartments on the fourth floor when the delegation burst in on him. He was awake, fully dressed and looking forward to his dinner, in keeping with his usual nocturnal timetable. His initial reaction was outrage, turning to anger as he realised why they were there. He tried to leave, but the doors were barred by the police officers.

Von Gudden, a short, bearded man in his early sixties, was polite and apologetic.

"Your Majesty, it pains me greatly to have to do this, but I must inform you that your uncle, Prince Luitpold, has assumed the regency of Bavaria as you have been deemed mentally unfit to continue ruling."

"What do you mean, 'deemed mentally unfit', you

pompous little coxcomb?" Ludwig shouted. "You haven't even examined me."

"We have overwhelming evidence from witnesses that you are suffering from an advanced case of what we alienists term 'paranoia'."

"What evidence, what witnesses?" Ludwig demanded. "Get out! I'll have you flogged for this, have your eyes put out."

"You need to come with us, Your Majesty," von Gudden said calmly.

"Come where?"

"We are taking you to Berg, where you can receive the medical attention you need."

"I don't need medical attention. I need my dinner. And I need you and your lackeys to get out of my apartments."

"I regret, sire, that this has become necessary, but you have no choice in the matter. You must come with us."

"I am the king. You do not tell a king what he must do."

"You are no longer the king, sire. As I have already said, your uncle is now regent."

"On whose authority? Who made him regent?"

"The proclamation was made earlier this evening in Munich, authorised by all your ministers."

"Those treacherous weasels? They don't have the power."

"The constitution gives them the power. It is all quite proper. Please, Your Majesty, it is for your own good."

Ludwig looked around the room. At the two doctors, the orderlies in their starched white uniforms, the police officers blocking the doors, and his resistance began to ebb away.

"This medical attention you claim I need. How long will it last?" he asked, his voice softer, more accepting now.

"I cannot say," von Gudden replied evasively.

"But when it is over, I will be king again?"

"I cannot comment on that either. It will not be my decision." Von Gudden glanced at one of the orderlies. "Help His Majesty with his coat. If you please, sire, your carriage awaits you."

Neumann cantered up the road in the darkness. The snow had virtually all melted away, but it was a cold, damp night. The moon was hidden by cloud. Rain was falling in a steady drizzle. He rounded the final bend, the sheer walls of New Hohenschwangau rising up in front of him, and found his path blocked by a detachment of soldiers. He dismounted and approached the sergeant in charge.

"My name is Major Reinhardt Neumann," he said. "I'm a police officer. I need to see the king urgently."

"That won't be possible, sir," the sergeant replied. "The palace is closed."

"Who's your commanding officer? Is it Major Hafner?"

"Yes, sir."

"Is he here?"

"He's inside the palace, sir."

"He can vouch for me. Can you tell him I'm here? Quickly, sergeant. This is important."

The sergeant considered for a moment, then despatched one of his men. Ten minutes later, Lukas Hafner emerged through the arched gatehouse entrance and strode down the hill. Neumann repeated his urgent request to see the king. Hafner shook his head.

"He's no longer the king. He was removed from the throne this evening on the grounds of insanity. His uncle, Prince Luitpold, has been declared regent."

"I still need to see him, Lukas. Can you get me in?"

"You're too late. He's just leaving with a team of doctors."

As Hafner spoke, a line of three carriages came out

from the palace and clattered down the road. The soldiers broke apart to let the vehicles pass.

"Where are they going?" Neumann asked Hafner.

"To Berg Castle."

"Where's that?"

"North, near Munich."

Inside the middle carriage Ludwig sat alone. The doors had been locked so he couldn't open them, but he pulled aside the curtain over the window and peered out. He craned his neck upwards to get a better view of his beloved new palace, wondering when, if ever, he would see it again.

The sentry outside at the front of the house raised his rifle and shouted a challenge as Neumann galloped onto the forecourt. Then he recognised the major and lowered his weapon. Neumann leapt down from his horse, ran up the steps to the door and rang the bell repeatedly.

Dagmar answered, looking sleepy and dishevelled, a blanket thrown hastily around her shoulders.

"Sir!" she exclaimed in surprise. "What brings –"

"Is your mistress in?" Neumann interrupted.

"She's upstairs, sir. Shall I fetch her?"

"It's all right, Dagmar, I'm here."

Sophie was coming down the stairs. "Let's go into the drawing room," she said to Neumann.

The room was cool, the fire just black embers. Sophie shivered, pulling her dressing gown across her chest and tightening the cord. Her hair was down. She must have been asleep, but she seemed wide awake now.

"I need your help, freiin."

"What's happened?"

He didn't know what to put in or what to leave out so he told her everything. He saw the shock in her face as he described von Auerswald's ruthless scheming.

"The king has been deposed?" she said incredulously.

"Just this evening. He's been taken to Berg Castle. Where is that?"

"On Lake Würm, about eighty, ninety kilometres from here."

"That's too far for my horse. Do you have a carriage I can borrow?"

"I have a two-horse trap. That would be better. It's much lighter, faster than the carriage. You're going to Berg?"

"I have to see the king. I fear his life might be in danger."

"Wait here, I'll get dressed."

"Freiin, there is no need for you to –"

"They're my horses," Sophie broke in. "They will not react well to a stranger. And besides, do you know the way to Berg?"

"Well, no," Neumann admitted.

"Without me you will certainly get lost."

She was back downstairs in ten minutes, her hair tied up again beneath a cap, a cloak over her trousers, riding boots and thick winter jacket. They went out to the stables and Sophie harnessed the horses to the trap. Then they clambered up onto the seat next to each other. Sophie wrapped a waterproof oilskin around their shoulders to keep out the rain and gave a flick of the reins. The trap rolled smoothly out of the yard, down the drive and onto the main road, heading north through the night towards Munich.

Of all the many royal palaces at his disposal, Berg Castle, on the eastern shore of Lake Würm, held a special place in Ludwig's heart. Acquired by the Wittelsbach family in the seventeenth century, it had been modified by Ludwig's father, Maximilian, who had added two towers and battlements to the building to make it look more like a medieval fortress. Ludwig had spent many happy summers there as a child and when he'd become king, he'd had a third tower constructed which he named Isolde, after Wagner's operatic heroine. The steamboat which he used for picnic excursions to the nearby Rose Island was re-christened *Tristan* and he had the interior of the castle decorated with paintings depicting scenes from Wagner's music-dramas.

When the carriages pulled in outside the castle in the early afternoon and Ludwig was allowed to disembark, he felt strangely calm. During the long drive from New Hohenschwangau his anger had dissipated. He'd slept for a lot of the journey and now he'd arrived, he was determined to challenge this outrageous medical assessment that had been made without any kind of examination. He wasn't mad. There were absolutely no grounds for declaring him unfit to rule and he was going to prove it. Von Gudden and his colleagues would have to reconsider their biased opinions and reinstate him to his rightful place on the throne.

But when he was escorted into the castle and upstairs to his apartments, he had a sudden pang of disquiet. Changes had been made since he'd last been here. The doors to his rooms had been tampered with so they could only be opened from the outside. Peepholes had been drilled into them to enable round-the-clock surveillance and metal bars had been fastened over the windows. It was looking less like a home and more like a prison.

Von Gudden showed him into his bedroom, as if he rather than the king owned the place. Ludwig contained his annoyance. He must conceal his emotions, he told himself, appear rational at all times if he were to have any chance of influencing the alienist's diagnosis of him. No fits of royal temper, no violent outbursts. He must ensure that there was never even a hint of anything that could be unfavourably interpreted as mental imbalance.

"Is Your Majesty hungry?" von Gudden enquired.

"Yes, I am," Ludwig replied, then added amiably. "Tell me, doctor. If I am no longer king, why do you still address me as Your Majesty?"

Von Gudden chuckled, a little taken aback by the question. He reminded himself that this kind of behaviour was to be expected. Patients, in his experience, were often cunning and manipulative. They could appear lucid or perceptive, but that didn't mean they weren't mad.

"It is merely a courtesy," he said. "But if you prefer, we could just call you 'sir', or even Herr Wittelsbach."

Ludwig smiled, to show he understood the humour in the situation.

"No, Your Majesty will be fine."

And when I'm back on the throne, he thought, I'll have my revenge on you, you jumped-up little quack.

They had dinner together in the dining room, an amicable occasion when Ludwig tried hard to be the urbane host – rather than an incarcerated patient – regaling the doctor with stories about the castle: the garden parties on the lawns, the firework displays on Rose Island, the steamboat trips across to Possenhofen where his favourite cousin, Elisabeth – Sissi – now Empress of Austria, had a holiday home.

Von Gudden listened with interest, relishing the opportunity to study the king in more depth. He was a conscientious alienist, renowned in medical circles for his wide knowledge and meticulous approach to psychiatric analysis. But he was aware that in this particular circumstance he had been pressured into giving a diagnosis based entirely on hear-say evidence rather than his own observations. That wasn't exceptional. There had been other situations when he had had to do something similar, but it was bad practise and he always followed it up with a full appraisal of the patient. Ludwig was going to be kept in the castle for the foreseeable future. Von

Gudden would use that time to establish whether he was really as imbalanced as the initial evidence suggested.

"I may walk in the grounds, I hope?" Ludwig said when they had finished eating and were enjoying a glass of brandy in the sitting room.

"Of course," von Gudden replied. "But for your own welfare and safety you will have to be accompanied."

"I understand. Perhaps later I might go for a stroll by the lake. Will you be good enough to join me?"

"It will be my pleasure, Your Majesty."

It looked as if it might rain so the two men donned overcoats and hats and equipped themselves with umbrellas. Ludwig seemed to be in good spirits, von Gudden noted, although whether that was purely the result of the copious amounts of wine and brandy he'd drunk at dinner was difficult to determine. Whatever the cause, the alienist was relieved that the king already appeared to be coming to terms with his situation, reconciled to the loss of his throne. That boded well for his treatment.

They emerged from the castle into an overcast evening, the sky and the lake just differing shades of grey. One of the orderlies fell in behind them, but von Gudden waved him away. There was too much of the asylum about the medical support staff. The orderly's presence would only remind the king that he was, in effect, a prisoner and perhaps make him belligerent or resentful. Von Gudden wanted his relationship with Ludwig to be professional, but also friendly and caring. The welfare of the patient was always his primary consideration.

They walked down towards the lake where *Tristan* was moored in the small harbour. Ludwig paused and gazed reflectively at the steamboat, remembering all the happy times he'd spent on board.

"I suppose I might be permitted the occasional excursion on the lake?" he said wistfully.

Von Gudden was struck by the king's choice of words. He wasn't dictating, as he might have done in the past; he was asking permission to do something that once had been his right.

"I'm sure that can be arranged," the doctor replied.

He sensed a mood change in the king, a hint of melancholy in his face. That wasn't good. It could so easily lead to depression which was never easy to treat. He tried a little distraction, initiating a conversation to draw the king out of his reverie.

"The vessel has an interesting name," he said.

Ludwig turned his head. "What?"

"*Tristan*. After Wagner, I assume?"

"Yes, indeed. He visited me here many times, you know. He would play the piano and we would talk long into the night. Such interesting discussions about music and mythology and philosophy. He taught me more about kingship than anyone else I've ever met. I remember once..."

And he was off, reminiscing about "The Friend." Von Gudden let him talk. It was good for the king to express himself, to recall memories that were positive and uplifting. They ambled away from the harbour and headed south along the shore of the lake.

The journey was exhausting for both of them. Cold, wet, dark, the road rough and pitted with potholes that sent jarring vibrations through the chassis of the trap every time they hit one. They huddled close to each other on the seat, their bodies touching, sharing their warmth, their fingers so frozen they had to take it in turns to hold the reins. It was unpleasant, but seductively intimate.

At a coaching inn near Schongau, they stopped to change horses and revived themselves by the fire while they had a breakfast of coffee and rolls. The innkeeper fussed around them, assuming they were man and wife, which made Sophie smile.

"You find that amusing?" Neumann asked.

"No, it's just a novelty for me."

"I imagine you've had offers."

"Not from the right man." Sophie sipped some of her coffee. Then she said gently, "How did your wife die?"

"Puerperal fever."

"What was her name?"

"Kristina."

"And the child?"

"Julia. She died two weeks later from an infection she'd caught in the hospital."

"I'm sorry."

"One moment they were both there. The next they were gone."

Sophie reached across the table and put her hand on his. Neumann turned his hand over and held her fingers tight, like a pledge. They looked at each other, sensing that something was changing.

It was light by the time they resumed their journey. They kept going for another twenty kilometres before Neumann suggested they take a break. They were both so tired they could barely keep their eyes open. Pulling off to the side of the road, they stopped and moved to the seat inside the trap, lifting the hood up to keep out the wind. Neumann spread the oilskin sheet over their legs and they fell asleep together.

The major woke first. Sophie was breathing quietly beside him, her head resting on his shoulder. He could feel the warmth of her body. He kept still, trying not to disturb her. Her cap had fallen off as they dozed. Her hair had come loose. A couple of strands dangled over her face. Neumann scooped them away, his fingers caressing her cheek. Sophie opened her eyes. She took a moment to work out where she was, then she tilted her head back and looked up at him. She made no move to pull away. Neumann cupped her chin in his hand and kissed her softly on the mouth. She gave a slight start of surprise, then her lips parted and she kissed him back, her arm curling up around his neck. Neither spoke. It wasn't a time for words.

The drive was easier in daylight. They could see the road; it had stopped raining. The temperature was higher, but they still had the oilskin to keep them warm. They changed horses a second time near Weilheim and by late afternoon they'd reached the southern tip of Lake Würm. The road here was narrower, less used, its surface uneven and muddy. They slowed down a little, giving the tired horses a breather, and followed the eastern shore until they reached Berg.

The castle wasn't difficult to find. In a village of just a few tiny houses, it was the only building of any size – set back from the road behind a high stone wall and accessible only through a gated entrance that was guarded by police officers. Neumann stopped the trap outside and went across to speak to the officers. They wouldn't let him in. He pleaded with them, explained how urgent his visit was, but it made no difference. They had strict orders to allow no one past without the permission of Dr von Gudden.

Neumann returned to the trap.

"Is there another way in?" he asked Sophie.

"We could try the rear, see if we can get in along the shore of the lake."

They turned the trap around and drove back the way they'd come. After a kilometre or so they pulled off the road onto a track through a small wood that gradually petered out, leaving them no option but to abandon the trap and continue on foot. Beyond the wood was a meadow leading down to the lake. The water was calm, splashed with the distant sails of fishing boats. On the far side, the land rose up into a long, forested ridge, a few roofs and a church spire poking up through the trees. To the south, the faint outline of the Alps was visible on the horizon, a hundred kilometres away but so big you could see the snow on their summits.

As they reached the water's edge, a launch came steaming past from the north. There were three men on board: one in the cabin at the helm, two others standing out on the stern deck. Neumann froze with shock as he recognised the taller of the two men outside – it was Captain Wilhelm Schirmer, his elaborate dress uniform exchanged for more practical green tunic and trousers, but unmistakable all the same.

Their eyes met across the fifty-metre expanse of water. Schirmer's face was cold, granite hard. He stared expressionlessly at Neumann and Sophie, his gaze never leaving them until the launch disappeared from sight behind a stand of trees.

"You knew that man?" Sophie asked.

"Schirmer, the king's adjutant."

"*Schirmer*? You mean the man who..."

Neumann didn't reply. He was already running north along the edge of the lake, an alarm bell hammering relentlessly inside his head. Schirmer here? On a launch on the lake? That was ominous.

The light was fading fast now. Up ahead, Neumann could see the towers of the castle, the battlements high enough to catch the last rays of the sun before it dipped below the ridge on the western side of the lake. Then he saw a dark shape on the path. It was a man's overcoat with a jacket tucked inside, as if both had been thrown off together. A few metres further on were two umbrellas and two hats.

"Reinhardt, look!"

Sophie came up behind him, panting for breath. She was pointing out across the water where what looked like two bodies were floating on the surface.

Neumann plunged into the lake and splashed out through the shallows. The first body was a short, bearded man he'd never seen before. The skin of his neck was still warm when Neumann touched it, but there was no pulse. He waded out to the second body which was clad only in shirt and trousers. He knew who it was before he rolled it over onto its back and saw the king's face staring lifelessly up into the sky. He felt for a pulse. Ludwig was gone. No possible hope of resuscitation.

"Reinhardt!" Sophie called.

Neumann turned. She was gesturing towards the castle where lanterns were glowing in the trees, coming towards them. He left the bodies and scrambled back to the shore.

"What's happened here?" Sophie asked. "Who are they?"

"The king's one of them."

"The *king*. Is he..."

"There's nothing we can do. We should go. We mustn't be found here."

"But if the king..."

"It's too dangerous, Sophie. We have to go."

He took her hand and dragged her away. They ran back along the shore, dusk falling so rapidly around them that when he glanced over his shoulder, the bodies had lost all human form and were just indistinct shapes, like driftwood on the surface of the lake.

THIRTY-FOUR

They took rooms at an inn in Starnberg, at the northern end of Lake Würm, and, over dinner, discussed what they should do. Sophie was in favour of going straight to the local police and telling them what they'd seen. Neumann had other ideas. They'd left the scene by the lake rather than report the incident immediately – behaviour which might be considered suspicious – and seeing Schirmer on a boat nearby wasn't proof that he had had anything to do with the deaths.

"But we can't just keep this to ourselves," Sophie protested. "That would be wrong. The king has been murdered."

"We might think that, but we don't know it for certain – not in legal terms. There could be other explanations. Maybe Ludwig killed the other man and then committed suicide."

"Stop being a policeman for once, Reinhardt. Look at the facts. The king dead in the water. Schirmer on a boat close by immediately afterwards – a man you suspect of killing several other people linked to Ludwig. What's the obvious conclusion to draw? We should tell the police."

"I don't trust the police," Neumann said.

"But you *are* the police."

"Not here I'm not. Not in Bavaria. This isn't some

random killing, Sophie. This has been planned, just as removing the king from the throne was planned. And it wasn't conceived by a lowly army officer like Schirmer. It comes from the top. You know already that Friedrich von Breckendorf was involved, but how many other ministers in the government are also complicit. Von Auerswald certainly is, and if he's involved, you can be sure his instructions have come from the chancellor."

Sophie stared at him. "From Bismarck? Bismarck is behind all this?"

"You see what I'm saying? The police do not act independently of their political masters. They will do as they're told, come to conclusions that are chosen for them by others – by those 'men who matter' you warned me about when we first met. We go to the police, we could be putting ourselves in danger."

"What do you mean?"

"It doesn't matter. You just have to trust me."

Sophie leaned over the table and looked him hard in the eye.

"What do you *mean*? You think they would kill us?"

"I don't want to frighten you."

"Then give me an answer. Then I know what I'm dealing with."

"Yes, they would have no compunction about killing us, if they deemed it necessary."

"So what do we do?"

Neumann took her hands and squeezed them gently.

"That's why I said you have to trust me. We will have to handle this ourselves."

Before breakfast next morning, Neumann went out into the town and bought a newspaper. The king's death was already being reported, though the facts were a little hazy. What was clear was that Ludwig and his doctor, Bernhard von Gudden, had gone out for a walk together in the early evening. When they hadn't returned to Berg Castle by dusk, a search party had been sent out to look for them by the lake where the lifeless bodies of the two men had been discovered floating in the water.

The cause of death wasn't known – and couldn't be properly determined until an autopsy was carried out – the newspaper said, but then, in true journalistic style, went on to devote considerable space to speculation about what might have happened, from a tragic accident through suicide to mysterious "foul play".

In a separate column was printed a proclamation from the government announcing that Prince Otto was now the King of Bavaria but, given Otto's mental incapacity, Prince Luitpold would continue as regent.

Neuman flicked through the many pages of tributes to Ludwig, and biographical details about his life, then a smaller, unrelated, story caught his eye. Two more deaths in Lake Würm. The bodies of fishermen brothers, Jan and Mirko Voight, had been found in the water after dark, their steam launch drifting nearby. Somehow, they'd fallen overboard and drowned. Neumann read the article with a grim feeling of resignation. Captain Schirmer had had a busy evening.

The journey back to Waldblick – with two changes of horses and a stop to eat – took them most of the day. Dusk was descending when they came up the drive to the house. Sophie noticed at once that something was wrong.

"Where are the soldiers?" she said.

"Round the back?" Neumann suggested.

"No, there's always at least one sentry at the front."

They drove round to the stables. There were no sentries there, either, and – when Neumann checked – no soldiers in the outbuilding that had served as their bunkhouse. Alarmed now, they hurried into the house and found Dagmar in the kitchen.

"What happened to the soldiers?" Sophie asked.

"They've gone."

"When?"

"This afternoon. A messenger came, ordering them to return to their barracks."

Neumann looked at Sophie, trying to appear unconcerned, but inside he could feel stirrings of anxiety, a cold dread. This was it. The start.

"Stay inside and lock all the doors," he ordered.

"Where are you going?"

"To check outside."

"I'll come with you."

"No."

"I know the grounds better than you."

"Stay here, Sophie. This is for your own protection."

Sophie glared at him. "I don't need protecting."

"Just do as I ask. I won't be long."

He slipped back out into the yard, drew his revolver and ran round the side of the house into the garden. He paused, keeping to the shadows near the building. His eyes scanned the lawn and flowerbeds, the first time he'd seen them without a covering of snow. It was dark now. The moon was stealing out from the clouds and in the faint silvery glow he caught a movement at the edge of the forest. Or thought he did. Was that a figure? A man? An animal? Or just a trick of the light or a bush twitching in the breeze? He peered hard into the blackness, but there was nothing there.

Don't imagine things, he told himself. Just stick to reality; that's more than enough to deal with right now. He flitted across the terrace, still close to the house, and along the path that led through an ornamental shrubbery, the foliage concealing him from view. As he emerged from cover, he paused for a second, checking the edge of the forest again. He saw nothing, heard nothing.

Darting across the gap, he ducked into the trees and stopped again, letting his eyes adjust to the darkness. Then he heard the click of a revolver hammer being thumbed back and a voice said, "Stay very still, major. Put your gun down on the ground slowly, then turn around."

Neumann did as he was instructed. Schirmer was standing three or four metres away, his revolver rock steady in his hand, pointing straight at the major's chest. Neumann was furious with himself. He *had* seen a figure moving at the edge of the garden – Schirmer showing himself deliberately to lure him into the forest. And Neumann had fallen straight into the trap.

"You disappoint me, major," Schirmer said, almost smirking. "You've made this too easy for me."

"My apologies," Neumann said dryly. "I didn't realise you liked a challenge. After all, your other targets didn't pose much of a problem for you, did they? An innocent young boy, a flabby jeweller, a middle-aged writer, an overweight king and his elderly doctor."

"I'm a modest man. I admit I had help with the last two."

"Ah, yes, the fishermen. And look how you rewarded them. Were Karl Schäfer and Frida Messer also your work?"

Schirmer gave a mock bow. "Credit where credit's due. And now it's your turn."

"Tell me something first," Neumann said. "To satisfy my curiosity. The ring with the letter 'W' on it that I found near Geissler's body. The Wotan Brotherhood ring. It was yours, wasn't it?"

"My only mistake, I believe. That was careless of me."

"What happened?"

"Does it matter?"

"Indulge me, captain. I don't like loose ends."

Schirmer shrugged. "I'd been to a meeting of the

Brotherhood the night before I killed Geissler. I was still wearing the ring. It slid off my finger without my knowing when I left his body in the forest. By the time I realised, the weather had turned, the snow had set in, blizzard conditions. I couldn't get back to retrieve it."

Neumann gauged the gap between them, wondering if he could get Schirmer off guard and jump him before he could shoot.

"Who else is a member of the Brotherhood?"

"Do you care?"

"Yes, I care. I care about those young women you violated."

"Whores," Schirmer spat. "They deserved what they got. And they deserve what they're going to get."

Neumann felt his blood turn to ice. "What do you mean?"

"I don't like loose ends, either. After I've finished with you, the women and the von Wildenstein bitch are next."

"You'll rot in hell for this, Schirmer."

"Maybe. But I won't be going there any time soon. Goodbye, major."

He took aim. Neumann heard a gunshot and flinched, expecting pain, blackness. But instead, he saw the side of Schirmer's head explode. The adjutant crashed to the ground. Sophie came forward out of the shadows, a revolver dangling by her side. She bent down, checking that Schirmer was dead, then looked at Neumann.

"I told you I didn't need protecting."

Neumann gaped at her, too stunned to speak. Then, instinctively, he stepped across and took her in his arms.

"My God, Sophie! Are you all right? You killed him!"

Sophie broke away. She was surprised how calm she felt.

"He was going to kill *you*."

"I know, but... but... I'm just shocked."

"I've been shooting since I was ten."

"You saved my life. Thank you."

He embraced her again, holding her tight.

"Such a touching scene," a mocking voice said behind them. "You make a lovely couple. Pity it won't last."

Neumann and Sophie span round. Von Auerswald was standing by a tree. A shaft of moonlight glimmered through the canopy of branches, grazing his face, accentuating his cheekbones, duelling scars and deep eye sockets so he looked like a cadaver. He flicked his hand slightly to make sure they'd seen the gun in his hand.

"I'm obliged to you, freiin," he said, glancing at Schirmer's corpse. "You've saved me the trouble of killing him myself. I'm impressed. You're a fine shot – for a woman."

"I'll shoot you, too, if I get the chance," Sophie said defiantly.

Von Auerswald chuckled. "I admire your spirit, but I think you've already used up all your chances. Drop your gun, you're making me nervous."

Sophie tossed her revolver to the ground.

"The freiin is nothing to do with this," Neumann said. "Let her go. It's me you want."

The prince's lip curled into a sardonic smile.

"A gallant gesture, major. But, alas, she is as much a part of this as you, and must suffer the same fate. She's far too dangerous to be shown any clemency." He gave a tiny shrug of regret. "I'm sorry it had to come to this, but you've been rather too persistent, Neumann. Your colleague, Colonel Wolff, would have been so much easier to deal with."

Would he? Neumann wondered. Could he have been any more stupid than I've been? A naïve fool who's done everything to deliver the result the legate wanted.

"So much death," he said. "Was it all really necessary?"

"I make no apology," von Auerswald said. "I work always for the greater good of the Empire."

"For the greater good of Bismarck, you mean."

"Well done, major. You're starting to understand how the world works."

"Fine words," Sophie sneered. "For such evil deeds."

"And all to destroy a harmless monarch," Neumann added.

"Not harmless," the prince countered. "Ludwig was a threat to the unity of the nation. He was arrogant, vain. He craved more power, he resented the dominance of Prussia, the treaty obligations that were imposed on him in sixty-six. He did not want to serve the Kaiser, he wanted to be his own little emperor here in Bavaria, an absolute monarch like his hero, Louis the Fourteenth. And there are people out there who would have supported his ambitions. People like the agitators in the Bavarian Freedom Party who want independence from the Empire and would foment a civil war to achieve that aim. We couldn't let that happen."

Neumann edged discreetly away from Sophie. He'd seen a metallic glint on the forest floor – Schirmer's revolver which had tumbled from his grasp when Sophie shot him. If he could somehow reach it before von Auerswald reacted, they might just have a slim hope of survival.

"And Christoph Geissler?" he said, keeping the legate talking. "Did you really have to kill him? Wasn't an affair enough to discredit the king?"

"That could've been swept under the carpet, easily covered up. No, it had to be serious enough to ensure that the Bavarians had no choice but to depose Ludwig."

"And Werner Graf and Norbert Ziegler and Bernhard von Gudden? How do you live with their deaths on your conscience?"

Von Auerswald laughed. "I don't have a conscience. Or hadn't you noticed?"

Schirmer's revolver was only a couple of metres away

now. Neumann readied himself to make a dive for it, but the prince brought him back to reality with a jolt.

"Stay exactly where you are!" he rapped. "Do you think I'm blind?" His gun swung in an arc from Neumann to Sophie and then back. "It's over. The only question now is which one of you dies first? I'm chivalrous enough to believe in ladies before gentlemen, but I'm not sure whether that really applies to murder. What do you think? I see you have it in your mind to do something heroic, major. Perhaps to save the beautiful freiin here. How romantic. And how futile." His revolver moved across to point at Sophie. "Time's up, my dear."

His finger tightened on the trigger. Neumann threw himself in front of Sophie and at that instant something erupted from the undergrowth. A grey, snarling shape that was like a moving shadow – a she-wolf with a white blaze on her forehead. Her jaws clamped around von Auerswald's arm, deflecting his aim so the bullet zipped away harmlessly into the trees. The legate screamed in pain, the wolf gnawing at his flesh. Neumann rolled over, snatched up Schirmer's revolver and shot the prince through the head.

The she-wolf backed away, startled by the gunshot. She and Sophie looked at each other, that empathy transmitting silently between them again. Then the she-wolf turned and bolted away into the bushes.

Neumann got to his feet. "What was…" he began. "A *wolf*?"

"A friend," Sophie said.

She came to him and wrapped her arms around his waist, her head pressed to his chest. He could feel her trembling. They held each other for a long time, then broke apart.

"What do we do with them?" Sophie asked, nodding at the two bodies.

"We'll take care of them tomorrow," Neumann replied.

He put his arm around her and slowly they walked back across the garden and into the house. On the landing outside her bedroom, Sophie took his hand in hers.

"Stay with me tonight, Reinhardt."

THIRTY-FIVE

"The chancellor will see you now, major."

Neumann went through into the inner sanctum, a huge, high-ceilinged room with thick rugs on the polished wood floor and three tall windows overlooking a courtyard at the rear of the chancellery, away from the noise and bustle of Wilhelmstrasse.

Otto von Bismarck was seated behind a leather-topped desk, studying a document through a pair of pince-nez spectacles perched on the end of his veined, bulbous nose. The last time Neumann had seen him – the only time he'd seen him in the flesh – had been from a distance at the Front during the French war, the chancellor a figure of fun to the soldiers, strutting about in his jackboots and spiked helmet.

Sixteen years had passed since then. Bismarck had changed considerably. At seventy-one, he was now a vast, bloated figure, his large frame hung with fat that squelched out over the sides of his chair like wet sand. His head was bald, except for tufts of grey hair above his ears, his moustache bushy and almost white, like the eyebrows which shaded his shrewd light blue eyes. Yet for all his age and size, there was still something of the bar-room brawler about him, although his fighting had always been done in the more refined – though no less vicious – circles of parliament and the court.

Certainly, he had an immense aura of power. Emperor Wilhelm was nominally the head of state, but everyone knew it was Bismarck who ran the empire – the ambitious Prussian Junker who had famously attributed his rise to listening out for God's footfall and then seizing the hem of His garment as it brushed by invisibly. The reactionary firebrand of his youth and bellicose warmonger of his middle years had metamorphosed into a grand elder statesman persona that was misleadingly benign. For he was still cynical and self-centred, a brilliant exponent of the art of the possible whose greatest skill was convincing others of his own infallibility. Though worn out by decades of scheming and in-fighting, he was still intent on creating his own legend in which everyone else would be bit-players. Events would not define him; he would define them.

He didn't get up from his chair as Neumann approached the desk – he was so obese he would probably have struggled to extract himself – but he waved a hand that was surprisingly small and delicate.

"Major, please be seated."

His voice, far from being the powerful bass Neumann had expected, was a high, reedy tenor. It was quiet, too. In a land, indeed a Germanic culture, of leaders who shouted, Bismarck was known – and feared all the more – for the softness of his speech.

"I've read your file," the chancellor went on. "You were in the army, I see. You fought in the French war and were decorated twice for valour." He shook his head regretfully. "An appalling business. So many casualties on both sides. We must never see anything like that again. Never."

"No, sir," Neumann agreed, although he knew better than to take the remarks at face value. Bismarck had engineered three wars to bring about his goal of a unified German empire. Now he'd achieved that, he was content with a period of peace – but only until he needed another conflict.

"I've also read your report on the... shall we call it 'The Geissler Affair'?"

Bismarck's piercing eyes came to rest on Neumann's face, sizing him up, the chancellor skilled at judging men and assessing who might be a threat to him.

Neumann said nothing. He was trying to control his nerves, the cramp in his stomach that was close to becoming nausea. He had to be very careful here. He had to protect himself, convince the chancellor that his version of events was true or he was in real danger – perhaps mortal danger.

"It seems quite incredible to me," Bismarck said. "This man Schirmer must have been seriously unhinged to commit so many horrific murders. I notice that you are cautious in coming to any conclusions about his motives."

"Yes, sir. I felt it best to stick to the facts, rather than indulge in too much uninformed speculation."

"Very wise, major. You're a sensible, astute police officer. But if you had to speculate, what might you deduce from those facts?"

Neumann considered his reply. This was particularly hazardous ground. "As you said, sir, he must have been mentally unbalanced. It's possible he may have been jealous of Geissler and his close relationship with the king. Embittered, too, about his status at the court. I don't think we'll ever really know for certain."

"And his end? You stand by your interpretation of the events?"

"Yes, sir. I reported my suspicions about Captain Schirmer to Prince von Auerswald and I believe he decided to take matters into his own hands. He met Schirmer out in the forest and confronted him with his crimes. I don't know exactly what happened, but from the evidence at the scene, it would appear that they shot each other."

"As in a duel, you mean?"

"Yes, sir. Both firing simultaneously, both hitting their target."

"How like the prince," Bismarck said admiringly. "Such a true nobleman. A duel is quite in keeping with his character. No messy court case, no embarrassing revelations that might be harmful to public confidence. It seems to me to be a most satisfactory conclusion."

He didn't believe it, of course, but that wasn't the point. Whether it was true or not was irrelevant to a man who'd made a career out of strategic lying. What mattered was whether it could be made to seem credible. And he thought it could.

"No one else was involved?" he asked, the casualness of his tone belying the significance of the question.

"How do you mean, sir?" Neumann replied innocently.

"Schirmer had no accomplices, he wasn't carrying out his crimes at the behest of anyone else?"

"I found no evidence of that, sir."

Bismarck nodded, apparently satisfied. Then he said, "And the king's death? The official explanation that he attacked Dr von Gudden and drowned him, then committed suicide himself. Does that seem plausible to you?"

"I obviously wasn't there, sir, but it seems to fit the facts. The king was much larger and stronger than the doctor. It's entirely possible he was able to overpower him and force his head under the water. The doctor's facial bruises and scratches were consistent with that hypothesis."

"And the suicide?"

"The king's mind was clearly unbalanced. Dr von Gudden and his fellow alienists had already deemed him insane. Taking his own life, given his fragile mental state, was not altogether surprising."

The chancellor nodded, pensive for a moment now.

"I met him only once, you know. Many years ago, when he was the crown prince. I dined with the family at the Nymphenburg Palace, in Munich. He seemed an amiable, charming young man. For his life to have ended in such a way, well, it is truly tragic. I'm sorry to have to say this, but his death is not without its benefits. Bavaria will be more stable without him and if Bavaria is more secure, the whole of Germany is more secure. That should be our paramount concern: the wellbeing and future of the empire. Wouldn't you agree?"

"Yes, sir, absolutely."

"Thank you for coming in, major. You've earned a long period of leave, I believe. I will clear the matter with Commissioner von Richthofen." He gave a ghost of a smile. "I'm glad we understand each other so well."

Neumann stepped out of the stagecoach and paused for a moment, feeling the warmth of the afternoon sun on his face. The winter was long past. Spring was racing by, even now giving hints of the summer to come. The Allgäu Alps still had snow on their summits, but Füssen was bathed in a golden glow. He looked around, remembering the first time he'd arrived in the town. The cold, the mist over the High Castle, young Jürgen Keller shivering by the carriage that was to take him to meet von Auerswald. He wondered what had become of the boy now the prince was dead. Perhaps he'd found a post with the new legate, perhaps he'd returned to his home in Prussia. Wherever he was, Neumann hoped he was warm.

Slinging his kit-bag over his shoulder, he walked along Reichenstrasse. He took his time. There was no hurry today. He looked at the shops, at the wares displayed outside, the pedestrians chatting to one another, the horses and wagons clattering past on the cobbled street. It all seemed the same as the last time he was here. Perhaps not so strange, given that it was only three weeks ago, but to Neumann so much had changed since then.

Ludwig was gone. He'd read the reports of the king's funeral in the Berlin papers: all shops and businesses in Munich closed; crowds lining the streets as the cortège moved slowly from the Residenz to the church of St Michael; the regent, Prince Luitpold, walking behind the hearse along with the crown princes of Austria and Prussia and nobles from all over Germany. But not Bismarck. The chancellor remained in Berlin. He'd got what he wanted and he was never a man to dwell on the past when there were schemes and plots to craft for the future. And what of my future? Neumann wondered as he walked down Lechhalde to Brotmarkt. What fate have the Norns spun for me? I'll find out tomorrow.

Axel was behind the reception desk at the Gasthaus Hoffmann. He greeted Neumann warmly, beaming with pleasure.

"It's good to see you again, major."

"You, too, Axel. You're working here now, then?"

Axel gave a rueful smile. "Mother persuaded me. She can be very persuasive."

"It must be quite a shock after all your years of service to the king."

"We have to move on, don't we?" Axel said with a shrug. "Besides, I didn't have much of a choice. All the royal staff lost their jobs. Prince Luitpold didn't need us. He's going to have a much smaller household than the king, a much more modest way of living."

"Well, that wouldn't be difficult. And the palaces? What happens to them?"

"They're renaming New Hohenschwangau. It's going

to be called Schloss Neuschwanstein now. And they're opening it to the public."

"Really?"

Axel nodded. "Soon you'll be able to pay to go round the king's apartments. I suppose it will help pay off the building costs, but it won't be the same without him."

"No more moonlit sleigh rides," Neumann said.

"No, thank God. Though, you know, I miss him. He was... well, he was Ludwig."

Johanna came out of the saloon bar and gave Neumann a hug.

"We've put you in your old room," she said, then she took in his clothes. "No uniform, major?"

"I'm on leave."

"For how long?"

"That depends," Neumann said cryptically, and left it at that.

He dined in the gasthaus bar – pork knuckle and noodles with melted cheese and onions – slept well, and when he came down for breakfast next morning, he picked up a copy of the *Füssener Blatt* that was lying on the bar. The main story, by-lined Gunther Krämer, was the tragic death of the Bavarian finance minister, Count Walther Ehrenbeck zu Freudenberg. He'd gone out for his usual early morning ride the previous day, fallen from his horse and broken his neck. There was nothing suspicious about the circumstances, but the police were anxious to speak to a young man who'd been seen in the area shortly before the accident and who, the police believed, might be able to shed more light on how it had happened. He was described as in his mid-thirties, medium height and slim, wearing a white shirt, dark jacket and trousers and a cap on his head.

Neumann left the inn after breakfast and walked down the hill to the bridge over the river. The Lech was in full flow, looking as cold and treacherous as ever. He crossed over and headed east. The new palace on the hillside gleamed brilliant white in the morning sunshine. He recalled what Axel had told him: the mad king and his extravagant life turned into a tawdry tourist attraction. That was surely a fate he didn't deserve.

Beyond Schwangau, he veered off the road into the forest, following the track he'd taken all those weeks ago when he'd come out to inspect the site where Christoph Geissler's body had been found. It still gave him a pang, the sacrifice of a young innocent boy for the political intrigues of a Machiavellian chancellor. Could he have done more to expose the reality of what had happened? Should he have done more? Those questions would haunt him for the rest of his days, but in a way, justice had been done. Wilhelm Schirmer was dead, so was von Auerswald. Bismarck had escaped untouched, but men like him always would. It was one of the laws of the jungle. And I am still here, too, Neumann thought. Sometimes survival is more important than the truth.

Gisela Winter was outside her hut, filling her kettle from the spring when he walked past. He stopped to exchange a few words with her, then continued on along the path to Waldblick. Gisela watched him go. She'd wondered for weeks what the runes had meant when she'd cast them across the table, thinking of death, and the signs had read new life instead. Now she knew the answer.

At the edge of the forest, he paused for a moment, remembering the evening Schirmer and von Auerswald had died. Remembering the she-wolf that had saved his life, and Sophie's. A *wolf*? He still found it incredible. A friend, Sophie had said, bringing home to him just how little he knew of her. Would he come to know her better? he wondered. Would she even give him the chance?

He walked out of the trees into the garden and found Sophie and her women busy in the flower beds –

weeding, planting, nurturing. Amalie was there, and Magdalena and Sabine and Kerstin, the other two girls who'd been rescued from The Wotan Brotherhood. They all looked happy and healthy, but none more radiant than Sophie. There was colour in her cheeks, her hair was glossy. If it wouldn't have been rude to comment, he might have suspected her of putting on a little weight. The House of Women, he thought. Am I an intruder here?

They went for a walk together into the ornamental shrubbery where the azaleas and rhododendrons were budding and sat down on a bench out of sight of the others. They kissed and held each other, then Sophie made him tell her his news, all the things he hadn't – or couldn't – put into the letters he'd sent since they'd parted, particularly his meeting with the chancellor.

"He believed you?" Sophie asked.

"He believes what is convenient for him to believe," Neumann replied. "What suits his purposes. But the important thing is that he knows his secrets are safe. And that means that we are safe, too."

"It's not right."

"No, it's not. But it is what it is."

"How can you be so phlegmatic?"

"Because I can do nothing about it. There's no such thing as absolute right or absolute wrong, black or white. Everything is a shade of grey."

"And if you like colour?"

"You look after your own garden." He took her hand and pressed it to his lips. "Speaking of which, I see you've got Magdalena and the others looking after yours. How are they?"

"Recovering well. Even Amalie. She's started speaking at last."

"That's good. I'm so pleased."

"And the men who did this to them?"

Neumann looked away, grimacing. "That's out of my hands now, but I don't think it's going to be pursued."

"So they get away with it?"

"As you said yourself, powerful men like them often do."

"Perhaps not all of them," Sophie said softly.

"What do you mean?"

"It doesn't matter. Where's your luggage?"

"I left it at the Gasthaus Hoffmann."

"Why?"

Neumann hesitated. "Well, I didn't know... I didn't want to presume anything."

Sophie kissed him. "Of course you're staying here."

"You're sure? You're not used to having a man around the house."

No, Sophie thought, but maybe I could get used to it.

"One thing at a time," she said. "You're here now. Let's see how that works out."

He nodded, knowing when to give her space.

"All right. But I don't want to just sit around doing nothing. Tell me what I can do to help."

She smiled at him. "Well, you could start by chopping some wood."

AUTHOR'S NOTE

This book is a work of fiction, but it is based partly on fact. King Ludwig II *was* declared insane by doctors who had never examined him, and he did die in mysterious circumstances in Lake Würm (now Lake Starnberg), near Munich. The events took place in June, 1886. For dramatic purposes, I have moved them to earlier that year, but the facts remain the same.

Ludwig was taken away by force from the palace of New Hohenschwangau (renamed Schloss Neuschwanstein after his death) in the early hours of June 12th by a team of doctors, asylum orderlies and police officers led by the psychiatrist Dr Bernhard von Gudden. They arrived at the king's castle at Berg, on Lake Würm, later that day. The following evening, June 13th, Ludwig and von Gudden went for a walk along the shore of the lake. On the psychiatrist's express orders, no one accompanied them. When the two men had not returned to the castle by around 8pm, the alarm was raised and search parties were sent out to find them. At about 11pm, two dead bodies were found floating in the water.

What had happened? The official story was that Ludwig had ventured out into the lake intending to kill himself. Von Gudden attempted to stop him and the king overpowered the psychiatrist and drowned him before wading out into deeper water and committing suicide. The death certificate for the doctor recorded death by drowning. The death certificate for Ludwig, however, was left curiously blank.

Is the official account correct? Was Ludwig trying to

commit suicide, or was he trying to escape? Boats had been seen cruising up and down the lake near the castle that evening and fresh carriage tracks had been found outside one of the gates to the estate that indicated the possibility of an attempt to rescue the king from his captors – or, equally, an attempt to assassinate him. Two local people who saw the bodies – a fisherman and a priest who had both seen many drowning victims – said that no drowned man ever looked the way Ludwig did. Whatever the truth, enough uncertainty remains to fuel speculation that the king may have been murdered.

At the time of his death, his uncle, Prince Luitpold, had already become regent of Bavaria – Ludwig's younger brother, Otto, technically next in line to the throne, having been certified mentally unfit to rule many years earlier. Luitpold's regency continued until his death in 1912 when his son assumed the title King Ludwig III (even though Otto was still alive, not dying until 1916). Ludwig III ruled until 1918 when he was dethroned.

Much has been written about Ludwig II, most of it in German. For a well-researched, engaging biography in English, I would recommend Christopher McIntosh's *The Swan King: Ludwig II of Bavaria* (Bloomsbury). Certain areas of his life will always remain controversial, not least his sexuality, his "madness" and his final hours, but to gain a greater insight into this man who has become a myth – and have some very enjoyable excursions into the bargain – you could do worse than visit his many extravagant palaces: Neuschwanstein, Hohenschwangau, Linderhof, Herrenchiemsee, Nymphenburg and the Residenz, all of which are open to the public.

ENJOYED THIS BOOK?

Why not try more of Paul Adam's acclaimed thrillers?

The Hardanger Riddle

Book Three in the Cremona Mysteries series

'This is a book that is exceedingly difficult to put down'
The Strad

Rikard Olsen, a successful violin maker from Norway, is found dead in the canal in Cremona – and it wasn't an accident. A mysterious, exquisitely-decorated Hardanger fiddle that he brought with him to Italy has disappeared.

Rikard was a former pupil of Gianni Castiglione, and Gianni and his detective friend, Antonio Guastafeste, travel to Norway to investigate the murder – a journey that takes them to Grieg's home at Troldhaugen; to Lysøen, the tranquil island retreat of Norway's Paganini, Ole Bull, and high into the remote mountains where memories are long and secrets easy to conceal.

The missing Hardanger fiddle had a carving of a hauntingly-beautiful young woman on the scroll. Gianni and Guastafeste believe that the woman may hold the key to the whole puzzle. But who was she and what made her so special that Rikard Olsen had to die?

ISBN 978-0-9571913-7-2
Available from all good bookshops or online
Also available as a Kindle ebook

Paganini's Ghost

Book Two in the Cremona Mysteries series

'Superb...captivating but never transparent...enriched by meticulously detailed historical intrigues'
Publishers Weekly

A dazzling young Russian virtuoso performs a sell-out recital on Paganini's violin in the cathedral in Cremona. Then one of the audience, a shady Parisian art dealer, is found dead in his hotel room, a fragment of sheet music belonging to the virtuoso hidden in his wallet. But how did the dead man get hold of it? And why?

Violin maker Gianni Castiglione is drawn into the murder investigation by his friend, detective Antonio Guastafeste, and the two men find themselves at the centre of a tantalising story of love, deception and greed. Following a trail that leads back to Paganini, his lover Elisa Bonaparte (Napoleon's sister), Catherine the Great of Russia and a long-lost priceless treasure, Gianni and Antonio must unravel another mystery that has gone unanswered for over a century, one that may hold the answer to the modern-day murder.

Filled with remarkable history and musical lore, *Paganini's Ghost* plays at a breathtaking tempo that will keep you reading until the very last page.

ISBN 978-0-9557277-2-6
Available from all good bookshops or online
Also available as a Kindle ebook

Knife Edge

'Paul Adam writes fiercely topical thrillers which deliver anxiety along with the excitement'
Literary Review

Knife Edge is a timely, chillingly plausible thriller that lifts the lid on the secretive links between people smuggling, illegal agricultural labour and Britain's supermarkets.

Crime reporter Joe Verdi investigates the murder of a Kurdish immigrant by Turkish people-traffickers in London. The dead man's wife Irena, the key witness to the killing, flees to East Anglia where she disappears into the murky underworld of gangmasters and exploited foreign workers.

The police are unable to trace Irena so Joe goes undercover as a migrant labourer to try to find her. But he's not the only one looking for her – the Turks are also on her trail.

Meanwhile, Joe's colleague Ellie Mason is following up an outbreak of typhoid. The only link between the victims seems to be the supermarket chain where they bought their food.

As the two reporters' investigations come together in a heart-stopping climax, the shocking truth about our industrialised system of food production is uncovered. There is a price to pay for cheap food – and sometimes that price is people's lives.

ISBN 978-0-9557277-1-9
**Available from all good bookshops or online.
Also available as a Kindle ebook**